S T A N

The
MANAGERESS

PENGUIN BOOKS

In association with
CHANNEL FOUR TELEVISION COMPANY LTD

PENGUIN BOOKS

Published by the Penguin Group
27 Wrights Lane, London w8 5TZ, England
Viking Penguin Inc., 40 West 23rd Street, New York, New York 10010, USA
Penguin Books Australia Ltd, Ringwood, Victoria, Australia
Penguin Books Canada Ltd, 2801 John Street, Markham, Ontario, Canada L3R 1B4
Penguin Books (NZ) Ltd, 182–190 Wairau Road, Auckland 10, New Zealand

Penguin Books Ltd, Registered Offices: Harmondsworth, Middlesex, England

First published by Penguin Books in association with
Channel Four Television Company Ltd 1989
10 9 8 7 6 5 4 3 2 1

Made and printed in Great Britain by
Richard Clay Ltd, Bungay, Suffolk
Filmset in Sabon

CHAPTER ONE

Gabriella was relieved that it wasn't raining. The combination of the darkly ceremonial Catholic funeral that had been her mother's request and bleak weather would have been hard to bear. Instead the clear spring sky which framed the Berkshire churchyard introduced a note of optimism into this depressing final ritual.

Gabriella tried to focus on this to stop the tears she could feel running down her cheeks. Her mother had always urged her to 'put on a brave face' throughout the disrupted life they had shared. But now, as the priest finished his remarks and nodded for the coffin to be lowered into the earth, Gabriella summoned the resolve which the 'English' part of her upbringing had given her.

An altar-boy, standing by the priest, held out a small silver dish containing earth for Gabriella to toss on to the coffin. But as she reached out, she became aware that the small clutch of family mourners behind her were shuffling and whispering. She looked around to see that they had parted to allow a passage to the graveside. Making his way through, dressed in an appropriately dark suit and with his eyes lowered, was a tall, broad-shouldered man of about sixty. Despite the greying moustache and spectacles, Gabriella recognized him as her father.

Gabriella had telexed Sergio's company in Italy with the news of the death three days ago. She could not depart from the regime of impersonal contact which her mother had laid down for her from the first weeks of the separation in 1960. These strictures had been reinforced anyway by a ten-year-old child's sense of confusion and resentment at a father's 'desertion'. The passing years did little to erode the jagged edges of the emotional landscape between them. Diana's death, in theory, had freed Gabriella from the obligations of emnity, but, seeing Sergio now, all she was aware of was a numbness so profound that her tears ceased instantly.

He stood over the grave and produced a single red rose from behind his back, dropping it carefully so that it landed across the brass name-plate on the coffin. Then he turned to give Gabriella a look of aching regret, and immediately started to walk away again without a backward glance. Gabriella stared after him, trying to untangle the knot of emotions his sudden appearance had generated. Simon, her husband, gently squeezed her arm as he stood supportively at her side.

'Talk to him,' he whispered. 'Go on.'

He gave Gabriella a discreet push in the direction of her father's departing figure. She stepped haltingly after Sergio, as he made his way towards the silver-coloured Porsche saloon parked ostentatiously at the churchyard gate.

'Father,' she called nervously. Sergio kept moving away from her. But then the chasm formed by years of separation was instantly bridged by a single child-like utterance from Gabriella.

'Papa!' she called.

Sergio stopped and stood still for a moment. Then slowly he turned. There were tears on his cheeks too. He looked plaintively at his daughter, swamped by memories. Despite the tears, and the severe, dark hat which framed her head, her eyes seemed as luminous as he remembered. Her skin was still beautifully pale, and her wide cheekbones continued to give her face the openness and innocence of childhood. Gabriella kept her distance from him, but now her eyes were locked with his.

'I'm sorry, Gabriella – I didn't know what to do for the best,' he said with a shrug.

Gabriella nodded. She understood his dilemma. If he hadn't turned up, he'd have been condemned as cold-hearted; yet, by attending his ex-wife's funeral, he risked similar accusations from certain sections of her family, who could never forgive him. Gabriella, though, was touched by the gesture.

'Will you come back to the house?' she asked him quietly.

'Thank you, Gabriella – but it's too soon.'

He nodded at the group of mourners beyond, picking out the tall, patrician-looking man with a shock of dark hair.

'That must be Simon – I recognize him from the wedding photographs.'

'Come back. Please,' Gabriella said, holding out her hand. After a second, Sergio took it tentatively.

He joined the other mourners at the startling art-deco style 1930s house Gabriella and Simon owned. Painted a stark white, it was entirely round in construction, with large areas of curved glass looking out on to the spacious gardens. In the panelled lounge, a small buffet lunch had been laid on. Sergio quickly found that the imposed formality of the event allowed Diana Rebecchi's other relatives and friends to maintain their hostile stance towards him and pass it off as English decorum. With Gabriella preoccupied by the other guests, Sergio clung to Simon, trying to get to know his son-in-law and, by extension, the daughter who was a stranger to him.

'I've a feeling I'm not entirely welcome here,' said Sergio.

'Well, not for me to say,' Simon countered carefully. He stared into his wineglass, a gesture that a long list of tedious, legal parties had honed into a reflex. It was intended to register boredom with the prevailing topic, and seven times out of ten the conversation would switch to some innocuous subject, such as wine itself. But Sergio persisted.

'Perhaps it would have been better for me to stay away after all?'

'Please,' insisted Simon. 'I really think this is a matter for you and Gabriella.'

Sergio registered the firmness in Simon's voice this time and fell silent. Instead he directed his gaze towards Gabriella, who was moving around the house's elegant drawing-room, exchanging quiet words with those who had come to mourn her mother. Without the severe hat and black shawl she had worn for the service, Gabriella's slim figure and classical beauty made her almost hypnotically watchable. Simon was lured to follow Sergio's look, and tried to imagine the impact of seeing this mature, self-possessed, 38-year-old woman when he had only previously known a child.

'She has grown into a beautiful, gracious woman,' Sergio concluded.

'Yes, like her mother.' The remark was unwittingly cruel, and Simon saw the hurt in Sergio's eyes, but because he thought he'd given him enough warnings to avoid the subject, he felt no obligation to apologize.

'If you'll excuse me, Signor Rebecchi.'

Simon wandered off with practised ease, jettisoning the intruder into that limbo in English social gatherings from which recovery is impossible. Sergio saw that Gabriella was still occupied, so he left the room with as much purpose as he could muster.

A trip to the bathroom and back gave him some time to recover his poise, and to look at the house. The circular exterior walls were matched by a wide spiralling central staircase. The furnishings blended judiciously with the light oak of the exposed, polished floorboards. Sergio was pleased: it showed both good taste and comfortable affluence. The taste, he knew, was his legacy. The money, he assumed – wrongly in fact – had come from Simon's partnership in a prominent London law firm.

He remembered from a Christmas card some years back that Gabriella had opened an exercise studio in the local town. Now, as he made a detour into what he guessed, from the family photographs, was her study, he was impressed by the evidence of its success. Photographs on the walls and between the shelves showed Gabriella, in leotard and training shoes, leading a class of prancing women; and there she was standing outside the premises which bore a neon 'GB's' logo. Gabriella

4

Benson's, thought Sergio, recalling her married name and concluding that perhaps a lot of this household's wealth had been created by Gabriella after all. His eye caught a framed certificate: 'Businesswoman of the Year Award' from a national paper. At once, this acclamation for his daughter made him feel proud, an emotion that was tempered only by a wistfulness for those years when he had had no part in her development.

He continued his journey around the room, aware of the pleasure he felt from piecing together these unknown elements of his daughter's life. One shelf of books confirmed the seriousness of her enterprise: aerobics, dance, Alexander Technique, fitness, anatomy; there were dozens of books on each subject. He remembered Gabriella as a single-minded, almost obsessive child, who had always followed her enthusiasms through.

On an adjoining shelf there was further evidence of this. A row of neatly stacked video-cassettes took up more space than the volumes of *Encyclopædia Britannica* below. Each cassette was labelled in Gabriella's handwriting. He tilted his head to read them: 'France v. West Germany, 1982 World Cup, Spain', 'Belgium v. USSR, 1986 World Cup, Mexico', 'Bayern Munich v. FC Porto, 1987 European Cup Final'. On and on they went, stretching back beyond the video age: 'Glasgow Celtic v. Inter Milan, 1967 European Cup Final'. Here was a collection of football games that had thrilled the world. Games in which the spirit of adventure and romance had matched the occasion.

'Ah, here you are!'

Sergio turned to see Gabriella at the door. She closed it behind her. He gestured to the corner-table, which bore images of their seemingly perfect family so long ago in Italy.

'Sorry to intrude – I saw the photographs.'

Gabriella looked at them too, almost unable to equate the man and the little girl in the pictures with the two people they were now. Sergio moved over to the framed award and held it aloft.

'You should have told me about this!'

'Haven't had much chance, have I?' Gabriella murmured, uneasy at having to explain herself to this man.

Now Sergio moved back to the shelf holding the row of video-cassettes, trying to take control of the conversation.

'Success and marriage don't seem to have dimmed your passion for football!' he said triumphantly.

Gabriella noted the elated tone of his voice. Football had always been a sort of tribal totem for Sergio. It represented manliness and power in Italian society, and when his older brother, Paulo, got to play for AC Milan in the early 1950s, Sergio had used his increasing wealth from the family construction business to buy *his* way into football too. Years later he became a committee member for UEFA. He loved the game itself, of course, and had passed on this enthusiasm to Gabriella. He had taken her to Italian league games from the age of eight until the breakdown of the marriage.

'You trained me too well,' Gabriella complimented him dryly.

'That wasn't training, Gabriella,' Sergio insisted. 'The game has always been in my life. I shared it with you the way any father would have!'

Gabriella gave him a rueful smile. 'Pity I was a girl, really.' Sergio looked hurt, as Gabriella had guessed he would. Even now, as a successful woman, the childish instinct to wound him remained.

'Don't worry, I don't resent you for it. After all I've kept watching of my own free will since . . . well, since May 1960.'

Sergio looked at her. They both knew the relevance of that date. The family had come over to England then, to visit Diana's parents at their London residence. Gabriella had felt a strange sense of disorder in their usually welcoming house. She'd heard whispered conversations and at one point found her mother and grandmother crying. The next day, Sergio took her on a plane to Scotland. He had a treat for her. They had seats in the VIP box at Hampden Park, Glasgow, for the European Cup Final. Eintracht Frankfurt v. Real Madrid, the great Madrid side which had dominated European club football for five years, and which boasted the dazzling talents of the explosive Hungarian goal scorer, Puskas, the sinuous Argentine centre forward, di Stefano, and the quicksilver Spanish winger, Gento.

Even though she was only ten, Gabriella had known she was privileged to be in the 135,000 crowd that night. And then the football itself seemed to respond to the electricity among the spectators. Real Madrid won by seven goals to three, with the chunky little Puskas scoring four and di Stefano the remaining three. The brilliance of the passing, the precision and power of the shooting, the non-stop movement of the players, the dazzling patterns they weaved across the pitch, the huge roars of appreciation from the crowd – all this was burnt into her memory.

The next day, Sergio had returned Gabriella to her English grandparents' home, and then flown back to Milan for a business meeting. Gabriella's mother took her out into the garden after he had gone and explained that they would not be going back to Italy to join him. The marriage was over. Gabriella was to be brought up in England. He would remain in Italy.

The looks they exchanged revealed something of their feelings now about that distant severing of relations. Gabriella seemed defensive, distrustful even, while Sergio's eyes were filled with regret.

'You must still have other resentments?' Sergio probed.

'We don't want to talk about them today, do we?' Gabriella said defensively. 'Least of all today.'

Gabriella bit her lip as she felt tears swell once again in her eyes.

'I just want you to know, Gabriella, that I loved your mother dearly,' Sergio said plaintively.

After this, they rejoined Simon in the main room, where the reception was dwindling away, and after a few more pleasantries with his son-in-law, Sergio decided to leave. Gabriella escorted him out to his car. She felt obliged to ask him to stay on for a few days, but he graciously conceded that this was 'too soon'. His real reason for being there then emerged. He was over on UEFA business, compiling a report on English hooliganism. Gabriella was stung by the realization that her mother's funeral had been accommodated into an existing schedule. Despite Sergio's considerable charm and visible sadness, her defences went up again. He paused as he reached his car.

'Nothing can make up for my mistakes, Gabriella. But I will do anything I can to ensure that you are happy.'

'What makes you think I'm not already happy?' she replied defiantly.

Sergio conceded the point with a smile. He was beginning to admire the spirit his daughter had acquired, though had he mentioned this, she would undoubtedly have told him that his desertion was the major factor in its development.

'Let's just stay in touch for now,' suggested Gabriella. 'It's a step in the right direction.'

Sergio leaned forward tentatively. After a second Gabriella moved towards him, and they kissed each other on both cheeks. Sergio was grateful for this first hint of warmth, and he knew that he very much wanted to see her again.

'What are you doing this Saturday, Gabriella?'

She frowned, trying to anticipate what he had in mind. She wasn't one for excuses or diversion, so she told him the truth.

'Supporting my local team. Perennial second division, but they're honest toilers.'

Sergio smiled. 'Very English!' He put his forefinger to his lips thoughtfully.

'Perhaps I could make that one of my inspection games and come with you?' He looked at Gabriella, whose face gave no clue to her likely answer, so he decided to try a further temptation.

'I could get you into the boardroom.'

Gabriella looked intrigued, and Sergio knew he had taken a small step towards winning her back.

8

Gabriella's affection for her local football club was, like that of most fans, based on a limited amount of contact. Certainly she went to as many home games as she could, read about the team changes in the evening paper, occasionally saw a player pick up his wife from her exercise studios, and received her monthly newsletter from the supporters' club (she was what they called a 'non-social' member, uninterested in snooker or drinking). But she had no direct contact with the club or its officials, and had little idea of the way the club was run or of how the players led their lives.

She'd heard rumours, of course, about the alleged disharmony in the team and their lack of faith in the present manager, Fred Taylor – which was only to be expected, given their disastrous position in the second division. But her perception remained very much that of an outsider looking in. That's how football clubs were run these days, she'd concluded. No sense of community, no shared experience with the supporters. The team was a private fiefdom except for the ninety minutes of a game. You bought a little bit of entertainment or masochistic pleasure from them once a fortnight and tried hard not to care, because caring wasn't really appreciated any more. Not very long ago, the fans would turn up to watch training *and* be welcomed!

.

There were no supporters watching the team training on the morning that Gabriella's mother was buried. The practice pitch on a windswept corner of the town, flanked by a trading estate, had few enough facilities for the players, let alone spectators. The first team squad went through the familiar rituals of training – five-a-side games, press-ups, 'defence' versus 'attack' – with only the barking admonishments of their coach, Eddie Johnson, to enliven the tedium.

Eddie was a lean, hawkish-faced ex-pro who'd done the rounds of the lower divisions as a player, cultivating a reputation as a 'hard man'. After retirement, he'd had several offers of coaching jobs, because he was exactly the sort of bloke

English football managers liked to have under them: loyal, a bit of a bastard to the players, and with no ideas of his own.

Fred Taylor would have been proud of Eddie as he quashed another minor outbreak of imagination among the players that morning. Tony Morris, a tall but muscular black forward and probably the most skilful member of the squad, had tried a fancy turn to beat his marker, the club captain, rugged defender Gary Halliwell, whose reaction in those situations was by now almost Pavlovian. He'd instantly responded with a spoiling foul. But Eddie's tirade was directed at Morris, not his assailant.

'How many times have I told you? Don't try to turn! Lay it off, son!'

As Trevor Coughlan, the small, barrel-chested, hard-tackling midfielder, and effectively Eddie's alter-ego on the field, lined up the ball for the free-kick, one of the other forwards, Keith Nicholl, mouthed a justifiable complaint.

'Come on, Eddie – there's not much point in attack playing defence if Trev gets the set-pieces all the time!'

Eddie eyed Nicholl with contempt. Nicholl had come into the professional game after university, and had his own ideas about training and playing which, to put it mildly, didn't coincide with Eddie's own. So the rebuke which followed had additional spite.

'Who's running this practice, Mr Professor – you or me? I'll tell you: it's *me*! Coughlan takes the free-kicks!'

Nicholl hung his head and Coughlan did what he usually did, ten times out of ten: he drove a hard shot straight into the defensive wall in the hope of finding a gap. All he found was the unprotected groin of defender Jim Wilson, who collapsed in a heap on the turf. The team's instinct for finding such banality amusing quickly produced a welter of wisecracks and laughter, and the training, already desultory, fell apart. Eddie raged at them.

'Come on – move, move! Every time you step on this pitch, I expect you to die! Y'hear me? Die!'

Eddie's bile was partly in response to what he saw as an affront to his authority, but he was also conscious of the flash Ford saloon belonging to Fred Taylor which was pulling into the training ground. He probably had as much contempt for Taylor as the players, but he was still the 'boss', and Eddie knew his place. The practice resumed with sufficient urgency to look impressive, as Taylor, unseasonally tanned thanks to a sun-bed, climbed out of his car and buttoned up his sheepskin coat against the chill February wind.

Eddie feigned preoccupation with the training as Taylor sidled up to him on the edge of the pitch, casting what was meant to look like a professional eye over the proceedings.

'All right, Eddie, how's it going?'

'Working hard. Most of 'em anyway. Nicholl's been mouthing off as usual,' said Eddie, offering a scapegoat for any deficiencies the manager might have spotted. But Taylor, who sported the jewellery and hairstyle of some of the more prominent members of his trade, had other things on his mind.

'He's not the only one. Did you see the *Star* this morning?'

Eddie shrugged diplomatically.

'Shit-stirring as usual. I'm not unpopular with the players, am I, Eddie?'

Eddie could hardly credit this sudden display of vulnerability from his superior.

'Paper-talk, boss,' he reassured Taylor. 'Take no notice.'

Taylor seemed satisfied with this, and resumed the appearance of deep concentration on the training.

'How's Dave McGregor shaping up?'

Eddie's gaze fell upon the young midfield player, one of the few to show any signs of eagerness for the morning's work. 'Not bad.'

Taylor snorted with amusement. 'In-depth analysis, eh, Eddie! Where would I be without you?'

Eddie refused to rise to the dig. Taylor suddenly seemed dynamic.

'Well, he still doesn't look fit to me, so let's have him back this afternoon, shall we?'

'Again?'

'Again,' said Taylor, firmly. 'I'll catch you later.' Taylor called out a greeting to the players but got no response. His eyes met Eddie's, but they gave nothing away, so he shuffled off back towards his car, packing his hands into the pockets of his coat. Eddie watched him go, his contempt softened momentarily by a stirring of pity for the man. Eddie knew what the players thought. He also guessed what Fred Taylor was up to that morning. He'd say nothing, because loyalty came with the job. For now, anyway.

·

Later that afternoon, the drowsy midweek atmosphere at the club was disrupted by the arrival of a telex. The deputy chairman, Anthony Coombs, was the first to see it, and he hurried through to the chairman's office, where Martin Fisher was dabbing at a computer. Despite his apparent concentration, Fisher had heard the telex come chattering through, and his first thought was that it concerned a potential transfer deal, since that was all the machine was ever really used for.

'If they want anything over thirty grand, Anthony, they can forget it,' Fisher smirked as he picked up the remains of a substantial Monte Cristo cigar from his ash-tray. Coombs, whose manner was generally that of a rather vague, minor public-school prefect, looked more puzzled than usual.

'Who, Martin?'

'I think Fred Taylor's been sniffing round the transfer market again — I presume that's the bill?' Fisher said, as he held out a hand for the telex.

'Actually no, it's rather odd really.'

'UEFA?' Fisher scanned the tear-sheet.

'What the hell does this Rebecchi bloke want with us?'

Coombs shrugged. He guessed it had something to do with the ban on English clubs from European competition. Fisher shook his head with a patient smile. Coombs made an ideal deputy — earnest and obedient — but his sense of humour wasn't sharp enough for Fisher's tastes, with the result that Fisher usually had to spell jokes out for him.

'He can't have seen our team, then, can he?' Fisher accompanied this sally with a suitably jocose expression, and Coombs finally saw the irony. What *could* a major UEFA official want with a club as obscure as theirs, which had rarely achieved success in English domestic competition, let alone threatened an entry into the European arena?

Nevertheless, Coombs found himself excited by the prospect of the visit and scolded Fisher for his cynicism.

'You never know what might come of it, Martin!'

Fisher screwed up the telex and flicked it into his wastepaper bin.

'A big drinks bill, Anthony, and that's about all!' He resumed his concentration on the computer screen in front of him. Intrigued, Coombs edged round behind him to see what looked like an impressive display of figures.

'Well, well – club accounts?' Coombs said archly, knowing it was a touchy subject at any time. Fisher gave him only a pained smile in response.

'Actually, Anthony, I was working out my annual cigar expenditure for tax purposes. Five and a half grand. Not bad, eh?'

Fisher sat back in his chair and smiled. He loved winding Coombs up with his profligacy. A bulky man with a large head, Fisher looked exactly like the contemporary stereotype of property developers who'd become football club chairmen: smug, carnivorous and hard-nosed. When they all met up for the League's AGM, it would be hard to tell them apart.

Coombs looked irritated by the revelation. At thirty, he was perhaps ten years younger than Fisher. Thanks to thinning hair and an active bachelor life, however, Coombs frequently wore a seedy, bag-eyed look that meant the distinction in their ages was not always apparent. As an accountant and Fisher's personal assistant, he'd become used to the man's cavalier attitude to money. Trying to impose some sort of restraint upon him had proved almost impossible.

He'd been firmly opposed to Fisher buying into this football club eighteen months ago, but now here Coombs was, working alongside him as deputy chairman, watching their property company profits swill down the drains of the club.

To Coombs, money was an exact science, to be controlled by logic and detail. To Fisher, it was simply a means to pleasure or, in the case of the club, local prestige. It was a subject to be joked about, as he did now by suggesting to Coombs that the UEFA man should be charged for his two match tickets. But Coombs didn't laugh.

Sergio collected Gabriella from her home on Saturday at lunchtime. Simon was happy to stay in and watch the England v. Wales rugby international on the television, because it was 'more my kind of game'. As Sergio's powerful Porsche 928S weaved its way through the narrow streets towards the floodlight stalks in the distance, Gabriella found it hard to believe that *this* was still Sergio's game. Little bunches of supporters spilled out of pubs and bent into the wind as they hurried towards the ground. Elderly programme-sellers, their noses red with the cold, barked their prices and stomped their feet. And on every street corner stood a hot-dog stall, each of which seemed to be staffed by the same unshaven, red-eyed man. Gabriella had immunized herself through practice to these images of the true status of her local club. Now, as she saw it all through Sergio's eyes, she felt embarrassed at her devotion to such a downbeat operation.

'Not exactly San Siro, Milan, is it?' she offered, knowing that the huge 80,000-seater stadium, home of Inter and AC Milan, was his more usual haunt.

Sergio shrugged and smiled diplomatically. 'It's a game of football – an oasis of excitement in a dull world wherever it's played!' He lapsed into Italian for emphasis. '*L'opera di popolo!*'

Gabriella smiled at the hyperbole, knowing he was performing for her benefit.

'How can you still be so romantic about it all?'

Sergio looked thoughtful for a second. 'Because it never disappoints me.'

For an instant, Gabriella thought she saw beyond this, to an ageing man whose life was empty despite his success. But then the invulnerable figure of the father she thought she knew was still sitting alongside her. Superficiality returned, as the car pulled into the tiny VIP car-park at one end of the ground, where an officious commissionaire looked as though he'd prefer death under Sergio's wheels to an unauthorized admission. The embossed UEFA pass, however, produced an instant salute, and moments later Gabriella was on her way towards the inner sanctum of the club.

In fact, her arrival with Sergio had already been spotted by Fisher and Coombs, who'd been looking out of the boardroom window, glumly estimating how low today's crowd would be. The sight of the gleaming Porsche with its exotic Milanese plates and Sergio in a fashionable trench coat, doubtless from the same town, had already excited their interest. When Gabriella stepped from the car, with her long golden-brown hair blowing in the wind, and wearing an immaculately cut jacket and trousers, she looked every inch a Vogue model. She oozed class, they both thought, and her association with this older, powerful man excited their taste for the big-time, to which, in their different ways, Fisher and Coombs had always aspired.

'What's his name again?' asked Coombs, eager to put on a correct performance.

Fisher stared down at Sergio, eyes drinking in the symbols of effortless wealth, which included the glamorous woman. 'Rebecchi. Owns a big construction company in Milan, apparently.' Coombs smiled to himself; for once, Fisher had done some homework. 'Look at him, Anthony – can't you just smell the power?'

Coombs nodded. 'His wife looks a bit tasty too.'

Fisher rounded on him with a glare. Sex was the one area where he couldn't quite get a bead on Coombs. He got hints of strange appetites from him, which made him feel uncomfortable. The thought of Coombs trying it on with this UEFA big-wig's wife brought out his puritan streak. Or maybe it was just jealousy.

'Hands off, Anthony. She looks too classy for you!'

In fact, for two of the older, crustier directors present, relics of the age before Martin Fisher, Gabriella didn't look nearly classy enough. As Fisher and Coombs made their way to the door to greet Sergio and Gabriella, the balding Mr Austin turned to the grey-haired Mr Deness and speculated sneeringly on the background of the chairman's new guests.

'What do you think? Property or second-hand cars?'

Deness, despite his years, recognized the man to be more substantial than that. 'Actually, I suspect he may be the official observer from UEFA,' he declared, pronouncing the acronym to rhyme with 'loofah', a throwback to the days when the Union of European Football Associations had been an English term, not French, as it was today.

Mr Austin admired Mr Deness's punctiliousness but wrinkled his moustache in agitation none the less. Rules had been broken by these intruders.

'He should know the form, then,' he growled. 'Women go in the Blue Room. They can't come in here!' He looked at Deness as if he were stating one of life's great truths, and Deness duly nodded in agreement.

As yet, Fisher and Coombs were unaware of the tensions their guests had created. The formalities had passed off smoothly enough, although Fisher was convinced Signor Rebecchi had noticed Coombs's predatorial smile when it was revealed that the lady was his daughter and not his wife. Coombs immediately tried to get more information.

'This your first football match, Miss Benson?'

Gabriella was familiar with the gambit and was unabashed. '*Mrs* Benson,' she corrected.

Coombs's face registered a moment's disappointment, and then in a second his patronizing assumption of Gabriella's inexperience had also been trumped.

'This your first football game?' he asked.

'Actually I've been a season-ticket holder here for nearly six years,' Gabriella said with a patient smile.

'My daughter saw her first match when she was eight years old,' smiled Sergio.

'Inter Milan against Atalanta, as I remember,' she said to her father, who nodded his confirmation. Fisher enjoyed seeing Coombs get his come-uppance so quickly and was keen to rub it in.

'We have an expert in our midst, Anthony!' Fisher smiled through a cloud of his cigar smoke. Gabriella demurred quietly, but a convenient social hierarchy had been created, and Coombs was quickly dispatched to fetch the drinks.

Gabriella looked around the panelled room with its pennants and obscure trophies and photographs of old teams. Apart from a waitress distributing sandwiches, she was the only woman there. Off the field, just as much as on, it was still a man's world.

Below stairs, in the team's dressing-room, the macho rituals of preparing the gladiators for combat were well under way. The club physio massaged Tony Morris's bruised legs, kicked so often in that week's training, in an effort to stimulate ninety minutes' worth of running from them. Other players performed their stretching exercises, straining muscles and tendons in calf and groin to elasticate their bodies for the explosive demands of the game. For a few, there was mental preparation to complete, clearing their thoughts, focusing on fears and wishing them away, trying to put the nagging injury or dog-tiredness out of the mind.

The atmosphere was routine and business-like. Half a season of morale-sapping defeats and scratched draws had stripped the team of any optimism and excitement. There was still a job to be done, of course – the senators upstairs required their entertainment to follow the whiskies and finger sandwiches. But if there was ever a team that was defeated before it set foot on the field, this was it.

Keith Nicholl, sitting sullenly on one of the benches, seemed to symbolize the disillusionment at the heart of the club. He'd found out through reading one of the morning's tabloids that he was to be dropped for this match. Fred Taylor had a weekly 'as told to' column, in which he imparted his 'thoughts' on the game to a reporter over the phone. The journalist then typed these into a semblance of coherence, with an emphasis on any item that might prove contentious or, even better, 'sensational'. For this he received one hundred and fifty pounds. Nicholl didn't get a share of the fee.

Therefore when Taylor wandered into the dressing-room, affecting an air of brisk *bonhomie*, Nicholl, who felt that the footballing profession had to earn his respect rather than take it for granted, was quick to state his grievances.

'Excuse me, *boss*' – he emphasized the title with as much irony as he could muster – 'why do I find out I've been dropped in the press, and not from you? 'Cos they pay you, is it?'

Taylor, sweating now under the weight of his sheepskin coat, glared at Nicholl.

'Shut it!'

'Is that it, then? No explanations or apologies – the footballing approach to man-management?'

Gary Halliwell stepped towards the two men, sensing things could get worse. If asked, he'd probably have said he sided with Nicholl, but the stern professional code, learned over fourteen seasons in the game, made him recognize that a ruck with the manager ten minutes before kick-off was way out of order.

'Leave it out, Keith,' he said, adopting the firm but reasonable tone he used when disagreeing with referees.

Taylor took this intervention as a gesture of support, however, and decided to have another dig at Nicholl. Authority had to be asserted, malice displayed.

'If you put as much effort into training as you do into mouthing off, you'd be in the team all the time, Nicholl!'

Nicholl found an extra notch up on his scale of irony, so determined was he not to be out-argued.

'Oh, that's the reason, is it? Because I happen to complain about the management round here, I get the chop! Well, you'd better drop the whole team in that case, *boss* – 'cos I'm only saying what everybody else is thinking!'

Nicholl got up and stalked out of the dressing-room, ignoring Eddie petulantly throwing the Number 12 shirt at him. He'd made his point but, in the eyes of everybody else, had picked the wrong moment to do so. Unnerving the rest of the troops just before they charged out of the trenches was not the way to get them on his side. For all his learning, Nicholl was insensitive enough to still think like an outsider, and that's what they couldn't forgive him for. In the circumstances, Fred Taylor's last-minute exhortations and encouragements rang more hollow than usual.

.

By now Gabriella and Sergio had taken their seats in the directors' box, with Fisher and Coombs sitting solicitously near by. As the teams warmed up, Gabriella gave her father a spontaneous analysis of the home side's strengths and weaknesses.

'Tony Morris is probably the most skilful player in the team, but they make him stay on the wing, so he never gets the ball. He should be in midfield, really, because the Number 6, Trevor Coughlan, is just a ball winner, but then he doesn't know what to do with it when he's got it! Their main attacking ploy is just the long clearance from Gary Halliwell. It's kick-and-run football! The English speciality.'

This was truly a fan's assessment: passionate in its intensity but critical in a reasoned tone which testified to years of patient watching.

Sergio studied her during this discourse. He said nothing to her about it, but he couldn't help remembering the times she'd sat at his side during the football matches he'd taken her to in Italy. *He* had been the master then, but now here was Gabriella telling him about facets of the game he'd neither considered nor cared about. As the referee's whistle sounded for the start of the game and Gabriella suspended her appraisal, Sergio smiled at her with paternal pride.

The game, as Gabriella had suspected, was undistinguished, dominated by scuffling, frightened football. At this stage of the season, the pitch still had its winter deadness, which, with a bone-numbing wind blowing through the ground, made control of the ball – the first object of the game – virtually impossible. The crowd, which Gabriella guessed was less than 3,000 strong, was restive and surly. This inevitably communicated itself to the home team, who grew more cautious and hidebound with every minute.

The opposing team began to sense the collective disarray confronting them and swept forward to exploit the confusion. Coughlan, whose role in the team – apart from taking futile free-kicks – was to cut down forwards before they became a threat to the defence, was suddenly exposed for pace and missed his tackle. A quick exchange of passes left Halliwell and Jim Wilson, the central defenders, becalmed, and the forward struck a firm shot high past keeper Brian Rimmer's left hand.

On the terraces behind the goal, the small band of travelling supporters celebrated the score with relish, while at the opposite end there was a dismayed lowing noise from the home fans. Gabriella restricted herself to expressing her sense of frustration to her father, but she couldn't help noticing, now that she was sitting so close to the club's decision-makers, that there was an expression of almost personal humiliation on their faces. She saw Coombs whispering conspiratorially into Martin Fisher's ear, while both their gazes were locked on to the back of Fred Taylor's head, sitting in the dug-out down below. It was retreating, tortoise-like, into his big sheepskin coat.

The second half continued in the same way. A brief flurry of excitement ten minutes from time resulted in Morris being harshly fouled as he prepared to shoot, but the resulting injury to his thigh forced his substitution, and the subsequent free-kick, blasted aimlessly into the defensive wall by Coughlan, provoked the crowd into outright mutiny. The chants went up on three sides of the ground, and then a fourth, as the visiting supporters joined in the baiting with glee.

'Taylor out! Taylor out! Taylor out! Taylor out!'

Gabriella turned to Sergio with an ironic smile. 'I think you may get some crowd trouble after all. Perhaps a public lynching of the manager!'

The recriminations continued after the match ended. There was a subdued muttering in the boardroom as the directors of both clubs had drinks, one lot trying not to look too downcast, the other not too superior, though, in truth, neither set was likely to be moved deeply by victory or defeat. The day out was what mattered – the chance to talk business with like-minded men of similar status to themselves.

Nevertheless, Anthony Coombs pressed drinks on Sergio and Gabriella in 'apology' for what he presumed to be a wasted afternoon. Then Martin Fisher insisted they join him and Coombs for an early evening meal. Sergio was happy to accept, so used was he to being courted and entertained, but Gabriella felt less comfortable about it. Fisher had gone off to 'discuss one or two team matters with the manager', as the chanting for Fred Taylor's sacking wafted up from the streets around the ground. Now Coombs was muttering about Martin's perception of defeats as 'letting the customers down'. While she sympathized with the fans who had wasted hard-earned money on the afternoon's spectacle, this clinical, business-like posturing grated on her.

What swung her round to the idea was the sudden intrusion of Messrs Austin and Deness, who were hinting broadly that a woman should not be allowed in the boardroom. Coombs graciously stood his ground, and Sergio weighed in with an amusing deflation of their rude chauvinism.

'You know,' he said languidly, 'I've always thought that if you English had allowed more women into your institutions, you'd have provided Russia with far fewer spies.'

Coombs smiled approvingly at Gabriella, and he began to share a sense of mischief.

21

'Mrs Benson was just telling me about her successful dance-studio business,' Coombs said conversationally, making it plain that Gabriella was his guest and was staying put.

Austin smirked at them, feeling an instant sense of business superiority.

'I wouldn't have thought there was much of a market for ballroom dancing these days,' he chortled to Deness.

'Actually, Charles, it's to do with fitness training. You've heard of aerobics presumably?'

'Yes, of course,' Austin blustered. 'It's one of those women's activities.' He turned a patronizing eye on Gabriella. 'Must be a bit of an eye-opener for you, seeing how fit these professional footballers can get. Some of our lads could run through brick walls!'

Gabriella gave him a sarcastic smile. 'That would account for their injuries, I suppose?'

Austin bristled at the insult. Gabriella decided on a little test for Mr Austin to rub salt into his wounds.

'Excuse me,' she said, 'but do you know if Tony Morris is all right?'

Mr Austin looked blank. 'Who?'

Gabriella continued innocently. 'He's one of your players – the winger; he got carried off this afternoon. Remember?'

Austin looked uneasy. Gabriella recalled the book that the old Newcastle player Len Shackleton had written in the 1950s. A chapter entitled 'What Directors Know about Football' featured a blank page. He was still right, it seemed. But now Austin was fighting back.

'Well – what do you make of our team's level of fitness, Mrs Benson?' He contorted his face with contempt. 'As an expert.'

Gabriella paused, but Coombs gave her a nod of encouragement.

'Well, in their present condition, I don't think they could raise a poke in a Cairo cat-house.'

Coombs and Sergio stifled their amusement, as Messrs Austin

and Deness shuffled off back to the security of the boardroom bar.

·

There wasn't much amusement in the air in Martin Fisher's office. He pulled edgily on a Monte Cristo as Fred Taylor casually wandered around, smirking at the executive baubels Fisher had awarded himself: the mahogany desk, the computer, the brown leather chesterfield. Small consolation for Fisher, really, as the rest of his money had disappeared into the club's long-running overdraft.

'What do we do, Fred?' growled Fisher, trying to exert some authority. Taylor looked at him confidently. He'd seen off a few pushy chairmen during his short managerial career, and, despite his imposing bulk, Fisher had always struck him as a wanker. So he tried defence number one.

'Nothing. It was only a few yobs on the terraces!'

'Which are getting emptier by the week –'

'They'll come back. Look, Martin –'

'Try "Mr Chairman" for once – and mean it,' Fisher snapped.

Taylor paused. This was unusually heavy for Fisher. He was obviously needled. So Taylor decided to try defence number two.

'I know you're under pressure. As chairman, you've got to be seen to do something! But leave it to me – I'll sign someone. That'll keep the bastards happy.'

Fisher's face remained stony. 'How are we gonna pay, Fred? Luncheon vouchers? We couldn't afford a free transfer on today's gate!' he shouted.

Taylor was worried now, so he attempted defence number three – the calm walk-out to be followed by the gracious apology on Monday morning when the defeat had faded from the memory a little. But just as he was about to open the door, he heard Fisher explode behind his back. 'I want your arse, Taylor!' Fisher screamed.

Fred wheeled round – no defences needed now. It was time for attack. He advanced on Fisher menacingly.

'Well tough!' he shouted defiantly. 'I've been doing some reading, club files and such. And I've enough shit on you to keep me here for life! You should have thought about that before you stuck *your* nose in the trough!'

For a second, Taylor thought Fisher might leap up from the desk and grab him by the lapels, so he swaggered out as quickly as he could. Fisher seethed with a volatile mixture of humiliation and anger. He slowly exhaled two cheekfuls of blue cigar smoke, and violently stubbed the remaining three pounds fifty's worth of Monte Cristo into his ash-tray.

.

An hour or so later, Fisher's ebullience seemed restored as he ordered a bottle of vintage Perrier-Jouet for himself, Coombs and their two dinner guests, Sergio and Gabriella. They were in the warm lounge of a country house hotel a few miles outside the town. A log-fire burnt in the grate, and waiters in tunics were bustling around as the Saturday night county set glided in for their weekly ritual of display and indulgence. Fisher, with the humiliation of the defeat and Taylor's grubby defiance fading from his memory, was in an expansive mood. There was little likelihood of being pestered by fans for sackings or transfer-market plunges in a place like this.

'Anthony and I always have a little get-together here after home matches,' he beamed, as a waiter distributed menus the size of the Magna Carta. Coombs nodded his agreement.

'We'd rather settle club problems over champagne than in a board meeting.'

Gabriella, now reconciled to enjoying their hospitality as best she could, decided on a policy of mild dissent in order to assert her independence.

'That sounds very civilized but not too democratic. I'd have thought that Messrs Austin and Deness are sticklers for little things like voting.'

'Indeed,' said Coombs blandly, smiling. 'Everything always goes to a vote. We just tell them when to put their hands up!'

Fisher and Sergio joined in the laughter, beginning to bask in the glow of each other's power and status. Gabriella recognized the start of a male ritual and found herself reacting with the usual twinge of irritation. Seven years of seeing her husband Simon perform the same 'dance' at assorted legal parties had given her a lower threshold of tolerance when men started to swap business stories. In an hour they might even be asking her to leave them alone and go off to powder her nose!

'Do you consult your supporters' club at all?' she asked Fisher.

Fisher scoffed. 'What do they know?'

'Well *I'm* a supporter,' said Gabriella sweetly. 'And there were plenty of us out there this afternoon who could see what's wrong with the team.'

Fisher bristled at the challenge, hoping that Sergio might intervene and quell his daughter's insolent attitude, but he found Sergio looking at him, awaiting his reply.

'Yes, well – with respect, Mrs Benson, they only *think* they know, but they don't really.'

Gabriella waded in again. 'Come on – don't you feel that the balance of the team's play is too negative and destructive? I mean, you've got a defender playing in midfield!'

Fisher shifted on the sofa and held up a hand in self-defence. 'Please – I leave team matters to the manager . . . more's the pity!'

Sergio came to his rescue. 'Gabriella, please, let's not abuse Mr Fisher's hospitality.'

Gabriella resented the paternal chastisement but recognized also that her earnestness, as often before, had got the better of her manners.

'Sorry – I was talking as a long-suffering season-ticket holder and not a dinner-guest. I apologize.'

Before she knew what she was doing, she found herself getting up and heading for the powder-room after all.

·

After the early squalls, the dinner passed off in a civilized and entertaining fashion. In some ways, it was easier for Gabriella to re-establish a dialogue with her father while two strangers were present, and there was no denying that Sergio had retained all the charm and elegance which had once captivated Gabriella's mother.

After dinner the quartet adjourned to the lounge for brandies, where Sergio and Martin Fisher sealed their courtship with very large cigars. They had, more or less, talked football all evening, with the occasional diversion to take in Gabriella's business. On a couple of occasions Gabriella had pulled herself up short, realizing that she was trading stories and opinions with three men who, in theory at least, knew more about the game than she did. The fact that they listened to her seriously – Fisher with an effort, admittedly – made her reflect how much she had absorbed in her own right since the early years with her father.

Now, over coffee, it was party-game time – your favourite team of all time, club or national, and why. Gabriella quickly nominated Johan Cruyff's Dutch side of the 1974 World Cup. Sergio made great play of feigning mortal injury, when she spurned the alternative of Italy's 1982 World Cup winning side.

'I just think the Dutch achieved the ultimate dream: having players who could operate all over the pitch. Total football!' Gabriella enthused.

Fisher, perhaps with his own concerns in mind, pointed out that they hadn't, in fact, won in the final. Now Coombs proposed the Hungarians of the 1950s, who'd come to impregnable Wembley and humiliated England by six goals to three. 'They would wipe the floor with the Dutch of the seventies!' he asserted.

'They wouldn't, you know,' said Gabriella eagerly. 'Because the Dutch are twenty years younger than them!'

It was a good note on which to leave – history was bunk, even footballing history. The three men stood politely as Gabriella shook hands with Fisher and Coombs, who took her hand and kissed it.

'Thank you for a splendid evening. I'm sorry I spoke out of

turn, but I get very wound up about my team. *Our* team, I mean.'

Gabriella gave her father a hug and a mild warning about the perils of staying up late drinking. Then she went across to the reception desk to call for a taxi. Once she had left, Sergio apologized more formally for his daughter's exuberance – a gesture that would have re-established their separation had she heard it – but Coombs was eager to make light of it all.

'Martin's only upset because Gabriella knows more about the game than him.'

Fisher gave him a reproachful smile.

'I'm sorry, Mr Rebecchi – old habits die hard. I just don't believe women have a place in football!'

'Really?' said Sergio thoughtfully. 'How strong is that belief, Mr Fisher?'

In the hotel lobby, Gabriella waited for her taxi to arrive. She turned to see the three men in earnest conversation, plumes of cigar smoke swirling slowly around them. Man talk, she assumed.

CHAPTER TWO

In the morning a bleary-eyed Martin Fisher was to be found waiting near the first tee of the imposing and exclusive golf club he'd joined when he became chairman of the local football club. In some ways, he'd had to buy into the latter before being admitted into the former. Being a rich property developer didn't always win you access to the more established English institutions, especially if you were Jewish. By committing his money to a sporting cause, however, he'd proved himself a 'gentleman', and Messrs Austin and Deness, before they'd had time to discover their reservations about him, had dutifully proposed and seconded his membership.

But golf seemed to be the last thing on his mind, as he stalked impatiently around the practice green in front of the white, Palladian club-house. From the pro-shop in the near distance Coombs now emerged, Pringle-sweatered, wheeling his golf trolley at a less than leisurely pace. He joined Fisher, panting slightly from the exertion.

'Sorry, I overslept.'

Fisher eyed him like a man remembering a bad night at poker.

'I don't think I slept at all. Takes some thinking about, doesn't it?'

Coombs shook his head emphatically. 'Personally, I don't see what we've got to lose.'

'What about Fred Taylor spreading our guts all over Fleet Street?'

Coombs assumed his most confident prefectorial manner. 'There's ways round that – aren't there?'

Fisher didn't feel so sure. Coombs brought a new sternness to his voice, although it came out sounding more like petulance.

'Anyway — it's not a reality yet, is it?' His eyes challenged Fisher's. For once this really was the accountant telling his client firmly how to run his business. Fisher looked completely thwarted, and reached into his golf bag to produce a slim-line portable phone. He tossed it across to Coombs in what seemed like an act of surrender.

'Go on, then — make it happen.'

As Gabriella drove her car along the gravel drive to the club-house at the ten miles an hour demanded by the signs, her mind raced with curiosity about this bizarre summons. She parked her car in a section reserved for lady members, hoping that nobody would spot her lack of a tweed skirt or an Arran sweater. She found the two men installed in the dark-panelled cosiness of the bar, with the portraits of former club captains glowering down at them from the walls. It was just gone twelve, so only a few ardent nineteenth-holers, all male, were dotted around. Her arrival provoked a certain amount of disgruntled muttering, but Gabriella ignored this and headed purposefully to Fisher and Coombs's table. In contrast to the tumblers of whisky and water which seemed *de rigueur* for the others, Fisher and Coombs were presiding over a bottle of champagne, which jutted out from an over-laden ice-bucket.

'Another board meeting?' inquired Gabriella.

Coombs attempted earnestness. 'Well, actually, this is rather serious, Mrs Benson.'

Gabriella took the seat they were offering her opposite them, with a serene view of the lawns and a large cedar tree beyond.

'Gabriella, please.' She wanted to make matters less formal.

Fisher leaned across and, unbidden, poured her a glass of champagne. As he wedged the bottle back noisily among the ice cubes, he gave her a nervous smile. They want Sergio, thought Gabriella.

'How full-time is your business, Gabriella?'

'As much as I want it to be,' she replied cautiously. As a short visit on Friday had confirmed, GB's dance studios were ably staffed and virtually ran themselves. Gabriella was unwilling to concede this here, however, since she now sensed it was *her* they were courting.

'Because we'd like to offer you a job,' said Fisher, almost in a whisper.

'Aerobics for footballers?' Gabriella tried not to smile at the notion.

Coombs still looked tense. 'That's only part of it.'

Gabriella gave them both a puzzled frown. They seemed tense and ill at ease, as though they had bad news to give her.

Fisher cleared his throat and flexed his shoulders nervously, as though he had a three-foot putt at the eighteenth for the Open Championship.

'We, er – want you to be the new team manager . . .'

His voice tailed off, or at least so it seemed to Gabriella, who was starting to feel slightly uneasy. The words *sounded* like mocking revenge for her previous outspokenness, but Fisher's manner was grave.

'We're totally serious, Gabriella,' Coombs confirmed.

Slowly Gabriella began to register the intensity in both their faces, then she was aware of her mind being swamped by an avalanche of calculations as to the consequences and causes of this offer. For at least five seconds she was unable to utter anything more than a strangled exhalation, and then after that only the most obvious of responses.

'*Me?* I don't know what to say . . .'

'You said enough yesterday. And from what your father told us, you have an insight into the team's tactics,' asserted Coombs.

'Well, yes – but so do lots of other supporters.'

Gabriella remembered the image of them huddled amid the cigar smoke last night: it had been more than just man talk, obviously.

'Did my father put you up to this?'

Fisher made what looked like a 'cross my heart' gesture with only one hand, the other being occupied by a glass of champagne.

'The decision was entirely mine and Anthony's,' he said firmly. The clarity of Gabriella's mind was returning now that she had got over the first shock.

'Come on – you can't tell me last night provoked this?' She gestured to the little groups of whisky drinkers to emphasize her point. 'It's a man's world, football. You're going to get ridiculed if you go through with it, so there must be something at stake. What's he offered you?'

Coombs smirked vacuously at her. 'We just think it'll be worth it. For the novelty! Shake 'em up a bit!'

This seemed a flimsy justification to put before Gabriella, and even Fisher looked disappointed by Coombs's efforts at persuasion.

'Forgive me,' said Gabriella, 'but while I recognize that you're both civilized gentlemen, I wouldn't put either of you down as card-carrying feminists.'

'We're not,' said Fisher smiling, confident in his words for once, 'but when we see the best man . . . sorry, *person* for the job, we like to move quickly.' Fisher looked pleased with his recovery, but to Gabriella the slip sounded rehearsed, a clumsy attempt at flattery.

Fisher leaned back in his chair, trying to signal that no further explanations would be forthcoming. 'So – are you interested?'

Gabriella had become slightly irritated by now, not just because of their evasiveness, but also because they seemed so certain she'd accept. So her reply, 'Well, it would be a challenge, to put it mildly,' referred not just to the obvious difficulties of working in such an environment, but also to the additional complications of having Fisher and Coombs looking over her shoulder.

'I wouldn't come cheap, you know, if that's one of the reasons you picked me!'

'The money is not a problem,' Fisher stated, with apparent sincerity. Gabriella's stream of doubts and queries was only just beginning to pour out.

'And another thing – as far as I know, you still have a manager.'

'That won't be a problem either,' Coombs said confidently, although there was something in Fisher's look that suggested the contrary. He continued quickly, 'I mean, you've no respect for Mr Taylor, from what you said last night.'

'I know – but I wasn't in line for his job then. If I don't take it, what do you stand to lose?' She noticed now that Coombs, who seemed to be more behind the idea than Fisher, had become edgy. He was obviously worried that she was about to say no.

'You sounded keen a minute ago.'

'I'd be keener if I knew what was really going on. Look, I'll need twenty-four hours to think about it anyway.' She started to rise from her chair, champagne virtually untouched.

'Maybe I should wait at home until you tell me.' Coombs stretched out a hand towards her. 'Gabriella, look – trust us. We're going out on a limb for you. I hope you can respect that.'

Gabriella paused and confronted the issue head on. Whatever backstage manoeuvres had occurred to bring this about, it was still an exciting challenge. It was a chance to slaughter a few well-fed sacred cows: not just women working in a man's sport, but also a *fan* being moved into an area which had always been the heavily guarded preserve of the so-called 'professionals'. The flow of questions in her mind had petered out, stemmed by the unassailable attractiveness of the notion. Gabriella lowered herself back into her chair.

Fisher immediately reached out for the champagne bottle again, his usual zest rising like the colour in his cheeks.

'Right, we'd better round up the other directors, and alert the cardiac arrest unit.' They all smiled at this. Fisher raised a glass to her.

'Think about it, Gabriella. It's your chance to make history!'

The whisky drinkers looked on, oblivious to what was going on. They were still muttering about Gabriella's intrusion into the bar when she left.

As Gabriella drove away from the golf club, she switched her thoughts to Simon's potential reaction. He'd backed her enthusiastically when she'd set up the exercise studios, indeed she probably couldn't have found her way through the tangle of leases and employment contracts without him. He'd also shown no sign of resenting her continued involvement in the business, although she suspected that part of the reason for this was that it got him off the hook for the long and frequently anti-social hours his law firm required of him. They had frequently discussed starting a family, but since neither of them seemed strongly committed to the idea as yet, they had postponed the decision. 'Dinkys', they'd be called in the cheap shorthand of the Sunday supplements when the feature writers came to profile 'The Manageress' – meaning dual incomes, no kids yet.

So, as she parked the car outside their eighteenth-century local, alongside the BMWs and Suzuki jeeps, there was no question in her mind of not breaking the news to Simon. She knew instinctively that if she wanted to do something, their trust in one another was strong enough for him not to stand in her way. At least that's how it had been up to now.

Simon was installed behind a pint of bitter and the *Sunday Times* in a corner of the dining-room. Gabriella had told him about her evening, and he had also assumed that some interest in Sergio had provoked the summons that morning. But as he looked up from his newspaper, he immediately noticed that she was tense and realized there had been something more to the meeting than they had supposed.

'Don't tell me, they're suing you for slander and you want me to defend you?'

Gabriella smiled, took a sip of his drink, and explained.

'How would you feel about me taking on another job?'

Simon shrugged theatrically. 'Anything short of stunt-work is fine by me. Come on – out with it? What do these football blokes want you to do?'

He reclaimed his pint from Gabriella and lifted it to his lips.

'Manage the team,' Gabriella said quietly.

Simon paused in mid-swallow and lowered the glass. His eyes were fixed on Gabriella's, looking for some indication that it might be a joke. There wasn't any.

'Run a football team? But . . . but . . . you're a . . .'

'That's right, I'm a woman.'

'I was going to say amateur. Bloody hell, Gabriella – it's a lunatic idea!'

'They're very serious. Tell me why I shouldn't do it, Simon.'

Simon's head spun with doubts. 'Because you've never played the game,' he said, expressing just one of them.

'Well, no, but all those managers who have keep getting sacked, so it doesn't seem like much of a qualification.'

'Yes, but dealing with fifteen or twenty *male* athletes on a daily basis? They're not going to take you seriously!'

Gabriella conceded that they might not at first, obviously – but she told Simon, or more precisely, told *herself*, that once she'd made them fitter and given them fresh ideas about the game, they'd probably feel better about it.

'I haven't been watching for over twenty-five years just to get a glimpse of men's legs, you know!' This was an ungracious remark, because Simon was primarily talking as devil's advocate, with a strong protective streak mixed in.

'But these men have been playing for a living since they were sixteen. They spend years with each other. It's a little, closed, masculine world. What are they going to feel like when a woman comes in telling them what to do? They'll destroy you!'

Gabriella knew by now that these instinctive reservations of Simon's would be surmountable in time. So she smiled, if only to display her confidence in herself.

'Right – now that your male indigation has fuelled my resolve, help me guess why they offered me the job.'

But Simon wasn't ready for such flippancy. His peaceful Sunday lunch-time ritual had been ruined.

'I don't bloody know! I should imagine your father had something to do with it. Ask *him*!'

He snatched his newspaper up in a gesture of exasperation and tried to focus his mind on less vexing matters. He found he was looking at the sports pages.

.

Eddie Johnson was halfway through the *News of the World* when the door-bell rang. Eddie's wife had left him a few years back. There was no one else involved in the break-up, just the invisible barrier which comes down between a couple in early middle age, when the dreams begin to fade. Eddie's devotion to a job his wife didn't rate was the catalyst.

Now Eddie was left with the bitter joke, 'My wife had ninety-two football grounds for divorce,' but no one he could tell it to.

He opened the inner front door of his small 1940s semi-detached and stepped into the ribbed-glass porch. The first thing he saw was a Rolls-Royce parked on the path – Fisher's Rolls-Royce. And there were Fisher and Coombs standing in golf sweaters, smiling at him. Eddie didn't expect visitors at the best of times, but to find his bosses on his door-step on a Sunday afternoon was a little unnerving.

'Mr Chairman! Mr Deputy Chairman!' he exclaimed.

Fisher marched in through the porch. 'Scrub the formalities, Eddie.'

Eddie watched, bewildered, as Coombs followed his master into the lounge. Eddie was trying to work out why they'd come out specially to sack him, when all it usually took was a phone-call. Fisher strutted to the centre of the room, cigar alight, turned his chilled backside to the fire and fixed Eddie with a stare that would have done credit to an Old Bailey judge.

'I know you, Eddie. And I also know that nothing happens at the club without you hearing about it.'

Eddie was quailing now. 'Sorry, Mr Chairman – but what have I done?'

Coombs loomed at his shoulder and gave him a reassuring smile. 'It's not you we're after, Eddie. Honest.' Eddie weighed up their faces – they didn't *seem* hostile. But then people of their background and wealth often stuck the boot in when they were smiling. Fisher put an arm round Eddie's shoulder to clarify their friendly intentions.

'I need Fred Taylor's balls on a plate – and you can serve them up, Eddie. Yes, you can.'

Eddie was electrified. For the first time in his career he was in a position to wield real power. He'd been able to suggest which player might be dropped, who might be picked, bought or sold, but never in a situation where he could lose somebody a job. Especially not a boss as bad as Fred Taylor was.

'And would I benefit from this service?'

Fisher smiled expansively at him. 'Name it, Eddie, and it's yours!'

Eddie needed only a second or two to summon his long-lost daring, after years of subordination.

'The job. I want the bastard's job.'

Fisher digested this without apparent shock. He looked across to Coombs for confirmation, then turned back to Eddie and nodded. Eddie's heart felt like it was doing hand-stands.

'Well,' he said slowly, milking the moment for all it was worth, 'it's only a rumour . . .' It wasn't really, because nobody else was talking about it. Besides Eddie *knew* what the reason was for Fred Taylor's recent absences from morning training. Fact not rumour, that's what Eddie dealt in. Fisher beamed at the prospect of a little insider-dealing. He took a cigar from his pocket and stuck it into Eddie's mouth.

'Get the kettle on, Eddie.'

Eddie should have noticed that it was a cheap cigar in a plastic wrapper – but he didn't know the difference.

·

Armed with the information they had gleaned from Eddie, Fisher and Coombs called what they might have termed an 'Extraordinary General Meeting' in the boardroom that same afternoon with the three other directors of the club. One of them, Edwards, whose cleaning company enjoyed frequent contracts from Fisher's assorted firms, was guaranteed to play it their way. Messrs Austin and Deness, dragged from their Sunday rose-pruning or bridge games, were predictably in less pliable moods, especially when the sex of Taylor's would-be successor was announced. Deness and Austin raged about the sheer absurdity of the appointment. However, Fisher insisted that Gabriella was an outstanding choice, that it was in the best interests of the club to select her – though he didn't specify why – and that the appointment should therefore be accepted immediately.

Austin attempted to stall the meeting on procedural grounds.

'Are we to be given the chance to meet this wondrous candidate?' he demanded scornfully.

'You did that yesterday and I gather you were very rude to her,' Fisher said brusquely. 'But no, we haven't got time for the luxury of interviews and all that bollocks. We decide today, and the recommendation of the chairman and his deputy, who *have* interviewed her, is for immediate acceptance!'

Deness went a shade more purple in the face before launching his final tirade against this imposition. 'Do you honestly think you can ride rough-shod over us like this? You will bring this club into ridicule. Do you think you can do this with no opposition?'

This sort of grandee tone always brought out the barrow-boy in Fisher, which was never far below the surface anyway. He turned on Deness. 'Listen, granddad, if it wasn't for my money, this club would be a supermarket site by now. It's all the old farts like you who brought on the ridicule! I'm trying to drag the place into the twentieth century before the hundred years is up! Now I suggest we move to a vote. Those in favour?'

Fisher thrust his hand into the air, followed by a smiling Coombs and then the tame Edwards, who delayed a little to make it look good. Austin and Deness shook their heads at one another in dismay.

'Motion carried,' crowed Fisher. 'Roll on Monday!'

.

Fred Taylor had ordered the first team squad to come in on Monday morning – normally a day off – as punishment for Saturday's dismal showing. A familiar tactic for beleaguered managers, it was designed to reassert authority over supposedly disobedient players and, when leaked to the journalists in the after-match press conference, to reassure the fans that something was being done to improve the team's morale and form. It usually improved neither, since the players resented their 'detention', and fans saw the move as further confirmation of the team's disarray.

But the mood of the players as they took part in a practice match was surprisingly purposeful, with a touch of cheerfulness. This was partly to do with the absence of Taylor himself, but mainly because Eddie, who was refereeing the 'match', had been dropping broad hints about an impending change of manager. Although it was the same Eddie barking commands and abuse at them, the players were subconsciously trying to impress their new boss. This meant going in hard, running hard, and shouting loudly for the ball.

Gabriella registered this as she casually approached the pitch, in the manner of a passer-by. The sight of her brought an additional edge to the play, for not too many strikingly attractive women in their late thirties ever bothered to watch the training. Charlie O'Keefe, a small but energetic teenager with a Bros haircut, and his marker Gary Halliwell were the first to spot the mystery admirer.

'Here, seen that, Charlie?' leered Halliwell, during a break in the action.

'Yeah, tasty,' agreed Charlie. 'I'm definitely into older women, you know, Gary.'

'Haven't much choice, have you son?' Halliwell broke into a run as the play moved in their direction. 'I saw her first!'

O'Keefe gave chase, and quickly beat Halliwell to a ball played forward. Halliwell jostled him from behind.

'Hey, Charl – do us a favour and boot the ball her way.'

'Sod off,' laughed Charlie as he launched into some impromptu ball juggling.

'Now, Charlie – *please!*' begged Halliwell, elbowing O'Keefe in the back. Charlie obliged and clipped the ball into touch close to where Gabriella was walking. Halliwell sprinted after it, accompanied by a knowing jeer from the other players. Gabriella had trapped the ball under her foot, and waited for Halliwell to approach.

'Your throw-in, I think.'

Halliwell grinned at her, unable to believe his luck.

'Well spotted, darlin'!' He put his hands on his hips and breathed heavily to emphasize the masculine nature of his work. 'You, er, watch football, then?'

'Now and again.'

'I can get you tickets for our next game if you want. I'm the captain, see.'

'I know – Gary Halliwell, isn't it?'

Halliwell's rugged face lit up. 'That's right!' He looked back over his shoulder, where the rest of the team were watching idly. Eddie tapped his wrist-watch for the fun to stop.

'Look, I've got to get back to work, but if you'd like a drink at lunch-time –'

'Sorry,' Gabriella said, pulling a convincingly disappointed face, 'but I've got to go to a meeting.'

'Never mind – we're here most mornings. Come again!'

Gabriella replied truthfully, 'I will, don't worry.' She flicked the ball up to Halliwell, who took a long run into the throw-in, then turned for a quick wink at Gabriella before rejoining the fray with a deliberately muscular tackle to impress both Eddie and his new admirer.

·

An hour later, Gabriella stood in Fisher's office at the club to give him her decision. He was anxious about her 'spying-mission' on the players, but understood her reasons for wanting to see them in that context. After all, that was where most of her work would take place. The ninety-minute public performances were based on perhaps twenty hours of private 'rehearsals' per week. If she couldn't manage these successfully, no amount of epoch-breaking appearances in the touch-line dug-out would make up for that failure. Fisher listened patiently to Gabriella's assessment.

'No wonder there are so many injuries – they're not warmed up enough, and they're diving into tackles like rugby players. They're encouraged to be aggressive for the sake of aggression. There's no work on set-pieces, and nobody's giving them any ideas. They're going through the motions of training, without achieving anything.'

Fisher smiled ruefully. 'Don't soft-pedal, Gabriella – tell me straight!'

Gabriella looked sheepish – her earnestness had got the better of her again.

'Sorry – but they are worse to watch in training than they are in a proper match,' she concluded.

Fisher was only half joking when he asked her if she would still take the job. Before committing herself, Gabriella wanted to discuss terms. In all the excitement about the notion of appointing a woman manager, there had almost been the assumption that she might do the work for nothing or without a contract. But she wanted a hefty salary, £35,000, and a two-year commitment from the club, so that if things went badly, or the club found the ridicule too much to bear and she was dumped, she'd get her £70,000 as compensation.

Fisher seemed remarkably affable about this, fuelling Gabriella's suspicions about his real motives for appointing her. They would emerge in due course, she felt, so no point in pressing too hard now. Instead, she went on to list her other conditions of employment: Eddie Johnson to reorganize the training as she wished or to ship out; no intereference with her team selections from any source; and general commitment from the chairman, manager and team to meet with the supporters' club on a regular basis. Gabriella detected that Fisher found this the most irksome of her demands.

They clashed over the responsibility for transfers, which Fisher, for reasons he wouldn't go into, regarded as his preserve, although, as he conceded, they were rather academic in the present financial circumstances of the club. This allowed Gabriella to bring up the touchy subject of Fisher's own finances. With Simon's help and contacts, she had established that all was not well with Fisher Property Services Ltd. With this and the club's debts in mind, Gabriella made it clear that she regarded finances as her concern as well – after all, she had set up and run her own business successfully.

'You need me *off* the field as well as on it,' she told Fisher with a hint of arrogance. She waited for an explosion, but there was almost a smirk on Fisher's face as he reluctantly agreed.

'Well, yes – I suppose you're right.' He knew just how true it was.

.

Having shaken hands with Gabriella on the deal, and notified her of a press conference to announce her appointment the next day, Fisher's last remaining impediment was Fred Taylor.

The afternoon light was fading rapidly outside the window of Fisher's office when the material he needed finally arrived. Fisher checked the contents of the brown envelope with its cardboard back. He'd had a phone-call from his man that morning to say that Fred Taylor was exactly where Eddie had said he would be. Now here was the last detail whereby the Football League's first woman manager would get her job.

Fisher was so pleased with the contents of the envelope that he lit a brand-new cigar before the old one was finished. He composed himself, tucked the envelope behind his back, and walked across the corridor to Taylor's office. He could see a light under the door and hear Taylor talking on the phone. Fisher walked in without knocking.

Fred had his shirt-sleeves rolled up to suggest hard work, but there was nothing on his desk apart from an open contacts book. He tried to wind up the phone-call, giving Fisher a hostile glare. Fisher pulled on his cigar, unmoved.

'Yeah, well fine,' said Taylor on the phone, 'talk to your agent by all means – but I need a decision soon . . . yeah, but can we talk about that later? Okay. Cheers.'

He replaced the receiver and, although he didn't feel like giving one, offered Fisher an explanation.

'Just chasing up a loan agreement on a first division lad.'

'And organizing your back-hander?'

Taylor wasn't prepared for this – but then he didn't need to be. 'You can talk!'

'You're still not calling me "Mr Chairman", Fred.'

'Oh, well – hardly matters now.'

Fisher took the envelope from behind his back, lifted the flap and gently shook the contents on to Taylor's desk. They were three long-lens photographs which featured Taylor arriving at the front door of a Barratt-style house and being greeted by an attractive young woman; the same woman in the process of drawing the curtains in an upstairs bedroom; and Taylor being kissed on the cheek by the woman as he left the house. In this shot she was wearing a dressing-gown. The woman was Lesley McGregor, wife of Dave, the player Taylor had asked Eddie to keep back for extra training.

For once Taylor looked defeated. The pictures needed no sub-titles, but Fisher enjoyed providing them anyway.

'Screwing a player's wife while he's busy training – you're more likely to win Shit of the Month than Manager of the Month!'

'You slimy –'

'Fred, please. Every insult will knock a grand off your handshake. And you're getting sod all anyway.'

Taylor looked at him with contempt. 'Who shopped me?'

Fisher smiled at him, trying to be enigmatic but failing.

'It's Eddie isn't it? He'd do anything for my job.'

'He's in for a bit of a surprise too, Fred,' Fisher said, relishing the feeling of omniscience. 'We'll tell the press it was "by mutual consent", shall we?'

Taylor was gathering a few files and books from his desk drawers and putting on his jacket.

'Tell 'em what you like.' Possessions gathered, he headed for the door. 'I know about your rake-offs, Fisher. I'll have you one day.'

Fisher patted the photographs which Taylor had left sprawled across the desk.

'Play the white man, Fred. If you live by the cock, you gotta be ready to die by it also.'

Taylor gave him one last spiteful glance and slid out.

·

Fisher had called the press conference for eleven thirty on the Tuesday morning, time to soften up the journalists with a few drinks and still get his little 'coup' into the lunch-time news stories on local radio. After that, the big boys would be down in the afternoon.

The boardroom had been laid out with a desk and three chairs at one end, with the chairs for the press facing them. Fisher and Coombs occupied two of the chairs, with the third vacant until the new manager was revealed. Fisher had got the idea of Gabriella making an 'entrance' from Lawrie McMenemy, the former Southampton manager, who'd pulled this dramatic stunt when he'd secretly signed Kevin Keegan back from Hamburg.

Now, as he read briskly through his prepared statement, he could feel a tingle at the base of his neck, knowing that Gabriella was only a few feet away, waiting behind a side door for her cue.

The dozen or so pressmen scribbled desultory notes or idly held up pocket-recorders. Every chairman who'd ever sacked a manager came up with the same old spiel. They hardly needed to listen.

'Low team morale, discontented supporters, and a severe reduction in attendance,' he said listing the grievances. 'With all these factors in mind, I'm afraid I had no option but to talk to manager Fred Taylor about the situation. And he has, like the noble person that he is, agreed to tender his resignation for the sake of the club.'

Steve Simms, the local stringer for the *Star* who had been running stories for weeks about Taylor getting the chop, felt he had the right to the first question. 'Was this by mutual consent, Martin?'

'You took the words straight from my mouth, Steve.'

Now the other reporters joined in the formalities, looking for little details which might make the dismissal of Fred Taylor slightly more interesting than the ten or so others which had already happened this season.

'How much of his contract was left, Mr Fisher?'

'About 25,000.'

This got a decent laugh, and Fisher was gratified. After giving them drinks, the best way to guarantee a 'good press' was to provide quotable copy. He was sufficiently astute, however, to know that some expression of regret was required in order not to come over as a heartless tyrant.

'No, but seriously – Mr Taylor has been a good servant of this club, and his contract will be honoured in full. And I hope that it won't be long before he's back in football management, where he belongs.'

Coombs decided to chime in with a 'hear, hear', which Fisher felt was overdoing the sincerity a bit. He quickly stood and asked the gentlemen of the press to prepare to meet Mr Taylor's successor. As he strolled dramatically towards the side door, the journalists seemed amused by the intrigue, when it was commonly assumed that Eddie Johnson would simply step in. The sly smiles and looks of boredom were still on their faces as Fisher now led Gabriella through and installed her in the vacant chair.

The first instinct of the press was to see this as a joke – a stunt, a laugh, a wind-up. Bring on a beauty queen first, then haul Eddie out in his still sweaty tracksuit – that must be the score, mustn't it? But no Eddie emerged, and Fisher and Coombs looked defiantly serious.

'What's this, Mr Fisher, *Candid Camera*?' asked Simms.

Fisher decided they needed it spelled out for them. 'Gentlemen

– this is Gabriella Benson. As of ten minutes ago, she is in sole charge of team matters at the club.'

The boys still weren't sure – the first one to take this seriously would look a right lemon, so they clung to the security of collective bafflement, now with a hint of hostility.

'If this is a joke and we go away and write about it –' threatened one, aware of the stunts pulled by the infamous 'Rocky Ryan'.

'It's no joke,' Fisher said firmly.

'Absolutely not – Gabriella was an outstanding managerial candidate,' said Coombs, who was aware of a few flash-guns starting to go off.

Slowly, there was a dawning realization among the journalists that this mundane morning was about to become probably the biggest football story of the year. One of them broke ranks and headed for a phone in the press-room to alert his editor. As the photographers clamoured to the front to get shots of Gabriella, a great barrage of questions swelled up.

'Who did you say she is? Where's she come from? Are you serious, Mr Fisher? Who did she manage before – anybody? Has she any experience of football management?'

It was impossible to distinguish who was asking what. So Fisher raised his hand and quelled the waves of questions. He suggested they direct their questions to Gabriella, one at a time. A line of hands went up – Fisher pointed out a man near the front.

'Er, can I ask, Miss Benson, is it?'

'*Mrs* Benson,' Gabriella corrected, hoping to forestall the inevitable questions about boyfriends or 'live-in lovers'.

This vital information was immediately transcribed into all the notebooks. The reporter, senses still fogged by the shock, reacted stolidly to the news.

'You're married, then?'

'Ye-es,' said Gabriella, as if she were writing it on a blackboard for them. Still they came back for more.

'Who to?'

'*Mr* Benson!'

There was general impatience with this line of questioning, and Simms, whose mind was already racing with the rich seam of possibilities to be mined, signalled urgently to Fisher and got the nod.

'Have you ever worked in football before, Mrs Benson? In any capacity?'

'No, but I've followed the game keenly for over twenty-five years.'

This was an open goal for most of them, but one of the older reporters got in first. 'I've done it for nearly thirty, Mrs Benson, but nobody's ever offered *me* a manager's job!'

There was cynical laughter – if Gabriella kept giving answers like this, they'd savage her. The great joy of journalism was that while you might be obliged to register quotes faithfully when in the presence of your 'victim', the tone of them could later be coloured by the copy which surrounded it. Already phrases like 'she trilled excitedly' and 'cooed the brunette beauty with the best legs in the game' were being stitched in around her very words.

Gabriella's concept of her qualifications – aerobics diplomas, training in Alexander Technique – also made little impression on these battle-hardened veterans of the press-box. And when she listed, in her defence, great players whom she thought possessed feminine grace – Cruyff, Antognoni, Netzer, Beckenbauer, Platini, Hoddle, van Basten – the reporters were convinced they were on to a 'lulu' of a story. Steve Simms had already got as far as her first day's work.

'How are you going to cope with things like swearing and nudity in the dressing-room?'

Gabriella should have suffered in silence or made light of it, but she couldn't resist a dig.

'Oh dear – and I was just beginning to think you were a sports reporter, Mr Simms.'

She was playing into their hands – meeting cynicism with earnestness and a superior tone. For a second they switched their attention to Fisher.

'Don't you think you'll have a revolt on your hands when the players find out their new boss is a woman?'

'I don't know, I haven't told them yet,' Fisher laughed, in a vain attempt to lighten the tone.

Simms was sure. 'I think you will, Mr Chairman.'

'Only if hacks like you stir it up,' snarled Gabriella. Fisher's restraining hand came too late. The bulk of journalists stood to leave. The next part of the story was getting the players' reactions – fast.

As it happened, the team coach was just pulling into the car-park, returning from training, as the reporters spilled out of the club's main entrance. Still in their mud-stained kit, the players looked bewildered by the fuss as they made their way towards the dressing-room.

'Hey, lads, better get smartened up before you meet your new boss!' shouted one of the press-boys.

Halliwell put an arm round Eddie. 'He's right here with us, tosser!' Eddie smiled at the vote of confidence being given. But the reporters persisted.

'Gary, as skipper, can you tell me what your reaction is to having a woman as your manager?'

Still the message didn't get through.

'Hey, Eddie,' shouted Brian Rimmer, the keeper, 'there's a joker here calling you a poof!'

It seemed like a press wind-up to the team – part of the ever shifting relationship between media and sport, where the only constant was exploitation by one side or the other.

The players all filed into the club, convinced that this was just a Fisher hoax on the press for the slagging they'd given the team since their last match. Only when Fisher and Coombs escorted Gabriella into the dressing-room and gave a brief introduction did the shocking truth begin to sink in. They sat on the benches, hair matted with sweat, knees scarred with mud and grass, feet aching, unable to grasp that this person was coming into their world. They felt numbed and humili-ated. Their very essence as serious professionals in a tight exclusive little world of male superiority was being challenged.

Nobody was capable of listening as Fisher went through the motions of introducing Gabriella to each player, and then this strange being was actually speaking to them herself, reminding Halliwell of her meeting with him on the training pitch yesterday morning, not that he cared for being reminded. Ringed by scowling or impassive faces, she tried to say something positive.

'I don't need an introduction, really – I've watched most of you playing for the past five seasons.'

This drew no visible reaction. In truth, it wasn't the best time or place to meet them. The air was heavy with the stench of male body odour mingled with antiseptic, and the drably coloured, wood-lined walls of the dressing-room seemed to close in on her as she looked around. She thought that the least she could do was be pleasant – though her heart was beating so loudly she could hardly hear her own words.

Halliwell, as captain, finally gathered himself sufficiently to issue the first challenge. 'If you'll excuse me, Mr Chairman, I've just finished training and I'd like to take a shower,' he sneered at Fisher.

With that, he began to strip off his kit, slowly, defiantly, in what an anthropology student would have recognized as a primitive declaration of territory. Fisher was unnerved and took Gabriella's arm, but Gabriella shook him off and stood her ground. If she walked out now, she'd have to stay out. Halliwell continued his strip, eyes staring into Gabriella's all the time. Gabriella remembered the previous night when Simon had made passionate, almost violent love to her in what she'd interpreted as a male statement of possession prior to her new career. He must have had situations such as this in mind. Had he been here, Simon would probably have been beating his chest at Halliwell right now. The thought of it sustained Gabriella for the moment when Halliwell was totally naked, still standing in front of her. It was pretty pathetic as intimidation went, and she felt she'd made her own declaration of intent by standing her ground. Now it was time to retreat with grace.

'Come on, you should all take a shower before you catch your death. I'll see you in the gym after lunch.'

She turned and headed out through the dressing-room door. Fisher waited until it had closed, then raised an angry finger and swung it round at every single player. He was a bulky, heavy-shouldered man, who looked like street-fighting was on his curriculum vitae.

'Before anyone says anything. I don't give a shit what you think. This decision was taken by me in the best interests of the club, and anybody who doesn't like it can ship out now! In addition, any of you who feel like squealing to the press can forget it! Talk to them, and you'll be in breach of your contracts!'

Eddie, who'd been standing in a corner, eyeing the proceedings with a chilling look, snarled at Fisher. 'Mr Chairman – I want to see you!' he spat out through jaws clenched with anger.

'I'll be in my office, Eddie,' Fisher said blandly, before backing out of the room with Coombs at his side. Halliwell picked up his muddy kit from the floor and hurled it with venom at the door. 'Fucking bastard!' the captain screamed.

Gabriella, standing outside in the corridor, couldn't help hearing. Then Fisher came out, trying to regain his poise.

'Sorry about that.'

'I thought they took it rather well under the circumstances,' said Gabriella brightly. 'Want to change your mind?'

Fisher shook his head.

'No. No way,' he asserted.

Gabriella nodded, looked at her feet, and exhaled to relieve the tension. She lifted her head and smiled defiantly at them. There was nothing else to be said. She had a job, and she had to get on with it.

'Right,' said Fisher, 'I'll leave you to it.'

He and Coombs walked off, up the stairs to their executive offices high in the stand, leaving Gabriella standing alone outside the closed dressing-room door.

CHAPTER THREE

While word of Gabriella's appointment spread around the club
and the world beyond, she decided her first move must be to
establish the true state of the players' fitness. It wasn't just
because her curiosity had been aroused by her incognito visit to
the training ground. Her own specialist qualifications were in
fitness and exercise techniques – they would give her a power
base at the club from which, if successfully achieved, she could
expand into other areas – tactics and team selection being the
principal two which concerned her.

She had an hour before her meeting with the players in the
gym, so she took the opportunity to introduce herself to the
club's physiotherapist, Norman Williams, a stooped, grey-
haired man in his mid-fifties who, despite his surname, spoke
with the hint of an Irish accent.

She'd located him in the small treatment-room which adjoined
the main dressing-room. It boasted a couple of treatment tables,
an exercise bicycle, all the bandages and medications of Norman's
ancient trade – no sign of a cold sponge, though! – and several
more modern machines for infra-red or electronic healing.

Norman seemed unruffled by the arrival of a woman in his
domain, which made a pleasing change for Gabriella after the
scene in the dressing-room. In truth, he was pleased to be
consulted after years of verbal abuse or professional indifference
from Fred Taylor. Gabriella was interested to know if he had
any record of the players' injuries and subsequent treatments.
Norman reached up to a shelf stacked with notebooks and
ledgers, and proudly revealed his collection to his new superior.

Gabriella leafed through the books – a file on every player, reserves included, and a season-by-season log-book which detailed players' injuries, how they occurred, the treatments applied, and how long the man was kept out of the game.

'You're very thorough, Norman.'

'Thank you, er, Mrs Benson,' Norman said, unsure of how he should address a female 'boss'.

Gabriella scanned the log-book for the current season. It revealed a catalogue of ham-string pulls and groin strains, and two Achilles tendon breakdowns, amid the predictable list of wounds and bruises. The current consequences of this 'battle fatigue' were that Dave McGregor had been out for the past five weeks, and now Tony Morris would be unavailable after his thigh injury the previous Saturday.

Norman tried to be philosophical. 'It's been a very hard season.'

'What do you put that down to, Norman?'

It was too soon for Norman to be disloyal in any way, so he contented himself with a shrug.

'Bad luck, I suppose.'

Gabriella suspected, indeed she knew, otherwise.

•

Gabriella prepared for her two o'clock session with the players by changing in what used to be Fred Taylor's office, and would now be hers. There were no real provisions at the ground for a woman changing and showering, so she'd been told to make do with the away-team dressing-room until a facility could be provided. As she slipped into one of her most modest tracksuits – she had no intention of trying to win the players over by squeezing into a skimpy leotard, the Page Three route to acceptance – she became aware of an increasing clamour outside. The window of the office overlooked the main entance, and there was a growing crowd of reporters, and now an I T N camera unit, being kept at bay by a single, dogged commissionaire. From across the corridor in Fisher's office she also became aware of other reactions to her accession. A shouting match was under way.

Eddie Johnson had gone in to confront Martin Fisher for his act of betrayal. Gabriella found herself trying to listen to the row and realized that Eddie was not just reacting with the same outrage as the players. She couldn't hear precisely what was being said, but she understood the venomous tone. She guessed that Eddie had been expecting the manager's job, which would make him a dangerous enemy to work with.

Indeed, Eddie was guilelessly declaring his intended disloyalty to Fisher, without seeing the trap he was setting for himself.

'You're gonna have a players' revolt on this one, Mr Chairman. And it's no good expecting me to deal with it, because I'll be on their side.'

Fisher was unmoved. 'They won't "revolt", Eddie – players are too thick to organize themselves. They get so used to being told what to do, that the small part of their brain which ever did any thinking withers away. In a couple of days, she'll have them eating out of her hand.'

'And you expect me to help her?' asked Eddie incredulously.

Fisher sprang the trap. 'Yes, Eddie – it's your job. If you don't do it, I'll sack you. Simple as that!'

It took Eddie several moments to recover from the realization that his career was now umbilically linked to Gabriella's in Fisher's eyes. But Eddie was a creature who had evolved over the years in order to survive, and his principal instrument of self-protection had been his ability to know when the odds were changing in his favour. He would never have ratted on Fred Taylor if he had been in a position of strength – like a hyena, he trailed his prey waiting for weakness to set in. So now he'd seen a way forward.

'And if she screws up, she gets sacked too?'

Fisher was cornered by the game's persisting logic – only a dozen of the ninety-two teams could win anything meaningful like promotion, a cup or their divisional championship, which left some eighty managers subject to the whims of their chairmen and their club's supporters. If Gabriella didn't achieve success, or at least respectable failure, she too would become a casualty. So Fisher shrugged and said, 'Yes, I suppose so.'

'Would I be in with a chance, then?' Eddie probed.

'Put it this way – I owe you one for dishing Fred Taylor.'

Eddie didn't believe this particularly, but it would give him something to bite on in the forthcoming weeks. He couldn't help pointing out to Fisher, though, the ambiguity of his role – a role Fisher himself had defined for him.

'Quite a challenge you've set me, Mr Chairman. Support this bird with my expertise, yet keep on hoping she quits or fouls up.'

'I'm sure somebody of your devious nature will be up to it, Eddie,' he said, as he waved him out of the office.

Fisher reflected on the possibilities – he didn't know enough about the game to be able to recognize when Eddie might be undermining Gabriella. But more importantly, would Gabriella be able to recognize it?

Meanwhile the players were busy working out their two-faced stance to Gabriella: to appear to be co-operating in order to keep their jobs but in reality giving less than their best to ensure that she lost hers. Sitting in the small canteen under the main stand where they had their lunch after training, the four major opponents to the appointment – they were known as the 'Rat Pack' to the rest of the team for their drinking and gambling exploits – discussed ways and means.

There was Captain Gary Halliwell, a rugged Scouser whose years in the game had seemed like trench warfare, and whose body and face now reflected that. Trevor Coughlan was the midfield 'hard-man' from London; his barrel-chested physique and cropped hair were often sufficient to keep opponents away from him without recourse to his usual kicking. Jim Wilson was Halliwell's partner in central defence – a tall gangly player with good skills on the ground, he lacked some of the bite of Halliwell and Coughlan, but had won his status as a 'good lad' by dint of his raffish obsession with horse-racing and a formidable capacity for drink. Finally, there was Brian Rimmer, a beefy, open-faced man from Yorkshire, who did his best to subscribe to the football myth that all goal-keepers were crazy.

Rimmer wasn't crazy, but he liked a laugh, and usually didn't mind how he got it or at whose expense.

They had finished their plates of pasta and fruit and jelly cooked for them by the ever reliable Mrs Hastings, and though she was still in ear-shot they had never got used to the concept of moderating their language in her presence.

Halliwell summed up the various options they had discussed.

'All we have to do is go through the motions in training, ask her lots of questions she won't know, and I bet she'll be off in tears by the end of the week!'

'It's dead easy you know, lads,' Rimmer said, grinning. 'If I let a few soft goals in, she'll get the sack!' He let out one of his booming laughs.

'Very good, wonder-brain, but you've been doing that all season, so why make a special effort?' asked Halliwell.

Jim Wilson chuckled. 'Besides, if you start chucking them into your own net, you're gonna get dropped, aren't you?'

Halliwell was warming to his theme now, convinced that the sheer realities and drudgery of training would be enough to see 'this middle-class bird' off.

'Look, lads, we don't have to do anything drastic. Let's see how she fancies the job on a Tuesday morning, when we're out training in the pissing rain; or in the dressing-room when there're fourteen hairy arses on display, three of which have just dropped enormous farts!'

The Rat Pack liked this notion and registered their approval with cackling laughter. Sitting near by, unable to block out this conversation despite concentrating on his copy of the *Guardian*, was Keith Nicholl. He lowered the paper in exasperation.

'God Almighty, listen to you! You're supposed to be grown men, not schoolboys!'

This was a familiar scene at lunch-breaks – the topics were usually television, music or politics (the Rat Pack were unabashed Thatcherites), but Nicholl nearly always held the opposite view.

Halliwell saw it coming now: this time about Gabriella.

'Here we go – the intellectual viewpoint! I suppose you're quite *stimulated* by the idea, you wanker?'

'Well, she can't be a bigger moron than Fred Taylor,' observed Nicholl, who had suffered more than others under the regime of the sun-tanned playboy.

'That's not saying much,' Wilson laughed.

Nicholl persisted with his defence. 'She may have some new ideas, you know. She's into aerobics and stuff apparently.'

Coughlan sneered. 'All that Jane Fonda bollocks? What's that got to do with football?'

Rimmer chipped in with one of his speciality bad-taste jokes. 'Didn't do much for *Henry* Fonda, did it?' As always, whatever the remark, it was followed by the Laugh, to let everyone know that it was meant to be funny.

'Sod off, Rimmer,' Nicholl snapped in reaction. He folded his paper and stood up. 'The least we can do is give this woman a chance.'

'There's only one thing I want to give her, and that's resting between my legs,' Rimmer said oafishly, accompanying the remark with the obvious gesture.

They loved winding Nicholl up like this, because he always fought back.

'Really, Brian? I thought it was between your ears,' Nicholl responded.

They jeered his departure, taking it as a concession of defeat. Mrs Hastings came across from the kitchen with a tray of tea and biscuits for them, and Halliwell put a protective arm round her.

'Now this is the right place for a woman, isn't it, Mrs Hastings?' he said with a grin.

·

Gabriella stood in the corridor outside the club's gymnasium, composing herself, breathing deeply and relaxing her neck. She pulled her hair back into a functional ponytail and tied it with an elasticated band. She knew that the players were already inside because she could hear the formidable wall of chatter and male laughter. She took one last deep breath and walked in.

All their gazes turned on her, as a silence smothered the room. Despite her modest tracksuit and severe hairstyle, she could feel the mixture of hostility and sexual assessment cutting her like a scythe. Her training in the Alexander Technique, which had taught her all about poise under pressure and positive voice projection, came to her aid momentarily, allowing her to speak to them with apparent confidence.

'Thank you, gentlemen! Now if you'd all like to come through to the back of the gym.'

She walked through to an exercise area beyond the weight-training machines. She turned to see that none of them had moved an inch, and they were still lolling against the Nautilus equipment. The peer-group pressure had even got to Nicholl: he looked as though he wanted to follow but was held back by his primary obligations to the team mentality.

Gabriella decided, not that she had much choice, to drop the 'brave-but-brittle' tone in her voice and attempt a reasonable manner with them.

'Look, if it's any consolation, this was as big a surprise to me as it must have been to you.'

There wasn't a flicker on any of their faces. She tried to hold off her dismay.

'I know you don't like the idea, but there's not much I can do about that now. All I ask is that you give me a fair hearing. What I hope to achieve is to make you better players, both physically and mentally. To exploit the potential that I know you've got.'

Suddenly there came the noise of a slow, ironic hand-clap. The source was Halliwell, who'd presumably been brought up on films like *The Blackboard Jungle* and *Rebel without a Cause*.

Gabriella tried to make the best of the insolence, while also chastising herself for her own familiar failing: over-earnestness.

'Quite right – too much talk and standing around.' She

56

snapped her fingers. 'Okay, I want you in rows of four here,' she said, gesturing to the floor-space in front of her.' Still nobody moved.

'Come on, please – the quicker you get this done, the quicker we can go home.'

Halliwell slid off his perch on the bench-press and wandered towards her. The rest slowly began to follow.

'Come on, lads,' Halliwell urged. 'Mrs Benson's got to get back and make her old man's dinner.'

The squad shuffled into position an arm's length apart from one another and waited impassively for the revelation of her intentions.

Coughlan, who had installed himself provocatively in the front rank, gave her a dead-pan look.

'So what are we doing, formation dancing?' Around him, smirks started to appear on various faces. Halliwell's initial note of hostility had been followed, but now they would take their cue from Coughlan.

Gabriella proceeded patiently. The worst thing she could do at this stage, she thought, was to lose her temper. She clung to what *she* knew, rather than concede to their strengths.

'Okay – we're going to have a spell away from the weight-training. For all the muscle power it gives you, pumping iron isn't much use to athletes like you. It shortens your muscles, tightens them up, whereas longer, more supple muscles, especially in the legs, will enhance your running, jumping and agility.'

It sounded like an Open University lecture, Gabriella thought grimly to herself, but she could tell that it had started to make at least a few of them think.

Not Wilson, though.

'What are you going to do, stick us on the rack and stretch us?' More smirks, as the Rat Pack followed the party line.

'No – but it will feel like it. And what we'll be doing before *any* exercise is a solid ten minutes' worth of stretches.' She gave McGregor a wry smile. 'Try to put a stop to all these pulled ham-strings. Okay – first position.'

They all looked at her blankly, until she'd realized her slip of the tongue. 'Sorry, that's a ballet term.'

This was seized upon instantly. 'That's what this is, a bleedin' ballet class!' exclaimed Halliwell. 'Look, darlin', do we have to do this stuff?'

By now the primitive minds at the front had managed to come up with an analogy for their current plight. They knew when they'd last been in a similar situation: school, junior school to be exact. Wilson was the first to establish the metaphor which would quickly become the standard work of reference for dealing with Gabriella.

'Watch it, Gary, or she'll send you out into the corridor!'

Gabriella persevered with her demonstration of the stretching exercise she wanted them to do. She talked them through it: feet at ten to two, heels together, bend at the knees, then slowly up on to the toes and hold!

There were assorted grunts and moans about the indignity of it all, but by far the biggest scowl was on the face of Eddie Johnson, who had sneaked in at the entrance to the gym to confirm his worst fears.

After ten minutes of novel stretching routines, some of the players were beginning to lose their balance, not just their dignity. The one that really threw them was bending down, straight-legged and laying their palms on the floor. Gabriella performed it with ease, before announcing a move on to general fitness improvement.

Coughlan was at her throat quickly. 'We're already fit.'

'Not from what I've seen,' she snapped back, as she moved into brisk running on the spot. The players grudgingly followed suit.

'Come on, put some effort into it!'

'You played ninety minutes lately?' Halliwell queried, as he eased into the jogging. Gabriella stared back at him, and decided this was the first opportunity to start spelling things out to them.

'No, I haven't – and neither have you. You've just run about in short bursts. I want you to be able to maintain a constant fluid movement for the full length of a match. Okay,' she challenged them, 'let's see how fit you *really* are!'

Gabriella launched herself into a sequence of wide 'star jumps'. The gauntlet had been thrown down, and the players, particularly Coughlan, began to put their bodies into what they assumed would be the simple business of out-staying this presumptuous woman.

Sequence followed sequence, flowing into one another with effortless grace, at least on Gabriella's part. The players, used to the explosive demands of shuttle-runs, press-ups and interval sprinting, were not really trained to sustain the constant level of physical commitment that aerobics demanded. Half an hour into the session most of them were becoming breathless, their movements increasingly ragged, their shirts and faces soaked with sweat. Gabriella kept going, seemingly effortlessly, with only Coughlan, who had fixed his eyes on her, showing no signs of distress.

She put them through a further ten minutes before announcing a wind-down period: slower movements, allied to deep breathing, in order to bring the heart rate down. When she next instructed them to lie on their backs, she took it as a little victory that none of them had the energy for a crude reply. She made them lift their legs slightly off the ground, lower them, then hold, putting their stomach muscles to the test. Finally she let them drop their legs and relax. With the entire squad flat out on their backs, exhausted, she felt she'd made a small, perhaps symbolic point.

'Okay, that was good for an opener. Tomorrow we'll put in some hard work.' And with that, she picked up her towel and walked gracefully out, leaving them to reflect that, whatever else the manageress might be, she was certainly fit.

While Gabriella had been locked in combat with the squad, the media had been gathering on the door-step of the club. Fisher, to his great delight, had been interviewed over the phone by BBC radio, and a girl from the local television news had been allowed up to his office to film a short piece with him.

The person they all wanted to interview was Gabriella, but she made a point of staying in her office after she'd showered and changed, leaving the press to fall upon the players as they left for home.

They faced a welter of questions. How is she doing? What has she said to you? Has she been in the dressing-room yet? How does it feel to have a lady boss? They deflected these on Fisher's orders with slightly self-conscious 'no comments'. But Steve Simms, who was at the heart of the throng, having been appointed 'number one Manageress man' by his editor, tailed Gary Halliwell to his car as the light faded into evening.

'Come on, Gary – give us a break. It's worse than trying to get info out of South Africa!' Not that Simms had direct experience, of course – South Africa Road, home of Queen's Park Rangers, was about as close as he'd got to the Dark Continent. Halliwell told Simms of Fisher's instructions.

'That's all right, Gary. Anything you say will be strictly non-attributable.' Simms was thinking of the old stand-bys such as 'sources close to the club' or 'an insider revealed'. But Halliwell was convinced this would still drop him in it.

Simms leaned in through the window of Halliwell's Sierra.

'I can probably find two hundred quid a week for you – cash!'

Halliwell's demeanour changed. 'That's what I like – non-attributable money.'

'We got a deal, then?' pressed Simms.

'Long as you keep me in the clear, yes.'

'Good lad! Now tell me – what was this afternoon like, then?'

Halliwell paused. 'Well, Steve – depends how hot your ballet is.'

Simms beamed. He could already see the headlines.

·

Gabriella sat behind her new desk in the cramped manager's

office. She'd removed the trade calendar from the wall which featured topless girls in industrial clothes, and had set about logging the first and second team fixtures into her Filofax. Her door was open, so she glimpsed Eddie as he went past, back in his nondescript 'civvies' and heading for dinner-for-one and *The Benny Hill Show* at home.

Gabriella called out to him, but at first she thought he'd ignored her. A moment later, he appeared in the doorway, his thin features sharpened by the light from Gabriella's anglepoise.

'Come in a second, would you?'

Eddie took a few paces forward and tried to anticipate her question.

'If you expect me to take 'em for the sort of nonsense you were giving 'em this afternoon, you can have my resignation now.'

'I wouldn't expect you to do that,'she said pleasantly. 'You're not qualified!'

Eddie was stung and declined her invitation to sit down. Gabriella pressed on, despite his dumb insolence.

'I'd like your opinion of the club's injury record this season.'

'It's average,' Eddie said, shrugging. 'It's a man's game, you know.'

'So I've heard. What about Dave McGregor? He's missed half the season, on and off. Is he injury prone or just a hypochondriac?'

'He's an injury-prone hypochondriac. Makes Trevor Francis look consistent.'

Gabriella smiled at the comparison. Eddie didn't return her smile.

'Do you have any idea how we can change his situation?'

'Aye,' said Eddie, lip curling. 'Sell him.'

Gabriella looked pained. 'I was thinking of trying him in midfield, actually. Channel his skill more – maybe that would improve his confidence?'

'The only thing that would improve is our chances of being

relegated to the third division,' scoffed Eddie. 'He fancies himself too much, see? Fart-arses around, and when it doesn't work out, blames it on an injury of some sort. The lads think he should skip the team bus and arrive in an ambulance.'

Gabriella saw another immediate point of conflict. Here was a player who'd showed flashes of great skill when she'd been watching as a fan. Now she had the power to exploit his potential, only to be told the 'professional' view – they didn't, as they said in the trade, 'fancy' him.

'But he's got ability,' Gabriella persisted. 'Maybe you and the team are undermining him?'

Eddie was stung by this, stung too by the thought that he'd been lured into talking to her as if she was an equal. He went for the lowest blow in his armoury.

'Actually, you're blaming the wrong people, missus. If the lad's been undermined by anything, it's the fact that his old lady's been screwing around with Fred Taylor! That's what got Fred the sack!' he finished cruelly.

Gabriella was clearly disconcerted by this news, and Eddie enjoyed the sight of it.

'Will there be anything else?'

'No thanks,' said Gabriella thoughtfully.

.

Although she escaped the attentions of the press at the club – a discreet exit on the other side of the ground saw to this – Gabriella discovered how quickly they could track down a home number, despite such a common name as Benson. As she and Simon attempted to complete their usual domestic routine of a quiet supper alone, the phone rang for about the sixth time.

Gabriella moved to get up from the table, but Simon threw his napkin aside and stormed towards the offending instrument. 'Can't even finish my dinner in peace,' he muttered.

A tired and touchy Gabriella suggested that he didn't have to answer it, but Simon pointed out, with overdone irony, that it might *just* be a call for him.

It wasn't.

'Hello,' he answered brusquely, and listened. 'No, I'm sorry, she's not here at the moment, who shall I say called?' Despite his tantrums in front of Gabriella, he had managed to be remarkably civil to the press so far – a lawyer's training, Gabriella assumed. But the line of questioning this time tipped him over the edge.

'No,' he snapped in reaction to a question, 'I am not the bloody butler, I'm her husband! We don't *have* a butler! No, I'm sorry, I've no comment to make about it, and if my wife were here, she wouldn't either, goodnight!'

He slammed the receiver down, and stalked back towards his rapidly congealing meal.

'I'm sorry, Simon. It'll probably calm down in a day or so.'

'I think I'll have ripped the phone off the wall by then.'

The phone rang again. Simon, still on his feet, made a theatrical turn and headed back towards it, now almost masochistically enjoying his descent into martyrdom.

'Yes?' This time he suddenly seemed relieved. 'Sergio! Yes, I'm afraid the media have been on the phone all night. Yes she is . . . hang on.'

He held the receiver up for Gabriella, anticipating a long chat between daughter and father which would allow him time to finish his supper and have the substantial drink he now felt he needed.

Gabriella seemed delighted that Sergio had heard the news – via the *London Evening Standard*, complete with photograph – since it saved her from lengthy explanations. There was also still the lingering desire of a little girl to please her father, which his return had evidently rekindled. Simon winced as she clearly began to revel in Sergio's praise for this new achievement; the years of neglect seemed to have been miraculously forgotten.

Gabriella, albeit light-heartedly, started to quiz her father about his involvement in the affair, which, as Simon had been trying to point out during their interrupted meal, looked ever more likely.

'You must have done more than just *talk* to them?' she said, but then, after hearing what must have been a brief disavowal, she settled for a mild warning.

'I hope you're not lying to me!' Another reply rerouted the conversation back towards their mutual euphoria, so Simon was almost glad that the persistent ringing of the door-bell spared him further exposure to this cosy family chat.

He made his way down the hall, glass of wine in hand, and somewhat naïvely, opened the door without asking who was outside. Immediately he was dazzled by the explosive light of several camera flashes. He couldn't help thinking that, with wineglass in hand, he might very well be mistaken for the butler after all – but in that instant, a darker thought hit him. His wife was now public property. Their privacy was permanently at an end.

·

The following morning the players' bus headed for the training ground. Eddie was on board, but not Gabriella. There was some speculation that she may have already quit, but then somebody else pointed out that Fred Taylor hadn't exactly been up here that often. Dave McGregor stiffened at the mention of the name. His wife Lesley had by now told him about her affair with Taylor. It had hurt him grievously, but the prospects of the other players finding out hurt even more in some ways.

Players derived a great deal of meaning from their manliness. While it was an accepted part of their tribal customs that they should, married or otherwise, pursue women, married or otherwise, at every opportunity, the loss of a wife through desertion or adultery brought them great shame among the other warriors. Although Eddie had been goaded into revealing the affair to Gabriella, he was inclined to keep quiet about it to the team, because he knew how McGregor must be feeling.

As the coach pulled into the training ground, there was general dismay and bewilderment as the squad saw that Gabriella was already there waiting for them. What's more, she was setting up a video-camera on a tripod on the halfway line of the practice pitch. Eddie bristled in the knowledge that another initiative had been taken, one which was likely to render their passive resistance less effective. Jim Wilson was the first of the Rat Pack to venture an opinion about this new development.

'I know the sort of video I'd like to make with her. She'd be a housewife in a nightie . . .'

McGregor suffered again at this, sensitive to any remark which suggested that the team might know.

As they shuffled suspiciously off the coach, Gabriella quickly called them to order.

'Right, lads – let's have a good ten minutes' worth of stretches like we went through yesterday.'

The players jogged across to the centre of the pitch. Eddie nodded at the camera.

'For your photo album?'

'No,' Gabriella said patiently, 'I'm going to record the play in the practice match, so I can point out their faults.'

'*I'm* pretty good at that already,' Eddie told her in a clipped tone.

'I know you are, Eddie – but if a player himself can see what he's doing wrong, then we'll all know what we're talking about, won't we?'

In the background most of the players had formed an arc and were beginning to embark on the stretching routines Gabriella had put them through the previous day. Eddie wandered off in their direction as Gabriella was joined by Halliwell, who had sauntered off the coach last of all. He carried a rolled-up newspaper under his arm.

'Excuse me, miss – I brought you a present.'

He unfurled the newspaper for her benefit. It was the *Daily Star* and on the front page was a three-deck headline NOT BALLET LIKELY! SOCCER STARS REVOLT OVER LADY BOSS. This was flagged as an 'exclusive' by Steve Simms. Accompanying the piece was a photograph showing Gabriella exercising in a leotard. It must have been taken at least six years previously, thought Gabriella, when GB's first opened. Now it had presumably been excavated from the cuttings library of the town's local paper and pressed into service for this contemporary 'scoop'.

Halliwell dropped it by the tripod like a cat bringing in a dead bird and jogged off to join the rest of the team. Gabriella left it where it lay, allowing the wind which swept across the field to blow it away.

After the players had finished their stretches, Gabriella called for them to gather round. They shuffled mutinously into position around her, waiting for her to pronounce on their game. Eddie pointedly lined up with the players. Gabriella registered this and was determined to make it an issue.

'Could I have you over here with me, please, Eddie?' she asked with a tone just short of hostility.

After a pause, Eddie took a few slow steps in her direction, arms folded across his chest, head hanging down, and stood near Gabriella, facing the players.

'Now what I want to try and do is continue the usual practice-match format, but I'd like to throw in a few positional changes and a new discipline.'

'Which position do you want me in before you discipline me, miss?' asked Rimmer, before emitting his usual loud laugh.

Gabriella took the joke well and warned herself out loud to watch what words she used in front of them. She didn't mind the occasional sexist *double entendre*, since they were inevitable in the circumstances, but the cumulative effect might be wearisome and demoralizing. Now wasn't the time to make an issue of it. Instead, she resumed briskly with the details of the changes she wanted to make to the team's structure. She asked Keith Nicholl to play as an out-and-out centre forward, pushed up on the defenders, and then pointed out Dave McGregor and suggested he try central midfield. Coughlan put his hand up sarcastically in the classroom idiom which had now been adopted.

'Excuse me, miss – but that's my position.'

'Yes, I know, Trevor – but I'm just trying out a few ideas.'

The sarcasm continued. 'Should I go in goal, then? Or do you want me to protect Dave from getting a knock?'

'No – I want you to play *behind* the back line as a spare defender.'

This wasn't just a positional change but an ideological bombshell, for it effectively represented the Continental-style system of man-to-man marking with a 'sweeper', and, as Halliwell was quick to point out, they didn't play it here.

By 'here' he meant not just the club but in England, indeed the whole British Isles. There was a deep distrust of this 'Continental' – they used the word as an insult – system within the British footballing establishment. It belonged in the same foreign dictionary as shirt-pulling, spitting and feigning injury, other despised 'Continental' practices. Gabriella might just as well have offered them a bucket of *moules marinières* for their elevenses.

She replied with a patient 'I know', which was pregnant with sub-titles, along the lines of: 'This system is played by most of the successful clubs and international sides in the world.' And: 'It doesn't have to be negative if it's operated correctly, because it demands that defenders *play* as well as tackle.' But these explanations for her change would come later – because she had another, even more contentious demand to make of them.

'I'd also like you to play this match without tackling.'

There was a ripple of bemused laughter among the squad. Eddie shook his head in dismay. In the space of three minutes this woman had challenged the team structure, the defensive system, and now its capacity for winning the ball from the opposition.

Eddie spoke for them all when he replied, 'Tackling is part of the game, miss. This is men's professional football!'

'Yes, but ideally you should be trying to win the ball by anticipation and interception. Interceptions give us faster possession, they catch the opposition off balance, and they reduce the chances of sustaining injury. Tackling should be seen as a last resort, not as an end in itself!'

She clapped her hands like an American basketball coach finishing a court-side spiel – only there was no team response, just a sullen silence. The players donned their coloured bibs, and with Eddie refereeing and Gabriella watching through the video, this bizarre first training session got under way.

It soon became apparent that the players were fighting to take it seriously. They moved around slowly and had to be bawled at by Gabriella before injecting even half-pace into the proceedings. The first potential tackle of the game fell to Halliwell, who was marking Keith Nicholl on the edge of the box. Ordinarily, in the same situation, Halliwell would have clattered him, taking ball and man too if necessary. Instead he pushed Nicholl over with both arms, then affected an effeminate voice and walk to the amusement of the rest of the Rat Pack.

Gabriella looked up from the video-camera, plainly not sharing the joke. As Coughlan strolled forward amid the laughter to take the 'free-kick' that Eddie had awarded, she called out loudly from the touch-line.

'Sorry – can Dave McGregor have a go at the free-kicks, please?'

Coughlan put his hands on his hips and shouted back at her. 'I take all the set-pieces!'

'I know,' said Gabriella, 'and how many times have you scored from them this year – twice in twenty-two games? It's time for a change.'

Coughlan had really got the hump now. Moved from his usual position to accommodate McGregor and denied his party-piece, he stomped off and lined up with the defensive wall. McGregor, obviously grateful to get the chance of some limelight, weighed up the angles on his free-kick before chipping a beautifully curling shot over the wall but just over the bar, with Brian Rimmer well beaten. Nicholl applauded the effort, but Coughlan was still seething. He called out to Gabriella again.

'You realize his foot'll be in plaster for a month now?'

McGregor turned as he heard the crack and mimed a 'big mouth' gesture at Coughlan. Gabriella noted the friction between them, which her changes had now apparently heightened.

Thereafter the session passed off relatively peacefully, although she retained the impression that, with the exception of Nicholl, McGregor and perhaps Morris, the players were treating her presence as a joke.

On the coach back to the club after training, the players studiously made for the rear seats, leaving Eddie up front near Gabriella. Eddie looked out of the window, examining the drab urban landscape as though he'd never passed through it before Gabriella felt it was time to go to work on him.

'Were you very pissed off at not getting the job, Eddie?'

Slowly, Eddie turned away from the window and gave her a forced smile.

'You could say that.'

'I'm sorry – I didn't know.' Eddie snorted and went back to factory-spotting. Gabriella decided that talking to the back of his head would suffice – it was certainly prettier.

'Look, I know this must be a bit difficult for you . . . but I really would value your support. I'm not wanking about here, you know. I believe that my ideas can make this lot a better team.'

Eddie stayed silent.

'I know you may despise me for what I am, but I expect a commitment from you. It's your duty as a professional.'

Eddie turned to her again, nodding insolently.

'Professional, yeah . . . the first coach in history who agreed to stop his players tackling.'

'In training, yes. I know you can't – but I'd like you to try and see the game from a woman's point of view. It's got so much skill, imagination and daring – it doesn't have to be turned into an initiation ceremony for manhood! Look, who's your favourite modern player?'

This was a question Eddie didn't mind answering. 'Bryan Robson. He plays for Manch –'

'Don't patronize me, Eddie,' she interrupted. 'Yes, great player, but a case in point. The aggression in his game is destroying him. You can see him thinking every time there's a fifty-fifty ball, 'I must go in here, it's expected of me.' Then, wallop, the poor sod's injured again. I don't want my players to think like that.'

There was a long angry silence, while Eddie digested not only her argument but also the expression 'my players'. Finally he looked at her, full face for once.

'You and me are on different sides of the planet, lady.'

As the players changed after a shower, there were the first small hints of a breakthrough. Nicholl and McGregor, who had adjacent pegs in the dressing-room, chatted quietly lest the Rat Pack overheard their heresy.

'I thought you showed up well, Dave,' said Nicholl encouragingly.

McGregor, who was grateful for any such boost in the circumstances, said, 'Ta, Keith!' Then he confided, 'Better than being stuck out on the wing.'

Nicholl nodded in sympathy but didn't want to take the conversation further, because in the centre of the room Coughlan and Halliwell were loudly rubbishing Gabriella's changes of formation, particularly McGregor's new midfield role.

'It's bloody stupid – the moment we get in a game, they'll stick somebody on McGregor, he'll bottle it, and we'll get stuffed in midfield!'

'Yeah,' agreed Halliwell, 'and you'll be able to do sod all about it while you're hiding behind my arse!'

Gabriella now appeared at the dressing-room door, edging in diplomatically. Those players who weren't dressed quickly picked up towels.

'Right, I've got some good news and some bad news for you.'

'You're leaving and Fred Taylor's coming back?' asked Coughlan, determined to take any chance to snipe at Gabriella.

'As training went so well this afternoon, I'm happy to give

you the afternoon off from the gym. However, I'd like as many of you as possible to turn up at the supporters' club meeting tonight – seven thirty.'

She tailed off as she saw the mixture of apathy and incredulity written on their faces.

Wilson put his hand up. 'Please, miss – do we get paid extra for this?'

'Well, no – I'd class it as part of your job to meet the supporters.'

Wilson looked round the dressing-room with a sardonic smile.

'Well, we'll all be there, won't we lads? We don't mind giving up an evening!'

A smattering of laughter accompanied Wilson's remark. Gabriella looked at them for a sign of interest or enthusiasm but saw only a surly, slack-mouthed resistance. She almost felt like quitting there and then, but after a moment her resolve returned.

'Right – well done and thank you.'

She walked out without receiving an acknowledgement in return. As soon as the door closed, the chatting and movement among the players resumed.

'I think she's beginning to feel the freeze,' Halliwell gloated to Coughlan.

'Yeah, we'll have her out in a fortnight!'

Rimmer now joined them and adopted his best leering expression.

'Here,' he whispered confidentially, 'I've had an idea – ten quid a head in the kitty.'

.

The rest of Gabriella's day continued in a rather down-beat way. The real reason she'd excused the players from afternoon training was that the family solicitor, Mr Habgood, was coming round to her house to reveal details of Diana Rebecchi's will. The elderly lawyer's fluting voice seemed to echo round the room as Gabriella tried to fight back the memories of her mother's life. Now it was all reduced to a few paragraphs on parchment.

Diana had left £5,000 to cancer research and a similar sum to her housekeeper, but the balance of the estate, roughly £200,000, would fall to Gabriella. The figure meant nothing to her in the circumstances – she was happy and comfortably off, so it was rather embarrassing to be the beneficiary of such unnecessary wealth. And of course, none of it could fill the gap her mother's death had left in her life. Mr Habgood registered Gabriella's blank expression.

'I hope you won't be frittering the money away on some overrated player from the first division,' he smiled.

The realization that even this elderly, cloistered country solicitor had heard the news of her appointment brought Gabriella out of her abstracted state.

Habgood continued to tease her. 'I suppose if this new career move had happened earlier, your mother might have disinherited you.'

'Nonsense, Mr Habgood – she'd have probably come along as my assistant!' said Gabriella, cheered, for the moment, by the thought.

Habgood offered her a document to sign.

'Now if I could just have your autograph, Mrs Benson.'

Nobody asked Gabriella for her autograph that evening at the supporters' club. There weren't that many people to do the asking, since only about twenty fans sat in the hall to listen to her. Of the fifteen-strong first team squad, just Nicholl, perhaps predictably, and, more surprisingly, Charlie O'Keefe had bothered to turn up. Nicholl made a couple of rather earnest observations about the macho image of the game, which Gabriella wished he'd made a little more light-heartedly, and perhaps more importantly, in front of the team. O'Keefe, however, just sat there staring at Gabriella in adoring fashion, and smiling and twinkling at her when she happened to look at him.

As Gabriella made her winding-up statement, she was aware,

out of the corner of her eye, that the electric bingo-machine was being prepared for action.

'Even though I'm the new manager, I won't forget what it's like to be a supporter of this club,' she declared. 'I know how depressing it is in town on Saturday nights when we lose . . . and I know how infuriating some of the team selections can be. So I hope that with the aid of these regular sessions, we can keep a channel open between the club and its most valuable asset – that is, you the supporters!'

There was a smattering of applause as she sat down, followed by a swift adjournment to the bar to stock up on drinks, as the bingo-machine was trundled on to centre-stage. O'Keefe offered her a lift home in his Escort X R3i, but she pointed out she had her own car. Nicholl slipped away with a faint smile of embarrassment. Gabriella made her way out through the bar, running the gauntlet of curious and leering looks from the lads who were sitting around. She drove away from the club and out through the other side of the town, feeling small even in this backwater of England.

There was a clipped response from Simon when she got home. He was stretched out on the sofa, leafing again through the day's papers with their garish headlines about Gabriella. He'd picked up a couple of Continental ones too at Paddington, and now proceeded to regale Gabriella with choice extracts from all of them, comparing the thick-eared tabloid responses with the more considered assessments made by such papers as *L'Équipe* and *La Gazzetta dello Sport*. His motives in doing this were clear – he wanted to let Gabriella know how *he'd* been traumatized by her sudden lurid fame. As he finished his over-ironic version of 'What the Papers Say', however, he registered Gabriella's subdued mood and softened immediately.

He got her to lie on the sofa with him, so he could stroke her head soothingly, as she told him what hard going the day, and now the evening, had been. He reassured her by telling her what she knew instinctively to be right, but which she'd begun to lose sight of.

'The only way you can prove yourself to them is by sticking at it and getting results.'

'But that isn't what you want, is it?'

He reaffirmed his support for her, genuinely, not just because it was a required gesture. It would obviously take time for him to adjust to her new role, and the hours it would demand of her. Simon knew that Gabriella had a dogged, almost perverse resourcefulness, which he had increasingly been able to ascribe to her largely fatherless childhood. They'd talked about it a few times, and Gabriella had recognized that a high percentage of the driving zeal within her was connected to a wish to display her resilience, to prove to her father that she hadn't needed him after all.

Gabriella seemed to be soothed and cheered by Simon's words, but then his reflections on her relationship with her father prompted remembrance of a small item in the morning's *Financial Times*.

Gabriella's face darkened again as Simon flicked the pages to find the story for her.

'Here it is.'

He summarized the item for her before handing the evidence over. 'English company called Solford Construction has made a £20 million tie-up with the Rebecchi Company of Milan, with a view to several joint projects.'

Gabriella was already on edge, trying to assess why her father hadn't mentioned this, but then Simon added, 'Apparently Solford are specialists in urban redevelopment. And there's your chairman owning a property company! You're more likely to be running a housing estate than a football club!'

Gabriella was now reading the story, which gave few more details than Simon's digest. She had a queasy feeling in her stomach, which undoubtedly stemmed, as it had done for many years, from a deep sense of distrust where her father was concerned. Where he declared one activity, there was always another, possibly more, going on which remained part of his private, furtive world. And now she'd gone and let him back into her life, with him clearly playing some deeper game and possibly using her for his own ends.

CHAPTER FOUR

After a restless night, followed by a perfunctory breakfast with Simon, Gabriella resumed her battle for the minds, if not the hearts, of her first team squad. She reasserted her insistence on 'no tackling' for the practice, and for a short while the players adhered to it with a growing fluency, and seemingly less hostility.

The player to benefit most from the less intimidating atmosphere was Dave McGregor, adapting well to his central midfield role. Soon, though, the freedom went to his head. He was a good-looking, obviously slightly vain boy, and the more he saw of the ball, the more of a swagger he assumed, because in essence, he was watching himself play.

This 'posing' eventually proved too much for Coughlan, who was still desperately adjusting to his position behind the defensive line, where the action was much more sporadic than he liked. Suddenly, McGregor dwelt on the ball yet again – controlling it with the sole of his boot like Graeme Souness – Coughlan exploded out of defence and snapped a double-footed tackle on McGregor, who hopped away in pain as Eddie blew for the free-kick.

'You twat, Trev! You've been dying to do that!'

Coughlan gave him a thin smile. 'You were just too quick for me, Dave.'

McGregor subsided to the turf, clutching his ankle, while Eddie crouched and rolled down his sock, administering the freezing spray. Gabriella had been watching the game from the touch-line and ran over in an agitated state.

'That's *exactly* the sort of situation I wanted to avoid in training!' she barked at Coughlan. 'You learn this discipline now, you'll be in better shape for deciding what to do in a match. And we wouldn't have a dressing-room like a field hospital!'

McGregor, still on the turf, looked up at Gabriella.

'With respect, Mrs Benson, you're missing the point here. Y'see, Trev is the self-appointed hard man of the team. Every team's got one, but second division outfits have the worst, because they can't play, they can only kick. So when someone with a bit of skill comes along –'

'Where? Where?' asked Coughlan sarcastically.

Eddie pulled McGregor to his feet, and tucked the spray back inside his tracksuit.

'All right, all right – back to work, eh?'

'And *think – anticipate*!' shouted Gabriella, dabbing her forefinger at her temple.

Coughlan's response to this was to fetch up a ball of phlegm which he projected with great relish into the air. Gabriella eyed him, wondering whether to confront him now, but decided that would be pandering too much to his image of himself. She allowed the practice to resume, and the remainder of it passed without incident.

But there was an odd tail-piece to the morning. As the team left the coach back at the club, and Gabriella complimented them, almost sincerely, on a good morning's work, Gary Halliwell followed his usual dig about Gabriella's new defensive system by giving her a large box of chocolates. Ordinarily Gabriella might have scoffed at such a traditionally male gesture, but in the circumstances she was quite touched, and despite her prevailing pessimism, she began to feel as though she might be getting through to the players after all.

Cheered by the gesture, she worked through lunch on preparations for her first League game. She also put in a call to Charles Austin, the director who had reacted so badly to her appointment; she had a proposition for him.

·

On Saturday morning at ten the team set off by coach for the drive up to Yorkshire, which, Gabriella reflected, was a pretty tough place for *any* woman to get taken seriously, let alone one who was a football manager.

She sat up at the front of the coach, allowing the players to preserve their traditional routines of card-games and joke-telling without any intrusion from her. As the journey progressed, she was aware of Brian Rimmer moving about, apparently collecting cash – gambling debts, drinking kitty? – Gabriella didn't care very much as long as it didn't affect their game. Then, later on, Tony Morris, the skilful black forward who was still unavailable because of his thigh injury, arrived at her side to present her with a pretty posy of flowers. That explained the collection, Gabriella thought, as she thanked Morris for his gift.

Morris returned to the back of the coach to be greeted by wolf-whistles and jeers. Gabriella, buoyed by their apparent good spirits, turned to look at them, and found Rimmer blowing her a big kiss. Gabriella put it down to playfulness, brought on by pre-match tension, and dismissed a nagging doubt that they were sending her up.

As the coach pulled through the streets around the cavernous northern ground, Gabriella felt a tingle of nerves for the first time. Although the rows of small terraced houses, with a pub on one corner and a shop on the other, were similar to those surrounding her own club, there was a different atmosphere here. She felt the urgency of the people, their desperation to see their team win. Football *meant* more up here, because for a lot of the supporters it was the major excitement in their lives.

The coach pulled in tight to the players' entrance in the main stand. The home fans gathered round, chanting the name of their team, and now hastily made banners were waved, poking fun at the lads with the first woman manager. Gabriella spotted one which would have done justice to a headline in the *Guardian*: YOU ARE MISS-MANAGED. Eddie led Gabriella off the bus.

'Quite polite so far,' he said, knowing the 'stick' the team and manager would get from the fans on the terraces.

As the team filed into the visitors' dressing-room and headed for the match programmes laid out for them, they were surprised to find Fisher and Coombs standing in the centre of the room, leaning on the treatment-couch. In front of them were a couple of piles of cardboard shirt boxes.

'Hello, lads, good journey?' Fisher boomed.

'Crowd outside's getting its money's worth out of our new mistress,' said Halliwell.

'They're not the only ones – look!'

And he gestured for Coombs to break open the boxes. Inside were a new set of team shirts in the usual royal blue with white piping – but there was an additional embellishment. The name SOLFORD CONSTRUCTION was emblazoned across the chest of each shirt. The players started to grab the shirt with their regular number on, and a few jokes started to fly about the new sponsors, including a pun from Nicholl about defensive walls, which got a jeer.

Gabriella arrived to hear the commotion, but her relaxed manner disappeared when she saw the name on the shirts. She made the connection immediately – the company her father had 'pacted' with earlier in the week. Speculation was unnecessary, since it seemed obvious to her that she had been an unwitting part of a business equation. Fisher and Coombs looked uneasy when they saw her reaction, and quickly started to leave.

'Good luck, Gabriella,' said Fisher as he passed.

Gabriella picked up a shirt and waved it at him. 'This was my price, was it?'

Fisher gave her an edgy smile and scurried out. As the players embarked on their pre-match rituals unbidden, Gabriella felt the clammy sense of compromise and deceit.

She gave the team little advice before the match other than the general encouragement. Then when she filed out on to the pitch after the players, accompanied by Eddie and Norman Williams, she was almost unaware of the flock of photographers and TV cameramen who trailed after her, exhorting her to smile for their benefit. The only thing she *could* focus on was the sight of Sergio, sitting up in the directors' box alongside Fisher and Coombs. He gave her a cheery wave, which she did not return, and then she installed herself in the visitors' dug-out, with the wolf-whistles and crude calls of the home crowd bombarding her ears.

The first half of the match duplicated Gabriella's confused and sullen mood, with ragged play from both teams, but, more importantly, little discernible improvement in Gabriella's team. The man-for-man marking system seemed only to increase Halliwell's propensity for destructive tackling, which invariably resulted in a free-kick for the other team. McGregor too seemed hesitant and overawed in his role as midfield play-maker. The sense of smug satisfaction which was oozing out of Eddie as he sat next to her in the dug-out was almost palapable to Gabriella.

Then, ten minutes before the interval, Gabriella's two principal initiatives of the week went badly awry. Bringing the ball forward from defence, McGregor dwelt a little too optimistically and lost possession. A pass was immediately threaded into the heart of the defence, for a forward to run on to. Automatically, Halliwell, Wilson and the two other defenders raised their arms in appeal – they knew from years of experience that the forward had run off-side before the ball was played up to him. But they hadn't learned quickly enough that Coughlan would still be behind them, 'sweeping'. Thus the forward was *on*-side, and the linesman's flag stayed down while the forward moved in on goal. Coughlan couldn't get across to him in time, and, although Rimmer advanced swiftly from his line, the low, firm shot beat him comprehensively.

The home fans let out a great roar of approval. In the dug-out Gabriella's spirits sank even further, as Eddie slammed his hand at the wall in silent frustration. On the pitch, while the home side celebrated, there were only recriminations among Gabriella's team. McGregor stood, head bowed with his hands on his hips, as Coughlan raged at him for losing possession. To make matters worse, as they regrouped for the kick-off, McGregor started to limp into his position. Gabriella waited for Eddie to say, 'I told you!'

At half-time, the players snatched their cups of tea from a side-table and began arguing among themselves. This was very different from the training, as different as warfare is to parade-ground drilling. Gabriella's head ached with the tension – she was learning the great reality of management, that you can't really control what happens on the pitch.

Amid the clamour, she tried to throw in some encouragement, although it seemed like she'd suddenly become invisible.

'If we can knock short balls in behind their back four, they're terribly slow on the turn,' she tried to suggest.

'It's *our* defence that's the problem,' screamed Coughlan, before pointing across at McGregor, who was hoisting himself on to the treatment-table. '*And* the prat who's supposed to be holding midfield!'

Coughlan strutted towards the table.

'Ah, look – he's had enough already!'

Norman got to work on McGregor – it looked like a knee injury. Gabriella encouraged them to stick to the same system in the second half but was shouted down by an angry Halliwell.

'Sorry – I'm the skipper on the park! If things so wrong out there, I can change what the hell I like!'

Gabriella walked away from the confrontation and went to check on McGregor, who was complaining that his knee went just before he lost the ball for the goal – now it felt swollen. Eddie was seething, all his prejudices about McGregor boiling to the surface.

'Run it off!' he snarled. 'Give him some spray, Norman!'

Gabriella intervened, trying to diagnose the injury.

'I've had this a few times,' McGregor said weedily. 'I just have to rest till it goes away.'

Eddie was disgusted now, and practically dragging McGregor up off the table.

'Bollocks, man! It's not a dislocation or a break. Run it off!'

Gabriella intervened again, and forbade McGregor's return to action.

'I'm not putting an unfit player on the park.'

Eddie glowered at her and stomped away. Gabriella ordered Kenny, one of the substitutes, to get ready. She saw Eddie make a masturbatory gesture to Coughlan, and presumed it was directed at either her or McGregor – probably both. The bell sounded for the players to make their way out again. McGregor lolled on the table: Gabriella looked at him, and tried to work out what she felt. Anger, sympathy, pity? She told him briskly that she wanted a word after the match.

As she walked back to the dug-out, she saw Halliwell calling the team together and issuing new instructions. When they lined up for the restart, all of Gabriella's positional changes had been overturned. There was nothing she could do about it, and she slumped back against the dug-out wall and stuffed her hands into the pockets of her anorak.

Whether it was Halliwell's battle cries or just a fierce desire to prove their new manager wrong, the players threw themselves into the fray with energy that hadn't been there in the first half. Eddie began to perk up as the tackles went flying in, with Coughlan resuming his usual role as midfield destroyer. It wasn't pretty to watch – even Eddie would have admitted that – but the sheer vigour of their play drove them forward and rocked the home team back on the defensive.

They pressurized the opposition all the way back to the penalty area, and after a scramble that would have made a pinball machine look organized, who else but Trevor Coughlan slammed the ball into the net for the equalizing goal. Gabriella remained unmoved, while Eddie clambered out of the dug-out and saluted his boys with a clenched fist, as they celebrated the goal with extravagance born of their half-time frustration.

Their collective anger vented, the team subsided a little into pragmatic, stifling play, aiming now for only an honourable draw. But with the excitement ebbing and time almost up, they won a lucky corner. From it Gary Halliwell, who'd lumbered up more in hope than anticipation, looped a header into the net. It didn't matter that he wasn't marked – it was the best goal of his life at that moment, and he was swamped by the other players.

Eddie whooped with delight, and found himself in the way of the photographers who were encouraging a similar reaction from Gabriella; she declined to give it to them. Halliwell gave her a sarcastic bow as he trotted back to his position. Moments later, the final whistle went. Gabriella's first game had resulted in a 1–2 win, but she felt completely empty and disappointed.

Gabriella stood on one side of the dressing-room as the players patted themselves on the back for their second-half recovery. She and the disconsolate Dave McGregor, now changed back into his suit, were the only two not sharing the victory celebrations. As the team made a move towards the communal bath, Gabriella took her cue to leave, but she wanted to give them a touch of the cold shower first.

'Right, I want you all in Monday morning at ten. Our positional play needs a lot of work, wouldn't you say?'

She headed for the door. Halliwell was angry at having the team spirit doused and shouted after her.

'Hey! When you go up and get your fanny kissed by the press now, just remember it was us who won the game for you!'

Gabriella glared at him – she was certainly upset by the team's betrayal, but she knew inside that a more personal betrayal was the true source of her discontent.

Gabriella made her way along the bleak whitewashed corridor outside the dressing-room and on to the staircase which would take her up to the well-carpeted rooms occupied by press, sponsors and directors. She passed a couple of elderly stewards who smiled their congratulations, which she accepted with as much grace as she could muster. The tinny sound of a radio echoed along the corridor. It was broadcasting the familiar martial theme to BBC radio's *Sports Report*, which then faded as the presenter's voice came in.

'The headlines this Saturday evening,' said the voice. 'It's a winning start for football's first woman manager ... just five days after taking over, Gabriella Benson sees her team win two–one ... We'll be talking to the first lady of football a little later in the programme.'

Gabriella reflected ruefully on the disparity between the simulated excitement of the broadcast and the mundane reality she felt and saw around her. Then another male voice intruded – her father's.

'Gabriella – my congratulations!'

He was coming down the staircase, beaming proprietorially at her. She stopped and looked up at him, challenging, hurt.

'I don't deserve them.'

'But you must have said something to them at half-time. They were inspired afterwards!' Sergio said as he continued towards her.

'So. How much did you put into the club to buy me the job?'

This brought Sergio to a halt. He shrugged innocently, spreading his arms. She remembered the gesture from times past.

'Look, I just happen to be one of the football managers who reads the *Financial Times*. Now when I see that you're doing a deal with an English company and their name suddenly turns up on the team's shirts –'

Sergio deflected the accusation with bland assurances.

'I'm sure you got the job on your own merits as well.'

'How much?' Gabriella persisted.

There was a pause. Sergio had seen in his daughter from the moment of their 'reunion' a steely, independent spirit. He was, at once, both proud and intimidated.

'My new English partners,' he said carefully, trying to disguise his share of responsibility, 'have agreed to put in £750,000 over three years.'

Gabriella tried to smile, to acknowledge his comparative honesty.

'I don't suppose I should be surprised. That's always been your answer to life, hasn't it – to throw money at it? A frigid wife, so buy yourself some whores; a daughter not a son, but take her to the best football games in Europe, and the problem is solved; and when she can't forgive, you try to buy her affection.'

Sergio looked at her sadly. She returned the look with defiance.

'Well it won't work this time, father. I love this game for itself, not because you made me. And I'm going to succeed through my own efforts, not because of your money!' She gave him a sarcastic smile. 'I suppose if I get the sack, you get a refund.'

Sergio started to move towards her again.

'Gabriella, you're my only child. Why shouldn't I help you? It's only money, for God's sake! Your bloody English upbringing makes you guilty about using it.'

Gabriella dodged past his intended embrace and carried on up the stairs – she was looking down on him now.

'Sorry – I have to talk to the press, otherwise they'll accuse me of being snotty.'

She disappeared up the staircase without a backward glance. Sergio followed her receding back with saddened eyes.

.

Gabriella dealt as tactfully as she could with the press – she didn't pretend that the tactical changes in the second half were hers, and admitted that the team had defied her orders. But she quashed further talk of 'revolts' with praise for their hard work and general goodwill towards her. Her best defence was that these were early days, and that it would take time for the 'woman's touch' to show through.

She avoided the drinks in the directors' lounge, and soon it was time for the team to leave for their long journey south. The players filed out of the lounge, where they had drunk with the opposition, and headed towards the coach. Norman pushed the team skip out, with Eddie giving him a hand. Gabriella stood to one side, trying to stay in the background as much as possible. Then Dave McGregor appeared. She beckoned him over, reasoning that a quiet word now would cause him less self-consciousness than a prolonged chat on the coach home, with the rest of the team leering in the background.

As McGregor shuffled over, limping convincingly, Coughlan was reduced to a single passing comment.

'I do believe she's gonna transfer the pansy!'

The Rat Pack bellowed their enthusiasm, and McGregor seemed to shrink even more.

'Look, sorry about the goal,' he told her.

'Forget it – you were unlucky.'

McGregor smiled at his reprieve, but the smile faded when Gabriella leaned closer.

'Dave – I don't want to intrude but I, er, know about the Lesley situation.'

'Who told you?' asked McGregor nervously.

'It doesn't matter,' she said, 'but I'll do my best to keep it quiet. I promise.'

McGregor seemed relieved to talk about it – and the humiliation factor was certainly less potent talking to a woman.

'Look – you might as well know she's going off with him,' he confessed, hinting at long nights of distressing conversations. 'Feels sorry for him getting the sack apparently.' He smiled at Gabriella, underlining the irony.

'Shit – I'm very sorry, Dave. If you want some time off –'

'Haven't got much choice, have I?' he said, gesturing pathetically to his knee.

'I know this sounds hard, but try not to let it affect your game. You probably feel angry with her, a bit humiliated maybe, as though nothing will go right for you.'

'I'll say,' McGregor confirmed, almost revelling in his misery.

'Well, escape into your playing, why don't you? You fancy it in midfield, do you?'

'Well, yeah – it's great.'

'Good. Believe in yourself a bit more, Dave. I'm sure it can ease your mind, and who knows, maybe give you a different attitude to injuries,' she added as tactfully as she could. 'I really want you to succeed in this position, you know.'

This confidence in him, shown by a woman too, cheered McGregor instantly. She took his arm and pushed him towards the coach, aware that she was acting out of selfish interests, but hoping that he would benefit in due course.

McGregor sat alone on the journey back, as did Gabriella – they both had a lot to think about. The Rat Pack resumed their cards marathon, while the rest of the players chatted quietly among themselves, looking forward for once to a Sunday free from the fans' insults in the pub, or on the golf course, or in the sedate modern estates on which most of them lived – suburban men with public lives.

They stopped for an evening meal at a plastic-beamed hotel in the east midlands. It wasn't wonderful – just steak and chips and a couple of pints of lager – but it helped to make them feel a little bit special. Gabriella kept her distance, although Charlie O'Keefe insisted on sitting next to her and ordering the same dish as her – *foie de veau*, or 'foy-dee-view', as he kept calling it. He joined her in a bottle of red wine too, politely topping up her glass whenever the level dropped, unwittingly amusing her with his two-handed grip of the bottle – a YTS trainee determined to go up in the world.

She observed them throughout the meal, and found herself warming to the vulnerability they didn't know they possessed. Ordinary lads whose horizons had been magically widened by their ability to kick a ball, and yet whose careers were constantly on the edge of a precipice. Injury, loss of form, marital breakups, a bad result or even an unsympathetic manager could send them tumbling into a void, where they would disappear without trace.

Gabriella discreetly ordered a few bottles of champagne from the waiter, and watched their reaction when it was distributed among them.

'Here, what's this?' asked a bemused Halliwell.

'A present from me – to thank you all for a winning start today.'

Coughlan frowned. 'I thought you were pissed off with us?'

'I am,' she said, raising her glass in a toast, only to find Charlie O'Keefe reaching across to clink his glass with hers.

.

The following morning, Gabriella embarked on an altogether more sober gesture. She found Trevor Coughlan standing on the touch-line of a public park football pitch, shouting his encouragement to two teams of boys as they played a game. His exclamations were just as fervent as he might make in a match of his own, although more tastefully phrased. The difference was that the boys in the teams were all handicapped. Gabriella tried to reconcile these two contrasting images as she came up behind Coughlan.

The moment he spotted her Coughlan became sheepish.

'What the hell are you doing here?'

'I phoned your home. I wanted to talk to you, your wife told me.

'Bloody women,' Coughlan muttered.

He turned his attention back to the match, where the boys, despite their physical limitations, were playing with a joy and a spirit that might shame their professional counterparts.

'Go on, Robert – don't be afraid to shoot!' Coughlan urged.

'How long have you been coaching them?'

Coughlan refused to look at her.

'About two years.'

'Do you mind talking now?'

'Get it over with,' snapped Coughlan.

'I don't find your attitude very helpful, Trevor. At the club, I mean.'

'Tough.'

He still wasn't looking at her. Gabriella decided to probe a little.

'But here we have the hard man with a heart of gold . . . so maybe there's hope yet!'

Coughlan gave her a chilling, hostile stare and returned to the game.

'Well played, Tommy – now support the man on the ball!'

'Dave McGregor's injury been diagnosed as possible cartilage trouble –'

Coughlan blurted out an ironic laugh. Gabriella persevered.

'If he'd turned out in the second half, he'd have been having an operation today.'

'An invisible injury,' scoffed Coughlan. 'That figures.'

'Well, yes, maybe a lot of his problems are in his mind. But why have you got such a down on him?'

Coughlan turned to her now and pointed an admonishing finger.

'Because he's got what these kids haven't, but he hasn't got their spirit! Football's full of wankers like him, I like letting them know that *I* know!'

On the pitch the final whistle blew, and the kids shook hands with one another. Eager parents in warm coats ran on with flasks of tea. One of the boys now headed for Coughlan, his face glowing with a broad smile.

'We won, Dad!'

This hit Gabriella in the chest like a punch. Coughlan was cuddling his son.

'Yeah, you did ever so well, Robert!'

'Yes, well played, Robert!'

Coughlan gave her another fierce stare – and this time she understood. She was trespassing on Coughlan's privacy and it was time to go.

'Right – see you tomrrow, Trevor.'

Coughlan was holding his son to his side, ruffling his hair. He slipped his hand over Robert's exposed ear.

'The team don't know, by the way . . . about him.'

Gabriella nodded tactfully.

'Maybe you should tell them – that's what a real hard man would do.'

She walked off, regretting her intrusion, but grateful for this insight into the life of a key member of her team.

·

The optimism that Saturday's unexpected away win produced spilled over into the early part of the week, with a relaxed atmosphere pervading the club despite the 'ideological' conflicts Gabriella had set in motion. It helped that some of the initial novelty of her appointment had worn off, and that the players were, quite simply, getting used to having her around. In a world where managers and players moved overnight to other clubs, even a modest level of regularity began to assume the status of permanance.

They reluctantly agreed to continue with her methods, but this time there was substantially more response – at least they were giving it a try. Or so it seemed. Halfway through the week, they had all returned to the club for lunch after training. Gabriella came out of her office to collect a file of training schedules which she'd left in the dressing-room.

In the corridor, she found Halliwell approaching her. It was unusual for him to be sighted 'upstairs', because he didn't mix well with authority. But here he was, in shorts and sweatshirt, smiling at her.

'Not having lunch, Gary?'

'Just on my way. I, er, wanted to talk about dinner first. You and me?'

He leaned casually against the wall, trying to summon all the charm at his disposal.

'Well thank you, but I'd better not.'

'Come on,' he cajoled her, 'we can talk tactics, morale, strategy – try and win me over.'

'I'd rather do that on the pitch than in a restaurant,' said Gabriella firmly, disliking his tone. This was meant to be the last word, and she brushed past him, but he fell in step alongside her.

'I could make things a lot easier for you with the other lads,' he said in a suggestive voice, with a distinct hint of sexual blackmail.

Gabriella gave him her sweetest, most patronizing smile.

'Actually, the other "*lads*" seem to be coming round to my

way. I've had four dinner invitations in the past week, chocolates, bunches of flowers – maybe in a few months, eh?'

She walked off, slightly disturbed that the sexual element of her relationship with the team might become an issue. She'd hoped that her married status, and the fact that she was some ten or twelve years older than most of the squad, would prohibit advances. Fortunately, only O'Keefe in his adolescent way, and now Halliwell, slightly more menacingly, had triggered her well-tuned alarm system. She confidently expected them to be the first and the last – there was a sort of symmetry about being chatted up by the youngest and oldest members of the team, she reflected with a smile to herself.

She made her way down to the dressing-room and called out a warning to any naked players inside, although she knew that most of them would now be in the canteen, wading through Mrs Hastings's homely creations.

She found her file where she'd left it on the treatment-table, and was just turning to go when she caught sight of her own photograph taped to the back of a locker door. She approached slowly – it was the photograph that had appeared in the *Daily Star*, clipped haphazardly from the paper. Beneath it on the door was pinned a hand-written chart with the title: GOAL OF THE MONTH COMPETITION: £150 TO BE WON IF YOU 'SCORE'! Beneath this were inked the names of all the first team squad, and a 'tick' if they'd made a ten-pound donation to the pool. Next to their names the competing players had written in their own comments along the lines of: 'turned down dinner', 'offered her a lift', 'thanked me for flowers', 'touched me in training'. Other entries, beside Rimmer's and Wilson's names, were more direct.

Gabriella understood now what all the presents and sweet-talk had been about. She ripped the cutting and the chart from the door and walked out.

The banter was in full flow in the canteen as the players, exuberant after a morning's work-out, discussed their afternoon off. An embarrassed silence fell when Gabriella walked in holding up the chart. She looked round at all of them and they averted their eyes.

'Is that all you could manage, then – ten pounds a head? I'd have thought I was worth at least fifteen! Well let me tell you now, nobody's going to win the money, because I'm not interested. And you want to know why? Because if you fuck like you play football, I'd be in for a big disappointment!'

'Come on, Gabriella,' Halliwell pleaded, using her Christian name for the first time, 'it was only a joke!'

Gabriella ignored him. 'Is that the only way you can deal with me: humiliate me or hump me? All you've got to offer? I'm working my adopted balls off for you lot, and if this is all the response I can get, then I'll be off after Saturday's game!'

She let the chart drop to the floor, turned and walked out on them. There was a sheepish silence. Nicholl was the first to speak up.

'You and your moronic games, Rimmer!'

'Just having a laugh,' he protested.

Now McGregor joined in. 'Yeah, a hundred and fifty quid's worth and it's still cheap. The lady's all right!'

'Just 'cos you got some time off, you prat,' sneered Halliwell.

'Shut it, skipper, eh? Some of us are actually feeling good about what she's trying to do for us,' said Tony Morris. His words had weight, because they all knew he was the best player in the team. It put Halliwell on the defensive.

'Well, it's not showing on the park!' Halliwell shouted, before stalking out.

The unified hostility and resistance to Gabriella were beginning to weaken – she now had three 'supporters' within the team. Maybe there were more who were afraid of speaking out? At least there were cracks appearing in the male monolith, which Gabriella could work on if she were clever enough. And if she stayed.

The next game was, as the sports pages had it, 'a make or break occasion for Gabriella'. By this they meant it was an FA

Cup fourth-round tie – a stage at which the winning clubs begin to feel electrified as the dream of playing at Wembley edges just a bit closer as a possibility. For the losers, there is only anonymity and the knowledge that, unless they are involved in the hunt for promotion or the fight against relegation, their season is virtually over.

Martin Fisher rather tactlessly put these thoughts into words as he strolled round the dressing-room before the game. It was meant as encouragement for the players, and as a sly warning to Gabriella, but the phrase 'joyless slog for survival' hardly lifted anyone's spirits. He sensed Gabriella's displeasure and she asked him to leave before she gave the players their final pep-talk.

She stood, still a little self-consciously, in the middle of the room, with thirteen tense faces watching her every move, waiting to be inspired.

'I'm not very good at "fix bayonets and over-the-top" type speeches.'

Eddie Johnson looked disappointed – a Cup tie? That's *exactly* what he thought they needed.

Gabriella continued. 'I just want you to close your eyes for a moment.'

After a certain amount of bewilderment, most of the players followed her instructions, although there were a few smirks and twitching shoulders among the Rat Pack.

'Now try to clear your mind of all the tension, and think about all the hard work we've done over the past few weeks. Remember what I've tried to get you to do, remember when it worked, and now think of that moment of fulfilment when it comes off in a big FA Cup game.'

She was trying some of the methods of sports psychologists, who'd proposed that fantasizing about success in periods of collective calm helped build confidence. Gabriella thought it was worth a try – but after she'd let a silence fall for 'contemplation' she clapped her hands and added one last exhortation, for safety's sake.

'Right – now I want you to get out there and run your arses off!'

The players laughed and sprang up from their benches. The studs of their boots rattled on the floor like a line of battledrums. They shouted enouragement at one another, clenched fists were waved and then 'over the top' they went.

The match was a tight, tense affair. Playing before your own crowd in a Cup tie had its disadvantages. They could spur you on to adventure, or their fears and expectations could act as a bridle on the team spirit. Today was a case of the latter.

There was lots of promise in their play, with Nicholl and the now restored Tony Morris linking up well in attack. Even Coughlan seemed to be settling into his new 'sweeper' role and made a couple of good interceptions to break up moves from the visiting team.

The game went into the second half with no goals for either side. But then the opposition staged a break-out after several minutes of sustained pressure from the home team. The defenders backed away from the man with the ball, too busy concentrating on marking the forwards assigned to them. Suddenly he'd got within shooting range and tried a long, low shot from around twenty-five yards. Rimmer didn't have the clearest of views with so many bodies in front of him, but he probably wouldn't have got to the shot anyway as it hurtled into the bottom corner.

A groan went up from the home fans, but there was no abuse or booing, because they appreciated that it was a good goal. There was even a ripple of applause for it – an echo of the distant days of sportsmanship. The players hung their heads, but there were no recriminations. Halliwell chivvied them back into position for the kick-off.

They poured forward into attack in a desperate bid to save the match. They could hear the whistling of the visiting supporters – a hint to the referee – and could see the policemen circling the pitch, so they knew the end of the match was near. In this last frenzied attack, Dave McGregor, who'd applied himself with vigour and no sign of injury, was pulled down just outside the box. This time there were no histrionics – he got straight to his feet and placed the ball for the free-kick. The home fans sent up a chant of 'Coughlan! Coughlan!' and the stocky little battler scudded forward.

On the touch-line, Gabriella leaped from the dug-out and yelled for McGregor to take the kick. She semaphored that they should try one they'd been working on in training. The players strained to understand over the noise, but eventually McGregor nodded, and Coughlan stood aside.

Gabriella climbed back into the dug-out. Eddie shook his head at her.

'Two minutes to go – I'd have gone for a direct shot on goal and looked for a fumble and the chance to kick their keeper into the net!'

'Well, we can't be purists all the time,' said Gabriella with an irony that was lost on Eddie.

The crowd hushed as McGregor ran up for the free-kick. He dummied over the ball and kept going, leaving Tony Morris to play the ball in towards Keith Nicholl, who flicked the ball up for the in-rushing McGregor. It wasn't as precise as it should have been. McGregor tried to adjust at pace, but couldn't quite keep the ball down as he volleyed it, just inches over the bar.

The crowd's excited roar died. The players clutched their heads in disappointment, and McGregor pounded his fist into the turf in frustration. On the bench Eddie spat laconically out on to the running-track.

'Well,' he said, 'we probably wouldn't have got to Wembley anyway.'

•

It was a dejected dressing-room that Gabriella walked into this time, and no words of pity or consolation were required. Fisher bustled in to give his verdict.

'Bad luck, lads! A good fight, though. Proud of you, I am!'

He joined Gabriella, who was standing to one side.

'Bit of a disappointment, eh?'

'They happen,' Gabriella said defensively.

'Of course. Not going to call a share-holders' meeting yet, am I?' Fisher smirked at her, pulling a little ego-trip. It wasn't a direct warning, just a trick the powerful tried when they were annoyed or undermined – passing their anxiety on to the underlings. Making other people feel bad made them feel better.

Gabriella was in no mood to take it, however, and retaliated quickly.

'Well, if you do call a meeting, I'll be there.'

Fisher frowned, and Gabriella went on to explain how she'd persuaded Charles Austin, the most disaffected director, to sell her his shares in the club. She'd used her mother's legacy, but she didn't tell Fisher that because she wanted him to think she was wealthy in her own right. The more she kept him guessing, the more chance she had of survival.

'You needn't have done that,' Fisher said, trying to inject a light-hearted laugh into the statement.

'Maybe not,' said Gabriella, 'but if you and my father are planning any little property schemes at this club, it'll help me put across my point of view, won't it?'

Fisher scowled at her.

'Let's hope you can be as clever *on* the pitch as off.'

He broke away from Gabriella and returned to the centre of the room, trying in his bullish way to cheer the lads up.

'Here, fellers! I thought we'd got the draw with that fancy free-kick. Who's idea was that?'

Coughlan nodded at Gabriella, without emnity or sarcasm.

'The boss's.'

Gabriella registered the use of the word. It could have been a slip of the tongue or just habit – *or* he might just have meant it.

CHAPTER FIVE

In her third full week at the club, Gabriella set herself the task of assessing the squad of players she'd inherited from Fred Taylor. With the initial shock waves of her appointment receding, she now had a little more time for considered thought. She knew, both instinctively and on the basis of her own views about the game, that certain players would probably never fit into her scheme of things. Some of the new training routines had started to expose the 'weak links' in the squad, not just in terms of ability and adaptability, but in more tenuous areas such as courage and will-power – what those in the game called 'heart'.

So as she watched training with Eddie on a spring morning cold enough to test *anybody*'s will, Gabriella was looking beyond the fancy footwork of Tony Morris and Charlie O'Keefe. Eddie kept up his usual barking exhortations, and the particular butt of his invective was Jim Wilson, the gangly defender, who seemed sluggish compared with the others.

He'd already missed a couple of interceptions, and then he generated further abuse during a set-piece practice in attacking corners. As one of the team's tallest players, Wilson was used to being sent forward for corners and free-kicks in the hope that his height might cause consternation in the defence. A knock-down to one of the forwards, a decoy run to take defenders out of position or even a direct header on goal – these were the sort of moves they expected of him.

In two successive routines, however, Wilson got into good position to strike on goal, but instead of powering a header into the net, he punched the ball with his hand. Eddie yelled at him.

'Wilson! Get it! Get the bastard in! No pain, no gain!'

Eddie turned to Gabriella, as if seeking sanction for his remarks.

'Well? Am I right or what?'

Gabriella nodded. 'There's certainly a lot of pain out there,' she said thoughtfully, making mental notes for her 'stock-taking' session. This seemed a little too philosophical for Eddie, who dealt only with what his eyes told him. That morning, all they'd really communicated to him was that Wilson was fannying about.

Later, as the team headed for the dressing-room at the club, Eddie collared Wilson in the corridor.

'What was all that about, then? Punching the ball into the net?'

Wilson shrugged and gave him a facetious grin. 'Well, if it's good enough for Maradona, it's good enough for me!'

Eddie glowered at him, waiting for a more convincing explanation, but Wilson just repeated his statement, only louder, as if speaking to the hard of hearing, and stalked off into the dressing-room. Eddie let him go, and climbed the staircase up to the floor where Gabriella's office was. She had asked him to come up on the coach journey back from the practice pitch.

He knocked on her door politely and edged in, guessing that the summons was something to do with the training, and therefore a matter of reproach for him. Gabriella had a yellow legal pad on the desk in front of her. Eddie's discomfort over the expected bollocking was augmented by the inevitable swell of resentment at seeing her in the boss's chair: it was still hard for him to accept that he'd been passed over for the job, in favour of this woman.

Gabriella leaned back in her chair.

'I want your considered opinion; whom we've got, whom we don't need.'

Eddie smirked at her grammatical precision.

'*Whom* we don't need?' he mimicked.

Gabriella gave him an unblinking stare, the sort Eddie hadn't seen since his secondary-modern days back in Liverpool.

'Don't piss me about, Eddie. Who've we got who's okay and we can struggle along with, and who've we got who needs to be on his way, and have we got anyone to replace him, or should we be looking to be buying?'

Eddie looked glazed at the welter of questions.

'You know, look at it as though you were in charge,' Gabriella said provocatively, paying him back for his earlier sneering.

'Okay,' Eddie said slowly.

'Wilson?'

Eddie thought for a moment. Despite his morning tirade, Eddie wasn't about to wash dirty kit in front of this outsider.

'Fair player. Good turn of speed. Reads it well, doesn't often get caught out. Skill all right. In fact, he and Halliwell have been holding us together for a good while now.'

'You rate Wilson,' Gabriella summarized.

'If we didn't have him, I'd buy him. *If* I was in charge.'

'You'd buy him, would you? Other people rate him too. The question is, if he's so good, why hasn't anyone come for him? Why isn't he doing any better than us?'

Eddie found it hard to follow her line. It was like being in court with a smart-arse barrister trying to get you to say things you didn't really mean. He maintained his defensive manner.

'There've been a few inquiries over the years.'

'And?'

'Ask your predecessor,' Eddie said with an insolent shrug, designed to give nothing away, but which any barrister would have recognized as a signal of withholding evidence. Gabriella didn't spot it.

'What is it? Does he drink? Is he a womanizer?'

Eddie grinned. 'Who? Fred Taylor?'

'Jim Wilson,' said Gabriella patiently.

'A *womanizer*?' Eddie savoured the phrase and the irony of its context.

'No. Drinks normally like the rest of them. Likes a bit of a flutter, I hear. I don't know . . .'

Gabriella resumed her courtroom manner, metaphorically fingering her lapels and addressing the jury.

'Here we have a player who's been on the fringe of international recognition, and yet he is still with us.'

'Maybe he lacks ambition,' said Eddie, in an attempt to sound helpful.

'I'll have a word with him. In fact, I'm going to have a word with each one of them, individually.'

Eddie digested this information silently. He didn't like the sound of this one-to-one approach. It threatened instability at the club, and who knows what else. But he was obliged to tread a narrow path between loyalty to the players and duty to his new boss. He thought a joke might throw the inquisitor off the scent.

'A *word* is all most of them can manage.'

Gabriella didn't even smile.

.

While Gabriella worked with Eddie on her assessment of the team, the club's other assets were coming under scrutiny in the boardroom. Chairman Martin Fisher, his deputy Anthony Coombs, and the two remaining directors, Deness and Edwards, were seated around the oval-shaped table. They all wore topcoats and scarves because, as Fisher explained, the Electricity Board had taken intemperate action in cutting off the supply while the most recent bill was being queried. They suffered as they waited for the sharp-suited young man from the auditors to finish his rather impertinent inspection of the boardroom. Fisher produced a hip flask and poured a slug of brandy down his throat, while Coombs warmed his hands on a polystyrene cup filled with coffee.

The accountant, Kenneth David, had nominally been sent in by Solford Construction, the club's new sponsors, but Fisher had guessed correctly that Gabriella's father Sergio had been behind the move. While he waited for the directors to settle and finish their moaning about the cold, David moved on to take in the club's trophy cabinet, which contained a few pennants provided by visiting clubs and a large, dull, silver shield of no discernible prestige. David's breath misted the glass panels of the cabinet as he turned to address the doleful-looking board members.

'What did you win the shield for, darts?'

The four faces stared stonily back at him. Fisher and Coombs looked at one another, but said nothing.

'You want to watch it,' he continued cockily, 'someone might break in one night and steal the shelves.'

In the absence of any other laughter, David chortled at his own joke. Edwards, grey moustache bristling, should have guessed from Fisher and Coombs's silence that this Mr David held a sufficiently good hand to have his repartee pass unchallenged. A lifetime of promoting Victorian values in his own industrial firm, however, had erased whatever small sliver of tact he'd been born with.

'Let's get on with it,' he barked impatiently. 'I've got a strike to break, young man!'

Fisher and Coombs were immediately grateful for this distraction.

'A strike, Charles?'

'Yes,' growled Edwards, 'my girls are out and US-fucking-DAW have made it official!'

Coombs looked baffled, not just by the acronym, but by the prehistoric tone which accompanied it. David, who had by now installed himself at the far end of the table before a stack of files and a yellow pad, caught Coombs's glazed eyes.

'The Union of Shop, Distributive and Allied Workers, to give them their proper name!'

'Time was when women didn't want to know about unions,' Edwards said mistily.

Deness leaned across to offer a word of support.

'Make the bastards ballot. It's illegal without a ballot.'

'They *have* balloted,' snarled Edwards.

Much as he was enjoying the pantomime, David suddenly seemed impatient to unburden his findings on the worthies before him.

'Gentlemen, please! Now I understand Mrs Benson will not be joining us?'

Deness snorted.

'If you knew anything about football, young man, you'd know that the manager is only present when the board requests his presence!'

'*Her* presence, surely,' David corrected Deness.

Deness gave him a contemptuous look.

'Okay,' said David brightly, opening his files,' let's kick some shit!'

The board winced at the brash manner and rude turn of phrase, so unbecoming of an accountant, no more so than Fisher and Coombs, who stiffened in preparation.

David quickly moved in to what sounded like an opening statement, which was littered with ominous phrases like 'pretty reading it does not make' and a rather pointed reference to the disappearance of the club safe. At this point Coombs found something terribly interesting in the desk's elaborate marquetry.

'Unconcerned as we are at Lyle, Hewitt & Dobbs,' continued David, 'with the circumstances of the dismissal of your previous manager, Mr Frederick Taylor —'

'Let's just say he was told to get on his bike,' Fisher interjected with a smirk.

David gave him a brief look and resumed in full, voluble flow. 'The circumstances of his management of the club's affairs, apart from his conduct of the playing side, give cause for concern. If I may enumerate —'

'Don't give us the ten-bob words,' pleaded Fisher, 'give it to us straight!'

David considered the suggestion, and resumed at a more deliberate pace.

'Gentlemen — you told Fred Taylor to get on his bike.'

Fisher nodded smugly, preening at this achievement.

'The fact is,' David went on, 'that, in going, he got on his bike, but also on your bike, your bike and your bike too!' he said, nodding at each of the directors for emphasis. Coombs kept his head lowered as the consternation broke around him, albeit slightly more muted from Fisher.

David went on to list some of the financial liberties which Fred Taylor had taken during his time at the club. Apparently he'd been sold the freehold of his club-house for a nominal sum; he'd also been provided with a new car every year for three years from a local hire company but had still managed to purchase each of the cars himself, again for a nominal sum.

Fisher tried to interrupt this catalogue of misdemeanours with a bland wave of the hand.

'Need we hear more? We can just read the rest of the report, can't we? We know the kind of bastard Fred Taylor is, don't we?'

Coombs nodded eagerly. The two other directors, however, seemed rather keener to have the details.

'Mr David, can you "nutshell" our position?' asked Deness.

'Without using any ten-bob words?' he smirked up the table at the now extremely restive Martin Fisher, who, despite the cold, seemed flushed.

'We are dealing here, saving Mr Edwards's presence, with a jack-fucking-daw. And if it hadn't been for the injection of Italian capital with the arrival of your new manager, you would have been left without, as we say in the trade, a pot to piss in!'

The four directors assimilated this 'nutshelled' information – Fisher avoided all eye contact as Deness and Edwards looked to him for some sort of explanation, while Coombs sank further into the upturned collar of his overcoat.

David got to his feet and began to stroll around the room again. 'There is the old story of the one-man-operated bus. For years, this man had been stealing from the bus company. Creaming off ninety per cent of the fares for himself and giving the company ten per cent. When they found out, they asked him how such a long-serving and loyal employee could do this to them – hadn't they always treated him well? Sorely aggrieved, the driver said, 'You should be grateful to me for letting you keep the bus!'' David gestured around him with a wide sweep of his arm, indicating the boardroom and, by implication, the whole club.

'Gentlemen, you should give Fred Taylor a vote of thanks for letting you keep the bus!'

David returned to his seat and watched the effect of his informally phrased audit ripple across the faces of the four men opposite him. Deness and Edwards began to focus their gaze on Coombs, who was emerging sheepishly from his coat collar. He was, after all, the club accountant, brought in by Fisher, so this was surely his responsibility. Fisher was therefore obliged to offer protection.

After a long pause, Deness made a tentative inquiry.

'What do Lyle, Hewitt & Dobbs think we should do?'

David stabbed them with a bright, earnest smile. 'We urge the swiftest possible return to accounting legitimacy, Mr Deness.'

There was another pause, while Edwards and Deness considered their next statement, and while Fisher weighed up the odds. To David, it looked like seriousness and an instinct for respectability had finally settled upon them. In fact, they were laying aside their stones to protect the glass house they all inhabited.

'Is there any way round that?' Fisher asked, trying to force a smile.

For once, Mr David was speechless.

.

As always, the players forged on with their routines, blissfully unaware of the goings-on 'upstairs'. You couldn't really say that they wanted to know about such matters, but in any case they were denied any knowledge by a censorious regime. They had simply got used to not being consulted about their own futures or the progress of the club employing them. Their passive acceptance of the almost feudal system which still applied to football had been instilled in them from their first days as apprentices, when they had to clean the boots of the first team. Non-conformity and individualism were stifled, both on and off the pitch. All but a tiny few would remain foot-soldiers, to be discarded or sacrificed at the whim of their generals.

The players had all taken a bath and changed after training. It was an afternoon off, so a quick exit had been made by most of them. The golf course beckoned a few, shopping a few more, but the majority had headed off in a group for an afternoon of play. Only Wilson remained in the dressing-room, looking smart but conventional in his grey slacks and 'Question of Sport' style sweater. He was sitting on the bench, staring fixedly at the tiled floor, unaware of the two apprentices who were cleaning up the dressing-room around him. One lad swabbed the area around the team's plunge-bath, while the other collected the players' boots and dirty kit – both were too cowed by the system to attempt a simple inquiry such as, 'Are you all right, Mr Wilson?'

It was left to Gary Halliwell, poking his head around the door in search of Wilson, to break the spell which seemed to have fallen over the room.

'Jim! Come on!'

Halliwell accompanied this with a swigging motion made with his right hand. Wilson looked up at his defensive partner and frowned, almost as if he couldn't see him. Halliwell came into the room, the two apprentices hastily clearing a path for him. He sat down on the bench next to Wilson.

'Bevvy time, old son.'

Wilson lifted his head and turned to look at him. There was pain in his eyes.

'It all goes to bollocks in the end, doesn't it?'

This wasn't the sort of response Halliwell was looking for – it sounded heavy, and Halliwell was unnerved by conversations that went any deeper than sex, drink or the game. He tried to coax Wilson out of his torpor, cajoling him like a window-ledge suicide. Wilson seized his hand and gripped it tightly.

'Do you ever *think*, Gary?'

'Sure – I think it's time we got outside a pint.'

'I mean *think*!' Wilson said aggressively. 'Do you? Don't you ever think that in the end it's all bollocks?'

By now, Halliwell was embarrassed, not only by the fervour in Wilson's voice but by the continuing grip on his hand. Out of the corner of his eye, he could see the two apprentices going about their duties, but they were plainly listening in and had spotted the hand-holding. Halliwell quickly pulled himself free of Wilson's grip and stood up.

'Come on, mate, bevvy time!'

Wilson snorted out a short, mirthless laugh. 'Yeah, bevvy time. That's the answer, isn't it, Gary? Bevvy time!'

Halliwell squirmed at the way Wilson called him 'Gary' and gave a little nervous laugh at the apprentices, as Wilson stood and headed for the door.

'Keep at it, lads!' he urged, attempting to combine both authority and blokishness, in the hope of stopping the apprentices gossiping about this bizarre scene. It said something about Halliwell that he was far more concerned with the masculinity of his own image than with whatever it was that was bothering Wilson.

Wilson and Halliwell caught up with some of the other players at a local pub, the Seven Stars, whose landlord gave the team privileged access to a games-room at the back of the building and allowed them to stay for as long as they liked, although 'ordinary' customers were bailed out at two thirty. Halliwell quickly abandoned Wilson at the television set which was broadcasting horse-racing, a passion he shared with the goal-keeper, Brian Rimmer. Tony Morris and Dave McGregor were at the pool-table, while at a corner alcove sat Keith Nicholl and Charlie O'Keefe, apparently deep in conversation, although 'deep' was not a word normally applied to O'Keefe.

Nicholl, the only graduate among the players, often enjoyed his chats with Charlie, because he knew that he could tell him anything and that Charlie would be impressed. This afternoon, he'd decided to tell Charlie all about a new trophy.

'For real mediocrity –' Nicholl said.

'And who plays for it?' Charlie asked, his open face betraying no suspicion whatsoever.

'Well, teams in the middle of each division. Two from each. It was in the paper this morning.'

'I didn't see it – it was "Brazilian Ace in AIDS Scare" in my paper.'

'It was on Radio Four as well,' Nicholl insisted.

'You've got me again there,' said Charlie, frowning. 'What did it say about it?'

Before Nicholl could reply, Wilson broke away from the television set and imposed himself on them, sitting down next to Charlie and unwittingly breaking the thread of Nicholl's story. Nicholl was irritated.

'Hello – racing lost its many charms for you, has it?' he asked sourly.

Wilson fixed him with an intense look.

'Piss off!'

'Right,' agreed Nicholl. He studied Wilson, who was peering into his glass of lager, frowning. Nicholl decided he'd try his story on Wilson too, in the absence of any other conversation.

'I was just telling Charlie about the new FA trophy for outstandingly mediocre teams.'

'Get on with it, then,' urged O'Keefe.

'Right,' Nicholl resumed, somewhat wearily, 'the eight teams, two from each division who are smack in the middle of their tables, will play for the trophy at the end of the season.'

O'Keefe nodded enthusiastically, obliging Nicholl to continue.

'You see, the teams at the top have the championship or promotion to play for, and the teams at the bottom have the relegation play-offs. So, the FA figured what have the middle-of-the-table teams to play for? They came up with this new competition.'

'What's it called?'

'The Dalkon Shield.' Nicholl waited for a reaction from Charlie, but all he saw was the information being absorbed.

'Middle-of-the-table teams, eh? So if we keep going the way we are, we're in with a chance?'

'Right,' said Nicholl, who was tiring of the joke a little. Suddenly Wilson eyed O'Keefe.

'Piss off, Charlie. Go on!'

O'Keefe shrugged and picked up his glass, pausing to confirm the name of the trophy with Nicholl.

'Something to play for, eh?' Charlie grinned, as he left Nicholl to deal with Wilson, and joined McGregor and Morris at the pool-table, loudly informing them of the team's candidacy for the Dalkon Shield. Wilson finally showed a reaction.

'That was tasteless, that,' he chided Nicholl.

'Oh, you've heard of it, have you, Jim? In *your* paper, was it?'

'Piss off!' Wilson snarled through clenched teeth.

'Anyone tell you you're a great conversationalist?'

Nicholl got up to leave, but Wilson leaned across and restrained him.

'What do you know about headaches?'

Nicholl took a moment to stop himself making a facetious remark, but he'd registered Wilson's anxiety.

'What kind of headaches? Tension? Hangover?'

'Just headaches.'

'Take aspirin,' shrugged Nicholl. 'They go.'

Wilson shook his head. 'They don't go. Or at least sometimes they do when I take pills, sometimes not.'

'Probably stress,' suggested Nicholl.

'Christ, I've got that all right. Buckets of it!'

Nicholl realized Wilson was about to unburden himself, and became uneasy. The players didn't talk to him that often, and when they did it was usually on the assumption that his university education could somehow solve a problem. He decided to flannel in the hope that Wilson would leave him alone.

'Relax about it, Jim. I know it's easy to say, but try it.'

'How do you do it, though?'

'There's courses for it. I've got a tape you can borrow if you want. It's done by this psychologist. Speak to the boss. She'll know about it. She's got these exercise clubs, hasn't she? Works it all off.'

'I can do that in training.'

'Patently you can't. We've just trained, and look at you.'

Wilson put a hand to his brow and grimaced. He bent over his drink, then looked up at Nicholl with a desperate look in his eyes.

'If only I could get some bread together.'

Nicholl put both hands up as a prelude to denying him any of his, but Wilson didn't even notice the gesture. He was miles away, talking to himself.

'If only I could get some bread. If only –' He broke off and gave Nicholl another stare.

'If only the wife wasn't such a bike, eh? If only –'

He gave Nicholl a grin of sorts and stood up, ready to head back to the bar with his empty glass. Nicholl had no real idea what Wilson had been rambling on about, and he didn't want to know. Players usually kept their private lives to themselves – to admit to problems was to invite scorn. And though they all trained, and drank, and gambled, and womanized together, they weren't really friends. Each of them was alone among the others.

.

It might have come as a consolation to Jim Wilson, if he'd known that he wasn't the only one at the club under stress for financial reasons. But as Anthony Coombs turned his silver Saab into a little, tree-lined road of detached 1930s villas, he was determined that nobody should know about *his* difficulties.

Mr David's audit meeting had broken up inconclusively,

thanks largely to the stalling efforts of Martin Fisher. Coombs had taken this as his cue to put as many things right in as little time as possible, before the auditor called again. As he parked his car, climbed out of it, and wiped away the line of sweat forming on his upper lip, Coombs surveyed the club-house that Fred Taylor had acquired for himself . . . with a little professional help.

Coombs logged the presence of a red Fiat Uno outside the house, parked next to a silver Metro. He was sensitive to cars and to Fred Taylor for a number of reasons, fraud being just one of them. Coombs marched purposefully up the drive, passing one of the offending Ford Granadas on the way.

He pushed the door-bell and heard the tacky chimes sound inside, which increased his irritation. He pushed the bell again and paced around, sizing up the front door for a kick. This proved unnecessary, as Fred Taylor himself now appeared, smiling smugly, hair tousled, and wearing a light-coloured mackintosh over nothing else but his black socks and grey slip-on shoes.

'May I come in,' barked Coombs, as he pushed aggressively past Taylor.

Taylor checked the street and closed the door behind him. When he caught up with Coombs in the lounge, he was standing in the middle of the room, pointing with a quivering hand at a squat green steel safe, standing to one side of the red-brick fireplace.

'That,' raged Coombs, 'is over the top! Pinching the club safe is just over the fucking top!'

Taylor seemed unperturbed. 'Too bad.'

Coombs tried to calm himself by settling on to the imitation leather sofa. He ran his gaze up and down Taylor, registering his unclothed state for the first time. The usual gold chains dangled across the ex-manager's artificially sun-tanned chest.

'I hope you're not thinking of making a day of this, I'm busy,' smirked Taylor.

'Oh yeah,' sneered Coombs. 'Doing what?'

Taylor pouted at him, flapping his trench coat as he plunged his hands into its pockets.

'I'm engaged in Ugandan discussions.'

Coombs looked at him blankly, trying to work out what he was talking about. The visual evidence before him suggested a more literal activity to him.

'Come off it! You're at it! That's what you are!'

Taylor cocked his head, trying to work out what route Coombs had taken to arrive at this conclusion, then he grinned at him brazenly.

'I'm at it.'

Coombs revealed his evidence anyway, despite Taylor's generous confession.

'I know that car outside. It's McGregor's. You're still bonking his missus, aren't you?'

Taylor beamed with pride. '*Bonking*. I like that word. Yes, I'm still bonking his missus.'

Taylor seemed unruffled – not just by the admission, but by Coombs's sudden appearance. Coombs was just dying to wipe the smile off his French-polished face, so he assumed a grave manner, hoping for the maximum impact with his next statement.

'We've got new accountants in.'

Taylor took this calmly, and wandered over to the semi-thatched cocktail bar standing in one corner of the lounge. He extracted a couple of glasses of whisky from the impressive range of optics fixed to the wall, and gave one to Coombs before sitting down in an armchair opposite him. The trench coat flapped open, and Coombs's face registered immediate distaste.

'Christ, Fred – cover yourself up. It's like a baby's arm.'

Taylor seemed pleased with this image and grinned. Coombs tried to bring the conversation round to the more pressing subject of the club's accounts.

'Who's idea was it?' asked Taylor.

'The wop. When we put his daughter in, he insisted on new accountants.'

'So?' Taylor shrugged, still seemingly impervious to the implications of this.

'So I can't keep putting off giving them the books. They've already found enough to queer us.'

'Like what?' Taylor asked, interested now.

'The club-house deal — at the moment they know only about yours. Then there's the cars —'

'What you're saying, Tone, is that your firm screwed up. You were supposed to cover up.'

'I did!' Coombs shrieked. 'But this lot they've got in are like crocodiles. You should hear this young bloke this morning. Nose like an ant-eater. What are we going to do, Fred?'

Before Taylor could answer, a woman's voice called out his name from upstairs, asking if he'd be much longer.

'*Much* longer,' Taylor leered.

'That's not McGregor's wife! It's McGregor's car outside but it's not McGregor's wife!' Coombs exclaimed.

'She's here too,' Taylor said absently.

'Too!' Coombs said, eyes boggling.

The door to the lounge opened and a slim, dark-haired girl in a leather skirt and white blouse came in.

'Come on, Fred,' she pleaded, and then saw Coombs.

'Oh, hello, Tone!'

'Hello, Mrs Wilson,' Coombs said, trying to bluff.

'*Tone?*' queried Taylor, unsure of himself for a moment.

Coombs was agitated now.

'Shameless. Bloody shameless!' he muttered to nobody in particular. He stood up, almost shaking, and pointed at the safe again.

'I want that round to my office tomorrow. I'll return it to the club.'

Coombs brushed past Pauline Wilson without further acknowledgement, and then paused at the door to address Taylor again.

'I'm asking you to think about what we've said, but I don't hold out much hope. I've always thought you were a dickhead!'

Coombs stomped out, glad to be clear of Taylor's squalid environment. As soon as the door slammed, Taylor flashed a sharply accusing look at Pauline Wilson.

'Tone?'

Pauline shrugged and went back upstairs.

.

At about the same time, Pauline's husband was arriving home from the afternoon session in the pub with the team. Wilson took his key out of the front-door lock, closed the door and leaned on it. He looked up the spotlessly clean hall for signs of life, but there were none. Three thirty in the afternoon. She should be home, he thought.

'It's only me!' he called out hopefully, but there was no reply. All he could hear was the deathly silence of a modern English suburban home.

Wilson made his way down the hall to the kitchen, where the silence was doubled in intensity by the overpowering whiteness of the units, the furniture, the fridge and the cooker. Everything was almost antiseptically clean. Wilson reached up into the cupboard close to the sink and fetched down a bottle of paracetamol. He shook three tablets out on to his palm and put the bottle back in its cupboard, then placed the tablets in his mouth.

Next he took a tumbler from the rack on the drainer, filled it with water and raised it to his lips. He tilted his head back and the water washed the tablets down his throat. He paused for a moment, leaning on the sink for support. Suddenly his face was creased with pain, sharp agonizing pain. His body shook. There was a crack and a tinkle of glass in the steel sink. Wilson looked down. He had squeezed the glass to breaking point in his hand, and now blood mingled with the water and trickled on to the bright, shining steel.

.

Although Fisher and Coombs had guessed correctly that Sergio had been the instigator of the new audit, they had assumed that by resorting to procedural niceties, such as not inviting the manager to the board meeting, they could stifle any dissonance and prevent it reaching both Sergio and Gabriella. The flaw in their reasoning, however, was in assuming that Sergio would be as secretive with his daughter over this as he had been over his involvement in her appointment. They did not know about the subsequent row this furtiveness had generated, nor of the crisis of conscience it had caused Sergio. Nor did they know of Sergio's insistence that Kenneth David share his findings with Gabriella. David dined with Gabriella and Simon that evening, and over coffee he passed the initiative to the new manager.

'It's up to you, really. Do you want a bit of carpet cleaning or the whole place washed out?'

'They're rotten through and through,' said Gabriella.

'That's a bit sweeping, isn't it?' asked Simon as he fetched himself a large cigar.

Gabriella looked to David for confirmation, but he shrugged.

'But what you've described is fiddling on a massive scale,' Gabriella reminded him.

'Not massive, no. Just with the club. Though if they conduct their lives outside as they've conducted the club's affairs, it does make one wonder.'

'One doesn't wonder from where I'm sitting,' Gabriella pointed out.

David pushed his pudding plate away and sat back. He enjoyed the sound of his own voice just as much here as he did in the boardroom – the expert, giving opinions, pontificating.

'You see,' he began, 'dictators are rotten through and through. Mass murderers are rotten through and through. But this crowd are just directors of a football club. They're businessmen. Rotarians and Freemasons. Upstanding chaps.'

Gabriella supplied the sub-text immediately. 'Yes, with a cut of everything, from printing the programmes to ground redecoration, to selling club-houses, to . . . what else did you say?'

'Yes, I know,' said David, taking her line. 'In other words, complete and utter bastards. But isn't that par for the course?'

Simon had been listening and watching with detached interest. For him it seemed to be a question of legal propriety rather than of the business environment his wife was expected to work in. He challenged David's assertion.

'How so?'

David admitted that this was the first football club his firm had investigated, but insisted that all the indications were that most club directors conducted themselves in this way.

'Your directors are just not as good at it as some others are,' he concluded.

Simon was beginning to bristle at his generalizations now.

'Good at what?' he asked, only to be met by surprised stares from Gabriella and David.

'I repeat, good at what? "Rotten through and through", "complete bastards"! When you two have finished exercising your gift for hyperbole, what in fact are you alleging? Except normal business practices?'

Gabriella shivered momentarily at Simon's ability to be so unconsciously disloyal. He didn't see her disapproving look, so he challenged David to prove that what they had done was dishonest or criminal.

Simon's reasoning was simple – if directors owned companies which could provide services to the club, then why should they not do so. There was no conflict of interest.

'There *would* be nothing wrong with the directors of the club providing services, but it isn't as straight up as that,' replied David patiently. 'They do furnish those services and the money goes to their companies, but they also get a kick-back from the club for doing so.'

'Ah! That I didn't get before.'

'And directors of a football club must not receive payment from the club,' David concluded.

Simon conceded defeat instantly, and with grace. 'They're crooks, then!'

Gabriella and David exchanged a weary smile at this conversion to their cause. Then Gabriella asked what might have happened to the club safe, and David guessed that Coombs was the man to approach.

'How shall I proceed?' he asked Gabriella.

'Do as you were instructed. Send the report to my father.'

David saw the chance for another of his discursive anecdotes as they sipped their coffee.

'Do you want a measure of how petty it all is? Of what a small-minded bunch of losers they are? There's a list of sundry expenditure payments to people. Names like A. *Salmon*. A. *Hare* and A. *Radish*! You wouldn't believe it, would you?'

By now Simon had finally become solicitous for his wife's working future. He turned to her, adopting an avuncular tone.

'And how shall *you* proceed?'

Gabriella remained optimistic, despite the evidence of wide-scale corruption on the part of her board of directors. She also knew that to strike a note of despondency now would be exactly the opportunity Simon was seeking to talk her out of continuing with this job.

'Me?' she said confidently. 'I've got a team to build!'

CHAPTER SIX

When Wilson came down to his kitchen the next morning, there was some life in it – in the pretty shape of his wife. She looked fresh-faced, sipping her cup of coffee, perched on a stool in her thick towelling dressing-gown. He tried to work out when she'd come in. He hadn't felt the warmth of her body during the night, so she must have only just returned from . . . Wilson didn't know where, didn't want to know where.

Pauline looked at him without any sign of nervousness.

'What happened to your hand?'

Wilson held up his left hand, where three of the fingers were bound together with a rather ragged bandage.

'I cut it,' he said mournfully.

'Accidentally, I hope?' Pauline asked, concerned for an instant. Wilson nodded.

'Makes a change from headaches, eh?' she said cruelly.

Wilson looked at her with pain in his eyes, only it wasn't from a headache this time. She sat sipping her coffee, remote and untouchable. He zipped up his bomber jacket and walked out of the kitchen.

'See you, then.'

Pauline didn't respond.

As he moved towards his car parked in the drive, he became vaguely aware of a small, stocky man, sitting on the bonnet of Pauline's Mini Metro. Wilson walked past the man, ignoring him. The man hoisted himself off the bonnet and pushed his hands into the pocket of his blue cashmere overcoat. The canary-yellow scarf tied at the neck and the little moustache

gave him a slightly flamboyant touch – almost as if he were a
night-club comedian. The man hailed Wilson cheerfully.

'Good morning, Jimmy!'

Wilson inserted his key into the lock on his car.

'I'm trying, Vincent, I'm really trying.'

'Yes you are, Jimmy. Really trying. And I'm fed up.'

'Not half as much as me, Vincent,' Wilson said wearily. He
opened the door of the car, hoping Vincent would take the
hint.

'Seven and a half thousand, Jimmy,' said Vincent O'Grady
firmly.

'What if I don't get it, Vince? I mean, what if I don't get it?'

'There'll be tears,' O'Grady said in a strangely reasonable
tone.

Wilson didn't register the tone – only the message.

'What will you do? My arms? My legs? Here, do you want to
make a start?'

Wilson held out his arms to O'Grady, who must have been
at least nine inches shorter than him and ten years older.
O'Grady seemed taken aback by the gesture.

'Jesus, man! What do you think I am? The Godfather? Pull
yourself together!'

Wilson leaned wearily on the car door – he genuinely didn't
know what recourse a bookmaker had to recover a gambling
debt.

'Then what?' queried Wilson, plaintively.

O'Grady shrugged and thought, then gestured to the car and
then the house.

'You've got assets, Jimmy. *Realize* them.'

'You can have them. Take them. It's all bollocks in the end,
isn't it?'

O'Grady looked unnerved by this – he didn't know how
empty Wilson's life had become – and he started to worry
about pressurizing the man too hard. He thought of an appropriate story to console the footballer in this moment of
despair.

'Now, Jimmy – do you know the story of the England international who had similar gambling debts to you?'

'No, but you're going to tell me.'

Indeed he was – because it seemed like a life-line for both of them.

'Ten grand he owed. He couldn't pay. The bookie had to get some lads to burgle his house. Pinched all his caps, medals, cups, the lot. All his mementoes.'

This obviously did not apply to Wilson – so he was puzzled by the 'moral' of the tale.

'So how did the guy pay?'

'He went to the club and told them he was in schtook and asked if they could lend him the dosh. They came over all righteous and told him to piss off. But the manager was sympathetic. So the player got the manager to sell him, he picked up the five per cent of the transfer fee, paid off the bookie and bingo! Everyone's happy!'

Wilson looked thoughtful, but O'Grady frowned.

'Well, not everybody. Not the player who had to leave the club he liked, and not his missus who was happy where she was with her kids in a good school and her mates all around her. She had a breakdown. But the bookie got his money so happy ending. See?'

'I can't ask to go on the transfer list, Vincent, because you don't get a cut of the fee if you *ask* to leave,' said Wilson forlornly.

'I know that, Jimmy. But you can sound out this tart you've got in charge, can't you? Put it to her. See if she'll play ball, put you on the list. Much against your will, of course, heart-broken at the prospect of leaving the club, the wonderful fans, et cetera – but you get the picture?'

'I get the picture,' Wilson said dourly.

O'Grady looked at him, smiled and punched him playfully on the arm.

'You want to cheer up,' O'Grady advised. 'Remember, there's an answer to every problem if you put your mind to it, Jimmy!'

'No kidding,' Wilson said as he climbed into his car. It seemed like a possible way out – but he knew that Gabriella wouldn't put him on the list. She was bound to want to hang on to him, wasn't she?

.

Gabriella had a lunch date that day and skipped training early, without giving Eddie any suspicious-sounding excuses. It would be her first dip into the transfer market, and she knew from the papers that these were often conducted in out-of-the-way locations, to prevent football-following wine waiters ringing the local news-desk with a tip-off. Negotiations would not necessarily be delicate, but any speculation in the press might upset the parties involved, and the 'commodities' they were trading.

Ben Thompson himself had suggested the smart but staid roadside restaurant for their rendezvous. He'd used it before when dealing with Gabriella's predecessor, and seemed, at least over the phone, charmed by the prospect of lunching with his female fellow-manager. For Gabriella's part, it was a chance to meet a hero. An international centre forward in the late fifties, Ben Thompson had risen through the divisions, learning his managerial trade. He'd survived and prospered *and* remained popular. His bluff, common-sense approach to the game had endeared him to most fans and won him a regular place on the television circuit as a 'pundit'. When Ben Thompson talked, the public listened – with the honourable exception of the Football Association, who found him rather blunt.

As Gabriella sat down opposite the now balding figure, with his club tie and club blazer worn proudly, she could still equate the face with the caricature on one of those fifties cigarette cards. He'd already ordered himself a bottle of Italian white. He now offered Gabriella a glass, which she declined in favour of mineral water. He may have been a hero, but she didn't want to negotiate with a mind befuddled by wine and worship.

She broke the ice by asking if he remembered a game he'd played for his club in 1959 in Italy, a game Gabriella had seen with her father.

'It was a club friendly in Florence. Only Manchester United and Wolves had played European sides up till then in competition. You took some stick in that game, as I remember.'

He puffed out his chest. 'It's the job of centre forwards to take stick.' He turned round to catch the attention of a waiter, which shouldn't have been difficult, as the place was almost empty.

'Young man!' he called, bringing the waiter over at a sprint.

'Two medium-grilled sirloins, no potatoes and two side salads, no dressing.'

The waiter hurried off with the order.

'You're used to ordering, are you?' asked Gabriella pleasantly. 'Ordering, that is, in the wider sense.'

'Look around you,' Thompson said grandly, 'I know this place. You don't. Looks like it got three stars in the good salmonella guide, doesn't it? Steak and salad's the only thing they can do safely here.'

He leaned back and resumed his reminiscence of the game in Florence, prompted by Gabriella.

'You nearly caused a riot. Gave that right back some mouth.'

'Aye, well, he was all over me. I had to speak to him. I said, "Look Pedro – you pull my shirt once more and you and me shall have words. We'll be sorting this out with gloves on after the game." Of course he didn't know our lingo, but he soon got the message!'

Thompson beamed at his ability to tell a good story.

'Oh, but he *did* know your lingo,' Gabriella said, smiling. Thompson looked stunned. 'He did know your lingo. He *does* know it. And his name's Paulo, not Pedro. He's my uncle, Paulo Rebecchi.'

Thompson stared at her. Since Gabriella had the initiative, she exploited it to top his anecdote.

'The way he remembers it, when you backed into him once too often, he grabbed you by the shirt and you said, "Listen, bastard-face, you stay away from me, or you'll be carrying your balls home in a bag!"'

Thompson was upstaged – probably for the first time in his entire career.

'You've got a very vulgar tongue on you, young lady,' he said with a dead pan expression.

Gabriella took this as approbation, and smiled at him. Thompson began to appraise her – his manner changed now. She was less the adoring fan, more the other manager on the opposite side of the negotiating table – to be treated with respect.

'So you want my lad, then do you?' he asked, getting down to business.

'For my *lad*, and a cash adjustment.'

Thompson considered the option, and the player Gabriella had nominated for the part-exchange.

'Wilson's got no heart. He's a symptom of the disease afflicting your team. He can play a bit but his head drops and he hides. Now why should I want him?'

He sat back and began circling his thumbs round one another – Gabriella interpreted the body language as 'no deal'.

'Okay – why should you?'

The waiter returned and began to lay out the two plates of food. Thompson resumed his earlier expansive anecdotal manner.

'You know I have a saying: "Nothing in football ever surprises me." But you did. When you got this job, that surprised me.'

'I nearly rang you when I took it, to ask for your advice. Dos and don'ts of management.'

'I'll give you them now. One, all directors are stupid; don't talk football with them except in the most general terms and don't let them near the training pitch or dressing-rooms. Two, all players are stupid; keep all team talks very, very simple. Any boozers or whore-mongers, get shot. Don't let them talk to the press. Three, get yourself a lawyer, *not* an agent – they take ten per cent for nowt. A hundred and fifty quid for pictures of yourself and the team, five hundred for your "as told to" column.'

'My what?' asked Gabriella, beginning to feel distracted by the avalanche of cynicism coming across the table at her.

'Your "as told to" column in the press,' Thompson explained, as if admitting a novice into the brotherhood of Freemasons. 'You know, ten minutes a week nattering to a reporter – reporters by the way are all bastards – for the local paper. A thousand, of course, for a national daily. All in *readies*. Now, make up your mind and stick to it even if events prove you wrong.'

The waiter moved away and Thompson began cutting into his steak with vigour. Gabriella had lost her appetite. He jabbed his knife at her.

'Now, you want a good lad of mine for Wilson. I could take him off you. If he got a game with me, I've got the players to cover for him, which you haven't. He couldn't take the ball off my mother, but he can play just a bit. So what are you offering?'

'Wilson, and £250,000 for Marshall.'

Thompson nodded. 'And?'

'And what?' asked Gabriella warily.

'What do I get?'

Gabriella got his meaning, and was outraged.

'Let's get this straight. You're asking – '

'In readies,' Thompson interjected.

Thompson didn't see the worship die in Gabriella's eyes. He'd survived so long in the game, he'd probably forgotten how it once was, to be in love with a sport and to have that love reciprocated. He leaned forward in an avuncular manner, impervious to the shattered dreams across the table.

'Gabriella – do you mind me calling you that? Now I'll give you my rule number four. It's all about money. Whatever you do, make sure you get the money!'

Gabriella looked into his eyes to see if he really believed this – and she realized that he not only believed it, he *knew* it.

Gabriella returned to the club after lunch and holed up in her office while she tried to work Thompson's cynicism out of her system. For a large part of the time she stared blankly at the walls or at the window, asking herself if she'd really heard Thompson say what he'd said. Of course part of her disappointment was fuelled by what she now saw as her own naïvety – a grown woman who still had heroes, and who expected them to behave as such.

When there was a sudden knock on her door, therefore, Gabriella came out of her reflections in a brusque mood.

'Yes?' she snapped at her secretary, Marjorie, who was leaning through the open door.

'Albert Salmon to see you, Mrs Benson.'

'Who?' Gabriella demanded tetchily.

'Albert Salmon. You know, the club's chief scout.'

Gabriella vaguely remembered the name from somewhere and asked Marjorie to bring him in. She was somewhat astonished to hear Marjorie ask for a hand, and leaped up in curiosity. Outside in Marjorie's office, supporting himself against a filing cabinet, was the hunched figure of 75-year-old Albert Salmon, seemingly weighed down by his black overcoat and greasy black trilby. He was out of breath. Gabriella and Marjorie helped him into the chair opposite Gabriella's desk, where he proceeded to have a coughing fit, tears streaming from his rheumy eyes. Gabriella thought at one point that he might die there and then in her office, but gradually the wheezing subsided, and he composed himself sufficiently to place a clenched fist on Gabriella's desk.

'I'm known as the *legendary* Albert Salmon among my contemporaries. I discovered Charlie O'Keefe, Tony Morris and that college pudding Keith Nicholl for this club.'

'Yes?' queried a numbed Gabriella.

'I'm still at it. I'd die for this club.'

'I believe you,' Gabriella said, trying not to laugh.

'But I don't know you, so I thought I'd come and have a look.'

Gabriella took this as politely as she could. 'Thank you for coming.'

Mr Salmon looked her up and down. 'Right. I've looked. Now I want to know, do I still get my twenty quid a week? That's what your predecessor paid me.'

'Twenty pounds a week?' Gabriella asked slowly, recognition dawning. 'You're A. Salmon. Tell me, is there an A. Hare and A. Radish too?'

Salmon nodded. 'Tony Hare. Tony *Raddich*, not Radish. We're all scouts, and I'm the chief!'

At least that was one less accounting deception for Kenneth David to consider, Gabriella thought, as she confirmed with Mr Salmon that they were each paid twenty pounds a week for their services – a staggeringly paltry sum.

Mr Salmon reacted to the note of surprise in Gabriella's voice, and took it to mean that she thought the payment excessive. His gnarled fist made a vain attempt to bang the desk.

'Twenty quid! I've got expenses to meet! I go all over the country for this club!'

Gabriella couldn't stop herself asking: 'How?'

Later, she reassured Mr Salmon that his retainer would be honoured and almost certainly increased. She couldn't help reflecting on the extremes of reward which the game generated in the endless business of searching for and trading talent. Albert Salmon's weekly stipend would barely buy a lunch for the likes of Ben Thompson. And would a Ben Thompson ever offer the scout who discovered a player whom he sold a percentage of the rake-off he took on the transfer? More importantly, could Gabriella herself bring some measure of integrity and order to a process which seemed more like a car-boot sale?

.

The next day, Gabriella began the first of her one-to-one talks with the players during training. Since he was uppermost in her thoughts, she selected Wilson first, and made him accompany her on a slow walk round the touch-line, while Eddie led the team in various practices on the pitch.

Wilson was in a defensive mood, and this increased noticeably when Gabriella turned their talk to the subject of transfers, as an oblique approach to letting him know her feelings about his future.

Wilson guessed that the reason he hadn't been bought before was that the offers had never matched the club's valuation of him. Gabriella contradicted him, and asserted that at least two reasonable offers had been made – so perhaps there was another reason.

'You didn't want to go?'

'Who says?' said Wilson quickly.

'I'm asking,' said Gabriella.

'I'd have gone,' Wilson snapped, unable to control a note of bitterness.

'What happened?' probed Gabriella.

'I'd still go,' he said, thinking of the escape route Vincent O'Grady had suggested for him. Gabriella ignored this for the time being – there was another level to this business which intrigued her.

'So,' she prompted.

'So, no one matched Fred Taylor's valuation of me.'

Gabriella gave him a thin smile. 'That's right – Fred Taylor's valuation. Which was the club's price plus Fred Taylor's price, right?'

Wilson batted it back at her in best 'loyal professional' manner: 'If you say so.'

Gabriella realized this was as much confirmation as she would get out of him. So why hadn't he gone above Fred Taylor's head and appealed to the chairman for a move? Wilson's eyes danced shiftily.

'Mr Fisher?' Wilson asked, unable to hide his incredulity.

In that instant Gabriella understood that, like a fish, a football club rots from the head. They walked on a little more while Gabriella pondered. Wilson gave her another reminder about his willingness to be transferred – not that he was *asking*, of course.

'I'm settled. We're settled,' he added, remembering he was married. He grasped for the memory of the lines O'Grady had used.

'I'd miss the club, and the fans like. But I'd go – if I didn't figure in your plans.'

Gabriella took a slow intake of breath as she walked, choosing her imminent words with precision.

'You're a deceptive player, Jim.'

There was not enough precision here – Wilson took it, as all players did, as a compliment. Gabriella moved closer towards her true meaning, trying to spare his feelings on the way.

'You deceive ... no, don't get me wrong. You've got the skill. You've got the pace. You read the game well. And you're thought a lot of.'

'Great,' beamed Wilson.

'But not by me, and that's what counts.'

They stopped and looked at one another. Wilson was reddening around the face.

'You lack something. Call it heart, whatever. You don't have it.'

'No one ever said I've got no bottle,' he bridled.

Again Gabriella tried to convey her precise feeling. She gave him a few examples, his lack of 'shouting' – warnings, encouragement, and such – during a game, he never ran for the ball after it had gone out when time was urgent, he didn't encourage his team-mates.

'I *play*. That's what I'm paid for. Not for shouting!'

'It's all part of playing, Jim. That's what I'm trying to say.'

'So where does all this leave me, boss?'

Gabriella considered her concluding statement.

'When I've got someone better, you'll go.'

'Someone better? So you're not saying I'm rubbish, then?'

Gabriella shook her head with a sigh – it was like trying to walk on eggshells, dealing with players, or with this one certainly.

'Jim, if I thought you were rubbish I wouldn't even have bothered to talk to you.'

'So I'm on the list officially?' he demanded gravely.

'Yes. With a bit of luck you'd have gone yesterday, I must be honest with you.'

This was the first time in ages Wilson had felt any hope, and he smiled broadly. His five per cent was as good as secured – O'Grady could be paid off, and maybe the change of club would help improve relations with Pauline.

'Thanks very much, boss. That all?'

Gabriella, bemused by his sudden enthusiasm, nodded, and he trotted off to rejoin the others.

•

Anthony Coombs was spending the afternoon in his wood-panelled office in the town, assessing where the tracks he and Taylor had made might lead the inquiring Mr David. His concentration was broken, however, by the appearance of Pauline Wilson, dressed for action in a black leather mini-skirt, black stockings and a short red top. She smiled at Coombs, who wasn't quite sure where he stood with her after stumbling across her at Fred Taylor's house. She made the first move by starting to remove files from his desk, clearing a space at one end – a routine they had shared over many previous afternoons. Coombs still watched her cautiously, hurt by her betrayal.

'Why?' he asked eventually.

'I wanted to see what he was like,' Pauline said in a matter-of-fact tone. She ferried more files to the shelves.

'Fred Taylor . . .' Coombs muttered to himself, with dismay. Pauline came back to the desk, gauging how much more space they would need.

'Aren't you going to give me a hand?'

'Why that bastard?' Coombs asked savagely.

Pauline stacked more files, turned and leaned back against the book-shelves.

'Because I like it, and he just happened to be there at the time. *Correction.* I *love* it, and he was there.'

'Happened to be there? It was his house,' Coombs exclaimed, having taken the literal line as always.

'Not *there*. At a game I was at.'

'He didn't just happen to be at a game, he was *supposed* to be! He was the bloody manager!'

Pauline half turned away from him, giving him a glimpse of her midriff, drawing his attention to her body, as she had intended.

'Are you going to give me a hand?'

Coombs seemed a little calmer now – perhaps the promise of sex with her had dampened down the jealousy which had been eating into him since the day before. He crossed to the door and locked it. He turned to her.

'There's nobody else, is there?'

'Silly!' she said, smiling. She began to unzip her skirt slowly.

'Like a baby's arm!'

'What?'

'Fred told me what you said.'

'Did he now?'

'I told him about yours. He was well chuffed when I told him you weren't in the big league.'

Coombs's face registered affront but also desire.

'Did you now?'

'But what I didn't tell him was that it's not the size of the boat, it's the motion in the ocean.'

With this she let her skirt drop to the floor. Coombs's eyes began to glaze, and a broad lecherous smile filled his face. She had him where she wanted him again.

⋅

Whatever personal conflicts and disturbing undercurrents had flowed through the club that week – and there'd been plenty – the number one unwritten rule of the business was that they should be suspended for the ninety minutes of a game on the Saturday afternoon. Strangers became team-mates, beleaguered directors became carefree fans, disillusionment was banished in favour of optimism, and transfer ambitions were laid aside for the common cause. But the trouble with unwritten rules is that they're easily broken, with the result that the game can become a microcosm of the cancers afflicting the body of the club.

The first indication of tensions rising to the surface came as Eddie burst out of the dressing-room with the team on their way up to the pitch. Gabriella stood to one side, encouraging them to slap their palms on a club crest which she had mounted on the wall above the tunnel to the pitch. Bill Shankly had installed one at Liverpool many years ago, carrying the legend THIS IS ANFIELD, and it had become a talisman – steeling the resolve of the home team, striking fear into the hearts of the visitors, by trading on the superstition of both.

Gabriella had borrowed the idea unashamedly, although she knew that there were light years between Liverpool and here. Eddie wasn't impressed by the idea, but he was more intent on registering his annoyance at news which had filtered through to him. He snarled into Gabriella's ear: 'I've just found out why Wilson's perked up so much.'

Gabriella thought this was neither the time nor the place – as per unwritten rule number one – to discuss such contentious matters, and swatted Eddie away. He stuck with her as they hurried towards the tunnel after the team, a wave of noise from the crowd flooding down on to them.

'You've put him on the bloody transfer list. One of our best players and you've stuck him on the list!'

Gabriella stopped directly beneath the club crest and rounded on him.

'I'd rather play Albert Salmon, if you want to know. He'd die for the team – Wilson wouldn't! Now come on!'

She reached up and patted the crest and paused, expecting Eddie to do the same. After a second, he did.

Wilson, bizarrely liberated by the prospect of his move, was the dominant player in the first half. He won tackles he had no right to win, distributed the ball well, and then sallied upfield before crossing for Charlie O'Keefe to strike a goal. Gabriella danced on the touch-line in celebration, but Eddie couldn't resist pointing out who'd created the goal.

The game fell away a little in the second half, with Gabriella's team sitting comfortably on their one-goal lead. Unfortunately

Wilson's rejuvenated performance may well have caused his defensive partner Halliwell to become over-euphoric. After neatly tidying up an opposition attack in the penalty area, he inexplicably attempted a fancy, back-heeled pass to the goal-keeper, Brian Rimmer. Rimmer was clearly expecting him to perform his usual duty and boot the ball as far as he could manage. He was unprepared for such subtlety, with the result that the ball shot past him and in to the net for a prize-winning own goal. Rimmer's expletives could be heard, even above the massed groans of the crowd.

This seemed to affect the delicately balanced morale of the side so catastrophically, that soon they were under considerable pressure from a team they'd had at their mercy. Wilson and Halliwell were called into desperate rear-guard action. They looked as though they were winning the battle, when suddenly Wilson clutched a hand to his head and let a forward away from him. Gabriella gave Eddie a fierce glare of vindication, before turning back to see Wilson win the ball, only to slice it drunkenly into the crowd. He clutched his head again, and gestured to the bench to bring him off.

Gabriella's jaw was set tight in anger at what she thought was his spinelessness, and she virtually spat out the instruction to substitute him.

Wilson staggered to the touch-line and headed straight for the dressing-room. Eddie climbed from the dug-out and gave chase, dismayed that his 'champion' had let him down.

'What's the matter,' he shouted, 'one minute you're playing a blinder – '

Eddie kicked open the dressing-room door as Wilson lurched in ahead of him, still holding his head. Wilson sagged on to the bench in a forlorn heap as Eddie stood over him, waiting for an explanation.

'My headache . . . my head . . .' Wilson mumbled, breaking down into tears.

'Your headache?' Eddie shouted contemptuously, looking at Wilson in disbelief. But then Wilson tilted his head back and

Eddie could see that the player's eyes had become sightless. Eddie recoiled in alarm, and then Wilson began to release a scream that chilled Eddie to the marrow. The screaming grew more intense, and Wilson's body convulsed as if trying to expel some demon. Eddie virtually fell out of the dressing-room and grabbed a steward.

'Get the doctor! For Christ's sake, get the doctor!'

Gabriella was summoned from the dug-out a few moments later. As she ran down the tunnel, she saw a little knot of white-faced people outside the dressing-room, including Fisher and Coombs, and two ambulancemen were urgently wheeling a stretcher inside. Eddie was pressing himself back against the corridor wall, quaking. There were tears in his eyes. Gabriella felt a cold, clammy dread come over her body.

'You got it wrong, he died for his team,' Eddie mumbled before his face began to crumple.

.

There was an official club funeral for Wilson – all the board turned out, and his team-mates carried the coffin. Eddie even read a short eulogy in the church. The disparate elements which made up the club became, for a short while, a family united in mourning.

After the service, a coach brought them all back to the boardroom for a simple buffet, and a hushed attempt to come to terms with Wilson's loss. Pauline Wilson joined them, in the absence of other relatives, rendering Coombs sweatily embarrassed at the thought of his own relationship with her.

Martin Fisher stepped out of the murmuring ruck to make a short announcement.

'I haven't got much to add to what Eddie said at the church. Anything else would be inadequate, if not inappropriate. Jim Wilson – smashing player, smashing husband, smashing man. 'Nuff said. Ladies and gentlemen – to Jim. God bless him.'

The response was duly muttered as the team raised their glasses or, in Eddie's case, a cup of tea. The toast completed, the various sectional interests began to resume their identities again, as they assessed reactions to Wilson's death.

The players stayed in one group, standing apart from the directors and Gabriella.

'I still don't know what happened,' Charlie O'Keefe chirped, unabashed by the occasion.

'It was in the paper,' said Gary Halliwell through clenched teeth, 'the post-mortem was in the paper.'

' "He Died with His Boots On!" was all it said in mine. And something about his head.'

Nicholl tried to stifle Charlie's grating Cockney insensitivity with a hushed but firm declaration. 'He died from a beri-aneurism.'

'Something he ate, eh?' Charlie asked guilelessly.

Nicholl tried to control himself.

'Not "*berry*". Beri-aneurism. A rupture of an artery in his brain.'

'You can't catch it, then?' Charlie persisted with a hint of anxiety.

Nicholl adopted the tone of a weary lecturer, faced by an ineducable student. 'It's a very rare condition. It's caused by a tumour. It won't happen to you, Charlie.'

Halliwell, who had been lost in his thoughts during this exchange, was suddenly ambushed by the sense of loss.

'Christ! Poor Jimmy. All that talent and then this.'

Nicholl interjected his own rather egotistical memory of a player who'd approached him personally about his health concerns. It was rather like hearing an eye-witness to an accident, jostling for the tribute of 'I saw it first'.

Halliwell resumed his melancholy summary, undeterred by this antiseptic intrusion.

'He never had no luck. He always bet on donkeys. Then Fred Taylor wouldn't let him away. He married a cow. They always tell you to cheer up, don't they? Your luck's got to change. Jimmy's didn't. Poor Jimmy.'

They fell into silent remembrance again, before Nicholl's tasteless joke of a week ago re-emerged courtesy of Charlie's child-like sincerity.

'He'll miss the Dalkon Shield, then.'

Across the room, Gabriella stood with a mournful Eddie, their differences temporarily laid aside. Gabriella stared down into her drink.

'Shit,' she murmured.

Eddie nodded in sympathy. 'I hate these occasions too.'

Gabriella realized their thoughts were at cross purposes, and fell into line with Eddie's for a moment.

'Yes . . . poor Jim.'

She then resumed with what was really preoccupying her.

'I'd better get on to Ben Thompson, see if he'll take a straight cash deal for his player.'

She gave Eddie a grim smile, inviting his agreement.

'What am I saying? Of course he'll take a straight cash deal.'

Eddie looked at her – he couldn't believe she was thinking of money and transfer deals at a time like this. Was that all Jim Wilson's death had meant to her – merely the loss of something to trade?

Gabriella didn't have too long to register Eddie's disapproval, because Pauline Wilson sidled up to her almost immediately.

'Could I have a word with you sometime, Mrs Benson?'

'Sure, Pauline.'

'It's about Jim's money.'

'You'll have his wages until – '

'Oh, no,' Pauline interrupted, 'it's not his wages. I get a lump sum, don't I? The club's insurance on him. I'll get that, right? It must be quite a bit.'

Gabriella suddenly saw her own attitude reflected in Pauline, and felt chastened. She reflected how this poor man had become a commodity to two different women. There was something seeping through from all the small-time corruption going on at this club, and which potentially threatened them all – a corruption of the spirit.

After the official 'wake', Pauline managed to slip away with Anthony Coombs, taking a ride back to her cold, antiseptic house in his flash car.

Coombs pulled up short of the house as he saw a stocky man in an overcoat hanging around the drive. The old jealousies rose like bile into his throat.

'Who's he?'

'I don't know – one of Jim's mates, perhaps.'

'Oh yes?'

'Christ, Tone – don't get paranoid! I'm not anybody's. Now what about the money?'

'Nothing! I've tried to tell you, the club's insurance on Jim comes back to the club. You get whatever he was personally insured for, and maybe whatever he had in his PFA scheme.'

'What's that?'

'The Professional Footballers' Association,' he said wearily, tiring of her mercenary attitude. 'They have a scheme.'

Suddenly his weariness broke into hostility. 'Look, I don't bloody know. You'll be all right. Now come on, get out, be a good girl. I'll call you.'

'When?'

'When I call you. You know how it is.'

She looked at him, gauging the strength of this rebellion. She knew his weak point, though. She knew the control she had over him.

'I won't be left in need, Tony. I won't.'

She climbed out of the car and walked towards the man on the drive of the house. Coombs felt as though invisible wires were attached to his body, and that Pauline Wilson was pulling them. He drove off quickly, trying not to think of what the man on the drive meant to her.

In fact, Vincent O'Grady had called by to pay his respects. More or less.

'I'm very sorry, Mrs Wilson.'

'Thank you.'

Pauline kept going, past him and towards the door.

'I just thought I'd offer my sympathy. That was Mr Coombs, wasn't it?'

Pauline stopped and looked at him – was this a threat? O'Grady saw he had her attention.

'It's horrible to mention this, but Jimmy owed me some money.'

'How much?'

'The horses, you see. Jimmy never could pick a winner. I warned him but he couldn't stop.'

'You sound all heart, mister – '

'O'Grady. Vincent O'Grady. I aim to please, Mrs Wilson.'

'Do you?'

O'Grady nodded.

'Then please piss off.'

'Jimmy owed me *money*,' he repeated.

'How much?'

O'Grady guessed how much more he could get out of her, over what Wilson had owed him – call it interest.

'Ten thousand.'

Pauline was shocked.

'I know it sounds a lot but we could come to some arrangement.'

Pauline looked at him scornfully, this little bookie with his cashmere coat and peacock style of dress.

'Now am I right or am I wrong – if he couldn't pay you, you couldn't have taken him to law, could you? Gambling debts aren't recoverable in law. So what were you going to do with him?'

O'Grady had become flushed with anger.

'I was going to remonstrate with him, Mrs Wilson. Most strongly.'

Pauline nodded. 'I thought so. *Nothing*. And with me that means double-nothing. So piss off, Mr O'Grady. Piss off, off my property!'

•

Fisher and Coombs were surprised, not to mention put out, to get a summons to Gabriella's office the day after the funeral. Fisher called meetings, and Coombs could call them on his behalf – but the manager? As they waited for her to return from training – still wearing topcoats due to the continuing dispute with the Electricity Board – Coombs broached the subject of Pauline Wilson and her request for money from the club. Coombs attempted to disguise his involvement with her.

'Bitch rang me up.'

'I hope you gave her the bum's rush,' muttered Fisher, wandering round the office in a sour mood.

'She's panicking. Says some gangsters were into Jimmy for an arm and a leg, and now they want her to do the decent thing and cough up.'

Fisher looked out of the window absently.

'Why is she ringing you, Tony?'

Coombs thanked God Fisher had his back to him at that moment. He shrugged anyway, to suggest mystification.

'Wants to know if we can help her. What shall we do?'

Fisher turned away from the window.

'What's an arm and a leg worth?'

'Fifteen thousand, she says.'

'Bollocks!' Fisher scoffed. 'Wilson was into a toe-rag named O'Grady for seven grand or so, tops.'

Coombs registered this dramatic disparity between Fisher's version of the debt and Pauline's. He challenged Fisher, but Fisher stood by his assessment. He had good information throughout town, and a good 'nose' to back it up. Which is why Fisher was instantly suspicious of Coombs's zeal for accuracy.

'You've been giving her one, haven't you?'

'Piss off, Martin. Fred Taylor was giving her one!'

'I thought he was poking McGregor's wife?'

'And Pauline Wilson too.'

Fisher didn't know whether to be impressed or outraged. He wondered if Coombs had seen the disgraced former manager. Coombs nodded and reported that Taylor appeared to be in demand with a foreign team. Fisher was intrigued by the man's seemingly limitless powers of survival, and wondered where this new opportunity lay.

'Uganda,' asserted Coombs.

Fisher chortled with laughter – for a second it looked like Coombs's ignorance of the *Private Eye* phrase was about to be exposed, but it soon became obvious that he wasn't aware of it either, which resulted in a rather bizarre conversation.

'No, not Uganda,' Fisher mused. 'You can bet your boots he's having you on. Portugal, Greece. Somewhere like that probably. One of those'll be talking to him. Real Subbuteo or some such.'

Then Gabriella arrived, with Eddie at her heel. She sat down and briskly started to talk transfer business.

'Sadly, we have to replace a player – but then I would have replaced him anyway.'

Fisher was aghast.

'Replaced Jim Wilson – one of our best players?'

'One of *your* best players, Mr Chairman,' Gabriella corrected him. 'One of my predecessor's best players. Not one of mine. He didn't figure in my plans for the team, and he knew it.'

'He *knew* it?' exclaimed Coombs. 'You may have hastened his end!'

'Oh, I forget,' Gabriella observed sarcastically, 'you weren't at the post-mortem, were you, Mister Deputy Chariman? You couldn't have heard. What hastened Wilson's end was a million-to-one chance.'

Coombs bridled at her resistance, and he sought desperately for a counter.

'I wasn't there because I was busy retrieving the club safe, as a mark of respect!'

The other three looked blankly at him, wondering if he was beginning to crack up. Gabriella tactfully resumed the transfer discussion, and asked Fisher if funds would be made available. Fisher hedged.

'That depends, Gabriella, on how much.'

'Whatever it takes, Mr Chairman. But you can rest assured that I will look for a fair deal,' she said firmly, eyeing Fisher as she spoke. 'I'll pay the price a club asks to that club, and nothing to anyone else. No kick-back to any manager *or* any director.'

'Then you'll end up with Douglas Bader,' Fisher laughed, although there was no mirth in his voice.

'I don't think so. There are a few good people in the game – '

'Name one,' Fisher snapped.

'What if I were to name those managers and directors who take a cut from transfers? Or who stop a player leaving a club because the buying club won't meet the manager's or the director's *private* requirements?'

Fisher began to perspire a little despite the chill in the room. It sounded to him like Gabriella had come close to discovering the very truth which Fisher had wanted to hide from Kenneth David. He hated the way she could out-manoeuvre him occasionally. Fisher caught a glimpse of a big smirk on Eddie's face. To complete his discomfiture, Coombs rather needlessly pointed out that such payments were illegal.

'Yes, and if I'm approached with such a deal in mind, I shall immediately report it to the League and the FA,' Gabriella smiled, completing her implicit warning.

'Is that all?' Coombs asked.

'Until I come to the board for the money for the player I want, Mr Deputy Chairman.'

Fisher recognized that this was her price for her silence over what she may or may not have discovered. He tried to lighten the atmosphere, but Gabriella quickly dismissed him and Coombs from her office. As soon as the door was closed, Eddie clasped his hands together in delight and laughed gleefully.

' "The management reserves the right to dip your head in a bucket of shite" ' he recited.

'What's that?' Gabriella asked.

'Something they said outside the picture houses when I was a kid in Liverpool.' Eddie winked at her. 'No, they used to have a notice saying, "The management reserves the right to refuse admission," ' he laughed.

Gabriella felt no such glee – she'd got only a few strong whiffs of the decay and corruption at the club, even in the game itself. The small stand she'd taken might have an effect for a while in controlling Fisher and Coombs's excesses, but she remembered Ben Thompson's words very clearly: 'It's all about money!'

'Open the windows, will you, Eddie? Let's get some air in here.'

CHAPTER SEVEN

By the end of her first month at the club, Gabriella had completed her assessment of the players available to her and had also conducted all of her 'one to one' interviews with each of her players. She now knew a little bit more about what made them 'tick', which ones responded to pressure and old-fashioned 'bollockings' – she'd got used to these as a staple of football management – and which ones needed a more circumspect form of encouragement.

The player that had surprised her the most was Charlie O'Keefe, the little seventeen-year-old Londoner who'd joined the team as part of a government Youth Training Scheme. He wasn't the brightest player in the squad; indeed, his naïvety had become the source of much humour among the other players, who loved winding him up, but he made up for this with an irrepressible cheekiness. He was a good little player too – 'nippy' the old-timers would have called him – though Charlie would have preferred 'tasty', the contemporary equivalent. He had a habit of scoring goals, which certainly helped, and Gabriella had convinced herself that he was worth a regular place in the team.

He'd missed a game through injury – a strain, nothing serious – so after a few days' rest, Gabriella wanted his fitness tested before deciding on her team for that Saturday's game up in Lancashire. Norman Williams, the club physio, put him through a series of quick sprints and turns on the touch-line, watching as Charlie shuttled between two marker poles for any signs of sluggishness or pain. After twenty minutes Norman was convinced he was fit for action and gave Charlie the nod.

Charlie stopped his running and launched himself into a Hugo Sanchez-style somersault, partly in celebration, partly because he loved showing off.

'Hey, who's only a good 'un? Who's only a good 'un, Norman?' he asked rhetorically, before patting Norman cheekily on the face and disappearing down the tunnel towards the dressing-room.

Thanks, Norman, Norman said to himself in the absence of any gratitude from Charlie. That's all right, Charlie, think nothing of it, he said, finishing the conversation which hadn't taken place. Norman collected the two marker poles and headed into the dressing-room. There was a reserve match that afternoon which he had to prepare for. The players would be roughly the same age as Charlie, but they'd know how to say thank you. Too much, too soon, thought Norman reflectively, as he walked off the pitch.

Charlie stayed on for the match after his shower, and installed himself near the front of the stand. He liked being close to the action so he could throw in his comments, and watching the reserves fuelled his sense of his own wonderfulness. As the opposition full back ran close by to retrieve the ball, Charlie gave him his view of his performance so far.

'Hey, kid – you're shit!'

Charlie chuckled as the defender glowered at him.

As play restarted, Charlie's attention wandered. Sitting twenty yards away were a couple of young girls, with Madonna-style clothes and hair-cuts. Charlie gave them his flashiest smile as he dangled his car keys ostentatiously.

When the game finished, Charlie leaned over the parapet wall of the tunnel and shouted to two of the younger players, Travis and Leffernan.

'Come on, lads, I've booked us a table.' By this he meant snooker rather than restaurant. The reserve-team manager greeted him and asked how the fitness test had gone.

'Fit as a butcher's dog,' Charlie grinned, then turned to see the two girls leaving their seats.

Charlie caught up with them in the car-park and invited them to inspect his F-registration Peugeot 205. He assumed they knew who he was and established their names: Michelle was the blonde, Sarah the dark-haired one. In a small town like this, footballers were the only heroes on the streets, *and* Charlie had a Bros hair-cut. The girls were flattered to be in his company, even though it was only a car-park, and the fading light was making the ground look even shabbier.

'I thought you'd have a bigger car.'

Charlie had a ready answer.

'This is my runabout. I'm waiting for my mates, Steve Leffernan and Roy Travis.'

'Oh, they're good!' Sarah exclaimed with delight.

'Yeah, but they've got a lot to learn, though,' Charlie said loftily. Then he called out as he saw the two apprentices emerging from the ground, carrying their sportsbags. The two lads approached, reacting shyly to the presence of the young girls. Travis was a tall, wiry Geordie; his companion Leffernan a little ginger-haired Glaswegian. They'd travelled south to get their breaks in the game, and Charlie, one year their senior, had taken them under his wing, and offered to show them the town. Not that there was much to see.

'This is Sarah and Michelle,' said Charlie.

Leffernan seemed ill at ease.

'Are we going, then, Charlie?'

'Where?' asked Michelle.

'We're playing snooker,' Travis said shyly.

Sarah pouted a little at them.

'We've got a snooker-table at our house.'

Charlie looked impressed and signalled his interest to the other two lads. Leffernan shuffled his feet.

'Yeah. But we're in a club, like. You can get a cup of tea there.'

'I can make tea,' said Sarah.

Charlie smiled. Travis moved away impatiently.

'Come on, Charlie!'

But Charlie stood his ground.

The team travelled north on Friday afternoon for the game on Saturday. In past years they'd often done this as a round trip in one day, but the deadening effect of the journey often took its toll on the players' minds and limbs. There were infamous stories of hard-men managers who made their teams get out of the coach and walk the last mile to the ground to get the journey out of their systems. Gabriella did not subscribe to this philosophy and had appealed to Martin Fisher's sense of style in order to win the players a night in a hotel before the game. The club could afford it, just, and Gabriella felt that the psychological effect of making the players feel a little bit special would show in their approach to the match.

The only snag was killing time in a strange town on a Friday night until the ten o'clock managerial curfew. While the rest of the population celebrated the end of its working week, the players were obliged to save themselves for the next day, ignoring the siren calls of pubs and discos. Gabriella had arranged to record a radio interview that evening with a prominent national sports journalist who was in town for the Manchester United match – her way of killing time. And probably his too. She'd delegated the responsibility of organizing the players' evening to Eddie and Norman.

The players hung around the lounge of the hotel, eyeing receptionists and waitresses who might just be impressed by the presence of a lower second division football team. Meanwhile, their shepherds, Norman and Eddie, were in conference over the films section of the local listings magazine.

'*Rumble Fish*?' suggested Norman.

'Come again?' said Eddie.

' "A monochrome tale of – " ' Norman read from the review.

'No,' said Eddie decisively.

Dave McGregor wandered over, waiting for the verdict.

'Where are we going, then?'

'*The Journey of Natty Gann*,' tried Norman.

'Go on,' said Eddie, interested.

Norman checked the caption. ' "It is 1935, and motherless Natty – " '

'Nothing historical,' Eddie decided with a shake of his head.

'What about something to make us laugh, Norm?' chivvied McGregor, as he went back across to rejoin the rest of the team.

'*Sid and Nancy*,' Norman announced.

'What's it say?'

Norman adjusted his glasses and began to read again.

' "Despite its age, this film is still a delight. A baby elephant with very large ears has a tough time until he discovers his protuberance comes in handy. The scene with the drunken cows is terrific." '

'I think I know that,' Eddie muttered. 'It's a good 'un.'

'Right,' said Norman as he stood up to approach the team with their selection.

.

Gabriella's evening promised to be no more enjoyable than the team's. David Greenwood, the journalist conducting the radio interview, had a good reputation as a sports writer and as a thorn in the flesh of the footballing establishment, but his oily charm and pretentious tone somewhat dissipated the impact of his words, whether written or, as they would be tonight, spoken.

His introduction of Gabriella included such gems as 'pulchritudinous', which Gabriella guessed would have most football fans switching off their radios before the interview got under way. To his credit, Greenwood obviously found no difficulty accepting the notion of a woman manager, and started his questions with a serious probing into the early influences which Gabriella had brought with her into, as he called it, 'the beautiful game'.

Gabriella decided she'd set him a conundrum, since he plainly enjoyed an intellectual joust – no 'Well, Brian's' would do for Mr Greenwood. She started to describe a man who had indeed influenced her approach to the game, but giving no names, only a few details each time, to see how long it was before Greenwood recognized whom she was describing.

'I was a child when I met him. My father knew him and told me about him. This was a man who knew everybody in his club, knew their problems and cared about them. The first job his board gave him when he took over the club was to sack a 63-year-old groundsman, who was the longest-serving member of staff. He told his board, "How can you expect me to get loyalty from the players if you treat a man who's given all his life to the club like that?" So he wouldn't sack the groundsman, but he promised the board he'd give them the best team in the country in five years – and do you know, David, it took him just three and a half!'

Greenwood listened intently across the green-baize-covered table, with the dimmed studio lights picking out only Gabriella's eyes. He hadn't guessed yet, but he wasn't going to admit that to the listeners.

'I think I know this paragon of all managerial virtues, Gabriella, but for the punters out there –'

Gabriella cut across him sharply. 'Don't call them punters, David. They're fans.'

Greenwood sniggered like a schoolboy. 'I stand corrected.'

Gabriella continued her profile of this mystery manager who had so influenced her thinking about the game, with Greenwood watching and listening for clues.

'I'm talking about a man who gave his time to talk to prisoners in gaols, who answered all his letters personally, who had the only official club chaplain in the country, who made sure his players had business training for their future careers outside the game *and* who gave them moral guidance. A man who made sure the mums and dads were kept up to date on news of their sons, and who sent flowers on their birthdays or anniversaries.'

Across the small table, Greenwood's face had been darkening with horrified recognition, and now he leapt in to challenge Gabriella.

'You are talking about a man who suborned the opposition, left the managership of the England team in disgraceful circumstances and was called a perjurer by a judge in the High Court!'

It was now like a game of chess, with the two protagonists hunched and facing one another, will-power and self-belief driving them on. Gabriella shook her head and counter-attacked.

'I'm talking about a man who visited a sick little girl in hospital with flowers and sweets. A man who did so much unpublicized work for other people when there was nothing in it for him. And, as a by the way, a man who had the whole ninety minutes of Real Madrid versus Eintracht on film. Such a man influenced me.'

'We are talking of Don Revie,' Greenwood announced in sepulchral tones.

Gabriella nodded. 'We are talking of Don Revie.'

The rest of the interview passed off uneventfully, with Gabriella asserting that her more personally involved, enlightened approach to management was a valid alternative to the dominating, patriarchal style preferred by most male football managers. Greenwood appeared to respect her opinions, which was a welcome change from the predictably sexist innuendoes which characterized most of the press coverage about her so far.

Unfortunately, Greenwood became a different man in the bleak, subterranean corridor outside afterwards. Taking advantage of the isolation, he leaned across her and put an arm on the wall behind her in a would-be seductive manner.

'I was just going to say *Quo vadis*.'

'What?' asked Gabriella uncomfortably.

'Where are you going?'

'Back to my hotel.'

Greenwood unleashed a leering grin at her.

'What for? To help the egregious Eddie Johnson trundle the lads to *Babes in the Wood*?'

'I hope he's trundled them by now.'

Greenwood leaned a little closer to her.

'Then what's the rush?'

There was a brief pause while Gabriella worked out how to handle this – she knew what he wanted but was searching for the most polite rejection.

'No thank you, David,' she tried.

This didn't discourage him, however.

'I know a place where the fettucine is divine, and with a Barolo or simple Lacrima Christi –'

He allowed his voice to tail off seductively. Gabriella propelled herself off the wall and past him.

'Goodnight, David.'

He called after her, ebullience intact.

'Signorina – you face an evening in a lonely hotel!'

Gabriella turned and wagged the finger bearing her wedding ring at him.

'*Signora*, David – you should know better!'

With that she disappeared through the fire doors at the end of the corridor, leaving Greenwood to assess his failure to lure the Manageress.

'Was it my halitosis?' he called out down the empty corridor. He cupped a hand to his mouth and breathed into it, before sniffing.

No, he said quietly to himself, it wasn't my halitosis.

And he sauntered off towards the doors, swinging his large leather bag jauntily on to his shoulder.

.

Footballers' wives hated Friday nights, when their men were taken away from them prior to battle, denying them access to social and sexual intercourse. Simon Benson, if he'd known more about it, would undoubtedly have sympathized with the abandoned women of football as he arrived home after a hard week of meetings and travelling to find Gabriella gone, with just a semi-literate note from the housekeeper, directing him to the delights of a chicken salad in the fridge, to console him.

Simon slung his mackintosh and overnight bag on to one of the kitchen-stools and poured himself a large slug of Laphroaig.

There was only the hum of the fridge for company. He had coped splendidly with the press exposure of his wife's new job and lifestyle, but in a way, now that the media fuss had died down and Gabriella's demanding work-routine had begun to become a hard reality, he felt more at a loss than ever about how to deal with it all. They rarely had time to have dinner together, and the weekends were always disrupted by preparations for a game, and the consequences of it. As he opened the fridge door, he thought he saw in the petrified chicken salad, sealed in cling-film, an image to sum up the current state of his relationship with Gabriella. The malt was beginning to release his resentments and frustrations as he took the plate from the fridge. Suddenly the door-bell rang. He put the plate back down on the shelf of the fridge.

'Go away,' he muttered.

There was a moment's silence. He picked up the plate again. The bell sounded again – this time continuously.

'Shit!' Simon exclaimed, closing the fridge door on his supper.

He made his way down the hall and switched on the outside light. He opened the door, but for an instant there seemed to be nobody there. Then a pretty blonde woman in her late twenties stepped out from the shadows of the outside wall and thrust an imaginary microphone at him.

'Simon Benson, I'm Roger Cook,' the voice chimed, 'and I'm here to record an interview with you *now* about the exorbitant fees you are charging.'

Simon grimaced in astonishment and irritation, and told her to 'piss off' as he tried to close the door on her. In a second, she'd wedged her foot in the door and was pointing at it.

'Watch my foot!' she trilled. The voice, Simon guessed, originated from a few hundred yards either side of Sloane Square, but the slightly crazed manner came from somewhere else.

'Move it!' said Simon, as he attempted to close the door again.

'You're supposed to say, "You're not Roger Cook," and then we take it from there.'

'I don't know you. I've never heard of Roger Cook. If you say you're Roger Cook, you're Roger Cook!' Simon said. 'Now move your foot.'

'You don't know Roger Cook?' the young woman asked. 'Look, I'm a journalist –'

Simon now knew where the bumptious manner originated: Fleet Street as was, 'Île des Chiens' as it probably is now.

'She's up north with the team,' he snapped.

'I know,' the woman smiled exotically. 'It's you I want to talk to, not her.'

Simon was surprised. The woman saw it and moved to take swift advantage.

'If it's any encouragement, I'm Institute of, rather than National Union of –'

Simon looked momentarily puzzled.

'*Journalists*,' she said helpfully. 'We tend to think of ourselves as a cut above the hacks of the Yellow Press.'

Simon edged the door back a little so she could release her foot.

'What do you want with me?' Simon asked cautiously.

'I'd like to take you to dinner,' the young woman exclaimed brightly, not realizing at this stage how vulnerable he was to her suggestion.

Simon accepted – and not just out of boredom or bloody-mindedness towards Gabriella. The girl's approach had flattered him and, to some extent, raised his tired spirits.

Within half an hour he was sitting opposite her at the restaurant of a local 'inn' – all hunting place-mats and horse-brasses, with an antique menu to match. The woman introduced herself as Camilla Price – the name fitted the identikit Simon was building of her – and she said she worked as a feature writer on the women's pages of one of the more respectable tabloids. Simon had marked her down as the sort of brainless bint who trails her shallow thoughts through the colour supplements, so he was slightly surprised, and intrigued, to discover that she worked nearer the coal-face, as it were. He ordered a Scotch to start, and she followed suit, in an attempt, Simon presumed, to cut the mustard with him.

She startled him by producing a small tape-recorder and plonking it on the table between them.

'Shall we begin?' she said, like someone presenting a children's programme.

'Okay,' Simon nodded.

She pressed the 'record' button, set the volume level and sat back.

'You've no children, have you? Is that a decision you both took or don't you want any? Or are you saving them for later – mind you, you haven't got much longer – or rather she hasn't if she's going to have any before she's forty. Or is it simply that you are in a no-lead-in-pencil situation?'

Simon sat back, recoiling at the onslaught.

'Jesus!'

He stared at her in something akin to shock, as she instructed the wine waiter to fill their glasses without prior tasting. Then she raised her glass to Simon in salute. Simon drank for respite. He needed it, because she quickly resumed in the same vein.

'What's it like eating out alone every night? Sitting alone in the Wimpy with your quarter pounder, your *Independent* propped against the plastic tomato?'

Simon just took another copious mouthful of wine and let her rant on.

'No, you're above the Wimpy,' Camilla corrected herself, 'but I bet I'm spot on about the *Independent*, though, aren't I?'

As it happened she was, and Simon couldn't hide it. He put down his glass.

'You have a funny idea of –'

'What? How you live? Come on, what was it tonight? A plate of cold meat and a video?'

Simon was silenced for a moment. He tried to regain his poise.

'What particularly do you wish to ask me?' he managed.

'What's it like to be married to that power-house?'

'*My wife*,' Simon stated emphatically, hoping to cut through the tabloid-speak. But she was soon off again, doing what most journalists do before their unwitting victims, writing as they speak.

'Yes. There you are. Settled. Rich. On this comfortable plateau you've reached. The little woman already successful with her studio, so it's time to have a sprog or two, then bang! Off she goes in a brand-new direction, in the public eye, and you're left to don the pinny and squirt the Fairy Liquid. So what's it like?'

'I don't think I want much more of this,' said Simon, failing to understand that he'd just heard most of the article out loud.

'Oh, goody, here comes the grub!' Camilla sat back as the waitress delivered two plates of roast beef with Yorkshire pudding.

'You were saying?' Camilla smiled innocently, pretending not to have heard his objection.

'Look. I'm not this lonely person, jealous of my wife's success – '

'I didn't say you were *jealous*,' Camilla cut in.

'We're both doing what we want to do. We're both happy with what the other does. We support and encourage each other in our various endeavours and all domestic chores are undertaken by the estimable Mrs Cassidy, our home-help.'

'Who is sixty years old, has a moustache, wears corrective stockings and is no temptation to me and likewise there is no temptation for my wife Gabriella Benson, although she moves in an all-male world, smirked 39-year-old company lawyer Simon Benson!'

Simon would have let his mouth hang open if he hadn't been so stunned by this display – *this* was actually what this woman thought about him, was it?

Camilla smiled at him as she attacked her food with gusto.

'Eat up, Simon, it'll get cold!'

After a few moments Simon did so, but without any great relish. Camilla kept looking at him between mouthfuls, this proper lawyer, this loyal husband, this liberal feminist man. Suddenly she slipped off the shoe on her right foot and raised her leg until her stockinged foot was resting in Simon's crotch.

Simon went rigid with surprise.

'What *are* you doing?' he whispered anxiously.

Camilla gave him a parody of a siren's smile and kept her foot exactly where she'd placed it.

'I hope this is what I think it is and not a collapsible brolly!'

Simon looked astonished. Then she leaned forward as best she could and whispered across the table, after switching off the tape-recorder.

'How would you like to fuck the socks off me?'

.

Gabriella returned to the team hotel and found that Eddie and Norman had indeed managed to chaperone the lads out somewhere, though the receptionist didn't know where, as there'd been some loud arguing about the choice of film. Gabriella retired to her room, had a light supper brought up, and stretched out on the bed in her tracksuit to watch television for an hour but then promptly fell asleep.

She was woken by the chimes of the Open University theme. She switched off the set, went to the bathroom to splash her face with cold water and began dialling on the bedside phone while she patted her face dry. The call was connected, but all she heard was her own voice on the answering-machine. It was five to midnight. She thought Simon would be home by now, although he hadn't been sure if his meeting might necessitate another overnight stay in London. Gabriella had left the hotel number with the housekeeper, so maybe he'd phone later. They hadn't talked for nearly two days.

Refreshed by her unexpected nap, Gabriella prowled the small room uneasily, until she picked up her key decisively and walked out.

She walked down the staircase rather than take the lift,

feeling the slightly ominous atmosphere of a hotel at night. The foyer was deserted and silent apart from a few muffled rings from the switchboard at the rear of the reception. A night porter sat at the desk, reading a newspaper. Gabriella turned and headed for the bar, which she could see was still lit, although a rather raucous echoing laugh suggested that few people were in there.

The laugh belonged to one of three suited businessmen who were finishing pints and glasses of spirits at the bar. They all turned to eye her, smirking as they did so. Gabriella saw that the barman had lowered the metal grille above the counter and was cashing up from the electronic till. She turned to leave, and then saw Eddie sitting alone in an alcove by the door. In front of him on the table was a pot of tea and a plate of digestive biscuits. Gabriella crossed to stand opposite him, as the businessmen returned to their drinks with a muffled jeer and knowing nudges.

'I never figured you as one for the late taste,' Eddie said, miming a glass in his hand.

'Oh, no – I just wanted some cocoa or hot chocolate.'

'You can order it from your room, you know.'

'Yes.'

There was a moment of abstracted silence, while they worked out who was embarrassing whom most by their presence.

'Look,' said Eddie gallantly, 'don't worry. We'll get a result tomorrow, don't you fret. We'll get a result.'

Gabriella checked her watch.

'It's tomorrow now.'

'Well, we'll get a result today, then,' Eddie smiled.

Gabriella looked down at the table. Eddie stood and moved aside.

'Hot chocolate. I'll organize it.'

Eddie gestured for her to sit down, while he wandered out into the silent lobby. This move was logged by the trio of drinkers at the bar, though Gabriella didn't see their gestures. A moment later Eddie returned.

'No one around.'

'It doesn't matter,' Gabriella said with a grateful nod for his efforts. Eddie sat down in his chair again.

'I counted them all out and I counted them all back,' Eddie said, and pointed up to the ceiling. 'They're all in kip.'

'Oh, right – what did you see?'

Eddie scowled.

'Something about bleeding drug addicts. Norman cocked it up!'

Gabriella gestured to the teapot.

'No late taste for you either, then?'

'I'm not a drinking man. Right from being an apprentice. It's the way I was brought up in the game.'

'Standards, eh? You can't whack 'em!'

Eddie looked at her – he was sure she was sending him up. Gabriella caught his look.

'I'm not mocking. Why I was only talking about standards tonight.'

'Oh, aye?'

'Aye,' she mocked. 'The interview with David Greenwood.'

'Oh, him. Gobshite Greenwood,' Eddie said with a curl of his lip. 'Beg pardon – Gobbledegook Greenwood. Read a match report of his once. Couldn't understand a word – and I played in it. Bleeding ... what was it ... *catenaccio*. Aye. *Catenaccio*. That's the system he thought we were using.'

'It means –'

'I know what it means,' Eddie said sharply. 'Bleeding sweeper. I'm not like them upstairs, you know. I'm not a *Sun* reader!'

'Sorry – I was only going to say that in Italian, it literally means "lock". A padlock.'

'Yeah?'

Despite himself, Eddie was enjoying her company, and out of the corner of his eye he enjoyed seeing the envious reactions of the other drinkers. He wanted her to stay a while longer.

'What were you saying about standards to Greenwood?'

'We were talking about influences. He asked me if anyone had influenced me, and I told him Don Revie.'

Eddie looked surprised.

'You're joking?'

Gabriella shook her head.

'Don *Readies*, they called him,' Eddie sneered.

'I know. Whatever may have been said publicly about him, he was a good man, a man who cared. A man who did lots of things for people for no reward.'

'Lots of bastards are nice to dogs and little children,' he said slyly.

'And lots of people are cynical old bastards,' she retorted accusingly.

'See you can talk all you like about standards, principles, whatever – but it's in here that counts.' He patted his chest in the area above the heart.

'That's what I'm saying – a man of good heart,' Gabriella said, taking a sneaky look at her watch.

'Good heart, bad heart, no heart,' Eddie said scornfully. 'It makes no odds. It's knowing *in* your heart that you'll never have a choice between good and bent. I've known plenty of "good-hearted people" in this game who are always first on the team list for a charity match, or who'll walk from Land's End to John o'Groat's for terminally ill kids, but are as bent as nine-bob notes.'

Gabriella blinked at the dated phrase.

'And some who are beyond even that,' Eddie added.

'How can you be beyond bent?' she asked.

'They're not conscious of it,' Eddie explained. 'It's not as if, like most bent people, they know they're bent. They just don't know there's a choice!'

'Born bad, eh?' Gabriella mused.

'No one's born bad,' Eddie asserted. 'No, it's just that they come into the game as kids and meet bent people, see how things are going and think, "Oh, I see, that's the way it is," and then follow suit. They're the sort who you say "but that's cheating" too, and they say "Eh? Come again?" Know what I mean?'

'Yes, Harry,' said Gabriella, sending him up with a Frank

Bruno imitation. Eddie sank back in his chair, and Gabriella stood up.

'Sod it,' Eddie said, feeling more alone in the game than ever.

'I'm with you,' Gabriella pleaded. 'I'm just going to give sleep another chance.'

Gabriella stopped off at a phone-booth in the lobby to make one more call home. When she got the answering-machine again, she retired to her room, trying to forget her disappointment and anxiety, and fell asleep thinking of tomorrow's game.

．

Simon woke the next morning to the sound of Camilla's voice talking into the phone.

'Of course. Must go, darling,' he heard her say merrily.

Simon gradually remembered the surroundings. The hotel room, the floral duvet, the large floor-to-ceiling windows that had put him in mind of Paris. Only he wasn't in Paris. He was in a room, in a hotel, not far from where he lived, with a pushy journalist called Camilla.

'Black, white, sugar, no sugar?'

Camilla was poised with a coffee-pot on the edge of the bed. Simon looked at her blankly. She poured the coffee.

'Here is a chap who is guilt-ridden, embarrassed and wondering how fast he can get the hell out of here and home. How do you like your coffee, or perhaps you don't like coffee?' The words slipped as volubly off her tongue now as they had done last night.

'Just milk,' said a subdued Simon.

She brought both cups over and sat down close to him.

'Thank you,' he said.

They drank their coffee. Camilla kept her eyes on him over the rim of her cup throughout. Then for the first time she spoke slowly, quietly – almost like a normal human being.

'Thank you for last night, Simon, and I hope you like the article I write. When you finish your coffee, you can just go if you want and it's okay. Okay?'

Simon tried to nod. He hadn't expected to get off so easily and didn't want it to show.

Camilla gave him a shy smile. 'Except – I'd like to see you again. On the quiet. No involvement. Just pleasure. Know what I mean, Harry?'

Camilla didn't attempt a Frank Bruno imitation. Simon looked at her and thought about what she'd said. This had been the first time he'd ever been unfaithful to Gabriella. He still couldn't quite come to terms with what he'd done, or indeed why he'd done it. The fact that Camilla had taken all the initiatives had helped, of course, and he told himself how vulnerable he was, thanks to Gabriella's new commitments. He wanted to think that he hadn't enjoyed it, but knew that he had. Not the feeling now, the morning after, nor the cruddy meal and his embarrassing behaviour last night – but the explosion of lust and the feeling of being physically wanted, they had pleased him. Now he could have it all again if he wished.

.

The team went through their usual Saturday morning routine. A lie-in, a leaf through the papers, the racing ones in the case of Coughlan and Rimmer, a light team lunch of scrambled eggs, toast and tea at the hotel, and then the thirty-minute coach drive to the ground with games of cards throughout the trip.

Once inside the routines continued. Players left tickets for friends and family at the door, then retired to the dressing-room to change and prepare themselves. Gabriella filled in her official team-sheet and headed off to hand it in to the referee. Outside the dressing-room, at the far end of the corridor, Fisher, in one of his more exotic topcoats, collared Eddie for a discreet word.

'Can you be at the boardroom tomorrow at twelve?' asked Fisher quietly.

'Lunch is it?' Eddie inquired, puzzled.

'No,' Fisher said gravely.

He took the large cigar from his mouth and put his forefinger to his lips.

'Say nothing, understand. Nothing to *nobody*.'

He drew Eddie's attention to Gabriella, who was chatting to the referee across the way.

'Nobody,' Fisher repeated.

Eddie got that message, and thought for a moment that he was being told about Gabriella getting the push. He attempted to clarify this with Fisher, but the moment was ambushed by the arrival of the chairman of the home club, who had an expensive camel-hair coat draped over his shoulders. The two chairmen immediately clutched each other in a handshake of recognition, forcing Eddie to stand silently by. They exchanged business pleasantries and moved off, leaving Eddie none the wiser but a touch more contemptuous about those who ran football clubs.

Fortunately, the opening half of the match restored some of Eddie's faith in those who *played* the game, and especially in Charlie O'Keefe, who managed to get on the end of a brilliant right-wing cross from Tony Morris and power a header past the spread-eagled home keeper. Gabriella joined Eddie in an excited jig on the touch-line, as O'Keefe celebrated his goal with his customary somersault, borrowed from Hugo Sanchez.

Gabriella's team remained in command throughout the remainder of the first half and the early part of the second. It looked as though the expense of bringing them up for the night before was paying off in terms of commitment. But then, mysteriously, it all began to fall apart. There seemed to be no apparent reason, just a collective failure of will, because the home team refused to accept the inferiority that had been imposed upon them.

It looked as if Gabriella's lads would hang on for the win, but with only a minute or so remaining Coughlan made a reckless-looking challenge in the penalty area, and the home centre forward dived to win a penalty. Coughlan and his fellow-defenders raged at the referee for falling for this professional con-trick, conveniently ignoring the certain fact that they would have tried *exactly* the same thing had they been in the same circumstances, and would have celebrated their achievement the way the home team was doing now.

Coughlan was booked for his protests, and his anger simmered while the teams lined up to watch the penalty-kick, which was dispatched comprehensively past Rimmer. Coughlan eyed the player who had won the penalty malevolently, and when he made a sarcastic gesture of thanks, the old red mist came up over Coughlan's eyes. He launched his forehead into the forward's face, sending him crashing to the turf. Immediately there was a mêlée that would not have disgraced two street gangs, and the referee bundled through it to show Coughlan the red card. Coughlan spat out his dissent and trotted off in a matter-of-fact manner, reconciled to the fact that he'd paid a price for exacting his own justice on the 'cheat'.

Gabriella and Eddie studiously ignored him as he came back to the dug-out. Seconds later the final whistle went. The three points that had been there for the taking had been reduced to one by an ill-judged tackle, and the disappointment had been compounded by a physical assault and a dismissal.

The sour atmosphere spilled over into the dressing-room afterwards. Coughlan sat with his shirt pulled up over his face, while Gabriella prowled the room. Eddie watched, grim-faced, from the sidelines. The silence was ear-shattering.

'I'm waiting . . . I'm waiting,' Gabriella simmered. 'Just for someone to tell me how you did it . . . no one? You had them cold and then what? They were dead. No need for anything other than keeping going as you were . . . So, come on – what happened?'

There was a long silence, eventually penetrated by Tony Morris mumbling into his chest.

'What?' asked Gabriella sharply. 'I didn't get that!'

Morris mumbled again, forcing yet more sarcasm from Gabriella.

'Come on, speak up! Let's all hear it. It's got to be good.'

'We got a result, didn't we?' Morris said, falling back on the familiar professional 'rationalization'. Gabriella repeated it scathingly, but it was clear from the faces of some of the players that they agreed with Morris. Without turning to look at him,

Gabriella summoned Eddie to hear his assessment, to see if this was the kind of 'result' he had promised her in the hotel bar last night.

'You,' said Eddie firmly, indicating Coughlan. After another silence Coughlan emerged from his shirt. Eddie's eyes blazed at him.

'I don't want to hear from you *ever* again! Do you follow? I don't think any of us wants to. I don't even want to hear you asking the time of day. Do you understand?'

Coughlan sat there with a dead pan look on his face. He wasn't going to be roused by the familiar post-match hyperbole of losing managers and coaches. *They* hadn't played the game.

'As for the rest of you,' Eddie continued quietly. 'In the second half there I thought, "Hang on, have I missed five goals here? Are we six–nil up?" 'Cos that's how you played. *Pissing about*!' he shouted, before allowing his voice to drop again.

'In fact, I thought to myself,' and he broke into a scream, 'diarrhoea moves faster than you lot!'

Gabriella watched him impassively. He actually seemed to be on her side, not just going through the motions of a simulated rage. It seemed like the only good thing to come out of the whole trip – that and O'Keefe's goal.

.

The following morning, Eddie kept his date with Fisher, arriving at the deserted club at noon, and making his way up to the boardroom. It was an unfamiliar path for Eddie. Fisher was waiting on the landing outside the fake mahogany door with its brass plaque. He looked tense.

'Anybody outside?' Fisher asked, somewhat melo-dramatically.

'Nobody out there,' Eddie replied, puzzled.

Fisher gestured him towards the door.

'We've got trouble.'

Eddie couldn't help smiling at Fisher's seriousness.

'Right here in River City?'

Fisher shot him a look and pushed Eddie in through the door.

Seated at the boardroom table was Fisher's ever-present deputy, Anthony Coombs, and to one side, by a window, a large, red-faced man in a nylon anorak, wearing what looked like an official tie of some sort. Eddie sensed the atmosphere and his levity disappeared.

'Eddie, this is Inspector Moyse. Mr Moyse – Eddie Johnson,' Fisher said with strained formality.

Eddie turned and nodded to Moyse, who was watching Fisher's every move. Eddie sat down in the proffered chair. Fisher slid an envelope across the table to him. The flap of the envelope wasn't sealed, and Eddie presumed he was to look inside. He donned his reading glasses and fished inside the envelope. He took out three polaroid photographs. He looked at the first one and reacted with shock. He caught Fisher's eyes – they were gloomy, pained. Eddie looked back at the other two photographs which, from his reaction, were just as shocking. Eddie looked at Moyse, who was staring fixedly ahead of him. Eddie took his glasses off in dismay.

'You recognize the players,' said Fisher, 'the gobb – '

'The fellatees,' Coombs quickly proposed.

Eddie nodded.

'Two are reserve players – apprentices.'

Eddie closed his eyes and shook his head slowly.

'The girls are fourteen years old. The . . . *fellator* . . . in one of the pictures is Inspector Moyse's daughter Sarah.'

Eddie looked from Fisher to Moyse in a gesture of frustrated sympathy, only Moyse was now crying silently, oblivious to Eddie.

'I'm sorry,' Moyse mumbled.

Eddie scooped the photographs back into the envelope. Moyse regained control and turned to Eddie.

'I want it stopped, Mr Johnson . . . And those lads, at the very least, I want them punished . . . I want . . . oh, Christ!'

Moyse broke down in tears again and lumbered out of the room, with Fisher giving assistance.

Eddie looked at Coombs.

'Christ – he's kept this from his wife?'

'That, thank God, is not a problem. He's divorced. She's in Australia with the youngest. Oh, we've heard the life story this morning!'

Fisher came back in, looking very flustered.

'Tony, what do we do?'

Coombs shook his head.

'*We*? What's *he* going to do?' snapped Eddie, pointing to the door where Moyse had just left. 'He'll have the bastards up in court. I hope they get locked away and good riddance.'

'Does he want that? Would he come here if he wanted that?' Fisher asked them both.

'Whatever he wants, we get shot of the bastards.'

Coombs made placatory gestures with his hands.

'Eddie! Bastards . . . bastards? Enough! My instincts are the same as yours, but my feelings are very different.'

'How so?' queried Fisher.

'This is going to reflect very badly on the club if it comes out.'

'Comes out?' said Eddie.

'I think Tony means the media, don't you, Tony?'

Coombs nodded emphatically.

'How are you going to avoid that once they've been arrested?' Eddie pointed out.

A silence fell upon them as they considered the matter in their very different ways.

'It's a bastard, all right,' mused Fisher.

'Cool heads needed,' said Coombs.

'What we need is to tell the boss straight away,' Eddie suggested.

Fisher snorted and mimed picking up a phone.

'There you go, Eddie. "Sorry to break into your Sunday, Gabriella, but we've got a slight case here of our players shagging little girls. Can you spare a minute?"'

He challenged Eddie with a sardonic look. The way forward seemed clear: it was a man's problem, and it had to be solved by men. In matters of sexual indiscretion, Gabriella had to be protected – or, to put it another way – she had to be kept in the dark.

CHAPTER EIGHT

It wasn't until Monday morning that Gabriella got round to mentioning her fruitless late-night phone-calls to Simon. He was busy in the hall, preparing to leave for work, and Gabriella was sitting in the kitchen, leafing through a great pile of the daily papers, reading them, like any good football manager, from the sports pages backwards.

'Cheerio, then,' Simon called.

'Yes,' said Gabriella absently, still absorbed in a football story in one of the tabloids. Then she turned to look at him.

'You're off?'

'That's the idea.'

'I meant to ask – how was the trip the other day?'

'Fine,' said Simon quickly.

'You were back late.'

'No, I wasn't,' he said defensively.

'When I rang, the answering-machine was still on.'

'Ah, that's because I was taken to dinner by a beautiful young woman.'

Gabriella smiled at him.

'Anyone I know?'

Simon shook his head slowly as if considering this.

'A journalist. She wanted to know what it's like to be married to you.'

'Poor you,' said Gabriella with genuine sympathy for what she presumed was an ordeal.

'Well, have a nice day,' Simon said limply, as relief surged through him. Gabriella held out her arms to him. He smiled and came across to her. They embraced, and kissed briefly.

'You have a nice day,' Gabriella said sweetly.

'Promise,' said Simon, backing out of the kitchen. He watched her return to the newspapers again and become lost in concentration.

.

Monday was generally a non-training day – a chance for the players to heal their bruises and spend a day with their families. At the club it was an opportunity to catch up on administrative details, so Gabriella spent most of the morning in her office. She thought she caught sight of Eddie – who wasn't due in at all – but she didn't meet up with him. Charlie O'Keefe did – largely because Eddie had called him in 'for a chat'.

Charlie came out of the tunnel from the dressing-room and looked around the empty stadium. Eddie was standing in the centre circle, looking dreamily around him. Then he saw Charlie and waved him over. Charlie walked briskly across to him, trying not to get any mud or soil on his loafers or white socks. Eddie looked smart too, in anorak, open-necked shirt and slacks.

'Reliving old glories, Eddie? Now what is it?'

'Just thought we'd have a chat,' he smiled at Charlie, starting to gaze around the ground again.

'Ever read that David Greenwood fellow?'

'Who's he?' asked Charlie with a frown.

'Bloke who interviewed the boss on the radio.'

Charlie grinned. 'Oh yeah, geezer talking Spanish.'

Eddie thought about telling Charlie that it was Italian, but decided it was not worth the effort.

'He's a journalist,' Eddie added.

Charlie nodded knowingly. 'Right. Scumbag, eh?'

Eddie almost wagged a finger at him.

'Not him, son. Most of them, but not him. Funny fellow. Uses ten-bob words when penny ones will do, but he says some right things.'

'Yeah,' Charlie said as he did a fancy back heel at an invisible ball, his attention span almost exhausted.

'He wrote a book,' Eddie continued. '*The People's Theatre.* *This* he meant.' And Eddie gestured around to the terraces at both ends of the ground and down one side. 'He gets it spot-on too. For instance, he thinks it's interesting the players other players admire. So do I. Who do you like, son?'

'Jimmy White,' grinned Charlie.

Eddie grinned back at him. 'No, serious, Charlie. Footballers you admire.'

Charlie pretended to think deeply about this for a moment.

'Me!' he concluded with a laugh.

'That's good, son. You've got to like yourself before others can like you. But come on, who do you *admire*?'

Charlie shrugged.

'Maradona . . . er, that Mexican feller who does the somersaults when he scores, Hugo somebody . . . I dunno . . . that old geezer with the beard they're always showing you on telly.'

Eddie nodded, guessing who he meant. 'George Best.'

'That's him. He looks a bit special.'

He gave Eddie a patronizing wink, because he knew that Best was of Eddie's generation. Eddie was thinking about Charlie's list.

'Maradona scored a goal with his hand, of course.'

Eddie began to wander down the pitch towards one of the goals. Charlie checked his watch – he'd obviously got a snooker-table booked, but he thought he'd give Eddie a few more minutes and walked after him.

'Yeah, but Shilton should have got that. He should have twatted him when he went up for the ball.'

'Maybe, son,' Eddie observed. 'Nice goal you got on Saturday, by the way.'

Charlie looked pleased.

'Yeah! Bit special, wasn't it?'

Eddie wandered on, leading Charlie towards the goal.

'Could have done with another, really.'

Charlie smiled. *This* was what Eddie had wanted to talk about.

'Right. I know what you're going to say, Eddie. The service I'm getting is pathetic. I'm working my bollocks off up front –'

Eddie turned to him. They'd arrived in one of the goal-mouths by now. Eddie's tone suddenly changed.

'I wouldn't be talking to you about the service you're getting, would I?' said Eddie, slapping him down. 'You a fan, son?' he asked, pointing to the terrace behind the goal. 'Are you still one of them at heart? It's important, you know. All good players are.'

'Sure,' said Charlie, thinking of ways to dip out of this sermon from Eddie.

'Do you know what I mean by a *good* player? Not just a player with skill. Not just a lad who can delight them.' He nodded at the empty terraces again. 'But someone who hasn't got the great skill. Someone who's maybe a lot short of technique, but who goes out and runs his bollocks off for *them*. Some lad who'd run himself into the ground for the team, and if he couldn't play, would be up there cheering them on. He gives it on the park. He gives it off the park.'

'Sure,' agreed Charlie, hoping this was the end. But it wasn't.

'You're not one of them, son.' Eddie said firmly, turning to face him.

'Eh?' reacted Charlie, surprised by this attack.

Eddie began to move towards him.

'You're a prick, son. Full weight. You're a shitehawk. You're a toe-rag. The best part of you ran down your mother's leg. I want you long gone from here, but it's not up to me.'

Charlie looked shocked by this assault, and began to back away as Eddie still moved towards him, his jaw rigid with anger and contempt.

'What's up, Eddie?'

'Little girls,' Eddie squeezed out through clenched teeth. 'Fourteen-year-olds! *Minors*. Not content with having it off with one of them, you have to have photographs!'

Charlie knew what it was about now, and looked terrified.

'They're not fourteen! I wasn't the only one,' he pleaded.

Eddie backed him up against a goal-post.

'Until you leave here, you will leave them alone –'

'There was Travis and Leffernan, they were with me,' Charlie protested. 'The bird had the camera. It was a laugh!'

Eddie ignored this, and moved his face up to Charlie's. 'You will stay away from those little girls. You will stay away from those other two. You'll lead a blameless life. Understand, son?'

Eddie was practically bursting to pound his fist into Charlie's petrified face.

'If not, I will break your legs and leave you somewhere where you'll get gangrene!'

Eddie stalked slowly off, leaving Charlie to sag against the goal-post. Charlie looked around to make sure nobody had seen this incident, but the terraces and ground remained empty. Eddie had laid out his idea of standards to O'Keefe, and he knew that the youth had got the message. He had two more lectures to deliver that afternoon.

.

The next day Charlie O'Keefe didn't turn up for training. Eddie didn't say anything when Gabriella asked if he knew why, and it wasn't until she returned to her office at lunch-time that her secretary Marjorie gave her the telephone message from O'Keefe.

'He's got a virus,' Marjorie reported.

'Has he?' Gabriella asked dubiously. 'I want to hear it from him. Get him, Marje.'

Marjorie pointed behind Gabriella, through the open door of the office.

'Someone to see you.'

Sitting across the corridor in the main administrative office was a quaintly dressed woman in her mid-forties, with auburn hair. Her black-stockinged legs were crossed, revealing a pair of expensive patent leather shoes.

'Mrs Fitzgerald,' whispered Marjorie. 'I couldn't get rid of her. Says it's *very* important.'

Gabriella went across and greeted the somewhat restrained

Mrs Fitzgerald who, with her black gloves and green jewellery, looked a little like a palm-reader. Having taken in Mrs Fitzgerald's grave manner, Gabriella ushered her into the office.

'How can I help?' asked Gabriella.

'I suppose we should have met before. You see I'm a club mother.'

'A what?'

'A club mother. I lodge players for the club. Young lads, apprentices, lads far from home. You know.'

Gabriella tried to shrug off her ignorance of this aspect of club life.

'Mr Taylor designated us "club mothers",' the lady said proudly. 'There are several of us. We have our own little corner at the back of the stand on match days.'

'Mrs Fitzgerald, what's the problem?'

She told Gabriella that she looked after the apprentices, Steve Leffernan and Roy Travis, whom she held in high regard, and whom any mother would be proud to have as sons. She then paused, obviously disturbed by something which had disrupted this cosy, chintzy picture.

'I came home last night to find them crying. At least Steve was crying, and Roy was pretty near it.'

Gabriella settled herself back in her chair, ready to hear some tale of homesickness or teenage crushes.

'What was the matter?'

'Mr Johnson had been round to tell them to get on their bikes. They were finished with the club. They were devastated. As you know, Steve was a Scottish schoolboy international, and Roy was snapped up by Mr Taylor under the noses of a score of club scouts.'

Gabriella hid her reactions to this news and put on an outward show of calm intrigue.

'Why did Mr Johnson tell them that?'

'Mrs Benson – if I may call you Gabriella –'

Gabriella gave so sign of assent.

'Well, before I say any more, can I just say that my two lads are the nicest pair you could ever wish to meet. They observe the curfew, they're always in bed by ten the night before a game. They only go out on Saturdays – and then only if they've won. They write home regularly, they –'

'Mrs Fitzgerald, what reason did Mr Johnson give for saying what he did?' Gabriella snapped.

'Before I tell you –'

'Mrs Fitzgerald!' Gabriella held up her hand impatiently.

'No, please listen. I've been about a bit, it's no use denying, so I've seen what I've seen. I was at the Isle of Wight for Dylan in 1968. As I say, I've been around and this is nothing.'

'What is nothing? Please tell me!'

Mrs Fitzgerald shook her head sadly.

'Girls. That's all. Girls. They got up to high jinks with a couple of girls.'

'And for this Mr Johnson told them the club was finished with them?'

She nodded.

'Mrs Fitzgerald – I decide who goes and who stays at this club. *Not* Mr Johnson. They haven't got these girls pregnant or anything, have they?'

'Good God, no!' she exclaimed.

'Then I'll speak to Mr Johnson. Tell that to Steven and Roy, okay?'

Mrs Fitzgerald bit her lip and then produced a polaroid photograph from her big hand-bag. She pushed it across to Gabriella.

'You can see they're slags, can't you? Just little slags.'

Gabriella studied the photograph on her blotter.

'Which ones are the slags?' she said ironically.

'Mrs Benson – I think Eddie Johnson hit Steve.'

'Is that all?' Gabriella stood up. 'Where are Steve and Roy now?'

'At home. Devastated.'

'Your house? Right, shall we go and talk to them?'

Gabriella opened the door for Mrs Fitzgerald, who smiled at

her, thinking she'd understood. What she didn't see as she left was that Gabriella's face was as grim as hell. It was on the drive over that Mrs Fitzgerald casually mentioned one more detail: that both the girls involved were fourteen-year-olds, although she was inclined to think they looked much older. Gabriella thought about slapping her but controlled herself.

Mrs Fitzgerald's Victorian terrace house – garishly modernized, it has to be said – was situated in a quiet but central part of the town. She ushered Gabriella into her front lounge, which seemed to be in a uniform shade of beige but which was offset by a padded, semi-circular bar in one mirror-lined corner. Mrs Fitzgerald went upstairs to fetch the boys from their room, while Gabriella took in the drabness of their surroundings. She pictured them sitting here, six nights a week, watching television, with Mrs Fitzgerald curled up on the beige sofa in her fluffy slippers, watching them.

Mrs Fitzgerald showed Travis and Leffernan into the room and made a big show of retiring to be discreet. The boys sat down on the sofa, while Gabriella installed herself in the big armchair across the room from them. On the low table between them, Gabriella had placed the polaroid photograph. Leffernan began to cry softly, while Travis looked white-faced and rigid. Gabriella looked at both of them expectantly, which was enough to produce their halting explanations.

'We just wanted to play snooker,' Travis said quietly.

'That's all. We didn't know –' Leffernan's voice trailed away as he dissolved into tears again.

'It was Charlie, wasn't it? He made you do it?' Gabriella asked gently.

'It was them girls,' Leffernan blurted. 'We wanted to play snooker.'

Gabriella looked at the two of them – sixteen years old, living away from home, vulnerable.

'If only you had,' she said regretfully.

Leffernan was rubbing his eyes with his knuckles, like a little boy after a playground accident.

'What'll happen, miss?' he asked. 'Miss' – that had been the team's running joke against her during the first few weeks, but here it was used unselfconsciously, by someone not long out of school.

'You both realize how serious this is, don't you?' Gabriella asked, sounding inevitably like a headmistress.

They both nodded.

'You knew they were underage?'

Travis, who seemed to be in control despite the whiteness of his face, protested angrily.

'You couldn't tell that!'

'It doesn't matter what they looked like, you committed a *crime*.'

'What'll happen?' asked Travis, staring at her.

Gabriella ignored this for now.

'I don't think sportsmen should behave like this,' she said, pointing at the photograph. 'I don't think *anyone* should,' she continued, 'but *particularly* not sportsmen who are supposed to set an example. Do you?'

They both shook their heads in dumb agreement.

'I don't think badly of you for it. You're young. You'll learn. You were led astray by a very stupid Charlie O'Keefe. And I shall tell him so. Don't worry.'

They both began to look hopeful at hearing such reasonable sentiments, especially after the tirade they'd suffered from Eddie Johnson.

'I won't tell your parents what happened, when I write to them.'

Leffernan looked alarmed. 'You're going to write to my mum and dad?'

'Why, miss?' asked Travis, equally unsettled.

'Because you're going, boys,' Gabriella said as gently as she could, which made it all the more final. 'I don't want you in my club.'

She called out for Mrs Fitzgerald, who appeared so quickly it was plain she'd been eavesdropping from the hall.

'Can you give these lads a hand with their packing? They'll be leaving tonight.'

Mrs Fitzgerald looked at her spitefully.

'They're slags, those girls!' she shrieked.

Gabriella pointed calmly to the bar in the corner, stacked with bottles.

'I don't think that's the sort of atmosphere I want my young players in. I don't think you'll be boarding any more, do you?'

She stood up. Mrs Fitzgerald wasn't even listening to her.

'Slags, do you hear? And as for that Moyse one, she may be a copper's daughter, but she's a little whore!'

This brought Gabriella wheeling round to look at her.

'What did you say?'

Gabriella called Moyse that night to assess his mood and to propose a meeting. He was slightly surprised to find her in agreement with him about punishing the players concerned. The question was, would their dismissals be sufficient? Gabriella wouldn't know that until she met him. She would also have to talk to Fisher, Coombs and Eddie – find out why they hadn't told her.

⋅

Simon Benson had finished a two-day meeting in the Midlands several hours earlier than expected, giving him an evening to do as he wished. The thought of seeing Camilla again had been nagging away at him, ever since he'd been able to breeze through the expected questions from Gabriella without creating suspicion. So he'd found himself calling Camilla and fixing a rendezvous with her back in London, fired by the prospect of further furtive excitement.

Now as he waited on the railway station platform for the trip back to London, he rationalized his actions with legal precision. One, Camilla was available, willing and a lot of fun in bed. Two, he, as the husband of football's first woman manager, had had an awful lot of strain to put up with, not to mention his wife's increased absence from home – he *deserved* a bit of escapist enjoyment. Three, since he was known as a loyal husband and a lawyer of integrity, it could be put down as only a moment of folly if he got caught. Four, it didn't look likely that he *would* get caught!

Simon had just reached clause four, when he felt a hand on his shoulder, and smelled drink-soaked breath and the odour of cigar smoke. A voice said, 'London bound?'

Simon's heart did a somersault, as he turned to see a well-lunched Martin Fisher at his side. Fisher beamed at him.

'Two people halve a journey, as I always say!'

For Simon, the trip back to London felt twice as long. Fortunately, Fisher was emphatically lubricated and in verbose form, so he was able to get by with a few nods and smiles without having to talk much.

As they got out at Euston, however, Fisher insisted on walking with him, and up ahead Simon could see Camilla waiting beyond the barrier. Fisher prattled on, while Simon flashed luminous eye-signals at her. He should, really, have been worried by the practised ease with which she registered and acted upon them – walking straight past Simon as if he wasn't there and waving to somebody non-existent in the distance. As Fisher finally peeled off in the direction of the taxi rank, Simon found her falling into step a pace or two behind him.

'Who's he?' she asked.

'The chairman of the club,' Simon said, not turning to look at her. With Fisher gone, she linked her arm through his.

'I've just got to make a call,' he told her.

'Pee or phone?'

'Phone.'

They headed across to the phone-booths on the edge of the station concourse.

'You can call from my place, if you like,' Camilla offered.

He stopped and looked at her.

'Just for my own peace of mind, I want this call to be one where the pips or whatever are clearly heard.'

He arrived at a booth, put his overnight bag down and searched for some coins. Camilla stood near by.

'Ah, that call! "Hello, darling – been delayed I'm afraid. Just going off to bang someone rigid!"'

Simon picked up the phone, inserted money and began dialling.

'Actually, I just want to know if *she* knows that she's about to sell a player.'

Simon was surprised he'd remembered this indiscretion of Fisher's, given the frozen state of his mind during the journey. Nevertheless, the call would be infinitely more plausible now – and he might win a few 'brownie points' for the information he conveyed.

．

Eddie was wearing a cardigan, slippers and reading glasses when Gabriella called unannounced at his house, so she knew she'd caught him on the hop as planned. The sprawl of newspapers over the sofa and the stack of video cassettes under the television set confirmed that Eddie had been found in an unguarded moment. The fact that the video playing was the epic 1986 World Cup game between France and Brazil, generally perceived as a tribute to romantic football, was surprising to Gabriella. In other times, she might have been delighted to talk to Eddie about it – but tonight she had other matters to discuss.

'Switch it off,' she commanded Eddie, pointing at the set. Eddie duly obliged with the remote-control.

'Sit down,' she said, taking complete mastery of his evening in seconds. Eddie was so taken aback by her manner that he offered virtually no resistance – besides, he knew why she'd come.

'Give me a reason, any reason, why I shouldn't boot you out of the club?' Gabriella stormed.

It was a strong opening gambit, and Eddie subsided quickly into mute apology. He stared at the carpet for a few moments, hoping she'd calm down.

'I'm waiting,' she reminded him tersely.

'Who told you?'

'A club "mother". Mrs Fitzgerald.'

Eddie snorted out a little ironic laugh. 'One of the ones Fred Taylor was always —'

He saw the thunderous look on her face, and he let the story drop. Gabriella resumed her indictment, the harsh light of Eddie's reading lamp sharpening her already angry features.

'I've seen the lads, Leffernan and Travis, who lodge with her. I've seen a photograph.'

'And?'

'They've gone,' she said brutally.

'Charlie O'Keefe —' Eddie said, barely able to speak the name.

'I've seen him. I've seen Coombs. Now I'm seeing you. I'll deal with Martin Fisher when he gets back. Do you know what he's doing? Oh, of course you do. He's doing some deal with another chairman, isn't he? So some other poor bloody ignorant manager will find he's making me an offer for O'Keefe. A bloody offer I can't refuse.'

Eddie had guessed from her tone by now that she'd felt the same disgust as he had about the incident. She obviously shared his sense of standards. Eddie relaxed a little, even feeling that he could confide in her.

'I was all for calling you in from the start.'

'Why didn't you?'

Eddie gave her an embarrassed shrug. He didn't like talking about sex in front of men, let alone a woman.

'Well . . . it was what the lads were up to . . . Not something fit for a woman to know about.'

Gabriella let out a sarcastic little laugh at this — Eddie Johnson, protecting her feelings.

'That's what Coombs said. "We didn't think a lady should have to deal with such things." But it's not that. This is them wielding power. This is them saying, "Oh, we give her her pretty little head now and then, but *we're* in charge." They must have *loved* this!'

It was all above Eddie's head — for him the issues involved were straightforward and nothing to do with power; just decency, and punishment.

'What about Charlie?' he asked, face hardening, hoping to hear that she'd castrated the little bastard herself.

'He's on his way too.'

Eddie nodded his approval.

'Good. Little scumbag.'

He smiled at her, convinced they were on the same wavelength. And then she revealed that they weren't.

'When I get somebody better.'

Eddie's face registered shock and anger. He spat out his next words: 'You what?'

'When I get a better player, he'll get sold.'

'Jesus!' Eddie exploded, 'he's a man, for Christ's sake. They were *girls*! Fourteen-year-olds!'

'I know. And I'm sick about it.'

Not enough, it seemed to Eddie, who got out of his armchair and stalked the room.

'Sick? What,' he sneered, 'sick as a parrot? I'll tell you where you're sick. Up there!'

He jabbed his finger into his temple. Gabriella looked at him, wondering whether to explain how it had hit her too, but he was lost in his own world of regret and bitterness.

'You know what's sick?' Eddie spluttered. 'Charlie can play a bit. From a lad pushing a brush in a sausage factory, to a YTS trainee, he's come on! I thought we'd found something in him. And now this – '

'I know,' said Gabriella quietly, hoping to calm him down, but the two simple words just provoked another torrent of bile.

'Oh, no you don't lady! You don't know. Not like I do in here.' He tapped his chest forcibly. 'You lot will never know!'

'What *lot*? Women?' asked Gabriella, bristling at this all-purpose display of spleen.

'Yes. Women. And your lot!'

'What is this, Eddie? A genderist attack, or a class analysis?'

This enraged him even more. 'You see! You get smart. You don't feel the game. Not like the fans, not like the players.'

'Any minute now we'll be on to "my dad's bigger than your

dad",' Gabriella observed, trying to stall this seemingly ridiculous spiral of venom into which Eddie had fallen. But he was off again, self-powered now.

'Directors, people who watch the game in heated boxes through a window, journalists ... Jesus! Women football writers.'

'Women managers?' Gabriella suggested as an addition.

'It's the terraces. It's the teams. There's nothing else!'

He looked at her, focusing his argument at her but not as a target – more as a potential disciple. 'You know everyone loves a player who can play a bit. The fans love him. And the players who are just average. We're all fans at heart. And that's the crime of someone like Charlie. Any player who whores around, is a piss artist, pill-taker, whatever; they shit on their fellow-pros, and they shit on the fans!'

He was left virtually breathless with the shouting, and Gabriella moved quickly to try and demolish some of this dangerous, self-righteous indignation.

'We can't all be as squeaky-clean as you, Eddie.'

'Me? I've pulled a few strokes. But I had respect for the game, I had respect for the people I played against, I had respect for the crowd. I had respect for myself. And that's deep down what people like Charlie O'Keefe haven't got. They don't respect themselves, so how can they respect anything else?'

Eddie leaned against the mantelpiece, drained by his exorcism. Gabriella took this as her cue to make a move. But he had one more concern to voice: 'What about the copper? Inspector Moyse.'

'Oh, I think you'll find he's got a nicer house or car, and his daughter's on the way to join her mother in Australia.'

Eddie still had the energy for a slavering sneer of disgust, directed at Gabriella.

'Don't look at me! Speak to Fisher and Coombs; they have the details,' she snapped at him, finally voicing her own frustrations at the 'executive action' which had taken place behind her back. She snatched her coat up from the chair.

'The point of this visit, Eddie, is to tell you that you're hanging on here by your finger-tips. You don't do anything in the club or about the club without my knowing it or without my approval ever again!'

She challenged him with a long, fierce look 'Understand?'

'Right, boss,' Eddie said quietly, and without sarcasm. The storm had passed.

'I'll see you tomorrow, then,' she offered as conciliation.

Eddie made a move towards the door to escort her out.

'I'll see myself out. Get back to the game.' She nodded at the frozen picture on the television.

Eddie had one more thing to get off his chest, though. The darkness and the emptiness of the rest of the evening were closing in on him. He trusted her enough now to confide in her.

'You know what I thought when I saw those pictures?'

Gabriella waited patiently – something was obviously troubling him.

'I was jealous. I thought, at least *someone's* getting some. That's what I can't get over. Thinking that.'

Gabriella looked at him. He hung his head. Now she understood his ranting diatribe and the disgust. Eddie had failed to live up to his own standards. She gave him a sympathetic nod and then left. Driving home, the thought of him sitting alone in his slippers watching football videos almost moved her to tears.

.

There was one more sexual indiscretion to be resolved. And it too had been kept from Gabriella, and would always be kept from her. Simon finally saw a copy of Camilla's article about him. It featured a cartoon caricature of Simon in which he was depicted standing over a sink, wearing an apron, with a dish-mop in his hand. The headline to the feature ran: SHE MANAGES, WHILE HE BEATS, AND HE SWEEPS, AND HE CLEANS. Simon recognized much of what ran beneath this as Camilla's impromptu ravings from their original dinner date.

Sitting in his City office, Simon cringed as he read it, not just for himself but for Gabriella too. It cheapened them both – it lampooned her through him. He was angry enough to phone Camilla directly to remonstrate, only to be told by her that it had gone down rather well with the editor. Criticism to her was futile, since she saw no 'lies' or 'shit' or whatever else Simon called it: only journalism. Simon's plaintive appeal to honour their short-lived intimacy was met with incredulity.

'Twice in the sack and you think you *mean* something to me?' she said over the phone, before hanging up on him. Simon wouldn't suffer the way Charlie O'Keefe would for his lapse, by having to uproot himself and work elsewhere, but the sense of humiliation would last an awfully long time.

Charlie O'Keefe, however, saw no lessons to be learned from his experiences. Collared by an intrigued Dave McGregor on the training pitch just a few days before he was transferred out of the club, Charlie had only one word to describe it all. '*Great!*' he said, then launched into one of his somersaults.

CHAPTER NINE

The sale of Charlie O'Keefe, which followed close on the death of Jim Wilson, seriously depleted Gabriella's options for her first team selection. She had only fifteen players with League experience to choose from, because, although the club still ran a reserve team in the Football Combination, that side was made up largely of apprentices and a couple of part-time local players on short-term contracts.

The enforced transfer of O'Keefe also produced another difficulty for Gabriella. His progress from YTS kid to full-time professional footballer had captured the imagination of the local public. He'd scored goals too, and celebrated them in a style designed to make the fans take him to their hearts. Therefore his sudden departure aroused a good deal of animosity, especially as no explanation for it was forthcoming. The tabloid press, who had all but exhausted their 'sex in the showers' angles on Gabriella, now thought they had another story with which they could exploit her presence in the game. In particular Steve Simms, who'd been assigned by his paper to come up with as many 'exclusives' about her as possible, saw a real opportunity to write about the Manageress in the same way as the ninety-one other male managers in the League would be written about at some time in their career. KNIVES OUT FOR MRS B? read his headline.

Gabriella caught sight of it in her early-morning trawl through the sports pages over breakfast. Her muted oaths were heard by Simon, who was getting ready to go to work.

'Why read them if they annoy you?' he asked.

It was a fair question – but then Simon didn't really understand that football was, in many ways, a branch of the entertainment industry. Most of the people were in it for success, money, prestige and a certain amount of fame. But, like others in the more obvious branches of that industry, football people also wanted to be liked, to get 'a good press', to be appreciated. Gabriella, despite her different background, was no exception at heart, but she wasn't going to admit it to Simon, nor indeed to herself.

'I suppose the Americans would say, "It comes with the territory," ' she rationalized for his benefit.

Simon bustled around the kitchen, helping himself to coffee and orange juice, noting that Gabriella had been too preoccupied to pour either out for him.

'Listen to this,' she went on, quoting Simms. 'Exclusive! Football's first manageress is about to find that stilettos don't only belong on her fashionable shoes.'

Simon considered this as he sipped his coffee. 'That's quite clever,' he said mischievously.

Gabriella tossed the paper aside in disgust – partly at Simms, partly at Simon. Simon was still wounded by his encounter with Camilla, which had taught him a couple of salient lessons, not the least of which was what a good relationship he had with his wife. He'd been aware of a desire to 'make up' to Gabriella, to re-establish the closeness they had previously always enjoyed, without attracting her suspicions about his motives. The most obvious route available to him was to show more interest in her work, which meant displaying an enthusiasm for football.

'Why does he foresee a conspiracy against you?' he asked, in his newly acquired seriousness about the game.

'Because *he's* creating it!' Gabriella said in exasperation. Simon maintained a studied air, allowing Gabriella to continue her complaint.

'Okay, no doubt some of the fans *are* concerned, but until they read this, I don't think any of them –' she picked up the newspaper again – 'will be doing a Henry the Eighth and crying, "Off with her head!" '

Simon stifled another comment on the apparent wit of Steve Simms, which was probably just as well, otherwise the crockery that Gabriella was now tossing carelessly into the dish-washer might have been directed at him.

'Do you want me to threaten him or something?' he asked, his playful tone masking the real urge to help.

'If anyone's going to thump him, it's going to be me,' she muttered.

'I meant *legally*,' he corrected. 'I could get one of the partners to write him a sort of warning letter.'

Simon's voice tailed off as Gabriella gave him a withering stare. It was a feeble notion, brought on by over-compensation, and he recognized it as such. He shrugged, affecting a hurt look. It didn't attract any response or affection.

'I don't suppose you want me at the supporters' meeting tonight either?'

Now this *was* suspicious. He'd never shown the slightest interest in attending what sounded to him like a seriously masochistic exercise.

Gabriella gave him a curious look. 'What for – protection?'

'No!' he said plaintively. 'Because I'd like to be there. So I can talk about *your* work, rather than the weather, or ... kitchen units!'

He gestured around him. It was an attempt to prod Gabriella into realizing the barrier that her new job had created between them – which had, he'd since thought, provoked him into his fling with the appalling Camilla.

Gabriella gave him a perfunctory kiss and headed out of the kitchen with her briefcase. She had no suspicions about Simon's lapse, but the other consequence of her obsession with the job was that she didn't sense his increasing alienation either.

'We might as well have a revolving door fitted out there!' he exclaimed petulantly, but Gabriella was already gone. He swept the offending newspapers off the table with his arm, but it didn't make him feel any better.

.

Gabriella went straight to Martin Fisher's office when she arrived at the club, determined to take an initiative against the press speculation. Fisher was on the phone, but gestured her in with the hand which was already cradling his first Monte Cristo of the day. Gabriella waved her arms to disperse the blue fug hovering in the office and sat down opposite the chairman's desk.

'Of course, I'm happy to be guided by you, inspector, but I just happen to think that fifty is rather overdoing it.' Fisher pulled an extravagant face for Gabriella's benefit, followed by a conspiratorial wink. 'Most of the trouble is likely *outside* the ground, as you well know – I'm sure some of your men could be used to give the railway station and the transport police some protection.'

A smile now appeared.

'Thirty-five? Done! See you Saturday morning, inspector!'

Fisher put the phone down with a flourish, as if he'd just completed a staggering property deal.

'He's a real hustler, that guy – trying to get some tasty overtime for his division. But I knocked him down!'

Gabriella had understood the gist of the conversation – he'd been arranging police presence for the next match, for which the club paid – and she gave him a terse, knowing smile.

'Cutting corners on public safety? You could wind up more unpopular than me if there's a riot.'

Fisher ignored this hint to change the subject to Gabriella's pasting in the press and ploughed on, warming to his theme of the moment.

'Listen – it's only a few hundred yobbos from London, of which maybe twenty are out for a bit of aggro!' He patted his desk-top computer. 'Besides, I worked out that we'll be making less than a pound a head off them after police costs have been deducted!'

Gabriella tried again, provoked by the sight of Simms's newspaper lying on his desk.

'You'll probably need most of them at the home end, anyway – to stop our fans getting at me.'

She turned the paper over to reveal the back-page story. Fisher did a bad job of feigning surprise.

'What's all this about?'

'A touch more incredulity there, and you might have got away with it. Conspiracies start at the top, Martin. When did you talk to him?'

Fisher knew well enough by now – especially after his attempted 'cover-up' over O'Keefe's escapades – that denials were counter-productive where Gabriella was concerned. He shrugged.

'I didn't say anything that the fans aren't saying to me.'

'Oh, of course,' she said, ladling on the irony, 'I forgot that you talk to them all the time ... at the country club, or at Tramps when you're up in London, perhaps.'

Fisher bristled – he didn't like being sent up by her, even if he'd invited it.

'They have every right to be concerned,' he said, with sudden gravity.

'I know, that's why I go and talk to them every month. Why don't *you*?'

Fisher interrupted quickly. '*Concerned*, about the way that this team seems to be run.'

Gabriella was becoming used to 'chairman-speak' and took every opportunity to let Fisher know her opinion of it.

'Ah, suddenly it's "the team" now, meaning me – not "the club", meaning you!'

'Look, sweet-heart,' he said, adopting a tone and text designed to provoke her, 'I know we had to sell that little toe-rag O'Keefe, but that doesn't alter the fact that we've got to give the punters something else!'

'So, let me have the fee to spend – ' She knew it was a forlorn hope, and Fisher's expression confirmed it. 'Sorry, the key word back there was "give", wasn't it?'

Fisher nodded slowly for emphasis. 'That's right – the cash has already gone into a big hole called our bank account.'

Gabriella got up from her chair, realizing that further begging would be futile and probably humiliating. There was nothing Fisher liked more than the conspicuous exercise of his power over her.

'So I'm afraid you're just going to have to make someone else a star!' he concluded.

'I'm already working on it,' she said defiantly, asserting *her* power.

Fisher was intrigued. 'Who've you got in mind?'

'Paul Kennedy . . . from the reserves.'

She had to give Fisher credit – he knew who she was referring to without too many mental gymnastics.

'Black kid . . . neat little player . . . gets the odd goal from midfield,' he said, looking pleased with his recall.

'I hope he'll get even more when I play him up front.'

A frown now formed on Fisher's ever-expressive face – he wasn't about to query tactics and formation, surely?

'Er, do you think it's wise to blood him in this game?' he asked.

Gabriella frowned now, unsure of his meaning.

'I mean, the visiting fans aren't noted for their tolerance where black players are concerned, you know?'

Gabriella did indeed know that Saturday's opponents had an established racist element among their followers. There were perhaps a couple of clubs in every division with such a reputation, but she'd never imagined that this would be a consideration when selecting the team.

'Hang on, a moment ago they were just a few yobbos to whom we weren't going to make special concessions. Now I'm picking the team to placate them?'

Fisher recognized he'd overstepped his mark, and put up his hands in apology.

'All right, all right – just a word of warning. It's your decision. Does he know yet?'

'Well, no – but I've told Eddie to pitch him in with the first team squad this morning.'

Fisher relit his cigar pensively, and Gabriella quickly abandoned the blue smoke of the office for the fresh air of the training pitch.

·

The seventeen-year-old Kennedy was having the time of his life playing with the senior professionals, even though it was only a fairly gentle mid-week practice match. Although small and slight, he showed considerable ability on the ball, which made dispossessing him a difficult task. Eddie watched studiously from the touch-line as Gabriella approached.

'Boss,' Eddie nodded, which for Gabriella was his equivalent of a red carpet and a bouquet of flowers. They'd come to respect each other a little through the tortuous decision-making over O'Keefe. They'd discovered that they shared a similar attitude to standards in the game, even though Eddie deplored Gabriella's pragmatic insistence on holding on to O'Keefe while the possibility of a purchase was explored. Neither of them had demonstrably acknowledged this new-found understanding – alliances in football were too fragile to be celebrated publicly – so Gabriella would have to make do with 'boss' for now.

'How's he shaping up?' Gabriella asked anxiously.

'Pretty good,' said Eddie, which was a rave review for him. They watched Kennedy for a while, playing unselfconsciously – diligent, confident, but not too cocky.

'Mind you,' Eddie added a few moments later, 'he thinks it's a bit of fun for the moment. He'll probably faint when you tell him it's for real.'

'When do you think I should break it to him?'

Eddie looked at Gabriella curiously – this was a bouquet heading *his* way?

'Hang on – you, asking me for advice?'

Gabriella gave him a quick smile. 'Don't let it go to your head.'

Eddie watched Kennedy again – this time assessing his character, not his ability.

'Tell him now – it'll give him a couple of days to get used to the idea.'

'And to enjoy it? You're a big softie, really, Eddie!'

Eddie's expression told Gabriella she'd misinterpreted him.

'It'll test his bottle! Press inquiries, family and hangers-on suddenly all wanting tickets, and being given responsibility by older players . . . soon sorts the men from the boys. Lots of his type haven't got it.'

Gabriella stiffened at this remark, getting a hint of Eddie's true meaning.

'His type being what?' she challenged. 'Midfield players, do you mean?'

Eddie looked at her, wondering whether to risk airing his views on the status of 'coloured lads', as he would call them, within the game. But he sensed her strength of feeling, and backed down with an insolent shrug. 'If you like.'

The uneasy alliance had suddenly become difficult again. Eddie forestalled further discussion by winding up the training session, giving out his usual round of ironic compliments to various players who'd pleased him during the morning's work.

'You were almost average, Trevor Coughlan!'

The players ignored all this, heading for the coach waiting to take them back to the club. Eddie, perhaps unsettled by Gabriella's instant hostility a few moments back, singled out Paul Kennedy and put a friendly arm round his shoulder.

'Hey! Hey!' he called out at the squad. 'What about a big hand for young Paul Kennedy here?'

Most of the players took the hint, and there was a smattering of applause. Skipper Gary Halliwell patted Kennedy on the back as he passed.

'Tasty, son.' The ultimate plaudit. Kennedy was chuffed by this, and then Eddie leaned down and whispered in his ear.

'Here, son – the boss wants a quick word with you.'

He pushed him off in Gabriella's direction. Kennedy trotted across to her, pushing his fashionably cut hair back from his forehead.

'You wanted to see me, Mrs Benson?'

'Just a private word, Paul.'

Gabriella thought about how to approach this – nothing too sensational was required, but at the same time it was a very special moment for this young professional.

'Do your mum and dad come to watch you play?'

'Well, they can usually manage the Saturday morning games but not the midweek ones.'

Gabriella nodded. 'Well if you call in at my office after lunch, I'll give you a couple of stand tickets for Saturday's home match . . . the afternoon one.'

Gabriella watched the realization sink in. Kennedy's face lit up.

'I don't believe it!'

Gabriella smiled at him.

'Well, you'd better start believing – I'm putting you up front with Tony Morris on Saturday. Think you're up to it?'

Kennedy beamed. 'Yeah, man – well hard!' He displayed a steady hand to demonstrate his resolve.

'Right, I'll talk to you about it all on Friday. In the meantime – back on the coach with the others. I don't want you catching anything expensive!'

Kennedy set off with a springing stride towards the coach, then turned as he kept moving.

'Hey, Mrs Benson? I've got three brothers – can I have tickets for them as well?'

Gabriella gave him a thumbs-up and he turned and disappeared inside the coach. Gabriella saw him get hit by a hail of shin-pads and assorted rubbish as he stepped up into the aisle, and an ironic chant of 'Super-star, super-star, super-star!' went up. Either Eddie had told them, or they had guessed that Kennedy was being promoted.

This was their way of welcoming him to the small fraternity of League football – he was a 'man' now, and the first 'test' was to see if he could have the piss taken out of him. Gabriella saw that the tribal initiation rite had just begun, but felt confident Kennedy could handle the transition. She headed for her car, pleased with the way the morning had gone after the sniping article by Simms. No wonder they continued to call football a game of 'ups and downs'.

•

The next 'down' wasn't long in coming, for at the supporters' club meeting that evening, Gabriella came in for rather hostile questioning over the sale of Charlie O'Keefe. Gabriella sat on the club's stage as usual, flanked by the well-meaning, protective chairman on one side and by a drum-kit, organ and bingo-machine on the other. Behind her sat Keith Nicholl and Dave McGregor, who'd developed a friendship on the basis of McGregor's quest for self-improvement after the failure of his marriage. Now McGregor followed Nicholl everywhere – the cinema, restaurants, theatre and even the monthly supporters' club meeting. They were the only two players present.

In the body of the room, hunched over their pints at the little circular tables, were about twenty-five supporters, joined this evening for professional reasons by Steve Simms, who was keen to monitor any discontent. Gabriella answered each question as honestly as she could, hoping that sooner or later the topic of Charlie O'Keefe would fade away. Another supporter raised his hand and stood, rather self-consciously, after being pointed out by the chairman.

'Is the manager . . . ess, aware that there are rumours around town that Charlie O'Keefe's transfer was to do with a bust up at the club?'

Gabriella gave him a patient smile, seeing that despite her intentions to have open and accountable management, she was now about to lie to the supporters.

'If I'm honest,' she heard herself saying, 'I'd have to admit that Charlie was in breach of club discipline a couple of times . . .' She saw Simms suddenly look up from his note-pad in anticipation of details, so she proceeded quickly to her main point. 'But this had nothing to do with his departure. It was simply a good deal for us.'

Gabriella looked away from the questioner and scanned the room for the next raised hand, thereby attempting to thwart any follow-up, a technique, she realized with horror, that she'd seen the Prime Minister use many times. She couldn't see a hand, but from the artificial gloom came a sour, aggressive voice.

'You don't get it, do you? Charlie O'Keefe was one of us, one of the lads!'

Gabriella located the 'lad' making his statement – a stocky figure in a sweatshirt and with close-cropped hair. He was surrounded at his table by four similarly dressed 'lads', who gave his remark what sounded like a couple of 'hear, hear' endorsements.

The youth continued his tirade, accompanied by a good deal of finger-pointing in Gabriella's direction.

'He come off the dole, and he went straight out on the park and did it! That's what was great about him – he was the best of British, he was!'

The other lads cheered their agreement. Gabriella directed her gaze at the youth, who was now on his feet, enjoying the attention.

'I'm not questioning Charlie's qualities or his achievements,' she said tactfully. 'I admire the way he forced himself into the game – but he's not the only one. So now another youngster has a chance to make a name for himself.'

The tact was wasted, however, as the youth snarled back at her witheringly.

'Well, who is it, then? You'd probably sign that cheating dago Maradona. He's your sort, isn't he?'

Gabriella tried to work out whether this reference to 'your sort' meant that she was a 'dago' too, but the supporters' chairman had already come to that conclusion and now intervened on her behalf.

'Order, please, gentlemen! Mrs Benson comes here to open a much-needed channel of communication with us supporters, and it's not helped if that channel's blocked with cheap abuse!'

From the back of the room came a very loud 'hear, hear'. It was Simon. Gabriella winced as she noticed that his hand was up, waiting to catch the chairman's attention, which he duly did.

'Can I just say,' Simon boomed, 'that in the sort of circles I move in, someone who acquired a property for nothing, developed it, and sold it off for £300,000 worth of profit would be hailed as an extremely successful business-person!'

Most of the supporters had turned to register this curious intruder in the smart suit, although it was clear from the silence which followed Simon's intervention that nobody saw the point of what he was saying. The chairman looked at Gabriella, obviously expecting her to react to the contribution.

'I thank the gentleman for his remark,' she responded in a clipped tone, 'but fear that he doesn't understand the essence of the game.'

She turned away from Simon and addressed the room in general.

'Now, what I was going to say before our friend across here became overheated,' she resumed, pointing at the table of 'lads', 'was that I've promoted Paul Kennedy from the reserves to take Charlie's place.'

She craned her head in the direction of Steve Simms.

'Got that, Mr Simms?'

Simms gave her a patronizing smile as she stared at him. Then she turned away again.

'I believe we have an exciting team in the making, Paul Kennedy included. So I hope you'll give him extra encouragement on Saturday.'

She gave the chairman a firm nod, and he rightly took this as the cue to wind up proceedings.

'I think we'd all second that, Mrs Benson,' he said. 'Thank you once again for coming!'

There was a ripple of applause, led by the chairman and the two players sitting behind him. The small group of dissenting lads stayed silent. Gabriella thanked Nicholl and McGregor for giving up their time, and she made her way through the room towards Simon, who was leaning against the door, looking rather pleased with himself. Gabriella eyed him irritably.

'In Parliament, that would have been denounced as a planted question.'

'Just trying to stick up for you,' Simon said with a smile, nodding over at the table of lads, 'somebody needed to. Anyway, I'm an expert now – read six back pages after you left this morning.'

'Well, guess which one he wrote,' she challenged Simon, seeing Steve Simms sidling towards her.

'You got off lightly there, if you ask me, boss,' he smirked. Gabriella forced a polite smile. 'Er, this Kennedy lad – he's black, isn't he?' he asked.

'Yes, what of it?'

'Nothing,' Simms said innocently. 'Abyssinia!' he added in a matey way and sauntered off. Gabriella was too weary even to consider what he might be up to.

'Er, *The Times*?' guessed Simon valiantly.

Gabriella shook her head slowly, took his arm and led him from the club. Behind her, the organ had been moved to centre-stage, and the coloured lights had been turned on. A throng of men and their wives were spilling through from the bar ready for the evening's more vital entertainment.

Gabriella heard her first warning bell of disquiet about Steve Simms's activities when she arrived for training the next morning. On the far side of the field she caught sight of Morris and Kennedy posing for a photographer, while a practice game was going on under Eddie's supervision. She guessed that Eddie had been 'bunged' for allowing this intrusion, and as she stormed towards the two black players, the photographer made himself scarce.

Tony Morris tried to allay her suspicions by suggesting that the photo-call was a boost for Paul Kennedy on the occasion of his first League game. Gabriella might have felt better about this if she hadn't then been told that the photographer waddling off into the distance with his camera bags worked for Steve Simms's paper. Morris and Kennedy seemed blithely unconcerned about what had occurred, and she dispatched them to continue their training. But Gabriella had an uneasy feeling that they might regret being so willing for a tabloid photographer.

By Saturday morning the man's handiwork was revealed, aided by a few distinctive touches from Simms himself. Paul Kennedy opened up the page for Tony Morris's benefit when he came to pick him up for the game. Morris leaned across and registered the photo – one of several taken – which showed the two of them posing as boxers, complete with boxing gloves and head-guards provided by the photographer. He'd brought them along, he'd told them, in case they needed a 'fun-shot'. While Morris admired the photo, it was clear that young Paul Kennedy was not amused.

'Read the shit they've put underneath,' he told Morris. Morris obliged.

'Seventeen-year-old new-boy Paul Kennedy gets shown the ropes by Tony Morris before today's clash at Princess Park. Striker Paul reckons the visitors are in for a knock-out time – and after them, it's roll on Honeyghan and Bruno!'

Morris chuckled to himself, unaware of the despairing look on Kennedy's face.

'What's wrong with that?'

'Well, it makes me sound like a right cocky, aggressive sod, doesn't it? I never said anything to him about boxing or knock-outs . . . *and* it sort of says that that's all black people can do.'

Morris handed the paper back to him with a shrug and started the car.

'It's only paper-talk.'

'Yeah, but it's the one Halliwell and Coughlan read, isn't it? They're gonna make my life a load of fun this afternoon,' said Kennedy, looking worried.

Tony Morris didn't see any need for a fuss. He'd been a pro for nearly seven years and was used to the press striking certain attitudes to black footballers. If he needed to, he consoled himself with the thought that he'd gone out and achieved something, become a full-time player, and was earning good money, probably as much as any second-rate journalist or photographer. For young Kennedy, though, on the threshold of his career, his image was a sensitive issue.

'Listen, you'll be getting stick whatever the papers say. You've just got to live with it, Paul,' said Morris blandly. He punched a cassette of modern gospel music into the stereo-player, and pulled the car quickly away from the kerb.

As they neared the ground, they passed a wedge of visiting supporters, mostly in their teens, being escorted to the ground by a phalanx of policemen. They were chanting the usual 'Here we go!' anthem, although they gave off a sense of menace rather than boisterousness as they waved Union Jacks and flags of St George, emblazoned with the name of their team. Kennedy also saw that quite a few bore the inked-in motif N F, letters he'd grown up seeing on every wall in his area.

By the time kick-off approached, when the dressing-room was bustling with activity, the various images of the morning had combined with a natural nervousness to leave Kennedy silent and tense. He stared vacantly ahead of him, trying to clear his mind for the game.

Gary Halliwell drew Gabriella's attention to this, albeit in his usual heavy-handed fashion.

'Here, boss – have a word with young Paul, will you? He's gone a bit pale.'

Gabriella didn't laugh at the 'joke', but she was grateful for the nudge in Kennedy's direction. She headed across to where he was sitting, noticing that he was nervously wiggling his legs to stop the muscles getting tight.

'All right, Paul? Or are you just reacting to being featured in the *Daily Star*?'

This was intended as a light-hearted slap on the wrist, but Kennedy was unable to discern the tone and took it solemnly.

'Sorry about that, boss. He fitted me up. Won't happen again.'

'Yeah, well – just be careful, eh? If those guys tried to photograph me, they'd have me in a gondola selling ice-cream.'

That was as far she wanted to take the issue – what was important now was to get the kid's mind on the game. She called Tony Morris over to join them. Morris broke off from his stretching routine and wandered over. Gabriella gestured for him to sit down next to Kennedy.

'I can't get near him with his knees knocking like that!'

He patted Kennedy reassuringly on the shoulder as he sat down.

'I hope you're more helpful on the pitch, Tone.'

Gabriella sat between them, anxious to cut the banter out and get them concentrating.

'All right, settle down now. Remember what we talked about yesterday. I want you switching all across their back four, go wide if you want, and don't be afraid to turn. You've both got skill, so use it! Paul – if a shot's on, take it! Just because it's your first game, don't feel you can't be selfish, okay?'

Morris winked at Gabriella.

'But if you don't pass to me, Paul, I'll never talk to you again.'

Kennedy smiled at this, the tension easing with the talk. Gabriella got up and left them to it, going round the dressing-room to give little talks to individual players, which was more her style than making gung-ho speeches to the team. Kennedy, meanwhile, started taking in deep breaths and exhaling loudly in order to slow his pulse.

'Were you nervous in your first game, Tone?'

'Yeah!' said Morris generously. 'The worst thing is there's no toilets out there! You'll be all right. Just do the simple things. Get a feel of the game. And don't pay any attention to the crowd. Especially not today.'

'I ain't worried about that lot,' Kennedy said defiantly.

'Well, they'll be after you, son. You and me are prime targets. I mean this visiting mob are more used to having black kids running *away* from 'em than running at 'em!'

Kennedy flexed his shoulders aggressively.

'Bollocks to that! Anyone starts having a go at me, I'll be in the crowd to sort 'em out!'

Although there were only a few hundred visiting supporters standing on the open terraces behind one goal, none the less the atmosphere was intimidating. They'd draped their flags over the wire fencing, and the tight little knot of hard-core racists behind the goal made a point of booing the names of the two black players in Gabriella's team more loudly than the others as they were announced over the tannoy.

Gabriella tried to shut her ears to it as she took her seat in the front row of the directors' box, especially as she saw Kennedy's family in their seats near by. But it was hard not to notice, as the game got under way, that every time Morris or Kennedy touched the ball, there was a chorus of monkey noises from the mob on the visitors' terracing.

The reception on the pitch was no less intimidating. The visiting team had a raw-boned, mean-looking defender, who seemed to make a point of jostling and niggling at Kennedy whenever he got the ball. It made professional sense to pressurize a new player, but it soon spilled over into unpleasantness. Kennedy had a ball knocked quickly up to him, while running out wide. He sensed the defender hurtling in for the tackle, and so turned and let the ball run past him rather than trapping it himself. The defender thus had no chance of winning the ball, but he made sure that he caught Kennedy with a scything whirl of legs and arms, sending him crashing to the turf.

As Kennedy writhed in pain and the referee blew for a free-kick, the defender quickly made token gestures of apology by standing over the stricken Kennedy and patting him on the shoulder. Only he and Kennedy, however, heard what was said to accompany the gesture. 'Don't take the piss, or I'll break your leg, you black bastard.'

Kennedy was in too much pain to react, and the defender now successfully avoided the booking his foul merited by putting a friendly arm round the referee's shoulder and looking contrite. While Kennedy received treatment, Gabriella couldn't help looking across at his family, and wondering how much they were suffering, seeing their Paul abused in this way. As Gabriella turned away, she caught sight of a policeman standing on a gantry in the roof of the stand. He had a video-camera trained on the end where the visiting supporters stood chanting, 'Let him die, let him die, let him die!' in response to Kennedy's injury. Gabriella tried hard to block out the anger and despair she felt welling up inside her – how had the game come to this?

Fortunately, as is always the case with football, the play itself provided the antidote to the poison threatening it, and in the second half a sweeping move involving an incisive pass from Nicholl and a clever flick from Kennedy left Tony Morris free. Morris moved quickly on goal and slammed a firm low shot under the body of the goalkeeper as he came out.

Most of the team jumped on Kennedy and Morris to celebrate a well-worked goal. Gabriella, still sitting in the directors' box, was restricted to applauding enthusiastically, but she had to smile at the sight of the Kennedy family up on their feet near by, saluting the goal, ignoring the pleas of a commissionaire for suitable decorum. The noise of the home fans' jubilation was counter-balanced, however, by another surge of ominous booing and chanting from the wedge of visiting supporters.

They had certainly noticed that the goal had been fashioned and executed by two black players, and so the level of vocal intimidation increased as the second half continued, especially as Gabriella's team was playing towards that end. It didn't seem to affect Tony Morris, who again broke free on the right, only to be prevented from crossing by a desperate tackle. But a corner was won, and this brought the visiting fans flocking down to the fence, so that they could get as close as possible to the pitch.

Kennedy, taking up a position at the near post, was aware of the movement out of the corner of his eye, but it wasn't until a torrent of spittle began to rain down on him that he realized they were directing their intimidation at him. He tried to concentrate on the corner-kick, as the defender jostled him from behind, but then bananas began to land around his feet, and he saw the faces behind the wire grunting their hate at him. Kennedy's mind was a swirl of images and noise – he was struck dumb. But then through the noise he heard the defender behind him, shouting in his ear.

'Oi, nigger! Feeding time!'

Kennedy snapped at this and drew his right arm forward before slamming his elbow backwards into the defender's midriff. The defender went down with a theatrical fall and a mêlée ensued, with various visiting players trying to get at Kennedy, while some of Kennedy's team-mates ran to protect him. The referee pulled Kennedy from the ruck and booked him instantly, ignoring Kennedy's forlorn gestures at the spittle on his shirt and the bananas lying on the edge of the pitch.

Gabriella was alarmed by the incident, and she left her seat in the box to make her way quickly down to the dug-out at the side of the pitch. The match had resumed by the time she arrived, and she sat down between Eddie and Norman.

'He was lucky not to be sent off!' Eddie shouted into her ear.

'It's those bloody animals behind the goal – he shouldn't have let them get to him!' she protested.

'Bollocks,' sneered Eddie. 'His bottle's gone!'

Eddie had obviously decided to make Gabriella's selection of Kennedy an issue of her professional judgement, because there was a distinct tone of 'I told you so' in his words. Gabriella was more concerned about the effect of the crowd's intimidation on Kennedy, and she could now see as she watched that his concentration had gone. He drifted out to the left wing, 'hiding' from further involvement. Now as a ball was passed to him, he was either too preoccupied or too scared to run for it, and the pass trickled lamely out of play. Halliwell ran towards the dug-out, screaming his frustration.

'Hey! Hey! Get him off!'

He signalled for Kennedy to be substituted. Gabriella stayed stony-faced. Eddie was at her ear again.

'The skipper's right! Leave him out there now, and he'll be destroyed! You got him into this – get him out!'

Gabriella weighed up the odds on the decision – could it demoralize Kennedy more or throw her judgement further into question? Or would bringing him off now save him from further punishment? Gabriella laid aside her own pride and muttered for one of the substitutes to warm up. He leaped out eagerly on to the running-track, while Eddie quickly located the numbered boards used to indicate to the crowd and the referee which player was being replaced.

Kennedy hung his head when he saw that he was to be brought off. Everything seemed to him to have fallen apart in the space of a few minutes. Tony Morris ran over quickly to offer consolation.

'Go on, son. You've won it for us! And for Christ's sake, *limp*!'

Kennedy looked angry at the suggestion that he should feign injury to save face. He ran off to the edge of the pitch with as much poise as he could muster in the circumstances. Gabriella waited to greet him, applauding his efforts for the benefit of the crowd.

'Well played, Paul!' she shouted encouragingly. 'Now straight into the bath!'

She tossed him a tracksuit top, and he disappeared down the tunnel, unable to hide his relief at escaping from the arena. The home supporters cheered him gamely, while the louts on the visitors' terrace saluted their 'victory' gleefully with more monkey noises.

Gabriella walked back towards the dug-out pensively. She felt the need to get to Kennedy now, in the privacy of the empty dressing-room, to talk to him before the rest of the team got in the way. She leaned into the dug-out.

'How long left, Eddie?'

Eddie checked his watch. 'About four . . . maybe five with injury time.'

Gabriella turned and walked off down the touch-line towards the tunnel, satisfied that the team would hold on for the win.

Eddie was astonished at her behaviour. He leaned out on to the track and yelled at her.

'You job's out here, lady!'

But she had already disappeared down the tunnel.

Gabriella found Kennedy sitting alone in the dressing-room, his socks rolled down to his ankles. He was slumped against the wall, obviously tearful. He sat up as Gabriella came in, wiping his eyes with his sleeve.

'Sorry, boss – I blew it,' he sniffed.

'Rubbish. You done brilliant!'

The attempt at humouring him with a football cliché didn't work, because he slammed his fists down on the bench.

'I should have just waited till I could do him in a tackle!'

Gabriella understood his feelings, but she didn't like the sound of his reasoning. She offered a slight caution, not wanting to be too hard on him at this stage.

'Maybe. I'd better get back. We can talk after the game if you like?'

'I don't want to talk about that shit!' he said angrily, hating her reasonableness. He got up and stomped off towards the team bath. He showed her his shirt, flecked with spittle.

'I'd better get this off before I catch rabies,' he said.

Gabriella gave him a challenging look but thought better of shouting him down. He was full of self-justification at the moment; the time for a bollocking would come later. Besides, she felt a lot of sympathy for him. Gabriella made her way out into the corridor. Moments later the teams came clattering in, as the match had just ended. Gabriella stood to one side, offering her congratulations on the win. At the end of the tunnel she saw Eddie walking towards her, still looking agitated. Gabriella pointed a warning finger at him.

'Another three points, Eddie – so don't say anything I can make you regret!'

Eddie had another weapon lined up to assault her with. 'The ref just told me he'd have sent Kennedy off, if it hadn't been his first game!'

'So, he got lucky,' Gabriella shrugged.

'No, *you* got lucky. You put a boy in to do a man's job, and he nearly drowned!'

As always, Gabriella responded to Eddie's attacks with a gut instinct to insult his intelligence. 'Pick a metaphor, any metaphor,' she mocked. 'He'll be *all right!*'

'You hope!' Eddie shouted, before pushing past her and heading in through the dressing-room door. Gabriella leaned against the wall and tried to gather her thoughts.

She hated being wrong, but she recognized that Kennedy had been let down by his temperament. He'd suffered appalling racist provocation, but she wished he'd behaved more professionally. The afternoon had hurt her – the stinging sense of a personal misjudgement, mixed with the nightmarish taunting from the terraces, had left her both confused and angry.

Gabriella changed and eventually made her way up to the boardroom to meet Simon, who'd insisted on coming to the match. He was standing alone, because, keen as he was to show some enthusiasm for the sake of his relationship with Gabriella, he didn't really enjoy talking to the director-types, who all struck him as petty criminals in expensive clothes. He was grateful to see her and offered a congratulatory kiss.

'What did you make of it all?' she asked, her normal teasing tone absent for once.

'Well, the football was fine, but the atmosphere' – he moved confidentially towards her – 'it was like a National Front rally!'

Gabriella nodded her agreement. Fuelled by Simon's reaction, she headed across to where Coombs and Fisher were sharing drinks affably with the chairman of the visiting club.

'Ah, here's the conquering heroine,' hailed Coombs extravagantly. 'Gabriella, this is Mr Hilditch, chairman of –'

'Scumbag United?' Gabriella suggested.

Fisher and Coombs looked pained, while Hilditch's face registered astonishment.

'I beg your pardon?' he stuttered.

'Sorry, it was a reference to that mob of Hitler Youth who follow you around,' she explained with an ironic smile.

'Well, yes, I know they can be a little hostile.'

'Ever done anything about it?' Gabriella demanded petulantly. 'Attacked them in the club programme, condemned them over the tannoy, told them you don't want them in your ground?'

Gabriella was well out of control, having found someone she could vent her frustration and anger upon. Coombs put a restraining hand on her shoulder.

'Gabriella, this isn't the time or the place,' he said firmly.

'There was a young player of mine in tears half an hour ago thanks to the racial abuse he got this afternoon!'

Fisher stepped between them making placatory noises, and gave Gabriella a smile that was intended to be light-hearted.

'Look Gabriella – it's part and parcel of the game – not to mention life! I've had "yid" and "Jew-boy" for as long as I can remember! It's character-forming!'

She gave him a withering look. 'Yes, I can see that.'

Disappointed by Coombs and Fisher's lack of support, she turned and stalked off. She knew she'd got on to her high horse about this issue and had transgressed against all sorts of footballing protocol, but, other than attacking the visiting chairman, there wasn't a meaningful course of action for her to take in defending her black players. She could hardly storm on to the terraces and attempt to engage the racist offenders in lively debate.

Fisher watched her leave and exhaled with relief. He escorted Mr Hilditch in the direction of the bar.

'Sorry about that, Mr Hilditch – she, er, staked a lot on young Kennedy today.'

Hilditch nodded unconvincingly. 'Well I've heard of bad losers, but I've never heard of bad winners before.'

Downstairs in the dressing-room the players were enjoying a long soak in the plunge-bath. Tony Morris lay next to Kennedy, who still seemed morose and detached, all the more so since none of the lads had come out and expressed sympathy with him. They all felt he was in the wrong to a certain extent.

Morris made a gallant attempt to shake Kennedy out of his torpor.

'Sod it, kid. We beat 'em, didn't we? They'll be going home sick and depressed because a couple of black guys turned 'em over!'

Kennedy said nothing, but then he didn't have much chance to think, as Gary Halliwell jumped loudly into the bath. Morris tried again.

'You've just got to get used to it, Paul. If they see it winding you up, they'll do it even more!'

'Yeah, that's a real winning argument that, Tone!' Kennedy said scathingly. 'Take the shit like a good boy!'

'Now watch it,' Tony Morris warned, seeing his good intentions mocked.

'*You* watch it, man!' Kennedy exclaimed. 'If some of you older guys had had more bottle, us younger kids wouldn't be facing this sort of filth!'

Everyone else in the bath had heard, and Halliwell, as captain, knew it was up to him to take action. He tossed a bar of soap into the water in front of Kennedy's face.

'Oi, that's enough! You don't slag an older pro, especially when you nearly lost us the game! Besides, I thought you were the little tough guy in this morning's paper?'

Kennedy shook his head disbelievingly, realizing that he would be lumbered for a long while with the newspaper caption.

Nicholl, who might have spoken up for Kennedy a little earlier had he not also taken the 'professional' view of events, tried nevertheless to redress the balance a little by offering evidence in Kennedy's defence.

'Hey, skipper – you didn't hear what that bastard said to him!'

'I don't care!' Halliwell said emphatically. 'His first responsibility is to the team!'

Nicholl's intervention roused Brian Rimmer, who just loved taking the piss out of Nicholl's 'leftie' sentiments. With his head bobbing on the surface like a great sea-lion, his eyes swivelled in Nicholl's direction.

'What are you getting all worked up about? It was only a few bananas', Rimmer boomed, to be greeted by a few laughs from fellow Rat Packers.

Hearing this, Kennedy stood up and waded towards the edge of the bath, pulling a surly face.

'Yeah, okay – nothing to worry about!' he muttered sarcastically as he slipped out.

Nicholl gave Rimmer an ironic smile as the keeper lay there, pleased with his contribution to the 'debate'.

'I'd have thought that, as a keeper, you'd have understood about stuff being thrown from the terraces – or are you so thick, you don't notice?'

'He collects all the coins, puts 'em towards his pension,' said Coughlan, to more laughter. Only Nicholl and his disciple, McGregor, seemed dismayed by the return to the usual post-match banter.

'That's it,' Nicholl said witheringly, 'sod reality, back to bloody play-time again! The kid's been hurt!'

McGregor saw his chance to back Nicholl up and to display some of his recently acquired learning.

'Yeah, I've been reading a couple of books about psychological scars,' he managed to get out, before Rimmer's head surfaced again.

'Oh, leave it out, Tweedledum! He's lucky it wasn't a coconut!'

The others all roared with laughter, while Nicholl and McGregor shrugged at each other in dismay, though Tony Morris couldn't help falling quiet. He was a fringe Rat Pack member, and ordinarily would be among the first to join in the jokes. But here he found them unhelpful – he was troubled by the incident with Kennedy, but not just by what it said about the kid's temperament. *He'd* found a way of dealing with racism within the game over the years, but now that was being challenged – not by white liberals like Nicholl but by an angry young black guy who had only just come into the game.

After their bath the team adjourned to the players' lounge: a small, formica-clad room under the main stand, where both of the teams and their families met for drinks and chat, with the enmities of the match put behind them. Bottled lager was the order of the day from the tiny counter which served as a bar, a sharp contrast to the opulence of the boardroom, thirty feet above. While Halliwell and the other senior pros mingled happily with the opposition lads, Kennedy sat as far away from the throng as he could manage in the cramped room. He was still lost in his thoughts as Tony Morris ferried another bottle over to him.

'Here, drown your sorrows,' Morris said in a conciliatory tone. 'Not that you should have any,' he added.

Kennedy took the bottle and drank straight from it, without any word of thanks.

'You could apologize to me if you wanted,' Morris tried.

Kennedy looked up at him and gave him a pained smile. 'Unfortunately, I meant what I said.'

'Look, Paul, if you're gonna stay in the first team, you have to learn to – '

Kennedy interrupted quickly. 'No, *please* – not the lecture about "taking stick". Tony, you heard it out there today. *On* the terraces, *on* the pitch – it was hate, man! And you expect me to hide my feelings and maybe come in here as though nothing was said?'

He waggled the bottle in the direction of Halliwell, who was chatting amiably with the defender who'd abused Kennedy, both verbally and physically, throughout the match. Morris took in the scene – for him it was normal practice now.

'It's the only way, Paul. Cyrille Regis did it, Barnsey's doing it, all the Arsenal lads – you let your football answer back! You wouldn't have got that shit today if you hadn't been playing well. You'd got them at it!'

Kennedy stood up, irritated. 'Where'd you grow up, Tony? Disneyland?'

Halliwell had been monitoring this row since it surfaced in the team bath, and in his basic captain's way, he saw an easy solution to it all. Paul just had to bite the bullet.

'Here, Paul – come over and have a drink with Mick.'

Kennedy looked at him scornfully. 'Sure, skipper – and we'll shake hands like men and forget all about it? Bollocks!'

Halliwell wasn't used to having his authority challenged, least of all by a player who was new to the team, and while he'd made concessions to Kennedy's youth, he felt the time was right for a captain's talk.

'Listen, you little prat, when you go out on that park, you put *everything* out of your mind, you understand, except the game. I don't care if your wife and family have been hit by a steam-roller the same morning, you don't show anything, right?'

Kennedy nodded sarcastically and made a great show of weariness. At the door, Kennedy's family had appeared, eager to join their son.

'You'd better cheer up, your mum and dad's here,' said Morris.

Kennedy saw them, and quickly his face changed to a confident smile, as he waved them over.

Morris nudged Halliwell pointedly. 'See? He can do it if he tries.'

That might have been the end of the incident there and then. Kennedy might have realized his concerns were selfish in the context of a team game, and by Monday morning it might all have been forgotten. But at that moment Gabriella was walking along the touch-line in front of the empty visitors' terracing. A groundsman was taking the net down from the posts as she walked behind the goal. He saw her register the bananas dotted around the goal-mouth, a surreal confetti left over from the match.

'Same every time they come – I could open a stall,' the groundsman observed.

Gabriella gave him a rueful smile and continued her stroll through the 'scene of the crime'. An instinct had taken her there – not so much her own guilt at the possibility of throwing Kennedy into a situation he couldn't handle, but more like a morbid wish to confirm that the evil she had witnessed had actually taken place.

Behind her two ground-staff were busy brushing up the debris from the terrace, the usual load of empty beer cans and litter. Scattered all over the terrace, though, were an unusual number of what looked like leaflets. She called through the wire fencing to one of the ground-staff, and he brought a handful down to her, passing them through the metal grilles.

Gabriella looked at one of the leaflets in horror. Printed at the top, in large letters, and underlined in red, was a simple, chilling slogan: KEEP FOOTBALL WHITE! Underneath, the text went on about the threat of yids and niggers taking over football. It went on to urge 'all true English supporters' to 'frighten the niggers out of our game'.

Gabriella shivered at the brutality of it. Most managers would have ignored them, assuming that they would have noticed in the first place. But for Gabriella they represented more than just a threat to the game she loved. She folded a couple of the leaflets into her coat pocket and walked away, back towards the security of the main stand.

CHAPTER TEN

By six thirty Gabriella was sitting in the office of Inspector Willis at the town's police headquarters. She'd got his name from Fisher back in the boardroom, where she'd also broken the news to Simon that their quiet Saturday-night dinner out would have to wait. Willis was the officer in charge of policing at the football club. The strain of coping with the visiting fans was written across his weary face, as he handed the leaflets back across his desk to Gabriella.

'Very distasteful – but there's not much we can do about it, Mrs Benson.'

Gabriella took the hint. 'By not much, you mean "nothing", I take it? Well, isn't an incitement to "frighten the niggers out of our game" at least a public order offence?'

Willis ran his hands down his face. His tunic jacket hung on the back of his chair, his tie was undone, and the white collar of his shirt was soiled with the day's policing. He was hardly looking at her as he spoke.

'Probably. Mrs Benson, I've had over thirty-five officers on duty at your match today. Two of them are in hospital now, one with stab wounds to his shoulder. Four shops were smashed and looted, and a railway ticket-inspector – a woman – was sexually assaulted. There have been forty-eight arrests. But I happen to think we got off lightly. We got a result – and so did you. Let's call it a day, shall we?'

Gabriella felt the sympathy he was trying to elicit turn to anger at his bland indifference to her visit.

'I sympathize with what you've been through inspector, but

I'm offering you a little job variation here. You see the "lads" who produce this sort of leaflet aren't your everyday hooligan. They're more of what you might call political activists.'

Willis's reaction to her lecture was instant. 'Maybe you should try Special Branch, then? 'Cos I'm just an ordinary copper,' he said sarcastically.

Gabriella realized she'd exhausted her initial approach and so tried a different tack.

'You videoed the match today, didn't you?' she asked.

'We video the *crowd*, not the match, Mrs Benson. A useful spin-off from Heysel.' He gave her a patronizing smile.

'I agree – so if I can show a mob of racists acting provocatively, I can get a conviction, can I?'

Willis shook his head slowly.

'Not in the real world. Now broken heads and knife wounds, those I can deal with. More importantly, so can a jury.'

'That's child's play compared with what this lot want to provoke,' she challenged.

Gabriella sat back in her chair and stared at him, defying him to throw her out. After a pause Willis pulled open a drawer and handed a video-cassette over to her. He nodded at the video-machine and television on the shelf in his office.

'Help yourself. I'm afraid I'm five hours late for my lunch-break.'

With that, Willis pulled his tunic off the chair and walked out of the office. Gabriella knew she hadn't got far, but at least Willis had let her put her foot in the door. Gabriella switched the television on and inserted the cassette, sitting back to absorb the 'other' experience that the football match had created that afternoon.

The video-camera had indeed, as Willis said, concentrated on the crowd, principally the open terracing where the visiting supporters had been massed. Gabriella pieced together the crowd reactions with the fragments of the match visible on the edges of the video picture. Throughout, the muffled noises of the crowd's monkey chants provided a nauseating sound-track.

Despite her fascination, Gabriella soon found herself stifling yawns, and she fast-forwarded into the second half and the incident which led to Kennedy's booking.

On the edge of the frame, she saw Kennedy take up his position at the near post. She saw a wedge of fans clamber on to the fence and pelt the young player with a hail of bananas, and then, seconds later, his violent retaliation on the defender standing close behind him.

Gabriella rewound the tape and ran the sequence again, this time concentrating on the 'fans' on the fence. About fifteen of them were directly involved in the throwing. She shook her head in despair, but then sat forward as she saw something strange. She froze the picture with the remote-control hand-set and studied the faces in the centre of the group. There, right in the middle, was the youth who had given her such a rough ride at the supporters' club meeting earlier in the week.

She replayed the 'action' several times over, revealing that it was definitely him, and that at least two of the lads on the fence with him had been at his side in the club. Gabriella began to consider the reasons why alleged supporters of her own team should be in with the opposing fans, abusing a member of their own team.

She was still preoccupied by this when she arrived home after ten. Simon had already gone to bed, presumably in a silent protest at her ruining his plans for a sociable evening. She found him reading by a bedside light, studiously avoiding looking at her.

'Good time?' he inquired ironically.

'Yes. Running through a video-nasty with an exhausted policeman. It's what Saturday nights are for.'

Simon looked over his book. 'I put your supper in the fridge.'

'Thanks. I'm too tired to eat.'

'And I picked up a barrel of beer for tomorrow. That's what they drink, isn't it – footballers? And a bottle of Malibu for the wives.'

With her strenuous day, Gabriella had almost forgotten that

she'd arranged for the team and their wives to come over for Sunday lunch. It had been an idea enthusiastically endorsed by Simon in his post-Camilla phase, in the hope of forging a better understanding with Gabriella. But at this precise moment Gabriella felt it was the last thing she needed. She began to undress, still thinking of the video picture.

'Curious,' she thought out loud, hoping to enlist Simon's interest.

His weary reaction told her that she hadn't. 'What?' he said, laying aside his book again.

'That lad, the one who gave me a hard time at the club the other night. He was in with the away fans this afternoon, throwing bananas at Paul Kennedy.'

Simon couldn't stop himself from snorting with contempt. 'Well, let's invite him round tomorrow. I'm beginning to admire the intellectual depths in football!'

This was pure petulance on Simon's part, and he regretted it as soon as he'd said it, particularly as it earned him a weary, hurt look from Gabriella.

'Sorry – I'm just pissed off at losing another night with you. I understand that you feel guilty about pushing Kennedy in at the deep end, but I don't – '

'*Guilty?*' Gabriella snapped, stung by the accusation.

'Oh, come on – even Martin Fisher noticed it! *Another* victim of your great obsession!' Simon accompanied this with an ironic salute.

Gabriella stopped undressing, turned and stalked off towards the bathroom. Simon threw his book on the floor. He attempted to make love to Gabriella when she returned in the hope of easing the tension between them, but she responded so blandly to his touches that he abandoned the notion. He turned over and went to sleep on the far edge of the bed, thinking of the Sunday, bloody Sunday, ahead of him.

·

The players and their wives and girlfriends duly turned up at lunch-time, more out of curiosity than loyalty, and spread themselves around the spacious rooms of Gabriella's house in awkward little groups. Most of the players quickly ditched their wives for the various male cliques that sustained them during the week, while the women were left to admire the furnishings and fabrics. Simon and Gabriella shuffled dutifully between them, serving drinks and trying to put them at their ease, without success in Simon's case. He had difficulty remembering Halliwell's name and could scarcely conceal a smirk when Halliwell's wife ordered a Malibu.

Gabriella made a point of talking to the women, but she couldn't really get beyond questions about her furniture or discussions about the whole salmon that was the centre-piece of the buffet. How had she been able to find the time to manage the team on Saturday and prepare this food, they wondered. Gabriella didn't want to say she'd done it all herself, partly because it wasn't true, partly because she felt it was intimidating to the wives to have this 'superwoman' paraded before them. On the other hand, the truth – that she'd hired someone to come in and help that morning – smacked a little too much of effortless privilege. So Gabriella shrugged the questions off with a smile.

Meanwhile the various team factions had consolidated their positions. McGregor kept within striking distance of Nicholl, while Tony Morris and Kennedy and their girls formed a group near the stereo, and the Rat Pack of Coughlan, Halliwell and Rimmer retreated to the conservatory, where Simon had placed the beer barrel.

From there the threesome could see out on to the spacious grounds which surrounded the house. Materialism was a common spirit among most footballers, who were aware that their often short careers had to be devoted to gaining as much financial security as possible.

Brian Rimmer surveyed the opulence of the house and gardens, and reflected ruefully on his lot.

'You know, I'd have to have my testimonial game against Real Madrid or someone to afford a gaff like this.'

Paul Kennedy had been monitoring the threesome for a while. He eventually broke away from his girlfriend and Tony Morris and wandered into the conservatory on the pretext of getting himself a beer. What he *really* wanted was to find out if he was still in the dog-house with the skipper Gary Halliwell. They didn't acknowledge him as he came in and began topping up his glass from the barrel.

'If you're gonna send me to Coventry, do I get a cut of the transfer fee?'

There was a grudging pause while they assessed the worth of this remark. It was still a little on the arrogant side, when what they really required of him was humility or an apology. Nevertheless, Rimmer felt sufficiently encouraged to talk to him.

'See you got a good write-up in the *People* this morning – seven marks out of ten!'

It was a clever gambit by Rimmer, inviting either further arrogance or a modest disclaimer from Kennedy.

'Yeah, well – the bloke probably left at half-time,' he said, pointedly admitting to his disastrous second half. He faced Halliwell directly. 'I'm sorry, skipper. I was out of order yesterday. I can't say it won't happen again, but –' Kennedy shrugged sheepishly. He'd gone through a lot of thinking the previous night, and had concluded that the team's welfare came before his own private concerns.

Halliwell held out a hand in response. 'That'll do, son.'

Kennedy shook it, and smiles broke out on all their faces.

'Here, Paul,' Halliwell continued pleasantly, 'now you're in the first team, you've gotta meet us tomorrow at three o'clock in the Seven Stars.' He accompanied this with a conspiratorial wink to the others.

'*Three* o'clock?' asked Kennedy puzzled.

'Yeah, we have a lock-in organized there, after all the normals have gone back to work. Monday's always a Full Bifters Day!'

Kennedy smiled and shook his head, getting the picture – they all laughed in recognition of their own waggishness.

The noise in the conservatory attracted Simon's attention.

He'd found himself trapped with Nicholl and McGregor, who were busy trying to show off their social mobility and reading power to someone they obviously felt was an equal.

'Funny – we don't socialize much as a team,' remarked Nicholl, gesturing at the 'occasion' around him.

'Well, Keith and I have started going to the theatre occasionally,' blurted out McGregor, 'but, er, don't mention it to anyone, though.'

'Of course not,' Simon said, smiling tactfully. 'But I thought you'd be out together all the time, as a team.'

Nicholl tilted his head back as he considered this. 'No, it's a popular misconception, really. We're just a bunch of blokes doing a job together. No reason why we should live in each other's pockets. I mean, do lawyers go round in packs?'

Simon smiled, at ease with this more fluent conversation than with the terse mutterings of Halliwell and Coughlan.

'Well, there're a few "hoo-rays" in my firm,' he chuckled.

McGregor nodded in the direction of the conservatory, where Kennedy was still chatting with Coughlan, Rimmer and Halliwell.

'They're *our* tearaways.'

Simon studied them. 'I thought the young black chap had only just come into the team?'

'Ah, but they'll be recruiting him now, I expect.'

Simon smiled but then looked more serious as Nicholl brought up the subject which had dogged his weekend.

'Bit bad the treatment he got yesterday, wasn't it?'

'You mean the animal impersonations?'

Nicholl nodded.

'Yes, I'm afraid Gabriella has become rather worked up about it all,' Simon added, looking for sympathy.

'Good for her,' said Nicholl heartily. 'About time somebody in the game took a stand.'

'Yeah, I mean he could have psychological scars after that,' McGregor added, seeing his opportunity to impress again.

Simon's ease had ebbed a little, as he sensed the conversation turning away from cheerful superficiality. Now Nicholl was wagging a finger at him.

'You see, the terraces are a real breeding ground for fascism. I mean, I happen to think it was symbolic that in Chile they shot leftists in a football stadium.'

Simon's eyes began to glaze over, but Nicholl was only just getting into his stride.

'And you realize that all this violence is seen by these racist thugs as part of their plan to disrupt the game on a European scale. Look what happened in the European championships! The German and English racists joined forces against the Dutch fans!'

Simon nodded with a fixed smile on his face, trying to disguise the fact that he was virtually asleep standing up.

After the players left, Simon stretched out on the sofa with the papers, trying to recover. Gabriella piled the dirty glasses and plates into the dishwasher and returned for a final scan for debris.

'Any more?'

Simon craned his head over the arm of the sofa and looked round. 'Don't think so – oh, there was one breakage by the way. I hope it isn't an omen, but your goal-keeper dropped a glass in the conservatory.'

'Only one?' Gabriella smiled. Simon's face lit up. She came and sat on the arm of the sofa, and he began to think she was actually going to relax.

'How do you think it went?' she asked.

'I think a "scoreless" draw is the phrase, isn't it? I certainly don't envy you trying to motivate them, though.'

Gabriella knew what he meant, because she'd felt the same way when she'd first met them. But now she'd got to know them better.

'They're not a bad bunch.' She began to stroke a bare section of his leg, just above the sock line. It was an absent, affectionate gesture, no more – but Simon felt instantly electrified.

'I don't suppose you fancy the rest of the afternoon in bed? Make up for last night,' he said, raising his eyebrows.

Gabriella looked at him mischievously, but then the shutters came down again.

'Sorry, I've got to go and see someone. Try to get to the bottom of this Nazi supporter business.'

He tried hard to hide his disappointment. 'Take that Nicholl bloke, why don't you? He could bore them into submission!'

Gabriella smiled and stood up. She kissed Simon on the forehead and headed for the door. He couldn't resist a last word, but it was said in sorrow rather than anger.

'You know, one day, Gabriella, you might eventually work out that our marriage is a good cause too!'

But he'd said it too quietly for her to hear.

.

The person she had to see was the chairman of the supporters' club. She'd telephoned him that morning, asking if he knew the name of the supporter who'd been questioning her so aggressively. She didn't mention his latest appearance on the police video, but as the chairman couldn't place him immediately, the question of why she wanted to identify him didn't arise.

The chairman led her through into the main room of the club, which was now deserted for a quiet couple of hours. Gabriella sniffed a little too loudly at the potent odour of beer and floor-cleaning liquid.

'Sorry about the smell. Sunday lunch is a big session for us. Sometimes I think most of 'em joined for the extra hour's drinking.'

Gabriella gave him an understanding smile. 'I can believe it.'

The chairman gestured for her to sit at one of the small circular tables which filled the body of the room. He wiped the surface carefully with his handkerchief, folded it away, and then leaned his forearms on the table.

'I think I've placed him now. Asked around a bit at lunchtime. Terry Ellis, he's called. Local lad. Printer. Been a member for about three years. Hadn't noticed him much, to be truthful, until he piped up against you the other night.'

'So there's no doubt that he's one of our supporters?'

'Well, no – unless he's – '

'Only here for the drinking, yes? Has he ever caused trouble?'

'Not that I know of,' said the chairman carefully. 'Can I ask what this is about?'

'I'd rather not say at this stage,' Gabriella said. 'Do you have an address for him, please?'

'It'll be in the office. Copley Estate, if I remember rightly. But if he's not at home, you could try the Eagle and Child – it's the only pub. I, er, wouldn't go unaccompanied, though.'

'Take a big dog, eh?' Gabriella asked, trying to keep the conversation light.

The chairman nodded emphatically.

'Eh! Didn't young Kennedy have a good game yesterday?' he suddenly exclaimed. 'Who needs Charlie O'Keefe?'

It was the nicest thing anyone had said to Gabriella all week.

.

Simon's wasn't the only Sunday afternoon disrupted by the Kennedy affair. Tony Morris had been dozing off in front of the television set when his front door-bell sounded. On the porch of his smart, modern home, he found Kennedy standing, still in the clothes he'd worn to Gabriella's party but looking extremely grave.

'Come in,' said Morris sleepily.

'No, I'd rather stay out here. I don't want to upset Beverley or nothing.'

Morris started to look more alert. 'What's the matter, kid?'

Kennedy shuffled around the porch a bit, head bowed. He shrugged, as if apologizing to himself.

'Well – I suppose I have to tell someone. When I got back home from the party, I found this on my welcome mat.'

From his jacket pocket he produced a leaflet – it had the same distinctive lettering and message as the ones Gabriella had found on the terraces. He handed it across to Tony, who started to read the printed text.

'Don't bother with that side – it's just general hatred . . . it's this that's worrying me.'

Kennedy turned the leaflet over for Morris. On the blank reverse side had been scrawled a personal message, which read: 'Kennedy – next time it's a poison dart!'

'Do you think I should take it seriously? I mean, it could be the lads doing a wind-up, couldn't it?' asked Kennedy with a hopeful rise in his voice.

'I doubt it,' said Morris, troubled now. 'I mean Rimmer and Coughlan can be a pair of sick prats at times, but that looks for real to me. I'm sorry, Paul, I never got anything as bad as this when I came into the game.'

Kennedy acknowledged the sympathy with a rueful nod.

'What do you think I should do? I mean, after yesterday, it looks like the more you try to fight back, the worse it gets.'

'You sound like me now!' Morris scolded. 'No, man – you're a professional footballer. You don't have to apologize for wanting protection from these headcases! I should talk to the boss, get her to approach the police.'

Kennedy thought about this for a moment. 'I think I'll sleep on it.'

But Morris grabbed Kennedy's arm urgently. His acceptance of assorted insults and outrages in favour of 'the quiet life' had been comprehensively challenged by the younger man's plight.

'Do it now, man!' Morris pleaded. 'It's later than you think!'

.

Gabriella had returned from the supporters' club, unsure of what to do about Terry Ellis. She now knew his address, that he was a printer by trade. She had some racially offensive leaflets as evidence, and she had access to the police video. It was a fairly convincing argument, it seemed to her, for his likely involvement in the National Front. But where could she go with that? To the police again, hoping to find Inspector Willis on a good night?

The arrival of an embarrassed and frightened Paul Kennedy cleared all the doubts from her mind. He tried to make jokes about the threats on the back of the leaflet, asking to be moved back into midfield if they were going to be throwing darts at him. Gabriella recognized the fear behind the humour and reassured him in determined fashion.

'Leave this to me to sort out, and I promise you I'll do as much as I can, Paul.'

Simon, making coffee in the kitchen for the three of them, winced to himself as he heard this further commitment from Gabriella.

'But you must promise *me*,' she went on to Kennedy, 'that it won't affect your game. In terms of confidence *and* in the way you conduct yourself. I understand the provocation, but I don't want a repetition of yesterday's incident.'

'I'll do my best,' smiled Kennedy, gratified that she was taking him seriously. This was in direct contrast to Simon, who plonked the tray of coffee down on the table, with a withering look at Gabriella.

'Ready for some coffee, dear? Or will you be popping out again?' he asked.

.

The supporters' club chairman had been right – the Copley Estate on a dark Sunday night, with a silvery drizzle wafting down in the glare of the sodium lighting, was no place to be unaccompanied. Gabriella got out of her car and surveyed the Eagle and Child pub. It looked like a besieged fortress, with its barbed-wire rolls on the roof and its barred windows. She wondered how safe her car, a late registration BMW convertible, would be in the pub's car-park, considering that there were two burnt-out hulks of automobiles near by. None the less she walked towards the pub, trying to compose herself.

She hadn't told Simon, because she knew that he would have come over all protective, and would have insisted on coming. But having a man around when you're confronting men, she'd reasoned, was likely to bring out the aggression in each side. So she was going into this dangerous territory quite consciously relying on her sex for protection. She snuggled into her coat, not just for warmth, as she walked hesitantly into the pock-marked pub.

It was still relatively early in the evening, and there were only a handful of determined drinkers in there, propped against the bar, haunted by the prospect of earlier closing that night. She kept walking, slowly, unobtrusively, around the central rectangle of the bar, until she reached a section of booths. Cigarette smoke was rising from one of them, and there was the sound of raucous laughter. A jarring, heavy-metal anthem crashed out of the video juke-box on the other side of the room.

Gabriella drew level with the occupied booth and saw that Terry Ellis was sitting there with four other friends. She thought she recognized at least three of them, both from the supporters' club evening and from the police video-tape. The lad facing her on the end of the bench seat was the first to register her presence.

'Hey, Terry – look who's here.'

The four other faces turned away from their drinks to see Gabriella. Even if she hadn't been the manager of the football club they claimed to support, she would still have looked an exotic, alien creature, with her expensive clothes and lean good looks. Gabriella stood still for a moment, letting them adjust to her being there.

'I don't believe it,' Ellis said with a leer, 'I had a wank about her last night!'

They laughed in unison. It was almost as if she was supposed to be deaf or insensitive as a prior condition of being a woman trespassing in this man's place.

'Are you Terry Ellis?' she asked firmly, looking at him. He seemed pleased with the recognition.

'Yeah – want a drink?' He made a move to slide out of the booth.

'No thanks.'

'Well, to what do we owe the honour, then? Come to continue the debate?' he smirked at her.

'Sort of. What did you think of Paul Kennedy yesterday?'

For the first time Ellis looked unsettled. It was clear that Gabriella had a purpose in being here, and from her manner it seemed a provocative one.

'All right,' he said defensively. 'Should have been sent off, though,' he said and leered knowingly to his pals.

'I don't know – I thought he slipped on a banana skin.'

It wasn't the most fluent of gambits, but, on the spur of the moment, it was the best she could manage. It certainly let Ellis and his friends know what was needling her.

'What's your game, missus?' Ellis said stonily.

'Not the same as yours. I know what you did yesterday, and I've a pretty good idea why you did it. As of now, you are expelled from the supporters' club, and if you ever show your face at the ground again, I'll have you arrested. The same goes for this lot.'

She nodded at Ellis's colleagues.

'You've got some front, talking like that,' Ellis sneered.

'But not "National", eh? You must have felt really at home with that lot yesterday.'

Gabriella was pushing her luck now, but she could see that the tough-looking landlord was hovering by the bar, sensing trouble. She assumed, rather hopefully, that he would leap to her defence, should Ellis have a go at her. For the moment, however, Ellis just pointed a warning finger. 'You're in big trouble, lady!'

Gabriella stood her ground. 'If you threaten me or my players in any way, I'll be only too glad to turn you over to the police before you can say "*Sieg Heil*".'

Ellis's face creased with hatred. 'You wanker! It's just a game to you, isn't it? Well it's our *life*! All we got, right? And we don't like it being taken over by niggers and yids. Or women. So piss off!'

'My pleasure.' She took one of the leaflets out of her pocket. 'Oh, and I'll be keeping this for reference.'

Gabriella put the leaflet away again, took a few steps backwards still facing them, then turned and walked as calmly as she could out of the pub. Ellis's colleagues looked at him in stunned silence, waiting for a lead, but he just pulled heavily on his cigarette and reached for his pint, with an expression of seething rage on his face.

Gabriella began walking quickly to her car. The cold night air brought a sobering reality to what she'd just done, and she could feel herself reacting to the shock of the confrontation. She climbed into the car and carefully locked all the doors, then started up and reversed. She was suddenly aware of dark shapes moving towards her across the shadowy car-park, and she slammed the car into forward gear. At that second there was a loud thump on the soft-top roof. She accelerated, and then the blade of a knife came ripping through the leather above her head. She could hear the car being kicked and hit by bricks or rubble amid a torrent of abuse.

She pushed the accelerator to the floor and the knife disappeared, along with the body attached to it. The car screeched out of the car-park and sped up the bleak street with its eerie yellow lighting. Two minutes later she was out of the estate and on a main road, where buses and pedestrians passed in what looked like a surreal display of ordinary life. Only then did she begin to slow the car and try to catch the breath that had seemed to disappear from her body.

After she'd parked back at the house and told Simon her story, he switched on all the exterior lights and paced around the car in horror and anger, seeing the damage.

'You're bloody mad! These people would think nothing of attacking a woman! What makes you think you're so special?' he raged at her.

'Sorry,' she said quietly. 'I suppose I should have asked you to come with me.'

Simon turned on her. 'Stuff that! I'm not getting carved up just because you decide to go on one of your mad bloody crusades! Now report this to the police and let *them* take the action!'

Gabriella gave him an ironic smile. 'I'm sure they'd be falling over themselves with excitement,' she said before going back into the house.

·

Mondays at the club were for catching up with administrative tasks. Gabriella used this an opportunity to send off letters to Inspector Willis, the supporters' club chairman and Martin Fisher, detailing her decision about Ellis and his cronies. It was a way, at least, of sharing the burden and provoking further official response. It was also, genuinely, what she wanted – to have people like Ellis out of the club she managed.

She signed the letters and handed them back to her secretary Marjorie. The phone rang on Gabriella's desk, and she groaned, resenting intrusions when she still had many more things to do that day. Marjorie put the letters down and moved to answer the phone.

'If it's press, I'm out please, Marje. Unless it's Steve Simms – I want to talk to him.'

Marjorie nodded and answered the phone with polite defensiveness. 'Just one moment please,' she stalled. 'It's your father,' she told Gabriella, cupping the mouthpiece in her hand.

Gabriella winced – her natural reaction to hearing from him now was one of suspicion.

'Oh, God – what's he up to now?' she sighed.

Sergio wouldn't tell her, but he insisted on seeing her for lunch in London later in the week. Gabriella put the phone down pensively, then shook off her unease and dialled Steve Simms's number – an act that, at any other time, would have made her even more uncomfortable. They arranged to meet in a pub near the ground at five thirty.

·

The Rat Pack had already gathered in *their* pub for the celebration of a 'Full Bifters Day' with new recruit Paul Kennedy. Coughlan, Halliwell and Rimmer had lined up various drinks in front of him as part of the initiation ceremony, and Kennedy, eager to become 'one of the boys' after his Saturday tantrum, was making a valiant effort to get through them all. He blenched as yet another pint of lager was placed in front of him.

'Come on, Paul,' urged Rimmer, 'get 'em down you, son. If you want to stay in the team, it's "Full Bifters" or nothing.'

Kennedy's cheeks filled out as he tried to store more of the liquid before swallowing. 'Must be worse than joining the British Army, this.'

Halliwell nodded in apparent sympathy. 'Time to get a few shorts in, I think!'

Kennedy groaned as Rimmer and Coughlan laughed at his discomfort. They patted him on the back as he took more sips from the pint glass.

'The idea, Paul, is to make you really sweat in training tomorrow – sort the men from the boys!'

'Which is why that tart Nicholl never comes!' Coughlan said with a sneering laugh.

'Yeah,' slurred Rimmer, 'he'd rather take Dave McGregor to a fart gallery.' As usual, he laughed loudly at his own joke.

Kennedy finished another gulp. 'What's Tony Morris's excuse?' he asked, trying to buy himself some recovery time.

'Common sense,' said Rimmer, who then pushed the glass back under Kennedy's nose. 'Come on, son, drink up!'

Kennedy bravely returned to his task. Meanwhile at the bar, Halliwell was collecting a tray filled with glasses of whisky for the foursome's next round. The barman nodded casually at the ritual going on at the table.

'Hey, Gary – I bet you five years ago you'd never have believed you'd have a sambo in the team. They're all over the place now, aren't they?'

Halliwell fixed him with an unblinking stare. 'That's because they're good. And he's not a sambo – he's one of us. Right, prick?'

The barman gave him an embarrassed nod and turned away. Halliwell returned to the table with the tray of drinks and raised a glass.

'Right, I propose a toast – to Trevor's stomach!' He gestured at Coughlan's girth, as Rimmer and Kennedy joined in the laughter.

·

Gabriella made her rendezvous with Steve Simms on time and persuaded him to sit in a corner alcove of the large, timbered pub. This only heightened Simms's sense of anticipation of what the meeting might concern. He gave Gabriella a mischievous smile over the lip of his glass.

'I'd have suggested the Seven Stars, but I happen to know that half your first team's in there getting pissed!'

Gabriella gave him a patient smile. 'Steve, if you told me today was Monday, I'd have gone out and bought a diary to check.'

Simms smirked, feeling, for once at least, ahead of the game. He gestured to Gabriella and the drinks on the table.

'So what's this in aid of, then . . . glasnost?'

'Have they put you on the foreign desk as well?' asked Gabriella with heavy irony, to which he was totally immune.

'I've got a story for you,' she said, getting down to business. 'Well, two actually.'

Simms took a sip of his drink and shook his head, eyes narrowing with suspicion.

'This isn't like you – what's the catch?'

'None. Except I'd like one printed and the other forgotten about.'

Simms sat back, sensing that she was playing games with him.

'If this is a wind-up –'

Gabriella stepped in briskly to reassure him. 'The reason I got rid of Charlie O'Keefe was that he was caught having it away with an underage girl.'

Simms digested this morsel with relish. 'Nice,' he said approvingly of the story, although not apparently, of the incident.

'Personally, I think it's a dead story round here. You'll get no one else to talk, and not many people to listen. But if you want to check out his progress at his new club –'

'I can bear it in mind,' nodded Simms.

They looked at each other, wondering where mistrust ended and necessity began.

'So what do you want me to run?' he asked, intrigued.

Gabriella took a manila envelope from her bag and passed it across to him.

'There's a name and address in there, a copy of a letter I've sent to the same, and a leaflet to get you going . . . the rest you can make up.'

Simms dipped his head in acknowledgement of her grasp of the essential relationship between football manager and football journalist – mutual back-scratching.

'You're learning, aren't you?'

Indeed she was, for Gabriella had come to realize, after the impact of the initial Simms story about her, that the press could be used to apply pressure on others too. Simms didn't care who he slagged or why, just as long as it made a big enough splash to keep him valuable.

The next morning his back-page special appeared under the inevitable 'exclusive' tag, with the headline screaming BOSS BOOTS OUT NAZI THUGS!, complete with NF and SS logos, and a picture of Paul Kennedy. The article took as its main theme, as Gabriella had hoped it would, her 'vigilante' action in the face of police apathy to the situation.

Later that afternoon a sheepish Inspector Willis phoned the club to ask Gabriella if she could drop by the headquarters on her way home to discuss the matter.

Gabriella assumed that they might now be prepared to listen to her story, but when she was ushered into Willis's office, she saw that they were already several steps beyond that. Lying on his desk was an assortment of articles sealed in plastic forensic bags – they included a wedge of leaflets identical to those found at the match, a display of literature with fascist logos, and a typeset list of names and addresses. Willis now dangled a nasty-looking combination weapon, knife-cum-knuckleduster, in front of her. Gabriella sat down opposite him.

'His room was a right little chamber of horrors.'

Gabriella understood that they must have moved in on Ellis today.

'What caused the change of heart?' she asked innocently.

Willis gave her an apologetic shrug. 'You know how it is – you've got a high-profile, media-conscious chief constable, who suddenly sees a story in a paper and wants action.'

Gabriella tried not to smile. 'And you have to jump?'

Willis nodded but then spread his hands plaintively.

'Not that I'm unhappy about it. This kid looks like a serious ring-leader.' He gestured to some of the material on the desk. 'Addresses for fascist groups in Europe . . . plans for attack and personal intimidation . . . not to mention a newspaper picture of your house.'

Gabriella deflected the inquisitive look with a shrug – it was probably better not to mention her direct confrontation at this stage. But it was suddenly brought vividly back to her when she first heard, and then saw, Terry Ellis being man-handled by two policemen down the corridor. He snarled at her as he glimpsed her through the windowed panel in the door of Willis's office, but he was quickly moved on. Gabriella shivered a little at the memory of the attack, and at how close she had come to injury.

The shouting receded. Willis caught the alarmed look on Gabriella's face.

'We're charging him now, and maybe we'll get him to finger a few more of these lunatics.'

'I doubt it,' Gabriella muttered.

Willis nodded. 'Me too,' he agreed, suddenly looking uneasy. 'Which is why, and I know this is presumptuous, we'd like you to attend a press conference with us . . . you know, to stress the nature of our co-operation on this.'

Gabriella got the picture – her presence would get them off the hook created by Simms's 'story'. She added a proposition of her own to the agenda.

'And our joint determination to drive this sort of influence from the game?'

It was a demand rather than a question, and Willis was obviously prepared to accommodate it.

'That sounds about right,' he said, nodding, before adding a quiet 'sorry' for the initial reluctance he had shown to take her complaint seriously.

'Will you do it?' he asked.

Gabriella, milking the silence, agreed.

·

For once, Gabriella's lunch with Sergio was about *her* achievements, not his. He studied the back-page story Simms had run and shook his head sadly.

'What are they trying to do to our beautiful game?'

'I'm sorry I had to do it,' she told him. 'But it seemed like the only way to prod the police.'

'I'm sure you were right, Gabriella,' he said, handing the paper back across the table. 'You know, at U E F A, we already have so many reports of the poison seeping into the game – racism in Belgium and Holland, anti-Semitism in Germany, fascism in Spain and Italy. If Hitler were alive today, he would be stalking the terraces.'

Gabriella nodded her agreement.

'But hopefully not at my club,' she added with determination. 'He'd never get past the commissionaires.'

This lightened the atmosphere a little, but Sergio was still obviously intrigued by his daughter's actions.

'I know you have my volatile nature,' he joked, 'but what made you take up this little crusade so passionately?'

'Well, I cared about the player, for one. A young lad. A talent. I didn't want to see it pissed on,' she said, before adding '*scusa*' in apology for her language.

Sergio accepted this with a smile and a gracious nod. Then he saw Gabriella take a breath and avert her eyes from his.

'And I also remembered when mama first brought me back to England,' she continued. 'There I was, ten years old, in this genteel, oh-so-British convent school in the countryside, being called "wop" and "Eye-tie" by the other girls.'

Sergio looked at her, grieved by this revelation.

'Sorry, but it's true,' she said.

'You have a lot to hate me for,' he muttered.

'Oh, shut up,' she said, taking his hand affectionately.

'But maybe it's not too late to make amends,' he whispered.

Gabriella's guard went up, although she tried to hide her distrust behind a joke.

'What have you done – bought me a first division club?'

Sergio shrugged mysteriously and smiled.

'I think you'll find your team will be invited to play in an end-of-season tournament in Italy, possibly in Milan.'

Gabriella was taken aback by this – and pleased for once with Sergio's machinations. If true, it represented a wonderful opportunity to display her team in the land of her birth.

She thought about how to break the news to Fisher when she got back to the club, but any happy announcement on her return was forestalled by the angry tone in his voice as he shouted for her to come into his office.

'What's the problem – cigar prices gone up?' she asked lightly.

'I pay you to manage this bloody team!' he screamed. 'Not to play Juliet Bravo with a bunch of Nazi hooligans!'

Gabriella adopted a more serious tone. 'Sorry – but it *affected* the team,' she said reasonably, but Fisher was too fired up to listen.

'And then you make it worse by going on television to shout about it and dragging our name all through the press!'

He gestured to a pile of the day's papers, all now following Simms's lead.

'Well, if that's what it takes,' she said tetchily, resenting his attitude.

'No, that's not what it takes!' he shouted. He picked up a telex from his desk and brandished it at her.

'Because I've now got a telex from the bleeding Football Association, demanding an explanation! They'll be coming here mob-handed for a bloody inquiry!'

'Good,' said Gabriella defiantly, 'it's about time they took some notice.'

Fisher's rage suddenly petered out like a storm dying.

'You just don't understand,' he said quietly. 'They'll come down on us like a ton of bricks ... they can close down the terraces ... they can fine the club!'

Gabriella had been trying to work out what was spooking him, and reckoned it was simply the thought of officialdom that was terrorizing him, rather than anything they might or might not do.

'Well, it'll still be worth it,' she said provocatively before walking out of the room, deciding to save the good news about Italy for another day.

Fisher breathed heavily and reached into his humidor for a soothing cigar. His hand grasped thin air, and the realization that the box was empty was enough to make him throw it across the room in pique.

.

Had she arrived in time for training the next morning, Gabriella would have been gratified by a small incident which took place involving Tony Morris and Paul Kennedy. As the squad climbed off the coach ready for training, Steve Simms's photographer colleague was back again, his car parked behind one of the practice goals.

He called Morris and Kennedy over, and, a shade reluctantly, they came. He led them round to the other side of his car and opened the boot.

'I'm talking five minutes here, and two hundred quid, cash.'

'Yeah – but I don't like your style of photo, mate,' said Kennedy.

Kennedy's reservations were instantly borne out as the photographer produced two Zulu-style shields and costumes from the boot of the car.

'Steve's doing a big feature on you two. How you saw off the white trash, right?'

He beamed at them expectantly. Morris and Kennedy looked

at one another, each knowing now what the other was thinking.

'Tell him Tone,' Kennedy instructed confidently.

Morris looked down on the photographer and gave him a fierce smile.

'Piss off, will you!'

CHAPTER ELEVEN

The details of the end-of-season challenge in Italy became clearer a few weeks later. There would not be, as Sergio had suggested, a tournament in Milan. For once his estimate of his own power had been exaggerated. But he did come through with a commitment from first division Atalanta to play Gabriella's team in a friendly. This was greeted with great excitement at the club; English clubs were still banned from competitive games in Europe, and only the bigger first division teams with European pulling power – Liverpool, Arsenal, Manchester United, Everton – usually managed to be invited out for such prestige friendlies.

The prospect of the trip had given Martin Fisher a renewed glow of self-importance. He really couldn't wait to hob-nob with sophisticated Italian executives, handing round his duty-free Monte Cristos. For Gabriella, the anticipation was just as sweet, albeit for different reasons. She saw the game as a real chance to measure her team's progress against the Italian foot-balling style: disciplined, overcautious occasionally, but blessed with great technique and passion. She was determined, both as a matter of professional pride and as an assertion of the English side of her upbringing, to put on a good show in Itlay.

With this in mind, she had been examining the possibility of taking a first division forward on loan, with a view to making him a permanent addition to the side. His 'audition', as it were, would be in the friendly against Atalanta.

First she had to clear the expense with Martin Fisher, so she prayed that his good mood still prevailed as she entered his office on a midweek morning before the last League game.

'You got five minutes, Martin?' she asked as she came in, trying to gauge his state of mind through his usual body language. He had a big cigar on the go, his jacket was draped casually over his chair, and he greeted her with an expansive smile, not the familiar suspicious frown. Things looked promising.

'Sure – best part of the year, this. Summer to look forward to. A break from the stresses and strains of the game.'

She gave him a tolerant smile, but couldn't stop herself letting him know that she'd spotted the holiday brochures fanned out on his desk.

'Sorry to drop football into your in-tray, when you're busy with other things . . . but I may have a loan deal lined up.'

'Good!' he smiled, lifting Gabriella's hopes even higher. 'Who are we off-loading?'

It had been too good to last. She shook her head, amused in a way by the thought patterns of his asset-stripping mind.

'Sorry – but we're doing the hiring.'

Fisher's usual frown appeared in an instant.

'Perry Gardner,' she said. 'Know him?'

She could see Fisher already preparing excuses.

'Well, yes – I mean, I've only seen him play on telly, and on that *Question of Sport* programme. Isn't he still a first division man?'

Gabriella saw the 'How much is this going to cost me?' calculations going on behind his eyes.

'Yes – but he's been out of the team for a couple of months, and I hear their new manager doesn't fancy him much. Well, I *know* that.'

'You mean you've already set this up? Won't his wages be a bit steep for us?'

'Well, I'm sure you can knock him down!' she said sweetly, appealing to his vanity.

Fisher looked flustered. He hated not having the initiative.

'Look – why do we need him? *And* at the end of the season too?'

Gabriella launched into her rehearsed argument, trying to make it sound as spontaneous as possible. 'Because Gardner's a proven goal scorer, and our present team hasn't got one. If we get him now, maybe I can show him off in Italy next week. And if that works, then the season-ticket sales will go up over the summer – '

'Yes,' Fisher conceded, 'but we could do without the expense.'

Gabriella started to run out of patience, and her tone became more aggressive. 'Martin – we're either trying to take this club into the first division or we're not! If not – then *you* might as well manage the club!'

'All right, all right, don't make me out to be a schnorrer! Do you have a rough idea of how much he'll cost?'

Gabriella picked up one of the brochures from Fisher's desk. 'About the same as a week in the Marbella Club, probably. Talk to his chairman first.'

She had deliberately handed the initiative back to him now. She knew that she'd set him a challenge to which he couldn't help rising. If he could hustle and haggle a little and convince himself that he, and he alone, had pulled off this deal, then she knew she would get her man. Gabriella headed for the door.

'I'll be back after training. Got to try and sell Eddie the idea now.'

She gave Fisher a confident smile and left him to get on with it.

Although Eddie theoretically had no power in the decision-making process, Gabriella knew that it was tactful to obtain his 'professional' view first. It would flatter him that he was being consulted, and this in turn would convince him that he *was* part of the decision-making process. Gabriella had also, despite her reservations, come to respect Eddie's opinion.

She floated the Gardner idea to him as they watched a 'shooting skills' training session, which she'd suggested, knowing it could be used as ammunition if need be. Gary Halliwell stood on one side of the penalty area, feeding passes to a player running in for a first-time shot. However, the goal-scoring touch was conveniently absent from the practice – which was just as well for her argument, because Eddie's reaction to Gardner's name wasn't favourable.

'He's a park-player,' Eddie said with a shake of the head. 'Probably looks great in training, then does sod all in a match.'

'He gets goals,' Gabriella countered.

'Yeah, I've seen 'em. Off his knee, rebounds off the keeper, tap-ins from three yards.'

'Who cares, as long as he's clocking them up?'

Eddie looked at her, puzzled to hear this functional reasoning from a state-registered romantic. Then he twigged that she was trying to sell Gardner to him in terms he might appreciate. Gabriella realized she'd been rumbled.

'Besides – I've seen him score a couple of fantastic efforts – he's got flair if he's allowed to use it!'

Her true colours were up on the mast now, allowing Eddie the chance to try and haul them down.

'You must have caught him on a good night,' he scoffed. 'Probably trying to impress some PR man in the stands.'

On the pitch, another goal attempt whistled over the bar.

'Keep your head down and use your arms for balance!' she shouted at the offending player, before turning back to Eddie. '*I* think we need him.'

Eddie shrugged insolently.

'You're the boss – it's your decision. I wouldn't have thought the lads'll fancy him much, though,' he added. 'Especially if you're keeping him on first division wages.'

This was an obvious declaration of Eddie's intent to stir it up among the players. Gabriella sighed wearily.

'I don't suppose there's much chance of you keeping that to yourself?'

Eddie's look told her there wasn't. She walked off towards the practice, clapping her hands for attention.

'Right! Now let's try the same thing with a defender up your backside – Italian style!'

Fisher's reluctance and Eddie's downright hostility only fuelled Gabriella's resolve to sign Perry Gardner. If they'd been smarter, they could have put her off by simply going along with the notion, but neither of them was capable of reacting with anything other than gut instinct.

The 'ceremony' duly occurred in Fisher's office the following day, with Gardner, flashily dressed in a 'Hey, look at me I'm nearly famous' style, making himself at ease in the executive surroundings. Fisher handed the draft contract across to him as Gabriella watched. Gardner simply folded the document and put it into the inside pocket of his Armani jacket.

'I'll show it to my agent tonight, if that's all right. He's at a snooker tournament today, handles a couple of the lads.'

'Well, let's hope you're fitter than they must be,' Gabriella said.

Fisher shook his head, supposedly in amused dismay, but really it was in admiration.

'You first division boys – like Hollywood stars these days you are. Agents!'

'Don't worry, Mr Fisher,' Gardner said with a self-confident smile, 'he's a pussy-cat. And anyway, I fancy this move. I can't get on with the new manager there – now, working for a bir –'

Gardner stopped himself just in time.

' – a woman here – well, should put me back in the limelight a bit, eh?'

He looked across at Gabriella, and gave her a winning smile.

'Yes,' she said back to him sweetly, 'if you make the first team.'

Gardner tried, but failed, to keep his smile intact.

·

Saturday's home game was the last of the season. The team had a comfortable mid-division place, they weren't playing a side who needed to win, and an exotic trip to Italy was coming up, so it was hardly surprising that the players seemed supremely unconcerned about the afternoon's proceedings as they lounged around the dressing-room with less than half an hour to kick-off.

Gary Halliwell was signing his name in a dozen or so autograph books which lay on the central table. They were always handed in by fans before a game and redistributed by a commissionaire afterwards, filled with their highly prized signatures. Halliwell quickly noticed that he was the only one doing this, with Coughlan and Rimmer, for example, huddled in conference over a *Racing Post*.

'Oi – come on, let's get these signed and out of the way!'

Rimmer and Coughlan ignored him, until Rimmer stood up decisively with his racing paper and headed for the dressing-room door.

'When you've got a minute, Brian –' Halliwell tried, but Rimmer was on his way to the phone to place a big bet.

'I haven't, skipper.' He turned back to his gambling partner. 'Oi, Trev! Sign these for us, will you?'

With that, Rimmer hurried out. Coughlan approached the table and picked up one of the pens provided by the club.

'What's Brian's signature like?' he asked Halliwell.

'A big X, I should think. Just put a couple of squiggles, they'll never know.'

Coughlan picked up an autograph book and began signing both his own and Rimmer's name.

The relaxed atmosphere of the room dissipated a little, however, when Perry Gardner walked in for the first time. The team had been told of his arrival by Eddie, who'd also trumpeted the incriminating details of his likely wage demands, so there was a distinct chill in the air – not that the ever cocky Gardner noticed.

'Wotcher, lads!' he beamed.

There were a couple of muttered greetings from the likes of Tony Morris and Keith Nicholl, but Halliwell hardly looked up from his signing session.

'Cop yourself a peg, then – assuming you're staying?'

'I'm staying,' Gardner said firmly. 'I've got very fond memories of you lot – Simod Cup quarter final. Somebody kicked the shit out of me, as I remember.'

Most of the team pointed at Coughlan, who put his hand up with a smile.

'Cheers,' Gardner said sarcastically. 'Well maybe we can stop now we're on the same side.'

Gardner felt he'd said enough – there wasn't much sentiment in professional football for arrivals and departures, since they were so much a part of the daily ritual of the game. He selected a vacant peg away from the body of the team and took his jacket off.

'Er, Perry,' Halliwell said, turning to him.

'Yeah – Gary, isn't it?'

'I know you're only slumming with us for a while, but if you want to put your wallet in a safety deposit-box – '

It was said loudly for the benefit of the rest of the team, and managed to combine two digs in one go: his temporary status and his pay level. Gardner smiled and decided not to rise to the bait.

'I'm strictly credit, Gary,' he said with a patronizing smile, before starting to change for the match.

The atmosphere lightened again as the players concentrated on their own diversions. In one corner, Nicholl and McGregor, who 'pegged' next to each other, had been chatting about the Italian game, and Nicholl had produced a phrase-book from his bag, asking McGregor to test him with it.

McGregor complied, nervous of both the dressing-room reaction and his own inability to read well.

'Right, Dave – just read out the English phrase for us, and see how close I get to the Italian below it.'

'Right,' McGregor muttered, head swimming with anxiety. Tony Morris had already overheard, and was quickly in.

'He can't understand *English*, let alone Italian, Keith!'

Nicholl gave Morris a pained smile and gestured for Mc-Gregor to continue with the exercise.

'Er, let's see – "Excuse me, is there a bank near by?"'

Nicholl smiled, pleased with himself.

'*Scusi, c'è una banca qui vicino?*' he said. 'How was that?'

'Yeah – sounded like what's written here,' said McGregor valiantly.

'*Bene!*' Nicholl congratulated himself.

'Is that Benny Hill or Benny out of *Crossroads*?' Morris shouted, getting laughter from the other players who'd been monitoring Nicholl and McGregor with glee.

Gabriella walked in immediately after telling a reporter in the corridor about the importance of the forthcoming match in Italy.

'Come on, come on! We've got a game today in case you hadn't noticed! Now move yourselves!'

While most of the players made a token effort to appear diligent, Halliwell carried on with his autograph-signing.

'You're wasting your time, boss. Last game of the season's always like Christmas. There's so much to be done beforehand, it's hard to concentrate on the thing itself. Now, if we were in line for promotion –'

Gabriella gave him a steely look. 'Finishing ninth will look better than finishing tenth to me.'

'If this game matters so much, what's he doing here?'

He nodded at Perry Gardner, who was pulling on one of the substitute's shirts.

'Because I want him for Italy, skipper.'

'I thought it was a friendly, not a modelling assignment?'

Gabriella had had enough by now.

'Shouldn't *you* be thinking of putting some work clothes on?' she asked sarcastically.

Halliwell finished his last autograph and tossed the book on to the pile, then headed for his peg.

Gabriella clapped her hands for attention.

'All right, let's start concentrating, shall we? As far as I'm concerned, we've still got two competitive games this week. Your summer holidays don't start till they're over!'

The players had begun to seat themselves on the benches which ran round the walls of the room. There were sniggers and tittering laughter, and Gabriella looked at the offenders angrily.

'What's the joke?'

Other team members were laughing now and pointing behind Gabriella. She turned to see Eddie trying to get through the door while he was being swamped by a large net full of plastic footballs. Eddie looked grim-faced and humiliated.

'What gives, Eddie?' she asked, trying to keep a straight face.

'Sorry, boss – the chairman wants the lads to kick these into the crowd during the warm-up. Sort of end-of-season present to the fans.'

Most of the team had dissolved into laughter, and Gabriella saw that any attempt at seriousness would be futile today.

Upstairs in the boardroom, however, Martin Fisher and Anthony Coombs were in a considerably more sombre mood. They stood together, almost huddled, in one corner of the room, keeping other guests at bay, while they conducted a hushed conversation.

'I told them not to start until after three, and to be out of the way by four thirty,' Coombs said quietly.

'Good,' said Fisher, smiling, 'and I hope they aren't poncing round in Range Rovers and fancy anoraks like they usually do!'

Coombs gave him a confident smirk.

'I'm sure they'll be discreet. I suggested to them that if anybody asked, they should say they were safety officers from the council.'

Fisher enjoyed this and began a story, unaware that Gabriella's husband, Simon, had entered and was heading their way.

'You know I got the idea from reading about a burglar who steamed into this Yorkshire mining town on the day the Rugby League team were down at Wembley.'

Coombs stiffened suddenly as Simon loomed within ear-shot.

'Ah, yes – Wembley!' Coombs repeated loudly. 'Well, we can all dream, can't we?'

Fisher's puzzlement at the remark was only solved when Simon appeared at his shoulder.

'Making plans for next season already, eh?' Simon inquired sociably.

Fisher was momentarily disconcerted – Simon couldn't have overheard *that* much, surely?

'What?' he snapped.

'Well – I heard Anthony refer to Wembley just now,' Simon explained.

Fisher and Coombs briefly shared a look of relief.

'No, you know us, Simon,' Fisher boomed affably, 'we're very modest about our ambitions!'

Coombs and Fisher laughed. Simon joined in with them, not because he saw the joke, but because it seemed to be the friendly thing to do.

.

Gabriella's fears that the players' minds weren't on the game that day proved well founded, and a dire first half of typical end-of-season football ensued. It spilled over into the second half too, with disjointed, apathetic play from both teams. Eddie and Gabriella sat impotently in the dug-out with Perry Gardner sitting behind them, itching to get into the action.

Eddie stood up and leaned out of the dug-out to articulate his disappointment, and to try to breath some fire into the team.

'I think you're wasting your breath, Eddie,' Gabriella said, as he slumped back down on the bench. 'Their heads are already on the beaches in Benidorm and Marbella.'

'They're cheating us, and they're cheating the crowd!' Eddie fumed. 'There'll be some bloody changes in the second half!'

They all stared at Eddie. Gardner leaned across.

'This *is* the second half, Eddie.'

Eddie looked stunned by his mental lapse, but then he decided that the football must have stupefied him.

'Look, after fifty-odd games, I can't tell day from night!'

Gabriella checked her watch and decided it was time for Gardner to make his entrance. He began to peel off his tracksuit top.

'Right, let's give'em something to remember over the summer, eh?' he said, then sprinted off up the red shale track around the pitch. Eddie scowled, his mind clear again.

'Thirty-five minutes of the season left, and now he's ready to pull up trees. The true mark of the fanny-merchant!'

Gardner duly came on for Dave McGregor, which allowed a quick reshuffle of midfield, with Nicholl dropping back and Tony Morris moving out wide. If Gabriella's hope was that the substitution would galvanize her team, it was just as well she didn't see Brian Rimmer take advantage of the diversion to ask the crowd behind his goal if they knew the result of a horse-race. Nobody seemed to be concentrating on the game.

In fact, the only player to show any sign of energy after Gardner's arrival was Gardner himself – running about fear-lessly, making himself available for passes and generally giving the visiting defence a hard time. The general lethargy of the team blunted his effectiveness in terms of strikes on goal. But then, just when the game looked to be heading for a scoreless draw, Paul Kennedy managed to get a cross in. Gardner, with his back to goal, controlled the ball in the air before swivelling into a bicycle-kick which sent the ball hurtling past the keeper for a spectacular goal. He jumped on to the fence behind the goal to celebrate, and Gabriella danced out of the dug-out in delight. Eddie stayed put.

'Jammy bastard,' he said sourly, 'it could have gone any-where!'

'It was a bloody dream goal, Eddie!' Gabriella enthused.

'Yeah, scored against defenders who've done ten times the running this season.'

'Anyway, if he's still doing it in the mud next January, I shall expect an apology,' she smiled, delighted that her 'investment' had delivered such immediate returns.

Outside the ground, behind the popular south terrace end, two gentlemen in brightly coloured lightweight anoraks were reminded by the roar of the crowd at the goal that the match was nearly over. One of the men reeled in a large surveyor's tape-measure, while the other closed the cover over his clip-board of notes and measure-ments. They checked their watches – Coombs had told them to be out of the way by four thirty. It was just on four thirty-two.

'That should be enough to be going on with,' the older man said, as they began to walk away from the ground, through the maze of terraced streets which surrounded it.

'It could certainly do with a few amenities, this area,' the older man observed.

'Wouldn't they say that a football ground *was* one?' said his younger colleague with a smirk.

'They'd better not – I'm hoping this'll be a quick in-and-out job!'

They turned a corner into one of the quieter side streets, still lined with cars belonging to the football fans at the ground. Parked on a double yellow-line was a smart Range Rover with a 'Disabled Driver' badge in its window. The older man saw that no parking tickets had been attached to the windscreen, and patted the badge through the windscreen before he opened the door.

'Best investment the firm ever made,' he said with a wink, as he and his colleague climbed into the Range Rover. Their mission completed, they drove off, safe in the knowledge that most of the people who might have been interested in what they were up to had been corralled inside the ground, watching a bloody awful football match.

.

The players had taken their baths and changed when Fisher appeared in the dressing-room, lugging a case of champagne, which he quickly proceeded to open. Once glasses had been distributed, he took the centre of the room and addressed them, with Eddie and Gabriella forced to stand to one side and suffer.

'I couldn't be more pleased by the way the season's turned out, lads,' he said, toasting them with his glass. 'I know we've had our sticky moments when I dropped our little bombshell here on you,' he continued, nodding at a stony-faced Gabriella, 'but I'm proud of the way you've responded. I really think we've turned the corner. So we've got a lot to look forward to next season – but before then, we'll have a few laughs and a good time in Italy! So toast yourselves, will you? The Team!'

There was a slightly awkward moment while some of the players muttered the toast and a couple of others attempted some misplaced applause. Fisher took his leave, passing Gabriella as he reached the door.

'I've got to nip back upstairs now. I'll tell Simon to wait for you, shall I?'

Gabriella smiled her thanks, but the moment Fisher left she replaced him, standing in the middle of the room with a less congratulatory look on her face.

'Right – before the champagne sets in, *I've* got a few words today too. With one or two exceptions, you were crap today. I don't want a repeat performance on Wednesday night in Italy, understand? And despite what the chairman said, it's a job of work we're going for, not a "lads' holiday" or some sort of bonus for tasks completed. You've finished ninth in the second division and won nothing. So this club owes you nothing. You still owe it a lot! Think about that! Now Eddie has the travel details.'

Gabriella turned away and walked out to a deafening silence, which she took as a sign that the message had hit home, but she didn't see the hostile glares at her departing back. Most of the team didn't feel they deserved a bollocking, especially not after the last, meaningless game of the season. And whether she liked it or not, yes, nearly all of them did look on their Italian trip as a bit of a lark, with a football match as an unnecessary diversion. So there was a collective moan as she left, which would have been the prelude to a session of whining had Eddie not stepped in immediately.

'Before anybody drops themselves in it, I agree with every word she said!'

Eddie eyed the players individually, daring them to challenge him. There were no takers, and a grudging silence was resumed.

'Now – report here ten o'clock Tuesday morning, latest, for the coach to Heathrow. Don't forget passports. If you had club blazers, you'd wear 'em – so it's jacket and ties while we're travelling.'

His gaze fell upon Paul Kennedy and Perry Gardner, who were wearing their most conspicuously fashionable clothes.

'And I don't want any of those big woolly jobs with the padded shoulders, right!' he shouted, eye-balling them like a crazed scout-master.

The players tried hard to stifle their grins as they each thought about the fun they'd have at Eddie's expense on the trip.

Simon drove Gabriella home, taking the 'country route' to get the full benefit of the bright, early-summer evening. Relations between them remained edgy – Simon still found he had difficulty getting close to her, and he wasn't sure whether it was his fault or hers. For Gabriella, Simon had become an increasingly distant figure, impeding her view of the horizon none the less, with his just-below-the-surface longing for her to give up the job. Simon looked at her nervously as he drove, trying to gauge her mood.

'Fisher seemed pretty pleased with things today,' he said, hoping this would relax her.

'So I noticed.'

'Kept going on about preparing the club for the first division.'

Gabriella shook her head with irritation. 'He's going to have to find some more money before we do that – and spend it properly. On the team, not on champagne.'

Simon allowed this minor tirade to fade before tentatively broaching the next subject.

'He, er, asked me if I was coming out to Italy for the game.'

'Oh,' Gabriella stalled. 'You don't want to, do you?'

'Well, it hadn't really occurred to me,' Simon lied.

'Sorry, Simon – I've just lectured the players on the need to treat this trip in a business-like manner. It wouldn't look too good if I turned up with you on my arm, would it? I mean, none of the players or directors are taking their wives.'

Simon looked wounded.

'No, well – "we" must stay at home, obviously,' he said.

Gabriella scolded herself for the unwitting comparison, but she knew what she meant.

'Look, it's just the way things are. I mean, I've never expected to go on business trips when *you've* been on them!'

'But have you ever wanted to?' he said, voice rising with irritation.

'Well, yes, of course. But I'll have so little time to spare on this, it's not like I can go off sight-seeing with you and turn up just before the match. The team needs me all the time.'

'Yes, to "mother" it, I suppose,' he said witheringly.

'Oh, don't be ridiculous.'

But Simon had found a theme. 'They're your little children, and whether they're good or naughty, or hurt, they all must get your attention!'

'You patronizing sod,' she said angrily, turning towards him in her seat. 'How many bloody lawyers' dinners have I been to with you, where your prime function has been arse licking? We all have to make sacrifices to earn a living.'

'Me more than most!' he yelled. Gabriella turned away and looked out at the peaceful countryside as it flashed by. An angry, bitter silence fell between them.

'I suppose I shouldn't mention this now – but I have a clients' dinner to host on Monday night, and I would value your company and your support,' said Simon eventually.

If he thought this was an olive branch, he was swiftly disabused of the notion by Gabriella's look of incredulity as she turned to him.

'Try the *Yellow Pages*, under "Wild Horses"!'

Gabriella retreated to her study when they got home, while Simon stayed sullenly in the kitchen. Gabriella battled with her feelings – she had a niggling feeling that she was in the wrong, but her natural stubbornness quickly stifled that. The problem was that Simon just couldn't envisage how much the job meant to her – his support seemed to be grudging, nominal, without any real understanding of the passion she felt for the game.

To soothe herself and, in a way, to reassure herself of the 'eternal verities' before the trip to Italy, she watched her tape of the 1960 Real Madrid v. Eintracht European Cup Final again. The skill and the exuberance of the play washed over her, every bit as strongly as when she'd seen the game herself as a ten-year-old. She wondered if she might be allowed to take it with her, should she ever be invited on to *Desert Island Discs*.

Coincidentally, telepathically almost, Sergio rang while she was watching the game. He was looking forward to seeing her in Italy, and promised to meet her at Milan airport before driving up to Bergamo, where Atalanta were based. She was genuinely touched by his support; he really did seem to want to make up for the past before he got too much older. She started to speak to him in Italian, just as she always had when she was a little girl – it would be good practice for her 'home-coming'.

.

All the first team squad managed to get to the ground on time for the coach as planned. Eddie made them line up to get on board, so that he could conduct a passport check. Eddie had adapted a blazer by having a club badge sewn on the breast pocket. The players had made no such effort, but they were smartly dressed none the less in lightweight suits of various colours.

Halliwell was next through 'Checkpoint Eddie', and he looked amused as Eddie studied the photo and tried to match it to the player in front of him.

'What's up, Eddie – not sure it's me?' Halliwell smirked.

'This photo makes you look like that Carlos the Jackal. I'll be surprised if they let you in,' Eddie said with a smile, as he handed the passport back. Perry Gardner now appeared. To Eddie's disgust he was wearing an opulent cream-coloured jacket with shawl collar.

'If that's a blazer, I'm a Dutchman,' Eddie sneered.

'Well, I wouldn't know until you showed me *your* passport, Eddie.'

Gardner started to get on the coach, but Eddie grabbed the passport, and Gardner hung his head, waiting for the outburst.

'Hello, hello,' shouted Eddie gleefully, 'Perry *Cyril* Gardner! We kept that one out of *Rothman's Year-Book*, didn't we?'

Gardner suffered impatiently as Eddie milked the moment to the delight of the other players.

'We have a Cyril in our midst, lads! As if we didn't know already –'

'When you've finished,' said Gardner sourly.

Eddie handed his passport back with a fixed smile.

'There's a mistake on there – it says "Occupation – Footballer".'

Gardner gave him an ironic look and stepped up on to the coach, knowing that, if past experience was anything to go by, the baiting about his name would run for ages.

'Right, who's after Cyril,' asked Eddie, getting the ball rolling.

Gabriella waited with Fisher in his office while he finished a phone-call, which, judging by the extravagant gestures of dismay, was a disappointment. It soon became clear that Anthony Coombs was crying off from the trip, pleading pressure of work. Fisher shrugged as he put the phone down, knowing that Gabriella had understood what had happened, but his invitation to bring Simon along wasn't the most useful suggestion in the circumstances.

Finally the tour-party pulled away from the ground on time, and headed for the M4 and Heathrow, pausing only at the supporters' shop so that Eddie could buy a set of pennants. In his brief experience of Europe – the Anglo-Italian Tournament of the early 1970s – Eddie knew that it was the done thing to exchange pennants with the opposition before the match. However, Fisher was unimpressed, especially when he had to hand over fifty pounds for a set of twenty.

.

Coombs gave the coach a good hour to get clear of town before emerging from his home and driving the mile or so to the office of 'Mills & Partners, Architects'. It was rather an unnecessary precaution, since very few people outside the club would recognize him, and certainly none of the fans.

Once inside he was shown up to the main office, where he met James Mills and his assistant Hugo Bremner, the two men who'd been busying themselves so discreetly around the ground at the last match.

Coombs was slightly disconcerted to find somebody else there besides Mills, and said so.

'It's all right, Anthony – Hugo's aware of the climate, shall we say!'

Mills turned to Bremner, to reassure him that no insult was intended.

'Sorry, Hugo – Anthony and I were at Haberdasher's together. "Outsiders" are not trusted easily!'

The moment of awkwardness passed, as Coombs apologized gracefully.

'Now, what do you have for us?' he asked eagerly.

Bremner moved across to a large table in the centre of the room, covered in a plastic sheet. Coombs and Mills followed. Bremner removed the sheet, revealing a scale model of the football ground. At the popular end, a rectangular one-storey building now stood where the terraces had been, and on top of it were two layers of glass-windowed executive boxes.

'It may look like a brick shithouse,' Mills said with a cheerful smile, 'but the building will be the last word in luxury.'

'That's right,' said Bremner, fanning his hand over their design for the 'redevelopment'.

Coombs saw that inside the boxes they'd even installed little toy executives.

'I mean, the notion of the executive box is almost passé-groovy now,' Bremner said emphatically, expecting agreement. 'But with individual food and drink bars, toilets, TV and video, telephone and fax, reclining seats, we think we can refresh a tired cliché.'

Coombs smiled and nodded, refreshed by the idea already.

·

The players made the most of the ninety-minute flight to Milan, flirting with the Alitalia hostesses, accepting anything free on offer, be it drink or food, while stocking up again on duty-free goods. The ordinary traveller might have taken them for a bunch of schoolboys off on holiday, but at the same time they strutted around the air-craft as if they were famous.

But as the wide-bodied bus transferred them from the plane to the terminal, they were suddenly hit by a blast of what true fame might entail. For as they moved down the grey corridor with its low ceiling and out into the arrivals area, they were met by a barrage of camera flashes going off and a good deal of shouting from a horde of Italian pressmen.

For a few moments they preened themselves in true Milanese style, until the words 'Signora Benson!' and 'Signora Manager!' began to be more distinguishable – it was her they were after, not them.

Gabriella was quite taken aback by it all. Although she knew how passionately the Italians took their football and how much press coverage it attracted, she hadn't expected this. From the scrum, Sergio now emerged, arms outstretched, walking towards her with pride glowing on his face.

'Did you organize this?' she asked with a smile.

'My darling, they've been camped here for days,' he said, with perhaps only a little exaggeration.

While the players and Eddie collected their bags and Norman took charge of the team-skip, Gabriella and Fisher were diverted into a room for an official press conference, which seemed to be expected of her. Sergio sat by her side as she faced a gallery of sports writers across a table studded with radio microphones. Gabriella gallantly conducted the conference in Italian, much to the pressmen's delight, and she noticed that the questions were engagingly serious compared with the trivia usually demanded of her by the British press.

'What is your aim when you play the Atalanta team?' asked one reporter.

'Simple,' she replied, 'to beat them, but to do it with style!'

'Signora – what type of football will your team play? English or Italian?' was the next question, which had a couple of hidden traps in it, she thought. If she said 'English', they'd probably write it up as a slur on Italian football, whereas if she said 'Italian' they would probably accuse her of arrogance.

'We will use the best of both,' she replied, 'the aggression and energy of the English game, the skill and wit of the Italian!'

Sergio applauded the tactful reply, which effectively drew the press attention to him.

'Signor Rebecchi, what part did you play in this achievement of your daughter's?'

Sergio shrugged graphically, capturing the attention of at least three photographers.

'Simply, I gave her a love of football. The rest is the result of her own strength and capabilities.'

Gabriella leaned across to add to this. 'He is being too modest – he trained my eyes to see the beautiful things in the game!'

'And will your team show these aspects too?' a journalist near the front asked.

Gabriella smiled. 'I hope so, certainly, but only if you excuse me now and permit me to get on with my work.'

She stood up decisively, receiving applause and cries of 'Bravo!' Sergio accompanied her to the door, where Fisher stood beaming, greeting her for the benefit of the cameras.

'She is the best decision that I ever made!' he shouted in English, intoxicated by the clamour. Whether it was the language, or just the fact that nobody knew who he was, Fisher's comment passed unnoticed, but Gabriella received a bouquet of flowers from the journalists as she emerged from the room to more camera flashes.

The coach pulled away from Milan's Linate Airport and headed north-east on the A4 autostrada, which brought them to the outskirts of Bergamo within an hour. While the flat landscape alongside the motorway had been dotted with factories and domestic-goods warehouses, the city of Bergamo loomed in the near distance, with the walled medieval part rising high above like a mirage. As the coach made its way through the wide, tree-lined boulevards of the modern city below, some of the players couldn't help comparing the scenery with their normal beat, deciding that the likes of Stoke, Sunderland, Walsall and Portsmouth just couldn't compete.

The coach parked outside a smart modern hotel on the edge of a piazza, halfway between the nineteenth-century civic buildings of the 'new' city and the dazzling ochre-coloured villas and turrets of the old city on the hill.

Nicholl and McGregor noted down the '*città alta*', as it was known, for an early visit, but the rest of the squad filed quickly into the hotel lobby, where Eddie began to allocate them their rooms. The players would share where possible, a footballing tradition which had hints of boyish innocence about it, but which was, in fact, designed to discourage not only incidents of maverick behaviour but also sexual adventures, on the assumption that not many players would be too tolerant if their roommate brought a woman back for fun on the single bed a few feet away!

Eddie had paired the players off with this in mind. Morris and Kennedy, the two black players, were put together, despite Kennedy's joke that this was apartheid, and Rimmer and Halliwell were roomed on the basis that only Halliwell might be able to contain the goal-keeper's quest for excess. Nicholl and McGregor made a natural pair, and Eddie had shrewdly calculated that nobody else in the squad would want to be lumbered with either of them. Finally, Eddie allocated Gardner to a single room, 'by popular request', which was half true but a little cruel in the circumstances. Gardner was too hardened a pro to take the insult badly, and he shuffled off with the others.

The squad adjourned to their various rooms to unpack and get used to the foreign plumbing.

McGregor looked on admiringly as Nicholl produced a fashionable light-weight suit from a bag.

'Trendy stuff, Keith!'

Nicholl smiled at the compliment; he liked to think of himself as a sophisticated traveller.

'Well, there's a smart restaurant I'd like to try tonight. It's in the *Michelin Guide*.'

McGregor nodded as if he knew what that was.

'Come with me, why don't you? Unless you want to join the other berks on the piss?' suggested Nicholl.

McGregor thought this was a good idea.

'Yeah. I think I'd like to see more of the town than just bars, Keith. I'm a bit like you really, Keith. Travel appeals to me.'

Nicholl nodded enthusiastically, but then noticed McGregor take two cans of baked beans and a packet of English tea-bags out of his case.

A few rooms along the corridor, Gary Halliwell stretched out on his bed, flicking through the television channels in search of the porn programmes somebody in the pub had told him they had in Italy.

Rimmer emerged from the bathroom, dripping wet.

'Remind me to put my teeth to soak in the bidet tonight, eh?' he asked.

'Beats crapping in it like you usually do,' Halliwell said, his attention still on the television set. Suddenly he reacted as a trailer for a women's professional football match appeared.

'Now why couldn't they have fixed us a friendly with that lot?' he leered.

'Suddenly, it doesn't seem so odd having a bird as boss,' Rimmer said pensively, before reverting to his more familiar manner. 'Here, I wonder if they swop shirts at the end! That reminds me!'

From his suitcase he produced a large box of Durex.

'I bought us a jumbo pack of johnnies – don't want AIDS as a souvenir, do we?'

Halliwell was impressed.

'God, that advertising campaign must work if it's got home to you, Brian! You used to protect yourself with some wire wool and a splash of Dettol!'

Rimmer grinned proudly at him. The Rat Pack were all fired up and ready for a good time. In fact, the first activity got under way quickly, with a mammoth game of cards in the elegant marble-floored lobby of the hotel. Morris, Coughlan, Rimmer and Halliwell were playing, watched by three or four of the others, while Gabriella and Eddie looked on from the reception desk, where they were sorting out the supervisory arrangements.

Nicholl and McGregor, both wearing shorts and Dr Scholl sandals, emerged from the lift, carrying guide-books, to be greeted by wolf whistles and jeers from the card players.

'Out jogging, girls?' inquired Halliwell.

Nicholl was used to being baited and preferred to play up to the part of intellectual, as he knew it annoyed them all the more.

'Actually we're going up to the old town to visit the Colleoni Chapel. It's got frescos by Tiepolo, apparently.'

'Has it now?' Rimmer asked, making a show of being impressed.

'Yeah, about St John the Baptist,' added McGregor.

Halliwell shook his head slowly. 'Well, I'd love to come along, but I've got my best hand of the day here, Keith!'

'I understand, skipper,' Nicholl said blandly, refusing to be goaded.

'What's the name again, just in case I want to catch you up?' asked Rimmer facetiously.

'Colleoni. Only make sure you pronounce it correctly, because it might sound like the Italian word for "bollocks".'

There was genuine enthusiasm for this news.

'Now that's what *I* call cultural information,' howled Coughlan. 'I shall use that during the game!'

'And I thought travel broadened the mind,' said Nicholl, unable to resist a put-down.

'All it broadens is his arse,' said Morris, nodding at Rimmer over his hand of cards.

'Where are the rest of the lads?' McGregor asked, hoping that one or two of them might be sightseeing too.

'Having a kip. Saving their strength, I expect,' Rimmer said meaningfully.

'You on for a bit of rape and ruin tonight, Keith?' Halliwell asked.

'Thought I might treat myself to a good Italian meal, actually. See you!'

He and McGregor wandered out through the large glass doors of the hotel and into the sunny piazza.

'Light a candle for us!' called Morris.

'What a pair of wankers!' said Rimmer in summary.

'Twist!'

At the reception desk, Gabriella finished going through Eddie's rooming list and handed it back to him.

'Seems fine. Right, if you take them for a few beers and have them back in bed by half ten, okay?'

Eddie nodded, but then he drew her attention to the card-school.

'Won't be easy. What are you doing tonight?'

'I've been invited to some sort of cultural reception at the Town Hall, so I'll drag Fisher and my father to that.'

'Carving up the club between you?' Eddie asked petulantly, disappointed at not being asked along.

'Not while I'm around, Eddie. Now you do your job and I'll do mine,' she said, putting him in his place, which she felt he deserved occasionally.

Eddie folded his list back inside his blazer pocket.

'Quite a welcome you got this afternoon,' he said, without managing to sound impressed.

'The passion goes deep here, Eddie. You know when Italy scored their third goal in the 1982 World Cup Final, the *President* of the republic stood up in the VIP box and cheered like an ordinary fan! Can't imagine Thatcher doing that, can you?'

'Aye, well, they're fine when they're winning,' said Eddie. 'Or when they're spending millions on fancy-dans from South America. There's no tradition, though, is there? Not like at home.'

'Three world championships would suggest otherwise, I think,' Gabriella corrected.

Eddie remained unimpressed and went on to list what he saw as the great dynasties of the English game: Newcastle in the fifties, the Busby Babes, Billy Nicholson's Spurs, and Liverpool. Eddie suggested that Italian clubs were all flash-in-the-pans compared with that list.

'I had you down as a student of the game.'

She checked the date on her watch: 5 May. It was a coincidence, but it could prove a point to Eddie. She reached across him and took a pink *Gazzetta dello Sport* from a rack of newspapers.

'Should be something in this – '

She began to leaf through the paper, while Eddie waited for her to explain the relevance of the date.

'Ah – here we are – '

She folded the paper and showed him a picture of a candle-lit procession outside a church. Next to it was a photo of an old football team, fifties vintage, thought Eddie.

'Looks like a religious service? What's it got to do with football?'

'In Italy, everything,' said Gabriella. She pointed to the photos to illustrate her story. 'It's a memorial service for the Torino team of the 1940s. They were all killed in a plane crash . . . thirty-nine years ago yesterday. They won six championships and were unbeaten at home for over eighty-five games . . . the players were nearly all internationals.'

'So this is some kind of Munich-type tribute?' Eddie asked, grappling with the concept of such a tragedy.

'Yes – but at least there were survivors at Munich. Nobody got out of this crash. Everybody felt the shock, the Milanese, Romans, Sicilians. All the achievements in the Italian game since then are, in a way, a tribute to them.'

She folded the paper and handed it to Eddie.

'I'm sorry, I didn't know about this.'

'That's the trouble with our game, Eddie,' she said sadly. 'We gave it to the world, but stopped looking to see what they did with it.'

Eddie nodded in agreement and pushed a handful of lira across the counter to buy the paper. Then a thought struck him, and he couldn't help sharing it with her, whether it was tactless or not.

'I'm glad you didn't tell us about this before we took off.'

And with that he wandered away. Gabriella sighed.

.

By about six thirty a gaggle of players, including Gardner, Kennedy, Morris and the Rat Pack, had gathered in the lobby near the reception desk. They were all dressed for a night out, as indeed was Martin Fisher, who wandered over to join them, keen to prove that he was just 'one of the lads' at heart.

'Fancy a drink with the boys, Mr Chairman?' Halliwell asked with a wink.

Fisher looked at his watch and pulled a put-upon face.

'I'm supposed to be escorting her highness to a reception, Gary.'

'Oh. Pity. 'Cos Perry's got a bead on some swish night-club he claims he went to once. Wall-to-wall crumpet, apparently. I knew he'd come in useful somehow!'

Fisher looked agonized. Normally he would have rejoiced in the formality and status of occasions like a civic reception, but being abroad had liberated him from his usual self. Tonight he just wanted to have fun.

'Well, I suppose I could manage one,' he wavered. 'For team spirit, like.'

Halliwell grinned at him. 'Quite right, Mr Chairman.'

'She'll only be talking football with the Eye-ties anyway,' Fisher reasoned.

'We could do without that tonight, eh?' said Halliwell, egging him on.

Fisher smiled and joined the group as it made its way towards the door. Rimmer immediately broke into a chorus of the football yobs' anthem 'Here We Go', but he was cut short by the sight of Eddie, in his 'official' blazer, waiting for them on the steps outside.

'Going out lads?' Eddie inquired, trying to sound innocent. 'I'll tag along if you don't mind.'

Nobody, not even Fisher, had the nerve to tell him that they did.

'Do you want us in pairs, holding hands, Eddie?' Halliwell asked sarcastically.

'Only on the way back,' Eddie said with a killing smile, as he gestured for them to lead on.

Moments later, Gabriella emerged from the lift, looking stunning in a blue velvet dress. The receptionist saw her and called out that there were some messages for her.

Gabriella guessed that one would be from Simon. The phone had rung just as she was leaving the room, and she'd presumed that it would be a weary Simon, on his own in the house, trying to make her feel guilty, so she'd ignored the call.

The first message was from her father, saying he couldn't make the reception that night. No reason was given. The other message was that Mr Fisher would be back soon.

'Where from?' inquired Gabriella.

'I don't know, he left with the players,' said the receptionist.

Gabriella tried to hide her disappointment and annoyance. Maybe she should have brought Simon along after all. She went to the bar to wait for Fisher, taking an evening paper from the rack for company.

She waited there for nearly an hour, finishing the paper with its ECCOLO LA SIGNORA MANAGER headline and photograph of her at the airport, and downing two stiff dry Martinis for resolve. The suggestive looks of a middle-aged businessman across the bar told her it was time to go. She pushed the bill across the counter to the barman.

'Put that on Mr Fisher's account, would you, please?'

Sod them, she thought to herself as she left the hotel and caught a cab to the Town Hall.

By now 'the lads' had reached their first port of call, a bar-cum-restaurant in a quiet street off one of the main boulevards.

The trouble was that it was too quiet – only a handful of locals were in, all of them middle-aged males – and the only beer they had was Italian bottled stuff. Worse still, Eddie seemed to think this was the height of Bergamo social life, or at least as high as he would allow them to reach.

The group sat around their beers – apart from Eddie and Gardner, who were on mineral water – trying to make conversation without revealing their true intentions to Eddie. Rimmer moaned about the bar being worse than any pub back home, then Kennedy moaned about the bland 'Euro-music' it was playing.

'It's handy for the hotel, though,' Eddie smiled, enjoying their frustration.

Fisher leaped up and clapped his hands decisively.

'Right, chairman's round. How about a few bottles of champagne to get us going?'

'You'll be lucky. It's strictly that Nasty Arsolo stuff here,' said Halliwell.

Fisher moved towards the bar anyway.

'Boss's orders were for a few beers only, Mr Chairman,' Eddie called from his seat, unsure of how to handle things with Fisher involved.

Fisher leaned on the bar and spread his arms plaintively.

'Come on, Eddie, we're away from home. Live a little!' said Fisher.

'*After* the game, fine,' Eddie said firmly, looking Fisher in the eye.

'All right, all right,' he sighed, conceding. 'Lemonades all round. You ready for a drink yet, Perry?'

Gardener shook his head.

'No thanks, Mr Chairman. I'll get stuck into the cocktails at the club.'

His voice tailed off as he realized what he'd said. The other players looked away in frustration. Eddie turned to look at him.

'Joke, Eddie, joke,' Gardner pleaded.

Eddie's face gave nothing away. Halliwell stood up to break the tension.

'I'll give you a hand, Chairman.'

The players resumed their drinking in a sullen silence, as Halliwell joined Fisher at the bar.

'Similar, *por favor*,' Fisher tried, gesturing to the previous drinks. The barman got the message and started taking the tops off more bottles. Halliwell moved close to Fisher's ear and nodded back at Eddie.

'He's like a terrier with his teeth in a bear's arse! Can't you just tell him to piss off and mind his own business?'

Fisher pulled a face. 'It'd be dodgy. I don't want to cross him too much. He's my main source of pressure on Gabriella.'

'We have to shake him off, though. I mean, us married men have got to get strumped tonight – no point in coming abroad otherwise!'

Fisher took the point. He looked through at the bar's upper level, where a table of middle-aged blokes were seated around a bottle of wine and a plate of olives. They were all about Eddie's age. Then Fisher remembered Eddie telling him about his exploits in the Anglo-Italian tournament.

'Listen, try this . . .' Fisher whispered into Halliwell's ear.

About five minutes later, as Fisher's round of drinks was running out, Halliwell went to the toilet and made his way back past the table of four men, pausing for a few moments, seemingly to talk to them. Then he came down to the main bar and approached Eddie excitedly.

'Here, Eddie, you're not going to believe this, but there's a bloke over there who recognizes you!'

'Where?' asked Eddie, turning to follow Halliwell's gaze. Halliwell winked to the rest of the party while Eddie's back was turned.

'Geezer with the droopy moustache. Reckons he played against you once – kicked him all over the park, you did. Anglo-Italian Cup, I think he said.'

Eddie sat up, interested.

'Aye, I played a few games over here actually. Did he say a name?'

He looked across at the man Halliwell had indicated, who was chatting away to his friends.

'Mario something or other. He's sure he came up against you, though. 1971 was it? Anyway, he'd like to buy you a drink. For old times' sake, like.'

Eddie stood up, cautious but intrigued.

'It could be a lad from Sampadoria. I gave him a bit of a pasting, if I remember rightly,' said Eddie, convinced now.

'Well, time to bury the hatchet, then. Make up for Heysel and that,' urged Halliwell.

Eddie made his way over to the table, going up a half-dozen steps to get there. He tapped the man with the moustache on the shoulder and offered a hand when he turned.

'Eddie Johnson – once of Blackpool! Inghilterra!'

There were blank looks all around the table. The man with the moustache looked at him, puzzled, and asked him something in Italian.

'You know – football! My team played your team. 1971!'

The man now turned away from Eddie and made a remark to his three colleagues, which had them laughing in ribald fashion.

Eddie persisted. 'Mario, isn't it?'

The man turned on Eddie, getting annoyed now and shouting something hostile. Eddie didn't know what it meant immediately, but then he remembered Italian players saying it to him when he'd fouled them during his Anglo-Italian Cup games. He backed away and turned into the main bar, angry at the public humiliation. But in front of him the tables were empty, the drinks abandoned. The 'raiding party' had slipped away.

'Bastards!' Eddie cursed.

Worse than the feeling of betrayal – he knew it was a team 'stroke' and he would get over it – was the realization that the players seemed to be over here for a laugh rather than a football match. It looked like only he and Gabriella were taking the trip seriously. That's what stuck in Eddie's gullet as he made his way out of the bar and headed forlornly back to the hotel.

CHAPTER TWELVE

Gabriella's taxi dropped her outside the illuminated Palazzo del Commune, and she judged from the host of limousines parked outside that the rich and powerful of Bergamo were all within. She made her way past the security guards and into a pretty courtyard. From there, a marble-lined staircase led her up to the room where the reception was being held. Chamber music wafted down. Gabriella braced herself and walked in.

A huge, dazzling chandelier dominated the room, which was hung with portraits of the town's heroes such as the composer Donizetti and one of the founders of the republic, Garibaldi. There were about thirty guests hovering around a long buffet-table. The mayor introduced himself to Gabriella and they quickly fell to talking about football, which cut across all classes and professions in Italy. Soon Gabriella was besieged with enthusiastic questions, which she dealt with good-humouredly in Italian.

One gentleman was baffled as to why she was teaching the game to the English: weren't they barbarians? Gabriella found herself defending her 'adopted' nation in the face of this Italian onslaught, and she joked that the English couldn't be that bad if the Italians kept trying to buy their players.

'We are rescuing the best,' her inquisitor said, 'and perhaps now we will rescue you! Come home!'

Gabriella saw her chance to escape this particular circle of conversation.

'Very well, if you'll excuse me for a moment, I must go and call the Agnelli family!'

They all laughed at this reference to the multi-millionaire dynasty which controlled not only Fiat, but also the famous Juventus club of Turin. Gabriella made good her escape and drifted over to the buffet-table, where she helped herself to some of the cold meats on display. As she filled her plate, she became aware of another guest standing alongside her, surveying the buffet. He was a tall, well-dressed man in his early forties with typically romantic Italian looks. He caught her eye and smiled.

'You seem to have quite a following,' he said in Italian.

'Oh, no – not really. It's just novelty value, I think,' she replied, also in Italian.

'Why, what do you do?' he asked.

Gabriella looked at him, but his open, sensitive face told her that he wasn't being facetious. He genuinely didn't know her identity. Relieved that she didn't have to talk football, Gabriella hedged her reply.

'Oh, I'm involved in sports, I suppose.'

He pulled a comic face at the mention of the word sport.

'I must be the only Italian male who isn't the slightest bit interested in it,' he smiled, and then added politely, 'until now that is.'

He asked what sport she was involved in, and Gabriella hid behind her 'aerobics' persona, telling him of the studio she ran in England. He seemed surprised that she was English, and Gabriella was flattered that her Italian had stood up to such close scrutiny.

'I'd never have guessed,' he said, breaking into English in deference to her.

'Well, I'm half-Italian actually – the half that spends money!'

He laughed and then surveyed the wilting buffet.

'I think the food could use some fitness training.'

Gabriella laughed and nodded discreetly at the other guests.

'It's an escape from talking . . . until now that is.'

The man nodded politely at the compliment and moved quickly to try and take advantage of it.

'Look, forgive my presumption, but would you like to dine with me, perhaps?'

Gabriella dithered. 'Well actually, I was about to go back to my hotel and order room-service.'

He reached across, took her plate from her purposefully and laid it to one side.

'Oh, no, you're far too beautifully dressed for a lonely supper in your room.'

Gabriella was cornered. She could have just refused, but the disappointment of being abandoned by Fisher and her father, and the stolidness of the reception, had left her vulnerable to the prospect of a pleasant night out with an attractive man in Bergamo. The man saw her resolve weaken, and he offered his hand in introduction.

'My name is Marco Custodero. I'm an architect. But I promise not to talk about it,' he smiled.

Gabriella shook his hand. 'Gabriella . . . Gabriella Rebecchi,' she said, adopting her maiden name.

Marco suggested a restaurant on the main square of the old town – the Plaza Vecchia – with views out on to a dancing fountain, where a trio of youths strummed guitars, interrupted only by the chimes from several church towers in the vicinity. Gabriella was quite intoxicated by the setting, and she was happy to respond openly to Marco's questions later as they studied their menus over glasses of champagne.

Marco continued to speak to her in his accented English, more out of politeness than a desire to show off or to flatter her.

'What brings you back here, then, Gabriella? Not nostalgia surely?'

She smiled at him across the table. 'No, I was only ten when I left, so not too many things stick with me. The church . . . the countryside . . . a certain passion for sport, I suppose.'

'And now you return to assess the competition?' Marco guessed.

'In a way, yes,' she replied. 'But I suppose what I'm really testing is myself. In England I grew up being challenged to prove that I was really English. Here, I seem to be challenged to prove I'm not a failure.'

Marco nodded his understanding. 'It always happens with exiles – you must justify your leaving! So, how many employees do you have in your business?'

Gabriella was enjoying the temporary anonymity too much to reveal the truth, but found she was none the less able to answer honestly.

'Over twenty.'

'Quite a responsibility. Do you manage to keep them happy?'

'I try,' she smiled, thinking of the team and all its problems. 'Some need a lot of encouragement, others need to be bossed – the trick is to know which ones are which. They're all like children, really. They need love and attention, but they can sometimes break your heart.'

'I'm glad I'm self-employed,' Marco sighed. 'The skills of management are out of my reach. Tell me what's the worst part of being a boss?'

Gabriella reflected on her present mood: away from home and shunned by the men around her.

'The isolation. That gap between you and them, because they know you can decide their future. No matter how sympathetic you are, you can't get too close, because sooner or later a decision will crop up. And when you make it, it will hurt you as well as them.'

Marco registered Gabriella's pensive mood, and let her reflect in silence for a moment, content to look at her in the candle-light.

'Forgive me, but to me you sound too sensitive for your job.'

Gabriella snapped out of her reverie with a laugh.

'Oh, if only you knew! I can be a real Italian momma at times!'

Marco joined in her laughter and brought his glass up to clink against hers in a toast. Gabriella smiled: it wasn't turning out to be such a bad evening after all.

Had she been seated facing the square, her mood might have changed, because at that moment a little crocodile of players, led by Perry Gardner and Martin Fisher, made its way across the plaza behind her. In a narrow passage off the square was Gino's Disco, the main tourist attraction for the Rat Pack that night.

The lads had trooped through the seventeenth-century town without a single admiring look at the architecture, but their faces registered eager anticipation as the neon sign beckoned them. Underneath a classy-looking awning, which covered a flight of ancient stone steps, stood a formidable bouncer in evening dress. Gardner tried to quell their boisterousness as they approached.

'Here we go, lads. Now, please, one promise: don't break the place up. They know me here.'

They were too entranced by the prospect of getting in among the signorinas to quibble with Gardner's view of his European status.

'Perry, we're footballers, not supporters,' Halliwell pointed out.

'And we're here to pull, not to fight,' added Rimmer.

'Yeah, but one usually leads to another,' Gardner warned.

'All right, lads, best behaviour,' urged Fisher. 'No getting your plonkers out until you're asked to.'

They hung back a little as Gardner approached the doorman.

'Is it all right if I bring the team in?' he asked.

'Team?' queried the bouncer, plainly oblivious of Gardner's identity.

'Yeah – football. English! You know, Bobby Charlton!'

The last phrase drew a smile and a nod of recognition from the bouncer.

'Ah, okay! Bobby Charlton – sure, sure. Hunky-dory!'

Gardner gestured the rest of the lads over, and they filed in up the steps in the direction of the throbbing music. As Fisher went past, the doorman smiled and held out a hand.

'Nice to see you, Mr Charlton,' he said in broken English.

Fisher bristled and produced a wad of lira from his back pocket that was designed to impress.

'The name's Fisher! El Presidente, sunbeam!'

He stuffed a wodge of notes into the doorman's breast pocket. 'Have a drink,' he muttered, before running up the steps after the players.

.

By now Nicholl and McGregor, who'd resisted all attempts to get them to go on the disco trawl for women, were smugly ensconced in their Michelin-recommended restaurant, studying the menu like the cosmopolitan Europeans that Nicholl, at least, wished them to be. McGregor, however, was having a little difficulty with the menu.

'Did you bring the phrase-book, Keith?' he whispered.

'I think I remembered most of the culinary terms,' Nicholl smiled reassuringly.

McGregor looked relieved. He glanced around the smart dining-room with its tables of businessmen, local worthies and tourists.

'This is more like it, eh?' he enthused to Nicholl. 'Two friends on a civilized evening out. I couldn't have faced sniffing round the disco for crumpet.'

Nicholl seemed distracted but nodded his agreement.

'Well, no, me neither. All a bit desperate, really.'

'Yeah, I made up my mind after Lesley left that I'd take my time before plunging again.'

'Sensible, Dave,' Nicholl muttered, looking beyond McGregor. Then he smiled and stood up. McGregor turned and saw a pretty blonde girl approaching the table, gushing smiles at Nicholl.

'How super to see you, Keith!' she trilled before kissing him fondly. McGregor averted his gaze and shuffled in his seat. Nicholl broke away from this embrace and ushered the girl into the seat next to him. Even McGregor could work out that she hadn't just stumbled in by accident, and he looked suitably cheesed off about it.

'Er, Fiona,' Nicholl said smiling, 'this is a team-mate of

mine, Dave McGregor. Dave, Fiona's an old friend from university. She teaches over here, so I thought I'd look her up!'

'Yeah – sensible,' muttered McGregor, wishing he could go home instantly.

'Are you a graduate too, Dave?' Fiona asked as she installed herself.

'Well, not in the same league as Keith, here,' he said, forcing a smile. 'Er, do you mind if I stay?'

Nicholl looked aghast.

'No, no, of course not. I wanted you to be here, Dave!'

McGregor smiled, feeling a little better about the set-up.

'Just as long as you don't mind covering for me later with Eddie,' Nicholl said with a wink. 'Fiona and I have a lot of catching up to do, see.'

McGregor nodded.

'I'm sure.'

'Shall we order? I'm famished!' Fiona said.

McGregor gallantly offered her his menu.

'Know it backwards, actually,' she said.

Nicholl leaned forward across the table, hands pressed together in presidential style.

'Now, Dave, *you* are going to order. In Italian. And then you'll see how well people treat you when you speak to them in their own language!'

Fiona gave McGregor a nod of encouragement.

'Yeah, okay!' he said bravely, returning his attention to the menu. 'Is *sorpresa* a surprise?'

In Gino's Disco, Fisher and the Rat Pack had taken themselves quickly on to the floor in an attempt to announce their presence to the local womanhood. Kennedy, Morris and Coughlan danced eagerly with each other, trying to build up their nerve, and hoping that their behaviour would attract adoring women. Brian Rimmer, however, had waded straight in among a circle of teenage girls, and was trying to talk over the pounding music to any one of them who might listen.

'I'm a goal-keeper!' he shouted into the ear of a pretty eighteen-year-old.

The girl frowned, unable to hear, let alone decipher his broad Yorkshire accent.

'You know, Dino Zoff!' he shouted, hoping the reference to Italy's famous World Cup goal-keeper would convey the message. To back it up, he raised both arms above his head and 'dived' for an imaginary ball heading for the top corner of the net. The girl took this to be a startling new dance step and immediately imitated it.

Over at the bar, Perry Gardner and Gary Halliwell stood watching Rimmer's antics on the dance-floor.

'I think it's gonna be hard work here tonight. If someone of Brian's class can't pull, there's not much hope for me,' Halliwell shouted.

Gardner, who was still sticking with soft drinks, enjoyed Halliwell's joke. The earlier animosity between them had been softened by the camaraderie of being in a foreign country. Gardner's smile disappeared, however, as he saw the tabloid journalist Steve Simms swan through the doors.

'Bleedin' press are in here now!' he cursed. Halliwell turned to see Simms heading in their direction with a smirk on his face.

'How's the training, lads?' he asked ironically.

'Leave it out, Steve, we're only having a laugh. And it hasn't gone ten yet,' Gardner said plaintively.

Simms put a reassuring hand on Gardner's shoulder.

'It's all right, Perry – don't panic. I'm here for the same thing as you are!'

'Yeah, but if you get your leg over, you don't wake up with your face plastered all over a rag like yours!' Halliwell said aggressively.

'I'm off-duty, Gary!'

To illustrate this, Simms began to eye the clutch of girls on the dance-floor and pointed one out.

272

'Now *that* has got to go! You know, whenever I go on a foreign trip, I have this pathological need to get my end away. It's like some people collect passport stamps. I'll even pay for it!'

'You may have to, son,' Gardner said, before wandering off in the direction of the toilets. He got to the door, and turned to make sure that Halliwell was still talking with Simms. Simms was handing over a drink. Satisfied they couldn't see him, Gardner slipped towards the exit and left.

.

After their meal, Marco insisted on walking Gabriella back to her hotel. She was touched by the offer, and once outside in the warm air, with the square packed with strolling families, Gabriella remembered the old Italian tradition of evening walks with friends and family – the *passeggiata*. Marco gave her a guided tour of the old town as they returned, passing pavement bars and restaurants packed with locals and tourists. Gabriella soaked up the atmosphere with a mixture of emotions: sadness that her father's indiscretions had robbed her of this aspect of life in Italy and pride that she could still feel a part of it.

'You know, Marco, it's strange,' she confessed to him at one point. 'But I suddenly feel Italian again!'

He was pleased with her response and saluted her enthusiastically. '*Va bene!*'

They said their goodbyes on the steps of the hotel. Gabriella offered him her hand, but he ignored it and kissed her on both cheeks instead. He stood and watched her as she climbed the steps and disappeared inside.

In the lobby, Gabriella's romantic intermission came to an abrupt end when she saw Eddie sitting doggedly over a cup of tea with his list of players and their rooms. He looked a forlorn figure.

'How's your evening been, Eddie?' she asked, without animosity.

Eddie looked sheepish. 'They gave me the slip. Sorry.

McGregor's in anyway – and Keith Nicholl got back before him apparently. But the rest . . .'

Eddie looked crestfallen, waiting for Gabriella to blow her top, but luckily for him she'd been soothed by her own evening out.

'Don't worry, Eddie,' she consoled him. 'The bastards were always going to stitch us up.'

'Aye,' he said with a sigh. 'Anyway, I'll sit up for a bit.'

Gabriella smiled at him. She almost felt like planting a kiss on his forehead, to ease his loneliness and his obvious distress.

'Goodnight, Eddie,' she said and walked over to the lifts.

Eddie called out to the receptionist.

'Miss – may I have another pot of tea, please?'

Gabriella watched him sadly until the lift came.

Inside, she stood alone, looking at her reflection in the mirror. She felt the isolation she had told Marco about descend upon her like a shroud. Her job meant no real companionship, only hardened professional relationships. Fisher couldn't be trusted, her father always let her down, and the lads in the team would never accept her as anything other than a tolerable oddity at best. She wondered why she let it take so much passion from her, when she only occasionally received some in return.

The lift door opened with an electronic 'ping', and she walked slowly down the darkened corridor, taking her key from her bag. She opened her door and was about to go in, when she heard the doors of the second lift open. Marco came out and stood for a moment, looking along the corridor at her. She had plenty of time to ignore him, to go in through her door and leave the night behind her – but she didn't. He began to walk towards her. Gabriella watched him and waited. He came straight up to her and embraced her, locking his mouth on to hers. She let her hand-bag drop to the floor as she embraced him in return. He began to undress her where she stood, lifting her off her feet. They moved slowly in through the door, still kissing. Marco flicked out a foot and kicked the bag in through the door as he closed it.

'Goal,' Gabriella murmured.

•

Downstairs Eddie's tea had arrived, but he stopped in mid-sip when he saw Perry Gardner come in. Eddie looked at him, not knowing whether to be pleased at his professionalism or angry at his part in the deception earlier. Gardner wandered over to him and gave him an apologetic smile.

'Sorry, Eddie – it was a shitty trick to pull,' he said.

Eddie accepted the apology with a shrug. 'I've had worse. What brings you back?'

'The game. Want to be right for it.'

'I think you're in a minority,' Eddie muttered.

'I know, but I don't want to let the boss down.'

Eddie watched his face, looking for signs of superciliousness, but there were none. Gardner was serious.

'Do you want to order a drink?' Eddie asked.

'Yeah! I'll have a tea!'

'You can have a beer if you want one – I won't tell.'

'Ah, but *I'll* know,' said Gardner. 'Tea'll be fine.'

Eddie gestured across to the receptionist, who nodded in acknowledgement. Gardner sat down opposite him.

'It counts tomorrow, doesn't it: the match?' Gardner said.

'They all do. If there's only one man and his dog out there, we've still got to put on a show.'

Gardner smiled at Eddie. 'I know you think I'm a fanny-merchant, Eddie.'

Despite the improved atmosphere between them, Eddie didn't leap to deny this.

'Well, I've got news for you,' Gardner continued, 'I'm going to get worse. I'll tell you why one day, if we're still speaking. But as from tomorrow, I'm gonna go out and shoot from every angle when I could pass. I'm gonna "nut-meg" defenders by the dozen, and scissor-kick anything above waist-height. *And* I'm gonna enjoy every minute of it!'

Eddie considered this declaration of intent without giving anything away. After a pause, he stretched back in his seat.

'I think I'd pay to watch.'

Gardner couldn't have been more pleased if he'd scored at Wembley.

·

During the next half-hour, Simon phoned Gabriella's room twice. The first time she didn't answer it because she and Marco were making love. The second time she answered it, still slightly breathless, but told him she'd just stepped from the shower. Simon had nothing to say other than to wish her goodnight, and Gabriella didn't have much to say either. She put the phone down and returned to Marco's arms.

·

The last act of the night was the return of the lads from the disco at well after two. They came in through the darkened lobby to find Eddie slumped in his chair, asleep. They all looked sweat-stained and exhausted from their efforts, but the 'raid' had been unsuccessful – no women accompanied them. They made shushing gestures to each other, and grinned as they realized that they'd got away with their escapade.

'He looks almost human,' whispered Halliwell.

'Here,' boomed Rimmer, incapable of being quiet, 'he won't be able to tell anybody that none of us pulled!'

Fisher, suit crumpled and tie and collar undone, shook his head, and tossed his cigar stub into an ash-tray.

'What a shambles!' he sighed with exhaustion. 'I'm going to bed!'

And he shuffled off towards the lifts, followed by the weary group of players. Eddie began to snore.

·

The team were allowed to lie in until ten the next morning, which was probably just as well. Then they were allowed the use of Atalanta's training pitch at Zingonia for a light, loosening-up, head-clearing session. They had lunch back at the hotel followed by a short nap. Then they changed into suits for the brief coach journey up to Atalanta's ground, the Stadio Comunale.

Gabriella had made no show of her displeasure at their behaviour, preferring to save it, should it become necessary later. Besides, she knew she was hardly on high moral ground herself now. But she was pleased with the tangible excitement the players began to display as the coach, with its police escort, turned off a wide street and gave the first view of the coliseum-style ground, with tree-lined hills rising behind it. They would have to be made of wood not to feel a thrill at the setting. There was even a group of noisy, flag-waving Italian fans to greet the coach as it pulled up outside the main entrance. English fans mingled peaceably with them, sounding an appropriate note for this friendly game.

Once inside, Gabriella and the team trooped along a long tunnel, at the end of which was a flight of steps that took them up on to the pitch behind one of the goals. This fitted the gladiatorial setting, for as they came up into the warm evening air, they saw the huge concrete amphitheatre of the ground wrapped around them. Gabriella watched with Eddie as the players walked the pitch, which was in magnificent condition: flat, well-grassed, neatly clipped. Eddie looked around, impressed with the setting and the facilities.

'It must be pretty hard to do anything ugly with this lot around you,' he said wistfully. Gabriella smiled at his lyricism – Eddie, *moved* by Italy? She felt personally complimented.

Unfortunately, the opulence of the surroundings and the passion of the crowd had the opposite effect on the team as the first half got under way. They reverted to classical English type – hard-tackling, harrying, scurrying football, with lots of long, aimless clearances from defenders and fruitless high balls down the middle from Rimmer.

Gardner, Kennedy and Morris, up front, saw little of the ball as it soared uselessly above them. The display was capped by a crude foul from Coughlan which earned him a booking, and drew shrill whistles from the crowd, who had presumably expected something different from a team managed by a woman.

Gabriella sat seething in the dug-out, flanked by Eddie and Martin Fisher, whose alliance with the 'lads' had spilled over into sufficient enthusiasm to make him forsake the comforts of the directors' box on this occasion – *and* no doubt he felt more important down on the touch-line! Gabriella didn't particularly like him being there, but had swallowed her objections for the sake of the match. She was also angered by the fact that there had been no sign of her father, when he knew how much this game meant to her. This too she pushed from her mind. But the match itself she could not ignore.

As the team trooped off at half-time to more derisory whistles, Gabriella ran after them and quickly followed them down into the dressing-room, slamming the door behind her. Several of the players had already started bickering among themselves, and the biggest complaints came from Kennedy and Gardner.

'For Christ's sake, Brian – *throw* the ball out, will you?' Gardner moaned to Rimmer. 'Some of those kicks are coming down with icicles on them!'

Rimmer was not impressed. 'Look – I know these foreign teams. They're no good in the air, *Cyril*!'

'Maybe not, but the two lads on me are about a foot taller than I am! If I was Mark Hateley I could probably piss on them!'

Halliwell stomped over to step between them, and poked his finger into Gardner's chest.

'Listen, cake-brain, if you found some space and showed yourself, maybe we could hit you instead of the bloody Alps!'

'I haven't had one ball to feet all half!' complained Kennedy.

Coughlan stood up from the bench and shouted. 'Oh, fucking listen to it, will you! It's only a poxy friendly!'

Gabriella had stood to one side and listened to all this, pleased in one way that some pride had been hurt, but deeply angered by the cynicism and apathy of most of the team.

'Right!' she shouted. 'Shut up, the lot of you! Shut up!'

A grudging silence fell as she walked through the narrow but well-appointed dressing-room. She turned and looked at them, and began speaking in an artificially calm voice.

'This game *is* important. Because if we don't win it, and win it in the style I want, then I'm packing it in!'

The players, most of whom had been hanging their heads trying to avoid her gaze, started to look up at this revelation.

'That's right, I'll quit,' she confirmed. 'All the work we've put in together over the past five months has suddenly gone out of the window. And only you, each of you, knows why. Maybe you're still pissed from last night, or not pissed enough,' she added witheringly.

'Maybe you're tired and your attitude's wrong; maybe it's instinctive English behaviour when faced with Italians to go back to street-fighting, alehouse football. But I don't care what the reasons are. If you don't give me some reward for all the shit I've been through with you lot, then that's it. You wanted me out when I arrived, and you can get me out tonight if you still want to. It's up to you.'

With that she walked out, leaving them with their thoughts, and headed back down the long corridor towards the pitch.

It soon became clear that her words had had a galvanizing effect on the team, for right from the restart they stormed into fluent attacking moves, keeping the ball on the ground and trying to unstitch the Atalanta defence with sharp passing and incisive running off the ball.

After five minutes of pressure, a move involving a quick interchange of passes between McGregor, Nicholl and Gardner set Tony Morris free on the left-hand edge of the Italians' penalty area. Morris shimmied as if going outside, throwing the defender off balance, and then cut inside and hit a firm low shot past the keeper into the bottom corner of the net. The players celebrated with an extravagance which suggested a common purpose had been declared.

The Atalanta team – who had recently been promoted into the first division – took this as a great affront, and took advantage of the greater openness of Gabriella's team to launch several incisive attacks of their own. At last, the crowd had a game, and they responded with a cacophony of noise.

The teams traded attacks like prize-fighters trading punches. Eventually Atalanta won a free-kick on the edge of the box, and even Gardner and Kennedy were pulled back for the defensive wall. This was to no avail, because the wiry little midfield player who took the kick calmly clipped the ball over the wall with enough swerve to send it away from Brian Rimmer's desperate dive and into the net — one–one!

Gabriella almost had to stop herself applauding the goal, since it revealed everything she admired about Italian football: precision and technique. But she wanted her team to win the game, and she quickly stood up in the dug-out to urge her lads on to greater efforts.

With less than ten minutes remaining, a good pass and a clever flick from Paul Kennedy sent Perry Gardner hurtling towards goal; he was at a difficult angle, but he confidently hit the ball on the run and sent it slamming into the Atalanta net inside the near post. Gardner skidded down to the turf on his knees in exultation, and was quickly swamped by jubilant team-mates. The game meant something to all of them now. Two–one was the final score, and Gabriella celebrated the victory modestly, as befitting guests in a foreign country. Inside, however, she was bursting with pleasure and fulfilment.

The team had a few beers in the dressing-room followed by a raucous sing-song in the plunge-bath. Fisher hob-nobbed with the Atalanta directors, feeling as big as one of his cigars. After this, both teams adjourned to one of Bergamo's smartest restaurants for a joint dinner, with club officials present. In these troubled times for the game of football, a spot of fraternization between opponents would do no harm, although Fisher fretted at the prospect of having to give a speech, and worked on Gabriella to take his place. The players too had their problems, not just with the stiff formality of the occasion — what they really wanted was to get back out on the town — but also with the difficulties thrown up by having each English player sit next to an Italian. There was a lot of miming going on, and only Nicholl really relished this opportunity to show off his linguistic abilities.

'The food here is good, isn't it?' he managed in Italian to the player sitting on his left.

The Atalanta lad shrugged and whispered to Nicholl in English.

'I think it's shit – but then they change the menu to English food for you.'

On another part of the table, Halliwell was seemingly lumbered with his Italian counterpart. In the interests of conversation, Halliwell nudged him and mimed a yawn.

'Boring this, isn't it?'

The Atalanta captain nodded and leaned across to whisper into Halliwell's ear in broken but eminently comprehensible English. 'Later we go out . . . all together . . . get pissed . . . and then . . .' He inserted his fist into the crook of his other arm and bent the arm over it, in familiar sexual semaphore. Halliwell's face lit up.

'Here, Brian!' he called across to Rimmer. 'I think these lads speak the same language as us after all.'

Gabriella was rescued from Fisher's nervous twittering about speech-making by a waiter who gestured that there was a telephone-call for her. She hoped and expected, as she walked out into the restaurant foyer, that Sergio was calling to offer his profound apologies for missing the game. But it wasn't Sergio on the phone – it was Simon.

For a moment she was irritated by him calling when she was 'at work', especially when he began to dither about how important this may or may not be, and then said something about having been shopping in the supermarket. Gabriella was about to snap at him, thinking it was another call to let her know how miserable he'd been, when Simon told her he'd just seen Sergio – there, in town, in England, going in to the rear entrance of this supermarket, accompanied by Anthony Coombs and two other men who'd got out of a Range Rover.

Gabriella couldn't begin to work out what was going on, so she promised to call Simon back once she'd confronted Fisher. She thanked him for his call, and walked pensively back into the body of the restaurant. She came up behind Fisher and leaned discreetly over his shoulder; he cocked an ear, used to being talked to like this by his many minions.

'May I have a word in private, Mr Chairman?' she asked quietly, determined not to cause a scene.

'Yeah, sure – my place or yours?' joked Fisher.

'You have got five seconds to get your arse out into that corridor before I break something heavy over your head!' hissed Gabriella.

Fisher tried to maintain his *bonhomie* as he shuffled up from his chair and followed Gabriella. Once out of ear-shot of the team, Gabriella told Fisher of this reported sighting of her father and Coombs, and asked calmly but firmly what they might be doing.

'*I* don't know,' Fisher shrugged.

'Martin,' Gabriella sighed impatiently, 'I accept that you've never played it straight with me, maybe because you actually can't do it. But tell me now, because I'll find out sooner or later, and if I know you've been lying –'

'You'll shout and scream and stamp your bloody foot like normal,' he said witheringly.

'No,' said Gabriella remaining calm, 'I'll have you out of this club.'

Fisher stared at her, and she looked back at him unblinkingly. She didn't have the power to remove Fisher – unless her father 'changed sides', as it were. Fisher reasoned that this was eminently possible, given Sergio's character, and his resolve instantly weakened.

'Okay,' he sighed wearily, 'your father, Anthony and I have formed a company to exploit that share of the freehold which used to belong to Solford Construction.'

'Used to?' Gabriella frowned. 'They only acquired it three months ago.'

Gabriella knew that the English construction company was effectively a puppet in her father's hands – hence their sponsorship deal for the club – but she couldn't quite understand why they had been squeezed out now. An image came into her mind: sharks that attack one another when one of them bleeds.

'Sergio decided to narrow down the parameters of ownership,' said Fisher, 'to just the three of us. And we are approaching a supermarket chain about developing a store at the southern terrace end of the stadium.'

Gabriella looked stunned by their deception.

'We didn't tell you, 'cos we knew you'd kick up a fuss,' Fisher said limply.

Gabriella digested the information: property developers and accountants teaming up with a construction millionaire and a rapacious supermarket chain. It seemed to her like the 1980s equivalent of a Black Mass.

'Let me guess,' she said eventually, 'there'll be executive boxes on the roof of the store?'

Fisher shrugged.

'Only they'll have a design fault in them, because they'll face the pitch, when the people who rent them don't actually want to watch football at all!'

'Come off it, Gabriella!' Fisher pleaded. 'If it goes through, it'll be a good deal for us. We could make up to a million quid on the supermarket development alone!'

Gabriella presumed that the 'we' referred to was simply Fisher, Coombs and her father – not the club, which would obviously be lucky to see much of the money.

'*Of course* the club'll get some!' Fisher exclaimed.

'Yeah, but what's the point of having that sort of money, when you'd lose twice as much when the *real* fans stay away? You're tossers, Martin. You understand nothing about the game, or what it means to a community. If you proceed with this, I'll fight you all the way.'

'How would you do that, without *Daddy's* help?' Fisher asked scathingly.

'Don't forget, I've got my block of voting shares, and I'll bloody well use them, and maybe I'll get more too. But I can do more than that – I can mobilize the very people you think so little of – our supporters!'

A thought suddenly occurred to Fisher, and he smiled.

'But what if I sack you?'

'Try it,' Gabriella said defiantly. 'After a result like tonight's I could really stir the shit. Because that's where the real power is in the game – on the pitch and on the terraces! That's my constituency! Tell my father that when you see him!'

She stalked off back into the restaurant, leaving Fisher to exhale deeply, making a noise which was a lot like the sound of wind coming out of sails.

.

The team flew back at lunch-time the next day, buying up copies of the local paper which carried a big story and pictures of 'La Signora Manager's' triumph. Fisher sat apart from Gabriella the whole way. She knew he would have spoken to Sergio by now, which would have left her father with a simple choice: to call the deal off or to 'lose' his daughter again, this time for good.

There was no sign of him at Heathrow when they arrived back, to be greeted by camera crews and a flock of celebrating supporters. Gabriella gave her usual round of interviews and noted the new seriousness with which the press were treating her here. Maybe it was because her signing of Perry Gardner had succeeded so quickly, or maybe it was just an early start to the 'silly season' – but she was gratified none the less.

The coach returned the party to the club, where the players said their goodbyes to one another extravagantly as the short close season began. They even had the grace to come and thank Gabriella for her help, but she knew in her heart that this euphoria wouldn't last long, and that she would have to start the battles all over again as soon as they returned for training. Gabriella drove home from the club, and on the journey her feelings about Simon, which she'd pushed to one side so successfully, came flooding back.

As she came in through the front door, the house appeared to be empty. She called out nevertheless.

'Hello?'

There was no reply.

Presumptuous cow, she muttered to herself.

Then Simon appeared at the end of the hall, emerging from the kitchen.

'Hi – good trip?' he asked stiffly.

'Tense,' Gabriella said, 'storm clouds on the horizon, I'd say.'

'Oh, dear,' Simon said with apparently genuine sympathy. 'Is this something to do with what I saw last night?'

'Yes – I'd have been well outflanked if you hadn't spotted them!'

'Good job I stayed put, then,' Simon said with an ironic smile. Gabriella noted it.

'Does this mean they want you out?' Simon asked.

'No – it's a different sort of battle. But I'll fight it, just the same.'

'Of course,' Simon said dryly.

A silence fell. They hadn't moved towards one another. They both recognized the 'demilitarized zone' which lay between them for the time being.

'I missed you,' Simon said with his head down, for fear of seeing her rejection.

There was a pause.

'Me too,' she said sincerely. Simon looked up at her and stared into her eyes to see if this was true. It seemed to be. They smiled at one another fondly, aware that there was work to be done, but that they both still wanted their relationship to last. There would be plenty of time for talk over the coming football-free weeks, and perhaps even a reconciliatory holiday.

'I've got a few decent bottles of Italian wine,' she said, holding up her duty-free bag. 'Maybe we could have dinner in tonight – now that you've been shopping!'

'Sounds good, though I'm sure there's a reserve game at Swindon or somewhere, isn't there?'

'I don't suppose my father's phoned?' Gabriella asked.

Simon shook his head, and saw the dismay in her eyes.

'Look, far be it from me to coach the coach,' he said quietly, 'but isn't it about time you kicked him off the team?'

Gabriella looked at him and gave a weary nod of agreement.

.

Sergio caught up with her that evening. She'd gone to the cemetery to place flowers on her mother's grave, when she heard the car draw up outside the churchyard gate. She heard his footsteps on the gravel path.

'Simon told me you were here,' Sergio said softly.

Gabriella turned away from the memorial stone and faced him defiantly.

'Go away, father. There's nothing left in this country for you now. Not mother, not me.'

'Try to understand, Gabriella, please – it's how the game is – it needs people like me and Fisher for its survival.'

'Maybe if you'd told me that as a child, I could accept it now. But you didn't. It was a dream to me. It still is.'

Sergio smiled, encouraged by her calm tone.

'I don't think it's so healthy, to be like that,' he said, trying to humour her.

'Maybe not. I'm planning to sell up the exercise studio and use the money to buy out your interests in the club. Assuming you have the decency to sell them to me.'

'Yes. Of course,' Sergio mumbled, realizing there was to be no forgiveness this time.

'Then you'll have wasted nothing.'

'Hardly.'

'Goodbye, father,' Gabriella said, walking towards him. She kissed him politely on both cheeks but made no move to embrace him. She walked away, then stopped and turned.

'Don't you want to know the result?'

Sergio looked quizzical.

'Of last night's game?' Gabriella prompted. Sergio was mortified: he had forgotten.

'We won two—one. Played beautifully in the second half. You'd have been proud of me.'

'Gabriella, forgive me,' he pleaded.

Gabriella shook her head.

'It's a pity you can't think as a fan any more. The game's so much easier that way.'

She turned and walked out of the churchyard without once looking back.

·

Gabriella went down to the club a few days later to clear up any business that needed attending to during the break. She escaped from the office afterwards and walked up the tunnel and on to the pitch. Eddie was there, leaning against the dug-out, watching the groundsman reseeding an area of the pitch which was being watered by a rotating hose. The goal-posts had been taken down, and the stadium had an atmosphere of quiet decay about it.

'Not taking a holiday, Eddie?' she asked as she approached him.

Eddie seemed lost in his thoughts. While other people measured their years from January to December, football people worked on seasons, each with its own emotional identity. The summer was a blank space in Eddie's life.

'I dunno,' he said. 'Might have a week at my sister's. Take her kids to the seaside. I hate the summer really.'

Gabriella smiled – but then again that's all there was in his life. Eddie nodded at the groundsman sprinkling the seeds.

'He didn't need to bother last year, there'd been so little football played on it.'

Gabriella took this as the compliment it was intended to be, and nearly blushed.

'So I blitzed the grass but I stopped the terrace from becoming the supermarket end – there's an ecological irony there!'

Eddie hated it when she was being clever.

'Talk football for Christ's sake – it's what you're good at!'

'Okay – what day does training start again?'

Gabriella walked back down the touch-line towards the tunnel. Eddie fell into step alongside her.

'Twentieth of July – I'll make the buggers sweat their tans off!'

'I'm thinking about playing with two wingers next season,' Gabriella said.

Eddie, engaged by the football talk, frowned.

'You'd have to bring Coughlan back into midfield to hold things together.'

Gabriella stopped and smiled at him, wagging a finger. He still hadn't learned.

'Nobody got anywhere by being cautious, Eddie!'

FOR THE BEST IN PAPERBACKS, LOOK FOR THE

In every corner of the world, on every subject under the sun, Penguin represents quality and variety – the very best in publishing today.

For complete information about books available from Penguin – including Pelicans, Puffins, Peregrines and Penguin Classics – and how to order them, write to us at the appropriate address below. Please note that for copyright reasons the selection of books varies from country to country.

In the United Kingdom: Please write to *Dept E.P., Penguin Books Ltd, Harmondsworth, Middlesex, UB7 0DA*

If you have any difficulty in obtaining a title, please send your order with the correct money, plus ten per cent for postage and packaging, to *PO Box No 11, West Drayton, Middlesex*

In the United States: Please write to *Dept BA, Penguin, 299 Murray Hill Parkway, East Rutherford, New Jersey 07073*

In Canada: Please write to *Penguin Books Canada Ltd, 2801 John Street, Markham, Ontario L3R 1B4*

In Australia: Please write to the *Marketing Department, Penguin Books Australia Ltd, P.O. Box 257, Ringwood, Victoria 3134*

In New Zealand: Please write to the *Marketing Department, Penguin Books (NZ) Ltd, Private Bag, Takapuna, Auckland 9*

In India: Please write to *Penguin Overseas Ltd, 706 Eros Apartments, 56 Nehru Place, New Delhi, 110019*

In Holland: Please write to *Penguin Books Nederland B.V., Postbus 195, NL–1380AD Weesp, Netherlands*

In Germany: Please write to *Penguin Books Ltd, Friedrichstrasse 10–12, D–6000 Frankfurt Main 1, Federal Republic of Germany*

In Spain: Please write to *Longman Penguin España, Calle San Nicolas 15, E–28013 Madrid, Spain*

In France: Please write to *Penguin Books Ltd, 39 Rue de Montmorency, F-75003, Paris, France*

In Japan: Please write to *Longman Penguin Japan Co Ltd, Yamaguchi Building, 2-12-9 Kanda Jimbocho, Chiyoda-Ku, Tokyo 101, Japan*

Cat Chaser Elmore Leonard

'*Cat Chaser* really moves' – *The New York Times Book Review* 'Elmore Leonard gets so much mileage out of his plot that just when you think one is cruising to a stop, it picks up speed for a few more twists and turns' – *Washington Post*

The Mosquito Coast Paul Theroux

Detesting twentieth century America, Allie Fox takes his family to live in the Honduran jungle. 'Imagine the Swiss Family Robinson gone mad, and you will have some idea of what is in store . . . Theroux's best novel yet' – *Sunday Times*

Skallagrigg William Horwood

This new book from the author of *Duncton Wood* unites Arthur, a little boy abandoned many years ago in a grim hospital in northern England, with Esther, a radiantly intelligent young girl who is suffering from cerebral palsy, and with Daniel, an American computer-games genius. 'Some of the passages would wring tears of recognition, not pity' – Yvonne Nolan in the *Observer*

The Second Rumpole Omnibus John Mortimer

'Rumpole is worthy to join the great gallery of English oddballs ranging from Pickwick to Sherlock Holmes, Jeeves and Bertie Wooster' – *Sunday Times* 'Rumpole has been an inspired stroke of good fortune for us all' – Lynda Lee-Potter in the *Daily Mail*

The Lion's Cage John Clive

As the Allies advance across Europe, the likes of Joe Porter are making a killing of another kind. His destiny becomes woven with that of Lissette, whose passionate love for a German officer spells peril for Porter and herself – and the battle for survival begins.

A CHOICE OF PENGUIN FICTION

The Ghost Writer   Philip Roth

Philip Roth's celebrated novel about a young writer who meets and falls in love with Anne Frank in New England – or so he thinks. 'Brilliant, witty and extremely elegant' – *Guardian*

Small World   David Lodge

Shortlisted for the 1984 Booker Prize, *Small World* brings back Philip Swallow and Maurice Zapp for a jet-propelled journey into hilarity. 'The most brilliant and also the funniest novel that he has written' – *London Review of Books*

Moon Tiger   Penelope Lively

Winner of the 1987 Booker Prize, *Moon Tiger* is Penelope Lively's 'most ambitious book to date' – *The Times* 'A complex tapestry of great subtlety . . . Penelope Lively writes so well, savouring the words as she goes' – *Daily Telegraph* 'A very clever book: it is evocative, thought-provoking and hangs curiously on the edges of the mind long after it is finished' – *Literary Review*

Absolute Beginners   Colin MacInnes

The first 'teenage' novel, the classic of youth and disenchantment, *Absolute Beginners* is part of MacInnes's famous London trilogy – and now a brilliant film. 'MacInnes caught it first – and best' – *Harpers and Queen*

July's People   Nadine Gordimer

Set in South Africa, this novel gives us an unforgettable look at the terrifying, tacit understandings and misunderstandings between blacks and whites. 'This is the best novel that Miss Gordimer has ever written' – Alan Paton in the *Saturday Review*

The Ice Age   Margaret Drabble

'A continuously readable, continuously surprising book . . . here is a novelist who is not only popular and successful but formidably growing towards real stature' – *Observer*

A CHOICE OF PENGUIN FICTION

Holy Mother   Gabrielle Donnelly

Every Friday night the Society of St Aquinas meets to discuss the Faith in the basement off London's sin-filled Soho Square. 'A raucously promising début . . . Full of intensity and high jinks, humour, warmth, crossness, crudity' – *Financial Times*

City of Spades   Colin MacInnes

'A splendid novel, sparklingly written, warm, wise and funny' – *Daily Mail*. *City of Spades*, *Absolute Beginners* and *Mr Love and Justice* make up Colin MacInnes's trilogy on London street life from the inside out.

Fiddle City   Dan Kavanagh

'Scary insider's data on the airport sub-world, customs knowhow and smugglers' more sickening dodges are marvellously aerated by bubbles of Mr Kavanagh's very dry, sly, wide-ranging and Eighties humour' – *Sunday Times*

The Rachel Papers   Martin Amis

A stylish, sexy and ribaldly funny novel by the author of *Money*. 'Remarkable' – *Listener*. 'Irreverent' – *Daily Telegraph* 'Very funny indeed' – *Spectator*

Scandal   A. N. Wilson

Sexual peccadilloes, treason and blackmail are all ingredients on the boil in A. N. Wilson's *cordon noir* comedy. 'Drily witty, deliciously nasty' – *Sunday Telegraph*

A Fatal Inversion   Barbara Vine

Ten years after the young people camped at Wyvis Hall, the bodies of a woman and child are found in the animal cemetery. Which woman? Whose child? 'Impossible to put down . . . she is a very remarkable writer' – Anita Brookner. 'I defy anyone to guess the conclusion, but looking back, the clues are seen to be there, unobtrusively but cunningly planted, so that it seems one should have known all along' – *Daily Telegraph*

Is That It?   Bob Geldof with Paul Vallely

The autobiography of one of today's most controversial figures. 'He has become a folk hero whom politicians cannot afford to ignore. And he has shown that simple moral outrage can be a force for good' – *Daily Telegraph*. 'It's terrific . . . everyone over thirteen should read it' – *Standard*

Niccolò Rising   Dorothy Dunnett

The first of a new series of historical novels by the author of the world-famous *Lymond* series. Adventure, high romance and the dangerous glitter of fifteenth-century Europe abound in this magnificent story of the House of Charetty and the disarming, mysterious genius who exploits all its members.

The World, the Flesh and the Devil   Reay Tannahill

'A bewitching blend of history and passion. A MUST' – *Daily Mail*. A superb novel in a great tradition. 'Excellent' – *The Times*

Perfume: The Story of a Murderer   Patrick Süskind

It was after his first murder that Grenouille knew he was a genius. He was to become the greatest perfumer of all time, for he possessed the power to distil the very essence of love itself. 'Witty, stylish and ferociously absorbing . . . menace conveyed with all the power of the writer's elegant unease' – *Observer*

The Old Devils   Kingsley Amis

Winner of the 1986 Booker Prize
'Vintage Kingsley Amis, 50 per cent pure alcohol with splashes of sad savagery' – *The Times*. The highly comic novel about Alun Weaver and his wife's return to their Celtic roots. 'Crackling with marvellous Taff comedy . . . this is probably Mr Amis's best book since *Lucky Jim*' – *Guardian*

Illusions Charlotte Vale Allen

Leigh and Daniel have been drawn together by their urgent needs, finding a brief respite from their pain in each other's arms. Then romantic love turns to savage obsession. 'She is a truly important writer' – Bette Davis

Snakes and Ladders Dirk Bogarde

The second volume of Dirk Bogarde's outstanding biography, *Snakes and Ladders* is rich in detail, incident and character by an actor whose many talents include a rare gift for writing. 'Vivid, acute, sensitive, intelligent and amusing' – *Sunday Express*

Wideacre Philippa Gregory

Beatrice Lacey is one of the most passionate and compelling heroines ever created. There burns in Beatrice one overwhelming obsession – to possess Wideacre, her family's ancestral home, and to achieve her aim she will risk everything: reputation, incest, even murder.

A Dark and Distant Shore Reay Tannahill

'An absorbing saga spanning a century of love affairs, hatred and high points of Victorian history' – *Daily Express* 'Enthralling . . . a marvellous blend of *Gone with the Wind* and *The Thorn Birds*. You will enjoy every page' – *Daily Mirror*

Runaway Lucy Irvine

Not a sequel, but the story of Lucy Irvine's life *before* she became a castaway. Witty, courageous and sensational, it is a story you won't forget. 'A searing account . . . raw and unflinching honesty' – *Daily Express* 'A genuine and courageous work of autobiography' – *Today*

PENGUIN BESTSELLERS

Goodbye Soldier Spike Milligan

The final volume of his war memoirs in which we find Spike in Italy, in civvies and in love with a beautiful ballerina. 'Desperately funny, vivid, vulgar' – *Sunday Times*

A Dark-Adapted Eye Barbara Vine

Writing as Barbara Vine, Ruth Rendell has created a labyrinthine journey into the heart of the Hillyard family, living in the respectable middle-class countryside after the Second World War. 'Barbara Vine has the kind of near-Victorian narrative drive that compels a reader to go on turning the pages' – Julian Symons in the *Sunday Times*

Rainbow Drive Roderick Thorp

If Mike Gallagher (acting head of the Homicide Squad, Los Angeles Police Department) hadn't been enjoying himself in the bed of a married German movie producer, he wouldn't have heard the footsteps and seen the Police Department helicopter . . . 'Quite exceptional . . . powerful, gripping and impressive' – *Time Out*

Memoirs of an Invisible Man H. F. Saint

'Part thriller, part comedy, part science fiction . . . a compelling, often frightening novel. H. F. Saint makes the bizarre condition of his hero believable' – *Listener*

Pale Kings and Princes Robert B. Parker

Eric Valdez, a reporter on the *Central Argus* has been killed in Wheaton. His chief, Kingsley, suspects he was involved in the local pastime – cocaine smuggling. But, knowing Valdez's penchant for the ladies, it could be sexual jealousy. Spenser is about to find out. 'The thinking man's private eye' – *The Times*

Pearls Celia Brayfield

The Bourton sisters were beautiful. They were rich. They were famous. They were powerful. Then one morning they wake up to find a priceless pearl hidden under their pillows. Why? . . . 'Readers will devour it' – *Independent*

FOR THE BEST IN PAPERBACKS, LOOK FOR THE

PENGUIN BESTSELLERS

Oscar Wilde   Richard Ellmann

'Exquisite critical sense, wide and deep learning, and profound humanity
. . . a great subject and a great book' – Anthony Burgess in the *Observer*
'The witty subject has found a witty biographer who is also distinguished
for his erudition and humanity' – Clare Tomalin in the *Independent*

Presumed Innocent   Scott Turow
The No 1 International Bestseller

'One of the most enthralling novels I have read in a long, long time' – Pat
Conroy. 'If you start *Presumed Innocent* you will finish it . . . it grips like
an octopus' – *Sunday Times*

Spring of the Ram   Dorothy Dunnett
Volume 2 in the *House of Niccolò* series

Niccolò has now travelled as far as the frontier of Islam in order to
establish the Silk Route for the Charetty empire. Beset by illness, feuds
and the machinations of his rivals, he must use his most Machiavellian
schemes to survive . . .

A Time of Gifts   Patrick Leigh Fermor

'More than just a Super-travel book . . . it is a reminder that the English
language is still a superb instrument in the hands of a writer who has a
virtuoso skill with words' – Philip Toynbee in the *Observer* 'I know of no
other account of pre-war Europe which conveys so much so powerfully'
– Peter Levi

A Fatal Inversion   Barbara Vine

Ten years after the young people camped at Wyvis Hall, the bodies of a
woman and child are found in the animal cemetery. Which woman?
Whose child? 'Impossible to put down . . . she is a very remarkable writer'
– Anita Brookner. 'I defy anyone to guess the conclusion, but looking
back, the clues are seen to be there, unobtrusively but cunningly planted,
so that it seems one should have known all along' – *Daily Telegraph*

FOR THE BEST IN PAPERBACKS, LOOK FOR THE

PENGUIN BESTSELLERS

Relative Strangers   Maureen Rissik

Angie Wyatt has three enviable assets: money, beauty and a tenacious instinct for survival. She is a woman fighting for success in a complex world of ambition and corruption. '*Relative Strangers* is a wonderful, intelligently written novel – a pleasure to read' – Susan Isaacs, author of *Compromising Positions*

O-Zone   Paul Theroux

It's New Year in paranoid, computer-rich New York, and a group of Owners has jet-rotored out to party in O-Zone, the radioactive wasteland where the people do not officially exist. 'Extremely exciting . . . as ferocious and as well-written as *The Mosquito Coast*, and that's saying something' – *The Times*

Time/Steps   Charlotte Vale Allen

Beatrice Crane was the little girl from Toronto with magic feet and driving talent. She was going to be a star. It was more important to her than her family, than friendship or other people's rules . . . more important, even than love.

Blood Red Rose   Maxwell Grant

China 1926. As Communist opposition to the oppressive Nationalist army grows, this vast and ancient country draws nearer to the brink of a devastating civil war. As Kate Richmond is drawn into the struggle, her destiny becomes irrevocably entwined with the passions of a divided China and her ideals and her love are tested to the utmost.

Cry Freedom   John Briley

Written by award-winning scriptwriter John Briley, this is the book of Richard Attenborough's powerful new film of the same name. Beginning with Donald Woods's first encounter with Steve Biko, it follows their friendship, their political activism and their determination to fight minority rule to Steve Biko's death and Woods's dramatic escape. It is both a thrilling adventure and a bold political statement.